Beatrice and Benedick

Beatrice and Benedick

MARINA FIORATO

HODDER &
STOUGHTON

First published in Great Britain in 2014 by Hodder & Stoughton
An Hachette UK company

1

Text and illustrations © Marina Fiorato 2014

A CIP catalogue record for this title is available from the British Library

Hardback ISBN 978 1 848 54800 8
Trade Paperback ISBN 978 1 848 54801 5
Ebook ISBN 978 1 848 54802 2

Printed and bound by CPI Group (UK) Ltd, Croydon, CR0 4YY

Hodder & Stoughton policy is to use papers that are natural, renewable and recyclable
products and made from wood grown in sustainable forests. The logging and
manufacturing processes are expected to conform to the environmental regulations of
the country of origin.

Hodder & Stoughton Ltd
338 Euston Road
London NW1 3BH

www.hodder.co.uk

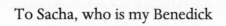

To Sacha, who is my Benedick

'Here's our own hands against our hearts.'
Much Ado about Nothing, V.iv

Dramatis Personae

Beatrice – a princess of Villafranca
Benedick – a gentleman of Padua
Don Pedro – a prince of Aragon
Claudio – a count of Florence
Leonato – the Governor of Messina
Innogen – his wife, aunt to Beatrice
Hero – their daughter and heir, cousin to Beatrice
Orsola – waiting woman to Hero
Margherita – her daughter
Friar Francis – Leonato's priest
Michelangelo Florio Crollalanza – a Sicilian poet
Giovanni Florio Crollalanza – his father
Guglielma Crollalanza – his mother
Ludovico de Torres – Archbishop of Monreale, uncle to
    Claudio
Diego Enrique de Guzman – Spanish Viceroy of Sicily
Philip II of Spain – a great king
Faruq Sikkander – a Moorish seaman
Faruq Sikkander – a water-diviner, his son of the same name
Borachio – a servant to Don Pedro
Conrad – the same

ACT ONE

Sicily: Summer 1588

Act I scene i

The dunes at Messina

Beatrice: I did not want to open my eyes. Not yet.

I sat with the sun gilding my lids, just listening to Sicily. The ebb and flow of the tide, the temperate winds breathing in and out. The scamels singing from the oleanders, and the crickets answering from the dunes. And underlying all, the beat of my own heart.

A bee bumbled into my cheek, singing his somnolent song, startling me. I opened my eyes and for a moment the brightness blinded me. But then the view assailed me at last. From my seat, high on the dunes, the isle was spread about me like the skirt of my gown.

To the south, in Taormina, the old honeyed stones of the theatre built by the Greeks. To the north lay the glittering seaport of Messina. In the harbour, a single Argosy slid into the bay, the sail flap-dragoned by the southerly wind. Away up the hill to the east, the sunlit courts of my uncle Leonato's summer palace, its stone walls as rosy as coral. And in the west, the blue slopes of a volcano, the mountain they call Etna, gently smoking with an ever-present threat. Above all, the sky; a hot high arc of stinging azure, reaching to the vault of heaven, blue as the Madonna's cloak. Sicily was beautiful. But it was alien to me, and I felt horribly alone.

My eyes began to water. It was the brightness, no doubt. Even the sun was strange here; here it was not the friendly planet which had shone upon me for nineteen summers, but a fiery orb that could pull strange spiny plants from the earth and ignite mountains. I blinked the unwelcome tears away; the sky was never so bright in the north, in Villafranca di Verona, my home. I *missed* it so. This sun was foreign, and the bright southern sea led to more foreign lands with stranger's names – Tripoli, Tunis, Oran.

My homesick gaze was drawn northward like a lodestone, and I turned to where the gradient of blue darkened to the north. Beyond the sapphire bay lay the perilous straits of Messina, with the rocks of Scylla hugging the mainland and the whirlpool of Charybdis nearer the isle. This legendary pair of troublemakers had been wrecking ships since ancient times. I had to sail between the two to get here, and I realised I was still between them now. Now I was in Sicily, more the fool I. When I was at home, I was in a better place.

I felt a pressure upon my boot, and looked down; an urchin was crawling over my toe. His coat was as spiny as the cactus plants that grew everywhere here. He snuffled his spiny nose at my sole, so I kicked him gently away and got to my feet, brushing the sand from my skirts. It was then that I saw two figures emerge from a little house farther down the yellow sands. They were a man and a woman, and they walked in my direction, holding hands.

I could have run, for I had time; but instead I dropped to the sand and crouched down guiltily. Had they been an ordinary couple I would have trespassed no longer and left them to their promenade, but what held me were their different colours. For the man was as black as his lady was lily white.

A Moor.

I watched, prone on the sand, my eyes peeping over a knoll, my hands parting the brittle grasses that hid me from view. I could see them clearly below me. They sank down in the powdery white sand between the hillocks only feet away and began to kiss.

My pulses thumped in my ears. I had seen a Moor before, of course. Moors walked about the streets of Padua or Bologna, as students, as merchants, as travellers, and no one troubled them. In Verona even the patron saint of our city was black; St Zeno, who was rendered in polished ebony in our basilica. But the Moors I had seen kept to their own; I had never seen a Moor with a white woman before.

The pair were dressed the same, in loose white cambric robes, as if they had only just risen from their bed to make a new one here in the dunes. Now they were kissing hungrily; him on top, her beneath. He seemed to be almost devouring her. He paused once, to look upon her tenderly and stroke her face as if he could not believe she was real. I noticed his finger-tips and palms were white, and her cheeks stained with a blush, as if his colour had transferred to her. She was a beautiful creature, with hair so fair it was almost white, and eyes as pale as a dawn sky. But it was his beauty that held me transfixed; his skin was as burnished as St Zeno's ebony, his teeth pearl. His eyes were dark and fathomless, his lips thick and pliant as they mouthed at her, hungry as a babe. His hair was close cut, almost shaven, and I could see the bones of his skull. Her white fingers clutched the back of it, and one of them wore a gold ring. A man's ring. *His* ring.

They looked like two urgent angels, one black, one white in their flowing robes. As I watched he moved his body over hers, and he raised her robe higher. I could see the shadow of hair at her groin, and her bone-white curves revealed. She raised his robe likewise, bunching his shift above his waist. I saw his ebony back and rump and averted my gaze, only to see a black hand close on her white breast. His hand wore a ring too, the twin of hers; and I thought for the first time – *they are wed*. She arched her back as his lips replaced the hand, and she clawed and clasped a handful of sand in her transported state, the pale powder flowing away through her fingers as the Moor became one with her. Then they began to move together like a bark riding the waves, higher and higher. At the pinnacle of their passion she turned her head in ecstasy and opened her eyes, and I was shot through with her blue gaze as her eyes met mine.

I scrambled down from my perch, blushing scarlet, my flesh afire. I crouched, frozen and listening, for them to rise and shout. But no, their passion spent, murmurs and soft laughter replaced it, sounds somehow even more intimate than before. They would not have seen me even had I stood above them, blocking the alien sun.

I scrambled down to the shore and hurried back in the direction of Leonato's house. In my sleeve I carried the horn of ink I had been sent to fetch from Messina, ready for a day of my cousin Hero's schooling. My flight had dislodged it and as I drew out the little bottle the ink stained my pale hand. Black on white; the Moor and his wife.

I had to walk, to still the roiling tempest of my humours. I strode along the frill of the ebbing tide, one foot in sea and one on shore, hardly noticing that one leather slipper became soaked in the brine. At length my heart slowed, my cheeks cooled, but my spirits were still in turmoil. I wanted to laugh and cry. I felt excited but desolate, suddenly even more alone, excluded by that union. I looked out to the limitless sea, my mind tossing on the ocean.

I had been in Messina for a month, sent to summer here as a companion to my young cousin Hero. My father, Prince Escalus of Villafranca di Verona, had sent me from the city to my uncle – Lord Leonato Leonatus, Governor of Messina – for reason of my safety. Verona, in recent weeks, had become a seething cauldron of feuding and violence. Some trivial quarrel had woken the age-old enmities of two rival Veronese clans and the sleeping lions had become scrapping cats. When I was actually trapped in our carriage, caught amidst a brawl in the very street, my father had me packed and shipped and speeded to the safety of Sicily.

I had been happy enough these past weeks – I loved my cousin and her family, the island was pleasing and the climate balmy. I had, for my own amusement and for her sake, taken Hero's education in hand; for I had been shocked to learn that my cousin had never read a single book. But I had of late become the victim of dolorous moods and shifts in my temperament. One moment I would rock with laughter; the next be swept away in a gale of tears. I had always been of a merry disposition; perhaps I needed a tonic to settle my humours.

Or perhaps it was my age; at nineteen I was well into my marriageable years. Yet my father had not yet drawn up any contracts or covenants for my marriage, for his position as Prince Escalus was difficult. The two other families of consequence in our state were at war, and our bloodlines were entangled with both. To wed me to one and not the other would remove my father's impartiality and the delicate balance of power in Verona. My brother his heir was unwed for the same reason, and would doubtless become a bachelor prince when my father died.

I had been most thankful, until now, for this. But now I thought of the white woman in the dunes, carrying the weight of a husband. She was my age. She had the blond hair and blue eyes of the north, as I did, and my pale skin too.

As I left the beach for the coast road, the whole island seemed indecently fertile, dotted with vineyards and row crops of vegetables. Along the way calendulas, rock roses and native blackberries bejewelled my route. Even the spiny cacti grew blooming yellow flowers and prickly green pears, seeming to mock my celibacy. I wondered what the Moor's child would look like; a handsome mixture of light and dark. My stomach turned over alarmingly at the thought, and my treacherous liver heated with choler. I resolved to visit the apothecary for a linctus.

By the time I had view of my uncle's house I acknowledged what the problem was, and no linctus would cure it. I wanted what the maiden had. I wanted the Moor, or my own Moor, or a man of any colour; just someone who would look at me as if I was the only woman in the world.

I sped through the archway and the courtyard in search of Hero. She was only sixteen, my cousin, but she was wise beyond her years, a funny, sober little thing, fiercely intelligent, but with a gentle sense of humour beneath her serious demeanour. She had become my confidante in the last month, and I knew my aunt and uncle were already thinking of an alliance for her, so I saw it as my duty to educate her in others ways beside the construction of Latin verbs. Truth be told, in the last week more of our lessons had been taken up with the recounting of my favourite Italian folk tales than Latin grammar. The subject of these fables was always the same: Love. And today I had another story to add to the canon – the unfolding story of the dusky Moor and his wife.

Act I scene ii

A courtyard in Leonato's house

Beatrice: The chapel bell tolled nine times and it was time for lessons to begin.

I mounted the steps to Hero's chamber, thinking, as I always did upon stairs, of my family name Della Scala, and our blazon of a ladder upon a shield. My father had told me often that in Roman times, our ancestor Cangrande had brought the sacred stairs of Pontius Pilate back from the Holy Land to Rome, the very stairs which Christ had descended on his way to be crucified. The emperor Constantine rewarded Cangrande with the name *Della Scala,* 'of the Stairs'. It was not just this singular name which set our family apart; our redstone castle in Villafranca was topped with a vast tower containing the highest staircase in the Veneto. 'Stairs separate us from the common man,' my father was fond of saying. 'The poor do not have stairs but live in hovels, grubbing about upon the ground. Princes have towers, and many floors; we are elevated. You may measure a man by the stairs in his house.' If this was true my uncle Leonato was doing tolerably well, for his pink palazzo was a maze of stairwells, and the house had nearly as many steps as our castle in Villafranca.

I took this particular flight two at a time in my usual fashion (which I know pained my uncle) but my way was blocked. My aunt Innogen, wife to Leonato and mother to Hero, prayer book in hand, was descending to mass and stopped me with a kiss. Her embracing arm turned me around firmly and steered me back down the stairs to the coloured courtyard, where the wondrous mosaics of dolphins, sea serpents and mermaids, much older than the house, wove about our feet in their seaborne measure.

My aunt drew me down beside her on a stone bench. Behind us, a hanging tapestry showed a woman petting a white unicorn with her white hand, and was animated in the breeze as if the figures lived. I knew that unicorns would only let maids touch them and was suddenly struck – I did not want to be wed to unicorns for the rest of my days.

I knew, before my aunt began, that I was in trouble; for my aunt Innogen was more like my own dead mother, her sister, than she realised. She had the glassy, blue-grey eyes of my mother, the same colour as the Venetian lagoon on a summer's day. But the calm, just as at those waters, was superficial. Below the surface swirled rip-tides of intelligence and penetration. Being with my aunt made me miss my mother less, for I felt that I was still under her eye. I knew, looking into my aunt's eyes now, that she had divined where I had been this morning, and what I had seen. My cheeks heated again. But when she began her discourse, again with my mother's trick of speech, my aunt talked of quite a different subject.

'I hear, Niece,' began my aunt, 'that you have become quite the teller of tales.'

I was silent, for I did not know what she had heard, and did not want to buy myself more trouble. Innogen raised an eyebrow at me. 'Let me see. *Love* stories. Not exactly Latin verbs, Beatrice.' She chided, but there was a smile in the voice.

'Hero told you of her schooling, then,' I mumbled.

'Do not tax Hero with this fault; she was naturally keen to share the fruits of her lessons,' I heard the gentle emphasis, 'with her mother.'

I did not blame my cousin, but had she told the latest tale?

'Furthermore,' continued my aunt, 'I myself overheard,

when passing Hero's chamber, the story of a gentlewoman who had contrived to get herself betrothed to a young count, who refused her hand, causing her to *chase* him in a most *ungen-tle* fashion.' She smoothed her hair, dark like Hero's but shot with silver, into its golden net, and managed with the gesture to communicate her disapproval. 'I did not hear the sequel to that one, for I understand the story has, thus far, been left unfinished.'

'Ah now, this is a fine story,' I babbled. The tale was begging to be told, as I had not yet finished it for Hero. 'The count falls in love with another, but his betrothed contrives to wait in his lover's bed, and he surrenders his family ring to her by mistake—'

'Enough!' my aunt cried, throwing up both hands in horror. 'This history is preposterous.' Her hands dropped to her silken lap and she fingered the bracelet she always wore about her wrist, a gold band with a glowing stone of green chalcedony. She laughed a little. 'As if a jewel could be taken from a person unawares!' She spoke softly, as if to herself. 'And bed-tricks are *certainly* not meat for maid's ears.' She sat a little straighter. 'My husband, your uncle Leonato, wishes Hero to be a model of modest chastity, with a maid's mild behaviour and sobriety. It is he who has forbidden her to read thus far, for this very reason; that she should not be exposed to . . . licentious stories.'

I caught a chime of discord in her voice and felt the tapestry behind us stir in the breeze and touch my shoulder. 'And what do *you* wish?' I asked, gently.

My aunt pursed her lips. 'Try not to be insolent, Beatrice. My husband's wishes are, of course, my own. That said, I . . . *we* . . . now want Hero to be educated, as you were yourself, in letters and arts as is befitting a well-born woman. And *you* would do well to remember, Niece, that you will never get a husband if you are so shrewd of your tongue.'

'But I do not *want* a husband. Why do you speak of husbands?' I asked, suddenly cold in that oven of a courtyard.

'Hero,' said my aunt carefully, 'is sixteen years old and may now, by law, become betrothed. Today we are expecting a progress of noble guests at our house for the Festival of the Assumption, and they will stay for a summer's lease. Hero will be thrown in the way of many a young sprig. And there may even be a man enough in the company for you, Niece.' There was a small significant silence, filled only by the gulls mewing from the sea. The tapestry behind us bellied like a sail in the warm breeze, and the unicorn lady brushed my shoulder with her skirts. Like a warning.

I breathed out slowly. 'Was *that* my father's design in sending me here?'

She raised a dark brow. 'I do not know. Was it?'

It all made sense. If I were packed off to find a prince or a count of the south, my father would not have been seen to give the crucial balance of power away at home. I smiled grimly. 'Come, Aunt. I am not my cousin, a child to be gulled into a union. I can see a church by daylight.'

'The prospect is not pleasing to you? To have a well-born man profess his love for you?'

I thought of the Moor with a shiver. Before this summer I had noted my father's reluctance to dispose of my hand with relief, and I could not admit, even to myself, that I might feel differently now. 'I would rather hear a dog bark at a crow,' I lied.

My aunt narrowed her blue-grey gaze at me against the climbing sun, and I felt, again, my mother regard me from her eyes. 'Well, Niece, for all that, I think that I will see you, before I die, fitted with a husband.'

'I dare swear it,' I agreed, 'at a hot Christmastide.'

My aunt laughed and made a gesture of resignation. 'Get to your lessons, wretch,' she said, slapping my behind with her prayer book as I jumped to my feet. 'And remember what I said.'

But as I ducked into the cool stairwell once more and out of the sun's burning eye, I thought perhaps I had been too glib.

Perhaps in Sicily, Christmas *was* hot; and I had just sworn to marry.

Act I scene iii

Hero's chamber in Leonato's house

Beatrice: I mounted the stairs again to Hero's chamber, more soberly now, to find Hero sitting in the window seat, her small frame hunched in the arched casement, looking down on to the sea road, waiting. She jumped up as I entered and ran to embrace me fiercely. 'Where have you *been*? I want to know what happened to the lady and the count. Did she ever get the ring from him?'

I waved away her question with a flap of my hand and drew her back to the window seat, instantly forgetting my promise to my aunt. 'Oh, my pretty little coz,' I burst out, 'I have *such* a tale to tell you today!'

She clasped my hands eagerly, and I admired, as I always did, her small bones (I was a carthorse to her destrier), her tanned skin (I was day to her night) and her eyes as black and bright as olives (mine were as blue as birds' eggs). Even our hair differed, for hers was black and shiny and fell in a smooth veil to her waist and mine was blond and curly and stopped about my shoulders. Furthermore, I was three years older than she. And yet, for all that, we were friends. I twined her fingers with mine and she asked the question I knew she would ask. 'How does it begin?'

'Well . . .' Then I remembered what my aunt had said. 'That is to say, it does not begin.'

I got up from the window seat, and went to the writing desk. A polished square on its surface shamed me when I picked the dusty Latin book up; it had not been handled for a fortnight. I took a breath, and spoke my duty. 'Not today, Hero. For my aunt told me to instruct you in strictly educational matters. Now construe.' I opened the book and coughed a little at the dust. '*Hic ibat Simois, hic est Sigeia tellus* . . .' I droned on like a bee in a casement, boring myself.

Hero folded her arms sulkily and sing-songed back to me. 'Here-ran-the-Simois-here-is-the-Sigeian-land-here-stood-the-lofty-palace-of-old-Priam. Beatrice, please! No more dead histories of dead lands. A story of our own dear Italy, and of our times, I beg you.'

I relented and shut the book. 'Very well, a tale, but a worthy one, of morality and religion.' I racked my brain, for in truth I didn't know any. I dozed through mass, and did not study scripture. So I told a legend that my sea captain had told me on the way through the straits. 'I can tell you a moral tale closer to home. In biblical times Our Lady herself sent the citizens of Messina a letter, written in Hebrew, rolled and tied with a lock of her hair. Mary praised their faith and assured them of her perpetual protection. Ah, here is some Latin for you; she ended the letter *Vos et Ipsam civitatem benedicimus*, that is . . .'

'I bless you and your city,' interrupted Hero. 'I *know* this. The letter is kept in the cathedral, and we celebrate the day it came every year. I did not mean pious parables, Beatrice. I want to hear a *love* story.'

I sighed. 'I was brought here to instruct you, for soon you may be lying between the sheets of a marriage contract with some young gallant.'

'Then teach me of love!' my cousin begged. 'That can be my education. Beatrice, I *need* to know.'

I looked at her, her dark eyes enormous with pleading. I sat down on the window seat again.

'Very well.' I lowered my voice, in case my aunt overheard us, and told the tale of the Moor and the lady in the dunes.

I told how they had lain entangled in the still cool shadows of the seagrass, kissing hungrily. 'And then he pushed her into the dunes, and moved atop her . . .'

'No more!' Hero jumped up from the window seat. 'Tell me no more. Love, yes, but no farther. My lady mother, Friar Francis, they would not approve.'

'Friar Francis!' I scoffed. 'He likes my tales as much as the next man, despite his holy habit.' It was true; Leonato's rotund little friar had become a good friend over the last month I had been in Messina. Partly because we shared a secret – I had more than once seen him playing *Scopa* with the sailors at the docks, the colourful playing cards weighted with pebbles against the wind, resting on an upturned bark. I had seen him there because I played there too, in the early morning when the catch had come in, and I had bought my horn of ink. The friar and I had an unspoken agreement, as our eyes met over the seven of swords or the five of cups, that neither of us would tell my uncle.

I said nothing of this to Hero now; but I need not have troubled myself, for my cousin had ceased to listen. Her eyes were on the sea road and her forefinger pointed. 'Beatrice!'

A distant glittering dragon curved along the sea road, the sun catching on hulme and blade. The dragon was tiny at the moment, but grew and neared as we watched. 'Your father's guests for the Feast of the Assumption,' I said with a catch in my voice. 'Your mother told me of their coming just now.'

Hero jumped up. 'Then we must ready ourselves.' She fingered her simple surcoat. 'My father will want us to change.'

I got up too, more slowly. 'Heigh-ho. Time for our finery.'

'And you must wash your hands,' urged Hero, 'they are all over ink.'

I smiled as I turned her round to unlace her. 'It is not the first time I have seen black cover white today.'

'What do you mean?' Hero asked.

'The lovers. The man is black, the lady white.'

'He is a Moor? The man on the beach is a Moor?' She tried to turn, but I pushed her back by the shoulders.

'Stay still, I am not half done. Yes, he is a Moor. What of it?'

'Well. It is only that . . . All infidels were cleansed from the island. I thought all Moors had been driven from Sicily.'

'Not this one.'

'Was he like other men?' she asked curiously.

'Not at all. In form and in all other ways, he was vastly superior. Now do me.'

I turned, but not before I could enjoy my little cousin's expression. 'Beatrice!'

'Yes?' I was all innocence.

'Moors are . . . *savages*. Surely the lady is in danger.' Hero's little fingers pulled fiercely at my lacings.

'Do not repeat the follies of your parrot-teacher elders.' I tried to express what I had seen on the beach, the couple's intimacy, their partnership. 'There is love in the case, and nobility, and respect.'

The fingers stopped. 'They are *married*?'

'They are.'

'I did not know that white and black could wed.'

'So now you do. I can tell your aunt, with good conscience, that I have contributed to your education. Now hurry; call Orsola to you and Margherita for me, for no one plaits my hair as well as she.'

We dressed quickly, in our favourite colours – coral for Hero, blue for me – all the time with our eyes on the sea road. Orsola, Hero's old wet nurse, was a talker, and answered our questions before they were asked. 'Their leader is a prince of Aragon, Don Pedro. Owns a big bite of Spain, and has the ear of the Spanish king hisself. All gold from crown to spurs, and a handsome fellow too. With him are some nobles of the north, who joined his train at Venice, come to stay a full month in his court.'

Margherita, Orsola's daughter, was Hero's milk-sister, and despite the difference in their class they were as close as you could expect two girls of an age to be when one has suckled from the left dug and the other from the right. Margherita's little fingers had the trick of my hair, and she plaited and twisted my locks, forever yanking my head around as if my braids were reins, for I could not help my head turning to the window and the colourful cavalcade that came. I could hear the trumpets sweet in my blood, and the hoofbeats in my chest, and, my toilet done, I joined my cousin at the window.

The Spanish were a fine sight. All scarlet, and gold breast-plates, and prancing Arab destriers of inky black. They laughed and jingled up the hill, white teethed, brown skinned and care-free. I could not, just yet, make out a single face from the melee. I wondered, giddily, whether my husband was in the company, whether, somewhere among that cacophony, I was hearing his hoofbeats, his laughter, the chinks of his fortune in his purse.

Suddenly moved to make a good show of ourselves, I rummaged into my coffer for my best combs – moonstones set in silver – fixed them in my hair, and picked out a collar of gold fili-gree for Hero. She lifted the dark waterfall of her hair and I was still fiddling with the fastening as we clattered down the stone stairs to the courtyard. Margherita had to help me for suddenly my inky hands were all of a shake.

Act I scene iv

A courtyard in Leonato's house

Beatrice: In the courtyard there was a press of people with my uncle at the centre of them all, as if he were the earth in the middle of a coloured cosmos.

I could hear his rich, sonorous voice, and knew he would be making one of his wordy speeches, for there was nothing my uncle loved so much as his own voice.

I rolled my eyes and Hero and I made our way towards the crowd, me pushing Hero in front of me as rank demanded. Soon we stood behind my uncle and aunt, in the shadow of his outflung arms, as he gesticulated and flourished like a player. Satisfied that all eyes were on my uncle, I was free to look about me.

My uncle's court and the Spanish court had now divided into two opposing ranks like belligerents, with their respective generals out front to give the parlay.

The man my uncle addressed was not, out of his saddle, particularly tall or broad but he was dressed magnificently in the scarlet of his pennant. This must be the prince of Aragon, Don Pedro. His sleeves were slashed to show black satin, and the material had the same oily sheen as his short black hair cut close as a cap, and his neatly trimmed beard. He smiled to show white teeth, and to his credit, kept the smile wide for the entire length of my uncle's windy welcome. Although, at the end of the elegy, I did see the corners of his mouth begin to twitch with fatigue.

In a heavy accent, the prince said something gallant and brief in reply, hoping that he and his court would be no trouble to my uncle in the coming month.

My uncle denied any such thought with a shake of his head, and the beard that he cultivated – just beginning, to his delight, to be shot with august silver – shook in agreement. 'When you come to my house, Prince, happiness rides in your company; but when you leave us, sorrow will occupy your room, for all contentment decamps with you.'

As he spoke again, I saw a figure behind the prince whom I had not noted before shift restlessly into view, fidgeting.

The young man was not in uniform, but would have stood out from the liveried company anyway, for he was the tallest gentleman in that courtyard. Southerners and Spanish seem to be pygmy peoples and of the entire company only my aunt or I could look the stranger in the eye. He had the blond hair of the north, the colour of winter wheat. It had a wave to it, and he wore it long enough to curl about his collar, not cropped like the Spaniards'. His brows were darker than his hair but his eyes were green, and although he did not wear a beard, his cheeks had not seen a razor for some days and an untidy stubble darkened his jaw. His attire was beyond reproof, though – he wore the tight-sleeved, knee-length jacket fashionable in Venice at this time, in a bottle-green silk, and his breeches and boots both were black deer-leather.

I was so busy studying him it was some moments before I realised that he was not alone. He had his hand resting affectionately on the shoulder of a youth beside him; not his brother, from the difference in colouring. These two, alone of the company, had left off the scarlet and half-armour of the Spanish. The youth looked about Hero's age, had a poll of curly black hair and wore the purple velvet of the Tournabuoni-Medici family, which told me at once that he was both a Florentine and a nobleman of some consequence. As my uncle droned on I saw the man give the boy a squeeze of his velvet shoulder. The boy looked up and saw, as I did, the man allow his eyes to flutter and close as if my uncle's droning was lulling him into a sleep. Then he stumbled half a step forward and his eyes flew wide, as if he'd woken with a start. The little play was enacted with great economy of movement, so only his audience of one would appreciate it, and he would not be caught in a breach of manners. But it was done with kindness as well as discretion, and I warmed to the fellow for making the younger man feel less nervous. The youth smiled, and the northerner smiled too. And, as though my own small movement had caught his eyes, he looked straight at me. I saw now his eyes were as light as my own, and very direct. They meant home to me, and I forgot to look away. Then one of them closed, quite distinctly, in a wink. I dropped my gaze, pursing my lips to hide my smile, and shifted behind my uncle so that I was completely hidden, my pulses beating in my ears.

Finally, when both Don Pedro and my uncle had finished their elaborate ritual, the introductions began; and my aunt, Hero and I were presented. The prince kissed my aunt Innogen and Hero's hands, and I knew I was next. I shamefacedly presented my inky fingers, hoping he would not notice. But the prince kept his gaze on my face as his lips kissed the air above my hand, raking me with his black eyes in a way that made me uncomfortable.

The Florentine youth, name of Count Claudio Casadei, shook my hand with a grasp as limp and clammy as a wet mackerel; but I smiled warmly at him, trying to ease his nerves.

Then, last of all, the tall young man was presented as Signor Benedick Minola of Padua. A northerner; I *knew* it. Padua was half a day's ride from my father's house and homesickness hit me like a blow.

He shook Hero's hand, and then took mine. His grasp was firm and dry, and he spotted my filthy hand straight away, making a little pantomime of looking at my fingers and me and raising one dark brow with questioning amusement. Then, very deliberately, he turned my hand over, to where my palm was clean and white like the Moor's. He planted a kiss on the very centre of my palm, not a kiss for the air like the prince's, but a warm, firm salute. He held the inky hand he had kissed in his for an instant, then let go.

The whole incident had taken no more than a couple of heartbeats, and I am sure that in the flurry of greetings and meetings no one else had noted the episode. But by sleight of hand he had left something in my palm where the kiss had been, and as Don Pedro led the company into the house I opened my hand and looked. It was a single *Scopa* card, the *settebello*, the seven of coins, the most valuable card in the pack. The card which, once played, won the game; and so was known as 'the beautiful seven'. I turned the card over, but there was nothing writ there, only the pattern and mark of the stationers.

I looked back at the design on the front – seven circles, rendered in red, blue and yellow, with a flower design on each face. The *settebello*. What did it mean?

For the first time that day I forgot the Moor. I looked after Signor Benedick of Padua and he looked back at me with a green gaze.

His lip had a slight stain of ink upon it, like a little bruise.

Act I scene v

The Great Hall in Leonato's house

Benedick: I had no stomach for my dinner, but I did want to see Beatrice Della Scala again.

It was fully a week until the Feast of the Assumption, with its attendant processions, feasts and rituals; but our host Leonato, Governor of Messina, had decided that the time should not go idly by us. He had organised a programme of entertainment so full that not a single day was to be left free of his amusements. Feasts, masques and tournaments were to be laid on for our pleasure, all of which sounded to me more like labour than leisure. But our host, frantic to prove his hospitality could equal that of the greatest courts of the world, would not be denied; and tonight he had promised us a dinner such as we had never tasted.

I filed into Leonato's great hall behind the primped and perfumed Spanish and found my place near the salt. The room was a good size, with dirty dogs under the table and hoodwinked hawks in the rafters. The tables were groaning with pyramids of figs, almonds, apples, plums and pomegranates, and decorated with vines twined with poppies. The long boards were ranged as three sides of a square, with musicians sitting where the fourth should be, infecting the air with their cacophony. I spied the lady Beatrice's golden head almost at once. She was standing at the head of the central table, which was set upon a dais, with her aunt and uncle and cousin, awaiting the entrance of the prince.

Don Pedro walked to the central place of the high table, where an ornate carved chair anticipated him and a fat cushion waited for his arse. Once he had seated himself, the company settled themselves in their places. The prince was flanked by Leonato's wife and her daughter, with the governor himself on the other side of his wife, near enough to the prince's ear to tire the hearer with his book of words.

Claudio, in his purple surcoat, was seated next to the daughter of the house as they were of an age, and there was some goodwife between us. He looked at me pleadingly as we sat and I smiled reassurance. At seventeen he was three years younger than myself, but I had grown to like the young fellow on our journey, once I'd discovered that his stiffness concealed a crippling shyness and his haughty manner masked a merry nature.

So, when we were all placed, the lady Beatrice was seated about six souls away, between her uncle and another bearded fellow who I took to be the governor's brother. I could hardly see her, even by constantly moving my head as if I had an ague. Every so often I caught a tantalising glance of her long fingers, now cleansed of ink, tearing a piece of bread, or her blond curls lifting and settling as she turned her head. I would have been remiss in my duty to Claudio, were it not for the fact that the little maid of the house was keeping him enraptured with her conversation. Strangely, they seemed to be talking about scripture, and I could clearly hear the lady tell him, in her girlish pipe, some coil about the Madonna and a letter and a lock of hair. I envied Claudio that he could speak with the companion of his choice but not I with mine. Frustrated, I sat through the endless procession of local delicacies, accompanied by strangers and trapped in my chair by propriety.

The Sicilians seemed fond of marrying foods together that should never even have met. I was served a cheese with a lime inside, pasta littered with raisins, and anchovies stirred with oranges. Leonato had promised us in his welcome food such as we had never tasted; and he had made good on his promise for I had certainly never violated my palate with a repast like this before. I sighed as the next dish arrived; a pale mass resembling pigswill, wrapped in a fatty filigree of cow's caul. '*Maco*,' said my neighbour helpfully, but I did not know if she named the dish or warned me against it. My innards rumbled and I would, at that moment, have given all of Don Pedro's fortune for a dish of doves. In the end, my stomach growled at me so much that I tried a tiny bit of the stew – just so much as I could take on my knife's point. It was bland and mealy and my northern palate rebelled. I was glad that I had thought to bring a little pouch of fiery Paduan mustard, yellow and hot as the sun, which I discreetly but liberally sprinkled on that platter and every one thereafter.

In the midst of this parade of strange dishes, I saw my chance, when the bearded fellow beside the lady Beatrice left his seat to speak to one of the servers. I rose and quickly nipped into the seat next to her, twisting into the chair like an eel so that the bearded gentleman, upon his return, almost sat in my lap. I grinned at him; he waggled his head at me in reproof and walked away to the other end of the board, muttering. I turned my smile upon the lady, but she regarded me warily. Close to she was better than ever – her blue eyes very direct, her coral mouth plump like a rosebud, her eyebrows dark and expressive. Her hair fell in wayward curls about her face, escaping from the constraints of combs and braids; not by any means a neat hairstyle, but one that suited her remarkably well.

As the servers brought new trenchers with another alien concoction, we were necessarily silent and I considered what I would say – rare for me for I usually speak extempore. Giving her the *settebello* card was a good start. It usually worked; ladies were intrigued, flattered, and full of questions. They always asked about the card first, and then I could get on with the serious business of making them laugh.

But this lady did not wait for me to marshal my wit. She spoke first. And she did not mention the card.

'Do you travel farther, Signor Benedick, or are you at the farthest?'

'Lady Beatrice, this very chair is my destination. I came to Sicily with no other object but to sit beside you in it.'

She did not smile. 'So you have no farther to travel?'

'I am to convey my young charge to Monreale in the morning to visit his uncle, who is the archbishop there.'

'But you do not stay at Monreale?'

'No, and nor does he. There is some great coil afoot, and *his* uncle thought it better that he stay with *yours*.'

'So you will be here for the month.'

'At the least. And I will sit by you in this chair for every day of it, if you give me leave.'

Now she smiled and picked up her knife, as if selecting a weapon. 'If you are to do that you must have many histories to tell, so that our evenings do not become tedious.'

'Lady Beatrice, I have been on this good earth for a score of years, and no one has ever taxed me with being tedious.'

The next dish and her next question arrived together. 'You must be a man of experience, then. What is your profession?'

'I am of no profession.'

'None?' She raised one arched brow.

'Is that so rare in one of our class? Do you not have idle brothers?'

'I have one, older than myself.'

'And what does he do?'

'He brawls mostly. He is a great quarreller, and goes to seek trouble if it cannot find him first.'

'But he has no occupation?'

'His occupation is to wait for my father to die.'

'And will his labours be concluded soon?'

'No.' She smiled. 'My father is not very obliging. He will not accommodate anyone if he can help it. Nothing prompts him to good health and long life as much as the idea of thwarting his heir.'

'And do you like your brother any better than your father does?'

'No. We fight like cat and cur.'

'Cannot argument be a sign of attachment?'

'Not in this case.'

'But in others?' I asked swiftly.

She leaned back in her chair, regarding me with her blue gaze. 'Call you *this* an argument, Signor Benedick? I would never favour an acquaintance with one of my arguments on a first encounter.'

'We must be friends, then, before I am admitted to the pleasure of disputing with you?'

'Precisely,' she said smartly. 'But I prize honesty in my friends above all things, and I am afraid you have not been honest with me.'

I spread my hands like a conjuror, hiding nothing. 'I have spoken plain and to the purpose. Tell me how I've erred.'

She looked down at her trencher. 'When you said you had no profession, you did not speak truly. If you are delivering a young count to his uncle, you are a nursemaid.'

'Like you?' I countered.

'I am my cousin's companion,' she corrected. 'I teach her English, a little Latin and less Greek.'

Now I had to change the subject, for I was a poor student, and could not parry with her in any of those tongues. 'I joined Count Claudio at Venice, as his father asked mine if I would accompany him to Sicily. I was his *companion*,' I said with gentle emphasis, 'and made him laugh along the way.'

'You are a paid fool, then?' Her coral lips curled a little.

'Is that not an honourable profession?'

I raised my goblet to indicate a dwarf in motley, who turned cartwheels between the tables before bowing deeply in front of the prince. But the fool was facing the wrong way, and at his cue the trumpets blared as if he had broken wind. Don Pedro played along, fanning his face with his long fingers. Beatrice turned to me. 'Honourable indeed,' she agreed, in a voice laced with irony. 'You are the prince's jester, then?'

'I hardly know Don Pedro. I have similarly only been in his company since Venice. We joined his company when he was collecting ships for his king. I have spoken no more than two words to him, but now I think of it, both times he laughed.' I poked at the next course set before me – some sort of meat, so rarely cooked that it was still bleeding. In our conversation too, the bloodletting continued.

'If you are of no profession, you must have other diversions. Do you have no interests, no hobbies to fill your hours? Do you enjoy music?' She nodded to the gap in the tables, where her uncle's musicians were torturing their instruments for our pleasure.

'I think it strange that they should serenade us upon sheep's guts while we eat the rumps. No,' I decided, 'there's not a note of theirs that's worth the noting.'

'And what of poetry?'

I shrugged. 'I am a man who speaks plainly. I cannot understand one word in ten that your uncle says. His words are stranger than his dishes.'

She laughed then, and I enjoyed the sound not just for its pleasing aspect but for the respite it bought me from her attack. I was beginning to feel like a man at a mark, with a whole army shooting at me.

'Are you a good horseman?'

'I know which end points forward, and which back.'

'You are a pilgrim then, and walk the silver road with a shell in your hat?' She was making fun of me.

'You sound like my young friend Claudio; he is quite the

devout. I will answer you as I answer him. God has no quarrel with me and I have none with him – we let each other alone.' I adopted a rich, rolling voice like her uncle. 'The God of *love*, who sits *above* . . . quick, ask me the poetry question again.'

She smiled but asked a different one.

'Are you a swordsman, then?'

'I refer you to my reply upon the subject of horseflesh; I know one end from the other.' I relented. 'I learned, of course; but if you give me a rapier and a dagger, and my enemy a parsnip and a stick of celery, he will come out the victor.'

'So you have never taken commission for a soldier?'

'No, but I think *you* should. Do you catechise your brother like this?'

'Signor Benedick, *we* are not brother and sister.'

'No,' I said, looking into her lovely face, her features alive with argument, 'that we are not.'

'But life in armour holds no attraction for you?'

I threw up my hands, in a mock gesture of surrender. 'You are hard on me, Lady Beatrice. Would it make you kinder, I wonder, if I was on the way to be lain low by some axe-wielding German, or scimitar-swinging Saracen?'

She seemed to be considering this. 'It is one way to measure a man, by his length on the battlefield.'

'And you find me wanting?'

She looked at me very directly. 'I have not yet made up my mind.'

Outfaced by her honesty, I took a drink of my wine. It was thick and red and sour like blood. 'More often than not soldiers are younger sons, bored by their homely hearths, looking for action. Hotspurs, roaring boys.' I banged down my cup. 'If I want to let off steam in an iron coat, I will put a kettle on the fire.'

'Ah, well.' She sighed gustily and shrugged her shoulders. 'Then I cannot give you a gage, if you are not a knight.'

'A what?'

'A gage; a favour that a lady gives a knight to wear when he rides into the lists. Usually a ribbon or a flower. Or sometimes,' she said with delicate emphasis, 'a *playing card.*'

There it was. She had mentioned the *settebello* card at last, but I had lost the advantage of my gambit. She had kept it in her hand, masterfully waiting, and only played it when I was already annoyed. I lost my head. 'Lady Beatrice. I was lucky enough to be born to a wealthy family. I do not have to till the winter fields like some peasant, nor slave under a hot sun. I take the view, and you may not admire me for it, that as long as I am no trouble to any one I may do as I like. I eat when I have stomach, sleep when I am drowsy and laugh when I am merry. In short, I am quite happy to wear out my youth with shapeless idleness.'

I realised that the room had quietened, and those near to us were listening closely. She heard me in silence, a little smile playing about her damned, beautiful mouth. She had won and she knew it. I lowered my voice to a hiss.

'But next time there is a muster, I will give up *your* name for a knight.'

I would have said more, but there was a little commotion as the prince began to rise. The hour was late and the little lady of the house wished to retire, and Claudio was holding her chair for her. My lady Beatrice rose gracefully to accompany her; clumsily, too late, I scrambled to my feet to pull out her chair with an ugly scrape. She turned to murmur her parting shot in my ear.

'If I am the knight, then I thank you for my gage.' She favoured me with a soldier's grin. 'But now our joust is at an end, and I am the victor, I have the honour to return it.' She nodded to my plate as she turned to go, and spoke her parting riposte over her shoulder. 'If you have no more stomach, *Lady*, you had better turn your trencher. Farewell.'

Disconcerted, I turned over my trencher, as was the custom when the meal was done.

And there was the seven of coins, the *settebello*, looking up at me.

ACT TWO

Act II ѕcene i

A ѕquare before a church in Monreale

Benedick: Having delivered Claudio to his uncle in the cathedral of Monreale, I kicked my heels in the cloister while I waited for him.

I had assumed that I would be required to attend mass and had prepared myself to yawn through the liturgy for a couple of hours. But the good archbishop, clothed in gold and sitting in his throne beneath a giant mosaic of Christ Pantocrator, wept and smiled to see his nephew, then turned dry eyes upon me. He thanked me most graciously for conveying Claudio to him safely, and bid me come back at noon. I looked in his closed face, and the eyes as almond and inscrutable as the eyes of the Christ that floated above him upon the golden walls, and felt, with certainty, that he had some secrets to speak to his nephew. And so I turned myself out of his holy doors, and wandered into the cloister.

The cloister was more like a garden than a holy place, a vast space planted with glossy-leaved orange, olive and almond trees. The quadrangle was laid with pale stone paths and inter-sected with tiny dark green hedges cut into intricate patterns and lopped at shin level, just the right height to trip a man. In the centre, picking at the hedges with their orange bills, half-a-dozen snow-white geese wandered, honking importantly. No doubt they were sacred or something, but the very sight of them made my stomach growl. I had eaten little more than bread and mustard at dinner, and drunk overmuch. No doubt the apothecaries would say my grumbling stomach was contributing to my morning melancholy.

I walked beneath the shady loggias, striding from one arched shadow to the next, dodging the climbing sun. On the long ride to Monreale, I had not been merry company for Claudio, brooding instead on what Lady Beatrice had said to me the night before, and I fingered the *settebello* card, where it sat in my baldric, a hard little rectangle just over my heart.

In that huge place, with everyone inside for mass, I could hear the soaring notes of the choir, and I suddenly felt very alone. Strangely, when the choir began their motet, even the geese had suddenly hushed their honking and disappeared. I was not accustomed to my own company, and I did not like myself as a friend. When I was alone my thoughts clamoured loudly into the silence. But I did not want to hear my own thoughts, did not want to peer into my own heart and did not enjoy searching my soul.

But however hard I tried to concentrate on the music of the mass, unwanted thoughts began to creep into my mind.

What is your occupation?

Since boyhood I had always followed wherever others led, like a leaf in the stream. I would have stayed at home for ever had not my latest companion Sebastian taken it into his head to travel; once he was gone then loneliness and dislike of my own company persuaded me to take my father's offer to accompany Claudio Casadei to Sicily. And now I had reached a new nadir. I had followed a seventeen-year-old *novellino* all the way to this alien place, and had now been turned away from God's house, to be told to return and pick up God's nephew in a brace of hours. Lady Beatrice was right. I *was* a nursemaid – a nutshell of a man, with no kernel, no substance.

If there had been a stone underfoot I would have kicked it, but the well-swept paths afforded me no such outlet. The song of the choir swelled in my chest like a tide of sadness and pricked at my eyeballs. I sought escape, and walked through a white archway into the bleached piazza beyond.

There there were people and bustle aplenty, and my melancholy began to subside. Here was colour and company and life and noise. Seeking diversion, I spotted a bright cart at the far side of the square and walked over to peer at it. The thing was large and bravely painted in red and blue and yellow, with carved curlicues of gilt and golden frames bordering fantastical scenes all round the sides. The side of the cart facing into the square was comprised of a stage with a pair of blood-bright curtains, closed at present. A bored-looking mule stood between the traces, and a knot of people gathered about the cart with an air of expectation, as if it was a conjuror's box.

I retreated to the fountain bowl and sat on the warm stone, trailing my hand in the crystal water as I prepared to watch the coming spectacle.

I had not long to wait. With a great fanfare the red curtains opened and a little manikin appeared, so cunningly contrived that it was some moments before I realised that it was not a dwarf but a large puppet. The puppet had a helm of gold, and gilded armour and a shield. I sighed inwardly – everywhere I turned was there to be a polemic of soldiery, to make me feel even less of a man? But I was diverted when the jaw hinged open and the thing began to speak. I could not understand above half of the odd southern dialect, but I could understand by the puppet's tortured vowels coupled with his blue blazon that he was supposed to be French. I began to smile.

The puppet was joined by a troupe of others, all with marvellously designed and jointed limbs. I could not understand how the little men were being manipulated, for there seemed to be no strings above or levers below. Only by narrowing my eyes against the fierce sun could I divine that each joint, large or small, was attached with a string as fine as a hair to control it. The scenery, too, was devilishly clever – rendered in relief, the buildings were somehow built on to backboards, set behind each other in layers so the tableaux could change. I recognised the fiery mountain above the bay and the very square where we now stood, the cathedral built in sandy stone, and a little ring of golden bells visible in the campanile. I began to enjoy myself.

It was some way into the performance before I noticed the man sitting on the fountain bowl a little way from me. He was laughing too loudly, with the confidence of a man who had been born with enough privilege that no one will dare to silence him. But it was a cheerful noise and it was that which drew my gaze to him first; I was disposed, that day, towards happiness and amusement, to pull me from my trough of misery. He was Don Pedro.

I was surprised to see him. The way is long from Messina to Monreale. Besides, he could, had he wanted, have travelled in mine and Claudio's train; but he must have had a clandestine purpose for he was without cortège or retinue. He was dressed in scarlet and black, but had left off his armour today – yesterday he would have resembled the puppets more closely.

When he laughed he threw back his head and opened his mouth to show all his teeth. His fangs made me think of a cat of the Africas that I had seen in a menagerie once. He was the same; an oily black pelt, pin-sharp ivory teeth, and easy grace as he relaxed his long frame along the fountain's edge. He could have been purring. Humbly, I looked away again – I was not sure if he would recognise me, as in his cavalcade from Venice he kept with his officers and when he spoke to us he spoke to Claudio, who was nearer him in rank. I did not wish to presume, and turned my attention back to the play in hand.

Now the ridiculous French had been joined by a band of handsome puppets with red bandannas about their foreheads and particoloured hose like harlequins. These, I supposed, were the Sicilians; the heroes of the tableau. The Sicilians seemed to be questioning the French – trying to get them to speak their language, to say a particular word. *Ci ci*, it sounded like; *Cici*. The French could not say it – *She-she*, they lisped. *She-she*. Don Pedro laughed at the hapless French. *She-she*. I laughed. Everybody laughed.

Then the bells of the little white church in the scenery swung and gave their tinny chime, and behind us, as if to assist the counterfeit players' pretence, the bells of the cathedral boomed fit to shiver my ribs. The French puppets knelt and placed their hands together, while the Sicilians settled down to sleep, the puppets collapsing as their strings slackened and their joints crumpled together.

Everyone in the crowd was curiously still and my hands were cold where they trailed in the fountain. I felt a sudden, unbearable foreboding. The puppets now seemed real to me, the play was real, and the soldiers were real. I could hardly breathe as I watched the kneeling French with dread and pity; and when the Sicilians jumped up and drew their knives I felt a sense of inevitability. I had known this would happen.

The Sicilians tore into the foil breastplates of the French and pulled forth little red paper hearts, with rolled red ribbons attached to them to represent the blood and shambles. The ribbons flew into the crowd and the watching children – who knew this story well, it seemed – gathered them up; the little maids even tied them in their hair. The crowd cheered and clapped and the puppeteers came forth to collect the adulation and the coins. There was just one greybeard and his son, to operate all those multitudes. Puppetry, like murder, was obviously a family business here.

Don Pedro clapped with the rest, rose and flipped the pair a silver *real*, a gesture so generous that both father and son removed hood and liripipe and bowed.

I stayed in my place, not sure whether to greet the prince, but he turned to me at once. 'Signor Benedick, is it not?'

Now I scrambled to my feet and bowed. The flourish of my

hand sent a few drops of water on to his surcoat, where they sat on the nap of the velvet like diamonds. 'Yes, Highness.'

'Take your ease,' he said. 'I am here incognito, as you Italians say. And having watched that little play, it might be politic not to let these good people know that I am one of the ruling class.' I smiled as I was required to; for Sicily had been under the Spanish yolk for nigh on three centuries; they were the latest in a long line of invaders from antique times to the hapless French. Even now that paper king, the viceroy, sat upon his borrowed throne in nearby Palermo. I thought little of Don Pedro's alias, though; from his dress and grooming, and his easy distribution of his pieces of eight, there could be no mistaking him for anything but a Spaniard.

The prince sat back down on the fountain and motioned me to sit beside him, seemingly content to rest and talk on. 'A cautionary tale, did you not think?'

'I did not understand all of it,' I confessed.

'The Sicilian Vespers. They tell the story to their children here like a bedtime tale.' He stretched out his legs. 'The locals asked the French to say *cirici*: chickpea. Those that could not were identified as the enemy, and that evening, when the bells chimed for vespers, they murdered every one of them.'

'Killed by a humble chickpea,' I mused. 'I knew the food here was poison.'

A little moppet tripped over my feet, and I set her on to her feet again with a smile. Her pigtails were tied up with ribbons of blood.

'It is no accident,' he said. I thought he spoke of the child, but his eyes were on the puppet cart. 'It is no accident that they enact this play now. The people are sick of conquerors. Romans. Greeks. Arabs. Normans. French. They put up with them for a while,' he shrugged expressively, 'and then they've had enough. The blood runs close to the surface in Sicily. Like that hill of fire over there.' He gestured to the volcano, sleeping on the skyline, a line of blue smoke rising to join the clouds. 'All quiet and calm, until, *bang*.' He opened his fingers in a spiky explosion.

I understood him now. 'And today, the archbishops and vice-roys and princes of Spain.'

'Indeed. God save us from such a fate.' He crossed himself rapidly, across and down, across and down, stitching his heart firmly into his chest with the warp and weft of faith.

I nodded in agreement, the foreboding and melancholy returning to shroud my own heart. I felt, suddenly, that some misfortune had befallen Sebastian, or he would have written to me – that he was shipwrecked, drowned, dead.

'Are you well, signor?' asked the prince, with more fellow feeling than I would have given him credit for. 'You were mer-rier on the road, I think.' I thought then, he is here for a reason, but, like myself, he has some leisure, and is content to while away the time catechising me.

'I was put in mind of a friend – more of a brother, to say truly – who is in danger's way.'

'A soldier?'

Was there no avoiding the subject? 'No, not that – an adven-turer, more.'

'This world offers no greater adventure than to ride into the field of battle. And you? Your city-states are quarrelsome, I believe; and for a soldier opportunity is all. Have you ever seen battle?'

'Why does everyone ask that?' I meant it for a jest, a diver-sion, but he leaned into me, so close I could see the dark whiskers breaking though his skin, and spoke in deadly earnest.

'*Because something is coming*,' he said. 'It is time to stand up and be counted. To pick your side.'

'Is that what you were doing in Venice?' I asked, without a thought for my insolence. But the prince did not seem to mind my curiosity.

'Partly, yes. Believe me, I have good reason for asking. Have you ever been a soldier?'

I was tired of all this talk of soldiery. 'I, Prince?' I said. 'Have I not been up and down the map, naked sword in hand, looking for argument? Have I not followed every colour of the rainbow, taking every prince's pennant as my own? Have I not worn mail so many days that my very flesh is patterned like a Turkey carpet?'

'Have you?'

'No,' I said. 'But I once heard a chestnut explode in a farmer's fire.'

Don Pedro laughed louder than he had when the French puppets expired.

'There, sir, you are your old self again.' He wiped his eyes. 'Believe me, I know your pain. I, too, miss my brother Don John; he is minding our estates in Aragon, where, I trust, he will prove a good and faithful steward. Perhaps we can be companions for each other for the while?' He looked at me contemplatively. 'And you may yet wear a soldier's coat, though you have not seen active practice.'

'What do you mean?'

He swung his legs down and sat straight, as if he was on his throne. The cat was gone. 'Only this. Not all battles are fought in the field. Your countryman, Machiavelli, taught the world that. Sometimes, in a great cause, a man needs a sword and cannon and horses, it is true. But sometimes he needs an affable fellow, a fellow who is amusing, who seems harmless; a fellow who can move among dukes and counts, make them laugh, make them confide in him. Sometimes,' he said carefully, 'even a prince needs a man who can hear things.'

'Are you talking about . . . a spy?'

'Let us say an agent, rather. You saw the play. Despite our long vice-regency, we are outsiders here, still. I need someone who can speak to these Sicilian lords in their own language. Someone,' he smiled briefly, 'who can say chickpea.'

I decided not to tell him that a Paduan was as much of a stranger here as a Spaniard, for I was intrigued by his sayings.

'*Something is coming,*' the prince repeated. 'Soon, very soon, we may have need of you,' he said enigmatically.

I considered. I was not thinking of danger, or intrigue, or even the purse I could accept for such work. Above all, I was thinking of Lady Beatrice. She had chided me with having no occupation. Well, now I was being offered the most dashing of all.

A *spy.*

That single, sibilant syllable sounded spicy, secret, enticing. All the things that I, Benedick, could be. Benedick, the Spy. What would Beatrice say to me then?

I began to smile. Don Pedro clapped me on the back, and, as if he had rung my heart in my ribs like a clapper, the great bells chimed behind me in the cathedral. I rose. 'I am to collect my young charge at twelve bells,' I said apologetically.

'Claudio Casedei is the young count's name?' It was not really a question. 'He is of a wealthy Florentine family, I think?' It was spoken very casually.

'The wealthiest.' I said. 'The Tournabuoni. And, through his mother's marriage, the Medici too. His uncle Ferdinando is the . . .' I began, and then stopped. Don Pedro slid his dark eyes to meet mine, and I realised with a jolt that my mission had already begun. 'His uncle is Ferdinando de' Medici, Grand Duke of Tuscany, and he holds the purse-strings of all Florence,' I said. 'And Claudio's uncle on his mother's side – whom he is visiting even now, in the cathedral there – is the archbishop of this city of Monreale.' I was sure that this second piece of information the prince knew as well as I; but the first I thought was news to him.

'I will go with you,' said Don Pedro. 'Our host Leonato has invited us all to a masked ball in his pleasure gardens tonight, and I must visit the tailors in Palermo for a costume. Why do not we go together?' He looked me up and down, from my Venetian suit of clothes to my Florentine shoes. 'And while we are there, as you are to join my cavalcade, we will get you caparisoned like a soldier, and mounted like a corsair. We will visit the barbers too,' he said balefully, eyeing my curls as the Sicilian puppets had eyed the French, 'for your fleece rivals Jason's.'

I mounted the steps to the church with him, and he stopped in the porch under the shade of an enormous palm tree, and faced me, as if we were to be wed. His mind clearly tended that way too, for he asked, 'And you are not married, or betrothed?'

The tree did not shade me and the sun was now at his highest; I quailed under his and the prince's eye. In truth, the lady Beatrice had jolted me, and I knew it would take very little encouragement to make me fall in love with her. But under the prince's gaze I felt suddenly sure that I must deny this. I shook my head. 'I have not yet seen that special face that I could fancy more than any other.'

'Not even the Lady Beatrice and her fortune?'

So he *had* seen us talk at dinner. I grimaced convincingly. 'Least of all she. Why would I betroth myself to unquietness? If we were but a week married we would talk each other mad.' Then I realised what he had said. 'Wait – what fortune?'

'Her father is Bartolomeo Della Scala, Prince Escalus of Villafranca. He is the kingmaker of Verona, for the other two great families are perpetually at war. She is not the heir at present, though – she has an older brother.'

'Ah yes, the great quarreller.'

He misunderstood me. 'Precisely. He does not have the gift of Prince Escalus, to stay out of the squabbles of the Veronese. He may not outlive his father.'

Now I am not a religious man, but this, said so coldly on the hot steps of a cathedral, was a little more matter-of-fact than I cared for.

'And if he does beat his father to the grave . . . then she will be a princess and a prize indeed. What do you think now?'

'I think, Prince, that if you know so much, you have no need of a spy.'

He laughed. 'Her great wealth does not change your mind?'

It did not. My own father was only a merchant, but he had chinks enough. 'I swear on my allegiance that I will die a bachelor. Else, what would all the other ladies of the world do? For they all adore me, and I am a confessed tyrant to their sex.'

He laughed once more, showing his teeth. 'That is well – for single men are single-minded. And you will need your wits about you for the task to come.'

And I entered the church, walking a little taller than when I had left the cloister; and whatever denials I had made to the prince, I had but one thought in my mind; how the Lady Beatrice would greet the new Signor Benedick tonight.

Act II scene ii

A masque in Leonato's garden

Beatrice: When I saw Signor Benedick, I laughed till I ached.

I'd had such good intentions too. I was genuinely contrite for the way I'd treated him the previous night at dinner, and had dressed with great care, determined tonight to make good.

The garden was dressed in its best too. The night was still warm and numberless candles, their flames amplified by halos of polished pewter, stood in each niche and rockery like tiny sentinel angels. Strings of lanterns reached from tree to tree, and torches flamed in wavering ranks set into the ground by each alley and walk. Musicians wandered about the gardens in little groups, so that, turning a corner in the maze or bower, you might come across a lutenist or a viol player, running the gamut of your conversation. Castrati, naked except for their loincloths, and painted white like statues, stood dotted around the garden in various attitudes, only to come to life and begin to sing when a guest wandered past, their clear pure treble voices floating up to the stars. The effect was magical.

Hero and I were charged to meet the guests and conduct them to where the masks were waiting for them. Hero had suggested, since at a masque we were supposed to dress as other than ourselves, that she should wear a gown of my favourite blue, and that I should wear a flame-coloured gown of Barbary silk, that had been bought from Tripoli for Hero but was too long. It was a beautiful dress, the bright silk cool and flowing. I wore strings of yellow diamonds and topaz about my throat which cascaded in a glittering firefall over my bodice, like the lava that spilled from the volcano. A cunning panel at the waist and flare at the hips made my waist seemed tiny. My inward humours matched my gown, flaming with excitement.

My uncle had had dozens of the finest masks conveyed from Venice, and all afternoon his gardeners had been hanging them about the low-hanging branches of the great mulberry trees clustered in the middle of his lawn, for his guests to pluck like fruits. Now, in the darkness, the varnished faces peeped out between the lanterns in their glowing, jewel-like colours; peacocks, lions, columbines, jesters. Here were celestial faces too; moons dusted with powdered pearl, stars sprinkled with glittering diamonds, and suns crowned with gilded rays. I could see, among the masks, faces from the picture cards of the *Scopa* deck, one king, one queen and one knave. I untied the queen and placed her face over my own. I wondered whether Signor Benedick would choose to be the king.

Or the knave.

It was then that I saw him, walking down the ride from the house, flanked by the prince on one side and young Claudio on the other. I began to smile, for he was changed indeed – the green caterpillar had become a brave scarlet butterfly.

He was wearing the livery of St James, with a Spanish doublet, sleeves slashed up and down and double breasts carved like an apple pie. The sleeves, tight from elbow to wrist, tapered like cannons. His hair was cut short around the ears, tamed, combed down with a pomade I could smell from where I stood, parted on the side and styled in a curl plastered on his forehead. He walked with great pride and importance, taller than ever in vertiginous boots with high block heels. The stubble of his face had gone to stuff tennis balls, and only the shadow of a moustache shaded his lip, with a small triangular beard below. He had turned, in short, into Don Pedro.

Hero curtsied to the prince and Claudio, who bowed, and she

conveyed them to the mask tree to choose their identity. I saw my uncle fawn upon them, and cry: 'Gentlemen, choose your visors!' as he helped them to the tree's most costly fruits. Benedick hung back a little, then walked over to me. He bowed with a complicated flourish.

Although he was not in armour, he was ready, it seemed, for anything; for a rapier hung from his baldric, a dagger peeped from his belt and there were several little Spanish knives stuck into his ceinture, as if it were a butcher's belt. 'Signor Benedick,' I said, badly wanting to laugh. 'Have you come to slay me?'

'I am dressed as befits my new occupation.' He looked about him as if the mulberries grew ears in place of leaves. 'It is a *very great* secret.' He looked down at me archly, and I realised even his eyebrows had been tamed. 'Do not you want to know what it is?'

'To look as foolish as possible?'

He bristled, and I relented. 'I assume,' I said, 'from the medal of Saint James about your neck, that you have taken the Spanish dollar and accepted commission for Don Pedro's army.'

'That is so, but my role will be much, much more than that.'

'Last night you had no stomach for soldiery.'

'Does not the appetite alter?'

'Apparently,' I said tartly. 'But, Signor Benedick, a soldier's colours are won in the field, and the bravest deeds often wear the meanest clothes.' I walked all the way around him, assessing his attire from all angles. 'The jay is not more precious than the lark, because his feathers are more beautiful, nor the adder better than the eel, because of his painted skin.' I was back in my place. 'The battledress alone does not make a soldier, but what is inside it. And your sword,' I touched the cool haft of it with one finger, 'is as yet untried.'

Signor Benedick raised his chin. 'I wear my wit in my scabbard, and draw it daily, and it is this the prince has seen in me.

The tongue can open a door to the inner chambers of government better than a key or a cannon.'

'There we may find agreement. For it seems to me that there are no fellows of action any more; men are only turned into tongues, and trim ones too.'

'Well, Lady, I had thought to ask you to dance. I was yours for the walk, but now I must walk away.' He thrust out his shorn chin. 'You did not like me last night, and you do not like me thus. I cannot imagine that there will be any day of the calendar when my presence is pleasing to you.' He turned on his heels and marched away, but the drama of his exit was ruined; he tripped on his foil and stumbled on his boots, measuring his length on the ground. He stood back up too quickly and got himself entangled in his silly little cloak, which swung around to the front. He tossed the thing back, and the lace caught afire a little on the sentinel torches, causing him to beat at himself frantically as if troubled by a wasp.

It was then that all my attempts at politeness left me and the laugh that had been threatening to burst from me during our exchange erupted like Etna. I brayed so loudly that my uncle, busily flattering the prince under the mulberries, looked over. But even with my uncle's stony eyes upon me, I howled, doubled up, beat at my skirts, tears spurting from my eyes. Benedick raised his chin, and righted his cloak, and stalked away.

I was sorry at once, and was about to go after him, when my way was blocked by a woman, dressed in the same colour as me. She wore a golden mask, tricked out with gilt sequins and fashioned like the face of the sun. The sunrays caught the light as she very faintly shook her head and she laid her hand on my sleeve as if to prevent me following in Signor Benedick's path. Then she squeezed my arm once and was gone, with a whisper of her flame skirts in the grass. I peered into the colourful throng. But it was too late. I had lost Signor Benedick.

He had his revenge, for a little later, as the pipers struck up, I saw he had found another lady to walk about with him; some duchess from Catania, who, from the way she was leaning on his arm and laughing up into his visor, had morals as loose as her bodice. I saw, as he turned, that he had chosen for his mask the king of the *Scopa* pack. I studied them for a moment; as he could barely walk in the boots I had not had high hopes for him as a dancer, but had to admit that he danced well. We would have made good partners. Well, I could serve him likewise; I just had to find a man to dance with me, and make sure Beatrice was looking.

Then Don Pedro himself was at my elbow, and asked me to be his partner for the measure. I could not have done better, for he was the highest picture card in the pack, for all that he had chosen for his mask, strangely, the knave of the *Scopa* cards.

'A knave, Your Highness?' I queried, as the music began and we did reverence to each other. 'Surely you could have found a more lofty disguise?'

'What better disguise than the opposite of yourself?' asked the prince. 'I am a king on working days; may I not be a knave at my leisure? And I see you have risen in the world – for tonight the princess is a queen.'

'My father still lives, I thank God,' I reminded him, 'and my brother too.'

'To be sure, to be sure.' He flashed his white teeth.

'And in truth,' I said, the mask affording me freedom, 'you are no more a king than I am a queen – for does not Spain have a king who is an emperor too?'

'It does. Philip the Second.'

'Is he a worthy ruler?' I felt daring. 'For I have heard he is only a king of figs and oranges.'

'He is much more than that,' he said lightly, 'for his lands stretch from one edge of the Mariner's Mirrour to the other.'

I tried to imagine such a sovereign. 'What is he like?'

He flung his hand high; part of the dance, part of his answer. 'He is the most powerful monarch in Christendom.'

I dismissed such hyperbole. 'Yes. But what *manner* of man is he?'

Don Pedro considered, as I turned about under his raised hand. 'A man of contradictions. He will cry cold tears at prayer or contemplation, then warm his hands on a burning heretic.' There was more candour in his answer than I had expected. 'On Christmas night he will watch the night offices with the monks in the freezing cold, and on Corpus Christi day process in the burning heat. On that day, they offered him shade, but I heard him say: "Today the sun will do no harm." He commands the very heavens, Lady Beatrice, and sits as far above us as the great golden orb.'

I didn't believe a word of this; I thought the prince a man of keen ambition and decided to try him. 'Princesses and princes are but ladies and lords in waiting. Perhaps, though, you may still climb to the top in our little Sicily, as the cock crows on his own dunghill.'

He looked at me through his knave's eyes. 'What do you mean?'

'I mean that Sicily has a viceroy, who is old, and ineffectual.'

He said nothing for a moment, and I wondered whether I had gone too far. But then he spoke again. 'There is something I forgot to tell you about our king; he will always try on the coat before he appoints the tailor.'

So whatever Don Pedro was doing in Sicily, he was to be tried and tested before he was given preferment. I sensed, though, that he would tell me no more. His tone lightened. 'It is strange to be so serious, when attired in such foolishness.'

I thought of Signor Benedick. 'As a seasoned politician, you should know that the most important pronouncements come from the most fatuous faces.' As the music prompted us, I linked my elbow in his, and we changed places with the next couple.

'Still, perhaps we should be trivial now?'

'If it pleases you.' I was biddable, anxious to make amends for any impertinence. 'What shall we talk of?'

'Do not ladies always wish to talk of love?' His teeth gleamed through the mouth-hole in the mask.

'I have little to say on the subject.'

'But you must have many suitors, Lady Beatrice?'

I thought of the *settebello* card, and Signor Benedick; but I had belittled and rejected him, and could hope for no more overtures. I hardened my face behind my mask, and repeated what I had told my aunt . 'I had rather hear a dog bark at a crow than a man swear he loves me.'

The prince gave a little bark of laughter from behind his visor.

'I amuse Your Highness?' I said stiffly.

'Only because my new companion is of the same mind.'

I stopped halfway around my turn and was bumped from behind by Orsola. 'Signor Benedick? What did he say?'

'That he had never yet beheld a face that he could fancy more than any other, and that as a professed tyrant to your sex, he could not take one lady to his heart for pity of all the others.' He chuckled at the memory.

'*When* did he say this?' I tried to keep my voice light.

'This very morning,' said the prince. 'And as he uttered it in a church porch I assume he spoke the truth.'

I set my teeth. That cowardly, heartless, hollow knave! To lay his heart upon my plate at dinner, then take it away at breakfast! And yet, I counselled myself, what had he promised me? He gave me a card which I rejected, he offered me friendship and I traded him insults, he asked me to dance and I laughed in his face. Yes, as usual, I had no one to blame for misery but myself. I danced the rest of the measure mechanically, and do not know what, if anything, I said more to Don Pedro.

As the music ended my uncle bustled up to me officiously. 'Niece, could you look to those things I told you of?' I looked at him absently; he had not asked me to do anything that I recalled; but he jerked his silver head with great significance. I understood when Hero was steered into Don Pedro's arms as soon as I had left them. My uncle did not want me to take another turn with the prince.

'Your mercy, Uncle.' I bowed to Don Pedro and I shook my head at the uncomfortable tableau as I backed away into the crowd. The marriage market among nobility was an odd business. I could not blame my uncle for being an assiduous father, I suppose, and ensuring that Hero did not lose a prince to her cousin, but still they made an awkward pair – I know many a Spanish infanta has been dispatched to the marriage bed even from her cradle, but still, it looked as if Hero was dancing with her father.

My aunt Innogen, in the company of another lady, was gesturing at me urgently across the lawn. As I approached, my aunt lowered her mask, a pearlised crescent moon on a stick. 'Beatrice, whatever did you say to Signor Benedick? The gentleman I danced with told me he was much wronged by you.'

My insides twisted, and I hung my head. 'He came to ask me to dance, and I laughed at him.'

'Then dance alone.'

The new voice was rich and spicy, and the dialect sounded alien to my ears. Its owner stood in the shadows, but my aunt drew her forward, and I looked into the face of the sun once again. She was the same lady who had prevented me from following Benedick.

'This is my friend, Guglielma Crollalanza,' said my aunt. 'She was the companion of my heart when I came here as a green girl from the north and a new bride.' She turned to her friend. 'Do not encourage my niece, Guglielma, for she is already a horse of your colour.'

The lady gestured to a passing servant, took a crystal goblet from his hand, and passed it to me. 'Why should she not laugh at a man? Men are amusing. And if a man is too frightened by her tongue to dance with her, I say again, she should dance alone.'

I was intrigued, and took a gulp of wine. 'Without a partner?'

'Why not? I did so as a girl; danced till I was dizzy.' The wine was making me a little dizzy myself. The sun mask came closer. 'And I have seen your aunt do as much too.'

My aunt shushed her friend. 'Guglielma. I was young, and my husband does not like me to speak of those times.'

It was odd to see the sun disputing with the moon, and as I met the black eyes again, I could see that my aunt's friend had no good opinion of my uncle. 'Why should it pain him to recall the woman he chose to marry?'

'Enough,' admonished my aunt, 'or I will not fulfil my promise to find you a house.'

I was not really in the mood for company, but in this lady, this Guglielma Crollalanza with her forthright manner and sharp tongue, I recognised a kindred spirit. Besides, she gestured to a server again to refill my glass. 'Do you no longer reside in Sicily, signora?'

'I am of an old Sicilian family – one of the oldest, the Archirafi. So Sicily is in my blood, though I have travelled widely since I was a girl who called the island home. And yes, I hope to live here again. My husband, my son and I were hoping to summer here – things got a little warm for my husband in the north.' She turned to my aunt as she made this odd statement and I saw a look of complicity pass between them. 'We are at the Mermaid in Messina until we hear of a house to lease.'

'There I can help you,' said my aunt, 'if you cease your

lionising of my niece. It so happens I have heard of a vacant house, not far from here on the beach. A dreadful circumstance that befell the previous tenants was prequel to this happy chance. But if you can overlook its sad history, the house has a pleasing aspect, and vistas of the sea.'

Guglielma Crollalanza seemed unconcerned. 'There is scarce a dwelling in Sicily that is not soaked in blood. Give me the direction.'

I excused myself and wandered off, bored with their house hunt. Clasping the goblet, hiding my melancholy behind my mask, I walked through the dancers, watching Signor Benedick whirling competently from one partner to another. A tyrant to my sex indeed!

Thoroughly miserable, I wandered into the maze, and drank the rest of the flask as I wandered through the fortress of turns. At last I found myself in the very heart of the labyrinth and sat unsteadily on the stone bench. A statue, frozen in one of the niches in the beech hedge, suddenly came to life and stepped down from his plinth. The pretty youth struck an attitude before me and began to sing. The words of his ditty crept into my ears, something about sighing ladies and deceiving men. Every line seemed to be about Benedick.

'Go away,' I said.

After that things became hazy. I remember the lanterns blurring before my eyes, and seeming to spin around. I was the axis of an orrery and the lights were the planets wheeling about me. The stone curved arms of the chair seemed suddenly as inviting as pillows – I lowered my heavy head to rest and the goblet rolled from my hand, breaking with a little tinkling crash.

'Here she is!' cried a girlish voice. 'Signor, can you help me? We must convey her to my room before she is seen by my father and mother.'

And so I saw, through half-closed eyes, Hero walk ahead of us in the lantern light, leading us unerringly through the maze she had grown up with. I felt my head loll back and the strong arms carry me, the grass whispering under his sure tread, then the crunching of gravel, then the ringing of stone stairs to Hero's chamber. *Stairs keep us safe, stairs keep us separate.*

I was laid at last upon mine and Hero's bed, and I dreamed of a shadowy figure who lifted the queen mask from my face, and lifted the king mask from his, and pressed a tender kiss to my cheek.

Act II scene iii

Leonato's house and the harbour at Messina

Beatrice: I did not see Signor Benedick on the next day (when I was keeping company with the worst headache I had ever had) but I thought of him without ceasing.

I had it from Hero that Signor Benedick had been most concerned about my whereabouts, for I had not been seen at the masque for above an hour. He had secretly carried me to our room, avoiding the beady eyes of my uncle, and laid me upon the bed. This alone was enough to make me blush, so I did not dare ask about the kiss. My drink-addled brain had surely created this fiction – I cursed my storyteller's brain and I saved a curse too for my aunt's friend, the mysterious woman with the face of the sun, who had so readily plied me with wine.

I would have kept my bed but it was Sunday and Hero insisted that we go to mass. I shuffled behind the family into the little chapel in its own tiny verdant courtyard, set back on a perfect square of grass. I bowed my head as we processed and lowered my eyes in an attitude of penitence, but in truth my head boomed like a tabor whenever I moved it the merest fraction, and I could barely lift my throbbing eyelids. I was glad, for once, of the veil of black lace that all Sicilian ladies wore to mass, and drew it over my face against the fierce sun.

Inside the church, I had hoped for cool and gloom, but beams of merciless light struck through the stained windows and split into all seven colours, and the gilt and brave paint of the saints who lined the walls hurt my bloodshot eyes. I closed them in counterfeit prayer.

Friar Francis, with one amused eye upon me, took as his text the marriage at Cana. Every mention of water gave me a raging thirst, but the very mention of wine made my gut roil. As we knelt for the sacrament, the fumes rising from the chalice turned my stomach, and I shut my teeth on the pewter. But Friar Francis, with a significant look, tipped the cup until I had to gulp. For one terrible instant I thought that I would spit the blood of Christ all over the chancel, but I swallowed that mouthful and the next. There was little left of Christ's blood for the rest of the family, but on me it worked a miracle indeed; in the space of a few more Latin responses I suddenly began to feel much better, and even to contemplate my dinner with an appetite.

Feeling a little better after we'd dined, I decided to walk down to the beach, for I could always marshal my thoughts better with the backdrop of the waves. Almost as an after-thought, I wandered past the house of the Moor, but there was no sign of the pied lovers.

I wandered all the way to the harbour in Messina, for I loved the place and there was always diversion to be found there. I found Friar Francis, in his respite between matins and even-song, playing *Scopa* with the fishermen, dealing the cards on the upturned boat. I kirtled my skirts and sat cross-legged beside him as I always did, and he crinkled his eyes at me in his friendly fashion. 'Are you feeling better, Lady?' he asked, amusement warming his voice.

I nodded, a little sheepishly. 'And I thank you for the good office you did me at mass.'

Now it was his turn to look sheepish. 'Not such a holy office, to my shame,' he said.

'But still, the act of a Samaritan,' I consoled.

'It helped, then?' he asked, dealing the cards with his chubby fingers.

'Yes. How did you know it would?'

He quartered the cards on the boat, four face up in the centre, and turned over the battle card. It was the nine of swords. 'I have not always worn holy weeds,' he said. 'I once wore armour.'

I was reminded, sharply, of my conversations with Benedick. 'I washed up here after the battle of Lepanto in '71. When you are a soldier you learn to fight, but you also learn to drink. When you win, you drink. When you lose, you drink too. And in order to fight another day you have to be able to jump out of bed at the bugle's call.' He piled the pack in front of me, for I was to begin the play. 'I helped you with an old soldier's trick. A hair of the dog that bit you.'

I said no more; for one of Leonato's Watchmen made up the four, a tiresome fellow who needed the rules constantly explained to him, while protesting all the time that he was a great proficient. I stayed to play a few rounds, but I was not on my game that day. Ironically, it was the *settebello* card, the seven of coins, that completely evaded my hand through each round, and I soon gave up and wandered home, my spirits much depressed.

I did not know what to think of Signor Benedick, but I now thought of the card he had given me as a prize; it was as if when I had given away the card I had given away my luck. As the waves soaked my boots, one thought washed over me with icy clarity: if the *settebello* was to be the only thing he'd ever give me, I wish I had not given it back so readily. I wish I had kept it.

That night dinner was a quiet affair – the regiment did not join us, for according to Orsola there was many a rancid breath and a slack cod among the soldiers today, and they were all taking their rest. My uncle, as part of his relentless programme of entertainments, had organised a fencing tournament to be held in the great courtyard the next day, and they were preparing themselves for that. 'There is such an oiling of blades and polishing of buckles and a spitting upon boot-leather as you have never seen,' said Orsola, 'for their prince Don Pedro has promised the victor a precious golden reliquary, containing the fingerbone of Saint James himself. And Saint James is the most honoured of their saints; to the Spanish he is better than all the other apostles packed together.'

I pricked up my ears at this. Surely Benedick would lay down his gauntlet with the rest, for I had huddled enough insults upon him about trying his sword. I excused myself and took myself off to my bed too, for I would not fail him at the tournament on the morrow.

Act II scene iv

A tourney before Leonato's house

Beatrice: The courtyard was brave with banners of blue and gold.

The colours of the flags tricked out the colours in the mosaic, colours that the Romans had stamped in the floor centuries ago as their imperial imprimatur.

And now, eons later, Sicily's latest invaders would try their skill with the sword atop those little tiles.

Yet there was something old fashioned about the trial that Leonato had planned. He had had a loge constructed at the south side of the courtyard, a wooden structure brave with gilt and hung about with his blazon. Leonato's arms, featuring a lion, went back to his brutish British descent many centuries before. His ancestors were painting themselves blue while the Roman masons were etching dolphins into this floor.

Above his standard hung not the flag of Spain but the Trinacria, the flag of Sicily, showing my uncle's primary allegiance. The flag displayed a three-legged chimera with a gorgon's head, on a yellow and red ground. The three legs, I knew, represented the three regions of the island, but I did not know the significance of the snake-headed woman.

The scarlet of Spain was diplomatically in evidence too, fluttering and flattering about Don Pedro, who sat on a great wooden chair at the centre of the dais. He looked well today, for over his damascene sleeves he wore a white tabard emblazoned with a device in red that I did not know; at first I thought it a dagger, but then the prince turned his body and I knew I had been mistaken. The thing was a cross fitchy, terminating in a point, with arms of a cross fleury, ending in fleur-de-lys. Above the dagger-cross floated a scallop shell; and then I knew; this was the cross of St James the Great. And at the prince's elbow was the saint himself, or at least, a little bit of him. The prize was a beautiful reliquary with a ruby as big as my thumbnail set into the top, with golden sunrays spiking about it, and a little window of diamond panes below. Through the window I could see a small dun bone, a contrast to the glory about it, which must be the fabled fingerbone of St James himself.

Leonato sat on the other side of the digit, in a chair nearly as grand as the prince's, my aunt Innogen on the other side. Hero, myself and other highborn ladies of the region sat on fat cushions at the feet of our lords, and I saw a lady in a flame-coloured dress at the far side of the loge who looked vaguely familiar.

She was *una dama in nero*; a dark lady. Her black hair was unornamented and left free to curl in a tumble of spiral ringlets about her shoulders. She had dark skin, full lips and a broad nose, and looked alien and beautiful. Her eyes, when she looked at me, were as black and soothing as the centre of the poppy. She smiled; but, caught staring, I averted my eyes. As I did so I noticed that the loge backed on to the arras that hung on the wall. The tapestried dame with her unicorn reclined with us, watching too.

The tourney was beginning. Leonato had charged his marshals that everything should be as it was in antique times, so each young squarer had to come to the loge to present himself to Don Pedro and Leonato, and to be given a sash of the prince's red or my uncle's blue to wear about their waists as they fought. I yawned through a roll-call of noble Spanish names, as young Alba de Listes, Requesenes and Guzmanes paraded before us, while the poor marshal of the lists struggled with his quill to spell their names on the roll.

Each combatant was given the right to crave a favour from the ladies on the platform. I relaxed, expecting all the young sprigs to flatter their host by approaching his daughter Hero, but, to my surprise, most of them lined up in front of me, and soon my dress was denuded of all ribbons, pins, sashes and tippets. I even had to give away my little gold brooch of the Della Scala ladder, and since all the combatants were masked I had little hope of getting it back.

I concluded that perhaps a blond head is a rarity in Spain; but I was pleased and flattered. All the time I waited, breathless, for Signor Benedick to step up, hoping he had seen my popularity. I arranged my features into an expression which I hoped conveyed modest politeness (without contrition) but to begin with I could not see Don Pedro's newest knight anywhere.

I began to feel a hollow disappointment. Perhaps if he was as terrible with a dagger and sword as he'd maintained – I remembered his sally about a parsnip and a stick of celery – then he might decide that it was politic to step aside if he could not bloom among these flowers of Spanish chivalry.

Amongst all the antique posturing I'd half expected to see broadswords and helms, but all the competitors wore their fencing plastrons of creamy white, with a toughened breastplate, a blade-catcher at the throat and a visor of iron net obscuring the face. This was sport after all, not warfare – these noble babies were as safe here as in their cradles. I might not have spotted Signor Benedick among the uniform throng, but my gaze found him at last by reason of his greater height among the tiny Spanish. I watched him await his turn, and even if he had been of Spanish stature I would still have known him, for he spent his time until his bout balancing his foil on one finger, adjusting his hand all the time to keep the sword in the air as if he were a Carnevale juggler.

I felt a little ashamed for him amongst all these soldiers. He was a clown, and I did not have high hopes for him in the match. I was, I felt, about to witness his humiliation; but now the longed-for moment had come, I felt strangely sorry for him.

Then he was suddenly there, before the loge, his visor under his arm. In his plain white plastron he could have stood up with any man alive, and looked vastly different to the primped peacock of the previous evening. He bowed low, and Don Pedro, anxious not to betray his preference, spoke to him as he had to every knight of either colour.

'Your name, señor?'

'Signor Mountanto.'

The Spanish yakked away like jackals and I curled my lip. It was a poor jest, and one that he had reckoned on only the menfolk understanding – *mountanto*, an upward thrust in fencing, was also slang for a gentleman's manhood. My scorn was magnified by the fact that he chose to fight for Don Pedro, his new sworn brother. True, the states of Padua and Sicily had little to say to one another, but Signor Benedick had clearly thrown in his lot with the Spanish, and I felt it a small betrayal.

'Would you like to crave a favour from one of the ladies who so ornament our loge?' asked the prince.

'I thank you, Your Highness,' replied Benedick in ringing tones, 'but one of these ladies already did me the honour of bestowing me with her favour; after dinner the night before last.'

The loge rocked with laughter at this bawdy jest, but there was no offence taken, as he was already, it seemed, an acknowledged wit. Not once did he look at me, and no one else could know of the episode of the *settebello*, but I shrank inside, and when he put on his visor and turned without giving me away, I felt nothing but relief.

Once the competitors stood in the circle of the mosaic, around the inlaid head of Medusa, there were no more names, just the scarlet and the blue. It was blood versus sea, Spain versus Sicily, and I thought now that I had been wrong to call it sport; it was much more serious than that. The courtyard was packed not just with Leonato's guests, but with the townspeople of Messina, none of whom had much reason to love their Spanish overlords. Many of them waved the Trinacria flag; all of them cheered for blue, and were silent for scarlet. Every dagger and blade wore a foil; this was a serious business dressed as an entertainment. The whole affair felt like a practice, a rehearsal, for a graver matter. But for what?

As the morning wore on the sun skewed round in the sky and lit the ruby in St James's reliquary, illumined like a flare, shining out like the grail to the worthiest knight, a prize to covet indeed. And, incredibly, as bout followed bout, it seemed inevitable that the saint's finger would be claimed by Signor Mountanto.

I could see Don Pedro sit forward on his wooden throne, delighted with his new protégé. For as the rounds progressed even I had to admit that Signor Benedick outclassed all those who stood up with him. Not that I had much admiration for the Spanish style of swordplay; it was too pretty, with too many flourishes. It was attractive to watch, but had not the strength and clean lines of good Italian combat, and the beautifying flourishes left the core open to blow after blow. So Signor Benedick was giving them a master class. His *stoccata* was impenetrable, his *imbroccata* impressive and his *punta reversa* impassable. Not only that, but he gave good show – he would throw his sword from gauntlet to gauntlet, even fight a round with his left hand. One fellow he fought with just his dagger and still his opponent's foil never touched him. Another he fought with his body entirely turned away from his adversary, literally fighting him behind his back. The tournament was becoming a joke.

The crowd fell silent. Leonato's face grew sourer and sourer, and Don Pedro's countenance brightened. Benedick might be an Italian, but he was fighting in the colours of Spain, and Don Pedro, at this rate, would win the day.

My own visage soured as much as my uncle's, for as I watched I realised that Signor Benedick had gulled me at dinner. For he had clearly downplayed his talents in swordplay, preferring, for whatever reason, to appear a feckless dilettante, rather than a young man who had clearly studied every aspect of the art of combat for all of his childhood. I do not know why I was surprised; boys of his class would have been routinely schooled by a fencing master – my own brother trained every day . . . I stopped, caught by an idea.

My brother's situation was singular, in that while his male cousins were sent to war to cool their heels, or even taken up for murderers after a bloody street brawl, my brother was left with no opponents to practise his swordplay on. So Tebaldo Della Scala, lord of Villafranca, sharpened his sword on his sister.

From a very young age I was taught how to block a blow with a dagger, how to circle my braids with a rapier, how to protect my chest spoon, how to jump with both feet above a blow. I too was taught the *stoccata*, the *imbroccata* and the *punta reversa*, and yes, the *mountanto* too. And I was well used to fighting a young man of twenty.

I looked across at Hero, but she was deep in conversation with Claudio. A week earlier I would have told her what I planned to do, but today I did not. She had become, almost overnight, much more like the young woman her father wanted her to be. But I did not think it was Leonato's influence. I think it was Claudio's. For that dinner on the first night with the Spanish had been as pivotal to Hero as it had been to me. The young man was devout, and he had dismissed her Italian lovers' tales but listened rapt to the story of Mary of the Letter. I sensed, now, that she would not beg me to hear tales of love, but rather of scripture; that she would pick up a gradual over a book of hours. For it was she who had, despite the disparity of our years, this very morning bullied me to church. Like an opal,

Hero had changed to Claudio's colour. Even now her head was turned to him, as she enjoyed the tourney not through her own observations but through his eyes. She would never notice my departure.

Slowly, slowly, I edged to the back of the loge and crept down the temporary wooden stairs. The lady with the unicorn watched me and I held my finger to my lips. I made my way through the lists and into the gatehouse which served as an armoury for the day. The marshals were in the courtyard and there were no more than a couple of kitchen boys guarding the foils. I picked a rapier, a dagger and a suit from the racks and swept out before the dolts could stop me, saying as I went: 'My uncle's orders; another knight has arrived.' Expecting to be stopped at all times I slipped through the archway, across the small cloister and into the unlocked chapel.

I carried my booty to the nave, which I knew would be empty at this hour, for the friar was not a man to wear out his knees with prayer between the bells – and, in fact, I had already seen him in the throng outside. Still, I went behind the rood screen to change, and a parade of saints in the fresco watched me with disapproval. One of those who looked down in judgement was St James the Great – admonishing me with perhaps the very finger that waited to be won in the courtyard. With shaking hands, I took off my gown as quickly as I could – and pulled on the suit and visor. If I was caught in the chapel as Beatrice I could say I was praying for the knights; if I was caught as a knight I could likewise say I was praying for my own success – but to be discovered in my shift and stockings would take a little more explanation.

The white plastron fitted like a skin. Fortunately I was tall too, and had a decent pair of shoulders, and small breasts, so once the suit was on and the breastplate was in place, there was nothing to betray my female form. I put on the helmet and passed a hand before my face – I was satisfied, from my observation of the other knights, that no one could see my face through the dense grille of the mask.

When I returned to the courtyard the servers were handing round goblets, and there seemed to be some lull in the fighting. I picked a fellow in the crowd I didn't know. He had a Trinacria tied around his throat like a kerchief. 'What is happening?'

He turned to me. 'Signor Mountanto has won,' he said sourly, 'unless another comes to challenge him.'

I walked straight up to the loge before my courage failed, and bowed to the prince.

Don Pedro put down his goblet next to the reliquary. 'A late-comer!' he cried, always diverted by novelty. He beckoned the marshal of the lists with his beringed hand. 'Will you show us your face?'

I held a hand to my visor, and shook my head. Don Pedro's interest was piqued. 'The unknown knight. Well, if we may not know your face, may we at least know your name, señor?'

'Signor Arcobaleno,' I said, lowering my voice to a growl, my tones obscured anyway by the visor. I'd thought the alias witty, and it had come to me upon the spur of the moment from the sight of all the different pennants flying here today. Signor Rainbow; I was not of one colour, but all of them.

There was a titter among the ladies. Don Pedro raised one dark brow.

'Signor Arcobaleno,' he said. 'Despite your name, you must choose a colour.'

'Since Your Highness is winning the day, I will wear the girdle of my host.'

Don Pedro, untroubled, nodded, and my uncle Leonato gave me my sky-blue sash without a flicker of recognition. I knotted it about my heaving stomach and turned to face Signor Benedick, who was busy juggling apricots.

He threw the fruits into the crowd, where three lucky

children caught them with a cheer, then he turned to face me. Only I stood between him and the priceless reliquary, and suddenly he was deadly serious. We bowed, then moved our weapons to the commencement position; rapier high, dagger low.

His first blow stung my arm all the way to my shoulder, and I knew from that first strike that I had made a mistake. He was taller than me, and tougher than I expected, and I remembered those strong arms around me when he'd taken me to my chamber. My knees buckled as with rapier and dagger I desperately tried to fend off the stinging blows. I had the advantage only in my weight and agility and I did my best to dodge the strikes by moving fast. I was also out of practice – it was a month since I had been at home and had taken up swords with my brother. In the end I had nothing else to give – Signor Benedick's rapier point touched my breastplate again and again, while the marshal counted the palpable hits. In the end I grappled with my opponent to buy myself a moment's respite; for an instant our arms were about each other as close as an embrace and we tottered together until the marshal separated us.

And then, a miracle. I do not know whether Signor Benedick tired or what, but the tide unmistakably turned. Suddenly I was breaking through his guard, his blows had no purchase and I made hit after hit upon his breastplate until the marshal raised his flag. It was blue!

Sicily was the victor, and the courtyard erupted. I was deafened momentarily by the blast of the cheers, and blinded by the dozens of Trinacria flags thrown to garland my victory. Before Signor Benedick could shake my hand I was carried up and away at shoulder height, around the courtyard in a circle of honour; before being deposited, breathless, before the loge to claim my prize. My uncle was beaming from one ear to the other, and even Don Pedro, to give him his due, could not forbear to smile.

'And now, surely, señor, you will show us your face?'

I merely bowed with a flourish, desperately hoping he wouldn't press the point. And he didn't. The prince turned to the crowd. 'He is as valiant as Hector but as modest as Jove!' he cried, as the crowd cheered again. 'Well, let it be enough to say that if you would ever take a commission in my regiment, I will write you the letter of marque in my own hand.'

I bowed again, and as I did so I saw the dark lady with the ringleted hair in the flame dress staring at me intently, a little smile playing about her lips. She held her hand up to me in a peculiar salute; every finger and the thumb tucked away, save the index finger and little finger, sticking up like a devil's horns. I was wondering what this tribute meant when it struck me like a sunburst – she was Guglielma Crollalanza, my aunt's friend, and the one who had worn the sun's face at the masque. And further, that she, alone of all the people in the courtyard, knew exactly who I was.

'Signor Arcobaleno?' Don Pedro was holding the reliquary as high as the host, and he handed it to me over the front of the loge as if he was handing me the True Cross. I grabbed the thing and ran, with probably not quite enough reverence for the Spanish, St James's fingerbone rattling in its little bejewelled housing. I was hotter than a lobster in a kettle in the accursed visor, but dared not remove it before I was under lock and key, so much did I fear my uncle's wrath. For a stunt such as this one was neither a good example of a maid's modest behaviour for Hero, nor was it what he would countenance in the behaviour of his niece.

Escaping though an archway, I cannoned into Signor Benedick coming the other way. Cursing, I tried to edge past him but he was as tall as he was broad and the way was blocked. He had removed his visor, and his hair now curled as it used to about his face. Two days' growth had consumed the ridiculous beard, and his colour was high from the exercise, in contrast to the white windings about his throat. He looked remarkably well.

'I commend you on your victory,' he said.

I nodded briefly in thanks and sidestepped, but he was too quick for me and moved the same way. 'You did the feats of a lion in the figure of a lamb.' His eyes raked my torso, and I squirmed as if I had fleas. 'Won't you remove your helmet, so that I can know my conqueror better?' He moved closer, and I could feel the heat of his body. 'For I must tell you, privately in your ear, that I have never been so overthrown. I might as well have been holding a *parsnip and a stick of celery.*'

Something about this tribute made me uncomfortable. I pushed past him, and he let me go this time, but I could feel him looking after me as I clattered up the stairs. Reaching mine and Hero's chamber, I shed the visor at last and loosened the breastplate. Something fluttered out of the doublet to the floor.

It was the *settebello* card – the seven of coins.

Slowly, I picked it up and stood, frozen, with the thing in my hand as the swifts called from the eaves outside the casement.

He had known.

I played the bout again in my head. When we had grappled, and been close as an embrace, he must have guessed then. For that was the turning point of the fight – after that he had changed, as if he had been deflated, he had made silly mistakes, swatted at thrusts that did not connect, parried blows that did not fall, tripped on stones that were not there.

He had known, and he'd let me win.

He'd known when my eyes met his through the visor, and flared blue, for no one else in the court had eyes of that colour. Then, in those few heartbeats, he had put the card in my doublet, right between my breasts. I blushed, even though I was alone, and the blood sang in my ears with the swifts.

He could have defeated me. He could have stopped the fight, taken off my visor, for by the rules of the tourney no woman could bear arms. He could have taken home the reliquary, and the honour of it, for his family's church in Padua. He could have exposed me to the wrath of my uncle. But he had not. He had let me win. The wretch had been more than forbearing. He had been *chivalrous*.

I was the victor, and as such he had given me back my gage. But he was the worthiest knight.

Act II scene v

A wedding at Syracuse

Beatrice: It had taken us only from dawn till noon to reach Syracuse in our train of carriages, but it was as if we had come to a new country, or rather, an old one; the ancient Greece of myth and legend.

The stones of the city were bleached to pale gold, ancient pillars and fallen temples were everywhere, strange spiky trees grew from the very pavings themselves and rock flowers garlanded the capitals of the temples, as if the roots were nourished by the stone. We left the carriages and crossed a causeway to an ancient island city called Ortygia, surrounded by a sea as pale blue as a duck's egg. It was the day after the tournament, my muscles protested and ached, but my uncle would not let us rest. We were to attend the wedding of one of the sons of the Duke of Syracuse, who was lately returned from a long sojourn in Ephesus.

The duomo was also a temple, giant pillars making up a vast cavernous colonnade, which in later eras had been closed over with a roof. There were hundreds of people crammed into the church – as was custom, the nobility sat at the front, with the merchants behind and at the back the peasants of Syracuse with their children and their curs and their hawks on their wrists, ready to leave once the coins had been thrown.

The Archbishop of Monreale was taking the service, and I watched him carefully as he droned through the Latin form. He took to the pulpit early on and seemed to have little intention of leaving it; for the bells rang twice during his sermon. He held forth on a familiar theme; the evils of women both in the single and the married state. He took as his text 1 Timothy, Chapter 2, verse 12: *But I suffer not a woman to teach, nor to usurp authority over the man, but to be in silence.*

Since his premise was so distasteful to me I stopped my ears and studied his form instead. The archbishop was a strange, reptilian-looking fellow – clean shaven, with full purplish lips and yellow almond eyes and pasty flesh – and it was impossible to tell his age; for all that he was Claudio's uncle he could be anything from twenty to fifty. As he descended to the chancel steps at last to begin the prayers I watched, along with all the congregation, for his trademark; for he was famous for a little physical peculiarity. Sure enough, as he spoke the paternoster tears began to swell and form in his eyes, and fall down his jaundiced cheeks. The congregation crossed themselves rapidly – for the archbishop was known as a true devout, and his tears were thought to bring down the favour of God. The frantic crossings of the people made a whispering sound throughout the ancient temple.

I did not copy them but instead sought Signor Benedick among the throng – he was easy enough to pick out among the swarthy Sicilians by reason of his blond poll, but he sat some rows away from me. I consoled myself that I would surely see him at the feast, and my heart gave a little lurch. I blinked my eyes to see him better; his head seemed to be lolling at an odd angle towards his neighbour. He was fast asleep.

A swift flew into the vast vault of the cathedral roof space, fluttering and twittering, and one of the peasants' hawks rose above it, the raptor striking the little bird with its talons. Blood spattered the bride's silver gown, and the unaccountable Sicilians cheered fit to raise the roof – apparently this was a good omen for the match. The archbishop laughed and beamed along with the rest, but when he gathered the little dead swift in his hands from the chancel steps, his tears flowed again.

After the interminable service the father of the groom led the company through this Grecian city. The procession was like a bacchanal of Dionysus for we were all given wreaths of flowers to wear about our necks and musicians played upon the gilded lyres that nestled in the nook of their arms. White peacocks pecked and strutted by our feet, glancing nervously at the white leopards straining at their handlers' leashes, answering their roars with pathetic mews.

We ended our procession at an imposing palace clad in white sun-bleached stone, set on a promontory thrust directly into the sea. At the great doors there was a brief confusion, as form dictated that we would enter by rank and seniority, but the two sons of the house were twins, and had of course been born together. We all stood about, baking like salt in the sun, while the niceties were decided; all too polite to tell them to get on with it. The matter was settled at last when the groom and his brother joined hands and walked into their house together, just as they had come into the world, while their wives followed behind.

In the great hall, where the feast and the dancing were to be held, there was a vast and ancient archway entirely open at one end so the room was light and airy. There was a pleasing vista of the Far, a rocky finger of land terminated by an antique lighthouse. In the hall itself long tables garlanded with vine leaves awaited our presence. I hoped Fate would seat me next to Signor Benedick at dinner but was not prepared to leave the matter entirely in the hands of that tricksy goddess, so I manoeuvred beside him in the melee, and landed in the chair by his side. A stranger who would not trouble us sat on the other side of me, so I looked forward to recommencing our merry war. We all stood, with a great scraping of chair legs, for the bride and groom to enter, and Benedick, released at last by his sponsor, turned to me. I caught an expression of surprised delight upon his face before his cocksure half-smile chased it away. He bowed with an ironic flourish. 'Signor Arcobaleno!'

I bowed stiffly and replied in kind. 'Signor Mountanto.'

His eyes raked my gown – I was back in my favourite colour. The blue of my bodice was as dark as midnight and sprinkled with a cluster of diamonds at the bodice, which fell in a cascade to stud the kirtle in lesser number like the evening sky. The skirt fell in graduating circles of lighter blues, like the night fading to dawn.

'You look even better than you did in the lists,' said Benedick, with frank approval, 'and today perhaps we will use our blades for eating.' He picked up his knife and speared a piece of bread. The Archbishop of Monreale, three places away beyond the prince, looked murder at him, for the grace had not yet been said. Benedick palmed the bread into his hand.

The tables were set with cups and goblets of coral and ivory and rough glass, all of which looked as if they had been preserved from antique times. The food was strange fare, another vestige, I guessed, of Greek rule here; for there were dried fruits and sallets and vine leaves aplenty but not enough, to my taste, of things that have wings and are more substantial. I picked at the dishes, but I was more anxious to talk to Signor Benedick than to fill my stomach. 'Thank you for the reliquary,' I began, all pretence abandoned. 'I will render it you again if you would like it, for it is yours.'

'Keep it, and the card too, for both were won fairly.' He made a little pantomime of looking beneath his trencher, where he had found the *settebello* once before, and I smiled. 'Besides, if that bauble contains the fingerbone of Saint James I am a Dutchman. Every church I have visited boasts another such. Saint James must have had as many arms as Briareus and a score of fingers terminating every one.'

It was said in an undertone, so that Don Pedro would not hear the denigration of his blessed idol, but the stranger to the right of me certainly heard, for I heard him chuckle in agreement.

'But the victory was yours,' I protested. 'Do you not deserve a prize?'

'If I may choose my reward, I would wish only that you admit that I may have more to offer the field of battle than perhaps you previously supposed.'

'That I will own, with all my heart,' I conceded readily, but he was merciless.

'Perhaps Don Pedro saw something in me that you did not.'

He was right. Shamed, crumbling my bread between my fingers, I sought to make amends, and thought I knew how. 'So now,' I said meekly, 'will you not tell me of your new employment in Don Pedro's army?'

He regarded me with merriment. 'Ah, but now that you wish to know, I do not wish to tell.'

My humility vanished. 'Signor Benedick, how you do delight in being contrary. But I must tell you, friendly in your ear, that perversity is no substitute for wit.'

'Dear Lady Beatrice, I was not attempting to be witty. If I were, you would be laughing already.'

I snorted at his arrogance.

'I merely came to a conclusion about my new profession which I will lay before you; a riddle, if you like, since there is always wordplay and sport at a wedding. Simply put; my profession is such that if I told you of it, I would instantly have failed at it.'

I sighed gustily. 'If I am to be so denied, what shall be our subject?'

'My dear Signor Arcobaleno, as a man you were mum as an oyster, but as a lady I know you never have any trouble in making conversation. You might remark upon the food, the company, the music.'

I was about to retort that there was no music, but as if Signor Benedick had conjured him a lutenist stepped forward. 'A hymn to the newly wedded,' the musician announced in a reedy pipe.

He struck the gamut and bowed to the couple at their garlanded table, and began to sing before the chord died.

The verses were beautiful and far better than the singer. His reedy voice soared to the coffined ceiling for his final note, and he bowed double as if burdened by the weight of the applause. I turned to my erstwhile companion. 'What do you think of this musician? Is he superior to my uncle's, for I remember they did not please you.'

Signor Benedick, who had been munching his bones throughout, pointed a lamb bone at the lutenist. 'That twangling jack? He is worse.'

'But the poetry?' I persisted. 'Was it not sublime? Did it not transport you?' I could not believe anyone could hear such words untouched.

He sighed testily. 'Lady Beatrice. You would have me a soldier, and I became one. Now would you have me be a poet too? If so I must enrol in a college of wit-crackers to learn the metre by our next dinner. But until then I will say simply that I did not hear a word of the verse for it was ill served by an ill singer.'

Now the stranger on my left laughed outright. As I opened my mouth to dispute with Benedick, Don Pedro broke off his conversation with the archbishop and turned to claim his friend. 'Signor Benedick,' he said, 'it is time.'

Without the least hesitation Benedick dropped our discourse mid-syllable for the society of his patron. He rose, and, barely excusing himself to me, he went to do his master's bidding, whatever it might be.

Frustrated, I lifted my chin; very well, I too would find diversion elsewhere. I studied the family at the wedding table. The women were separated and pinned either side of their husbands. They sat, as I did, looking about them, glassy eyed, without even each other's society to comfort them.

I wondered whether sisters or female friends had the same bond as men; but I did not think so. I recalled with a pang how few hours Hero and I had spent together since the Spanish had come to the house. Instead we had spent our days thinking of our new companions Claudio and Benedick, and what little time we had together was spent talking only of them. But this was time wasted. Women did not stand a chance of penetrating these binding masculine friendships. Men were tied together by blood, by their banner, by the garter of their order. 'Brothers in arms,' I said aloud, scornfully.

'Yes,' said the stranger on my left. 'The strongest bond of all.' I turned to look at him, but he was already occupied in writing down either my remark or his reply. He had produced a horn-book with a neat little trimmed quill – heaven knows where he got either of them – and I studied him as he wrote.

His head was down over his scribblings so I could see that his dark locks grew somewhat thin on top. His hair was worn long about the sides, and where it curled over the scroll of his ear I noted that he wore a single drop pearl in the lobe, which shivered as he wrote. His doublet was oxblood brown, and around his neck he wore a ruff in the English style, a fashion that was a little outdated. His fingers were long and fidgety as they spewed the spidery writing.

He must have felt me observing him; for he looked up and it was then that I saw that despite the thinning hair he must be no older than Signor Benedick. He had handsome if slightly weak features, and a little pointed beard and light moustache. Around his neck hung a curiosity; a leather capsa containing a spare small quill and a slick of ink in a tiny crystal bottle. Courtesy fought with curiosity; curiosity won. 'What is that?' I asked.

He smiled and the expression seemed to lift his slightly sad features. He had been the mask of Tragedy, for his mouth had a downward droop to it and the corners of his eyes folded down. The smile gave everything an upward tendency; his eyes and mouth lifted and it was as if his whole countenance opened up; now he was Comedy.

'It is the insignia of my profession. Not a regimental medal or a garter, or even doctor's spectacles. Just a pen and some ink.'

I was reminded of my conversation with Signor Benedick. This fellow must be a lawyer, or perhaps a scrivener. 'And what is your profession?'

'I am a writer,' he said. 'A poet and a playwright.'

'A poet?' I said, diverted. 'Would I know anything you have written?'

He indicated the lutenist with his quill. 'I wrote the wedding hymn that your companion so enjoyed.' But he smiled; no offence apparent.

This impressed me, for I had enjoyed the ode whatever Benedick thought. 'And you write plays too? That must be very . . . difficult?'

'Not so long as you follow the rules. In a tragedy, everyone must die. And in a comedy, everyone must marry.'

It could not be that simple. 'What if some characters expire, and some wed?'

'That would be more of a problem.'

I thought upon what he had said. 'I wonder what my play will be.'

He did not reply to this, but just watched me speculatively. I found it unsettling, so questioned him to distract him. 'And where do you find your muse?'

'Italy is my muse,' he said. 'I am a collector of stories. I read Dante, Boccaccio, Bandello . . .'

'Bandello!' it was an unmannerly shriek. 'He came to my father's castle once.'

'In Verona?' asked the poet, turning towards me eagerly.

'Villafranca, just outside the city. I am Beatrice Della Scala.'

It was not the fashion for the lady to make the introduction, but I had little patience for such niceties. 'Are you Sicilian, then, that you wrote this tribute to the couple?'

'I was born in Messina, but taken to the north for my education. I was schooled in England, then studied in Wittenberg. Then I was court poet to the Danish king in Elsinore.'

'Then I may truly claim you for the north. I am glad to make your acquaintance, Signor . . .?' I let my voice drift upwards in a question. It was a hint; for he was clearly as much of a stranger to proper forms as myself. Somewhat belatedly, he held out one inky hand.

'Michelangelo Florio Crollalanza.'

The name flared in my memory. 'Then your mother is . . .'

'Guglielma Crollalanza.' He pointed across the room. I looked to where the ringleted woman sat beside my aunt, in her favoured flame-coloured silk.

'And is your father at the feast?'

'No,' said the poet. 'He does not enjoy society. He likes to keep at the inn with his books.'

'Reading or writing?'

'Both.'

'And he found the north too hot for him?'

He looked puzzled. 'How did you know . . .?'

I smiled. 'So you are acquainted with the family?'

'My mother knows the groom's mother well.' The young man had a strange accent, each cadence earned upon his travels like a pocket coin of each nation, collected to jangle together in their own particular music. 'But I do not know a soul in the wedding party.' He pointed his goose feather to the high table, where the Spanish and Sicilian nobles clinked their golden goblets. 'What is this constellation of nobility, Lady Beatrice? The dramatis personae have changed since I last saw this play.'

I studied the golden company. 'You think them players?'

'We are all players; but that board is groaning with particularly tasty meat for a plot. Politics, ambition, greed; all writ upon these fine features.'

I looked anew at the brave figures on the high table, the

paper kings of the *Scopa* deck all huddled together, and named them for my new acquaintance following his device, as you might read them on the first quarto of a play. 'Don Pedro, a prince of Aragon.' Benedick hovered at the prince's shoulder, close as a shadow, but I left him off the roll. 'Ludovico de Torres, Archbishop of Monreale. Next to the prelate is his nephew, Count Claudio Casadei of Florence, and beyond him the viceroy himself.' I pointed to the portly fellow with impressive moustaches. 'Diego Enrique de Guzman. Leonato Leonatus, my uncle, is beside the viceroy, and the father of the groom – Egeon, was it? – you know. Those are the players. But what are their parts?'

The poet turned his dark eyes on me. 'That I cannot tell, for I feel they are only in the prologue of their drama. Their story is still in train, their characters mere sketches. On so short an acquaintance I cannot tell you what each man is, but only what he loves.'

'Say on.'

The poet drew a long breath, and pointed his goose-tip at each player as he spoke. 'The prince loves himself, too well to admit room in his heart for another. The archbishop loves God and gold in equal measure. The young count loves God only. The viceroy loves his king, but would rather be one. Your uncle, saving your presence, loves his own voice.'

I was intrigued by his words, by him. 'And what do you love?'

'Words,' he said, 'words, words.'

'And how do you know these men's hearts?'

'Observation chiefly, and a little catechism,' he admitted. 'I questioned the count about his home in Florence, and as all conversations about that city must, our discourse turned quickly to art. I asked him if he'd seen Signor Botticelli's *Pallas and the Centaur*, as the subject of Pallas Athena holds a particular interest for me. He admitted he'd seen the painting, but said that to his mind Botticelli's devotional work was superior, and pointed to the fact that the artist himself, by the end of his life, had denounced his pagan work.'

I thought of what Hero had said when she had met the young count at dinner; that he did not wish to hear tales of love but of the scriptures. The poet had seen into Claudio's soul. I wondered what he had divined of the count's nursemaid?

With a great commotion and clatter all the company stood for the dancing and would soon divide into ladies and men. I had to ask.

'And Signor Benedick?' I spoke casually.

'Who?'

'The prince's companion. The tall blond northerner, hovering at his master's shoulder like a Barbary's parrot.'

'Ah, now that is easy. He loves *you*.'

And with that, he was gone, with a dramatist's talent for ending a scene.

Struck by what the poet had said, I sought Signor Benedick at once. Could it be true that he loved me, even though he had made denial to Don Pedro? He had given me a priceless reliquary, and a worthless playing card that even now I wore in my dress, under the starburst stomacher. He had rescued me from the maze and saved my blushes at the tourney. Was Michelangelo Crollalanza right? He could be gulling me, of course, but the poet did not seem of humorous bent.

My search was in vain, for Benedick was way out on the Far, standing sentinel a little way from the nobles, and looking as forlorn as a lodge in a warren. So I went to join the ladies, acting, for once, as form demanded; but only because, as Benedick was engaged in the service of his master and Signor Crollalanza had vanished, I had an urge to seek the society of the poet's mother.

My aunt was beside the lady, and the evident closeness of their bond was almost enough to make me reassess my earlier musings on feminine friendships. 'Aunt.' I greeted my aunt

Innogen with a kiss on the cheek, but Signora Crollalanza, who always seemed to speak candidly, did not waste time on niceties. 'Lady Beatrice. You look better without your mask.'

She might have been speaking of my disguise as the Queen of *Scopa* at my uncle's masque, but I knew she was talking about my appearance at the fencing match as Signor Arcobaleno.

'Signora Crollalanza. So do you.' It was true. Her black hair, unornamented as ever, had a nap and texture such as I had never seen.

'I have been making the acquaintance of your son,' I said.

The jet-black eyes softened. 'I am glad of it. Michelangelo thinks too much.'

'Is that possible?'

'For a woman, no. But for a man, yes.'

'He seems to enjoy observing others.'

'He has little to divert him here, so I am glad he is enjoying the festivities.'

I caught her tone. 'And you ?'

She smiled and spoke in my ear. 'It is more comfortable to observe than to be observed. In answer to your question I am enjoying myself much more *now*, now that disapproving eyes have taken themselves off to the Far.' I looked out to the group of noblemen on the rocks, gathered together like cormorants. 'I am speaking, you must know, of the archbishop.'

I had formed an unfavourable impression of that prelate on the grounds of his sermon alone, but was surprised that Guglielma should find his attack so personal. 'Why should he dislike you?'

'He has many reasons to hate me. One, that I am a woman. That would be enough. But I am free, in behaviour, in dress, in speech. I am part Moorish, and he had pledged to cleanse the island of my kind. I am from a family of slaves, and no one enjoys their freedom quite so much as those who have been denied it. And beyond that, I am married to a Calvinist who does not share the archbishop's faith and is articulate enough to proselytise. And lastly I am raising a son in the image of his father.'

I was struck – I had never considered any faith but the Catholic Church and had closed my ears to the teachings of the Protestants. Slowly I remembered the poet's education. England, Denmark. Cradles of Protestantism. And Wittenberg, famously the home of Luther's heresy. Guglielma's thoughts had kept step with my own. 'The sunrays that burned too hotly on my husband in the north were the fires of faith; but I feel, I dread, that they will burn here too.'

I hoped she did not have the gift of prediction. Her words and her prophetic tone gave me an urge to cross myself, but given the subject of our discourse I refrained.

Now she smiled, like a naughty child. 'Your uncle disapproves of me too. He thinks I am a bad example for his daughter, and lead his wife astray.'

'And do you?'

Guglielma glanced over her shoulder but my aunt was preoccupied with tying Hero's slipper, for my cousin had little to do, as Claudio, unlike Benedick, had been invited into the inner sanctum of the conference on the Far. And so Hero regressed to the schoolroom, whining and fussing and bothering her mother for ribbons and comfits.

'Your uncle does not like Innogen to remember her history, but as women our history is part of us. Let me tell you a little of your aunt.' Guglielma took my arm and led me beneath a Grecian arch loaded with ginestra blossom. 'When they were first betrothed, your uncle gave her a bracelet, the one with the chalcedony stone that she wears every day.' I knew the jewel well – the stone was beautiful, jade and opaque like the eye of a cat. 'She lost the thing for a time and your uncle thought her untrue; but she pursued him till her good name, his favour and the bracelet were restored.'

I thought of my aunt; so correct, so mannerly. I could not imagine her wantonly pursuing my uncle. Was theirs a happy ending? Had it been a comedy, their story? Guglielma echoed my thoughts, her eyes on her friend, on the jewel. 'The bracelet has become her shackle. And it reminds your uncle of a time when she was free.' Her honesty robbed me of breath, and as we returned to my aunt's side I could say no more, but I thought much on the price of a marriage which meant giving yourself away.

As the light thickened outside, the gentlemen returned from the Far and joined the throng. Claudio lined up with Hero at once, and she was once more transformed from a mewling child into a young woman; but, to my irritation, Signor Benedick did not seek me out. I saw him, after the first measure, in close conference with Duke Egeon.

Determined to enjoy myself I joined the fray, dancing with my uncle's brother Antonio, young Claudio, several of the Aragonese, and several times with the poet Michelangelo Crollalanza, who was very light on his feet.

Later, much later, in the middle of a vigorous jig, I changed partners to find myself joining hands with Signor Benedick. Flushed, happy and with my hair coming down my back, I was ripe for our next bout. But his mien was frosty, as if an ill wind had blown him back from the sea. His first words told me he had seen my long conference with the poet at the table.

'Where is your scribbling friend? Does he tire of the dance? Or is he waiting for an ink-a-pace?'

I ignored his poor jest. 'I suppose you mean Signor Michelangelo Crollalanza.'

He snorted. '*Gesumaria*. His name is more of a mouthful than my dinner was.'

'And where are your costly friends? I hope they had a satisfactory conference on the Far.'

'I do not know,' he admitted stiffly, 'for I was charged with guarding the shore path, to see that nobody came near.'

'Doubtless a very *important* office.'

'Indeed.'

At this point in the dance I had to walk about him behind his back, and it was just as well, for I had a smile to hide.

When I returned to face him the subject had changed with the tempo and he returned to his theme. 'Who names their son Michelangelo? Do his parents hope he too will become a dauber of chapels?'

'You may ask his mother if you like. She is somewhere in the measure.'

I turned around under his raised hand, and caught a glimpse of Signora Crollalanza's flying ringlets. As I peered at her I saw that she was without a partner, but was alone in the centre of the floor, whirling and whirling like a dervish, her flame-coloured skirts flying out to describe a circle. She was the sun in the centre of the sky, and, like sunflowers, many heads turned to regard her. She looked wonderful, and free. I would have remarked upon this singular sight, even though Signor Benedick was being such a crosspatch at present, but events interrupted our measure.

The Archbishop of Monreale made his way through the dance with his entourage, deliberately disrupting the measure. There was confusion as the couples stumbled and stopped, and the pipers struck discords and silenced themselves. The archbishop stopped before Guglielma Crollalanza. She ceased her whirling and met his eye. I felt the weight of an old enmity in their glance.

'Wives,' he quoted so the whole company could hear, 'be subject to your husbands as you are to the Lord.'

There was no novelty in his homily, and the text was commonly heard at weddings; but the tone of its conveyance chilled me to the very bone. It did not seem to be generally meant but directed at this woman and this one alone, this woman who was here without her husband, and who dared to dance alone.

But Guglielma seemed sanguine – she merely smiled a little, and then bowed to the archbishop, folding from the waist like a man, as if he had favoured her with a compliment. He looked at her with scorn and then raised his voice to where Duke Egeon was seated in his stone chair on the dais.

'Your pardon, my lord, but this measure is not to my taste.' And he and his retinue left the place.

Immediately there was a lightening of the mood, and the company looked to their host. The old duke waved his hand and called in his querulous voice: 'Strike up, pipers!'

Leonato, who had been looking on with a shocked countenance, took his wife from the floor.

As we began to dance again, Benedick was seemingly unmoved by what he had seen, but I had been deeply affected. I gave myself a little shake. My partner looked at me with amusement, and spoke in more friendly tones. 'You cannot wonder at such a correction, considering the archbishop's sermon.'

I looked at him over my shoulder as the ladies took a turn. 'You think him right in his censure?' I asked.

He shrugged. 'A man and a woman should stand up together. We all have our roles to play.'

'He said that too,' I exclaimed.

'Who?'

'Michelangelo Crollalanza. The poet.'

Anger shuttered his face once more. 'Then if *he* said as much, you will no doubt pay *him* heed, for you have never thought a word of *mine* worth the noting.' I could see he was angered by my mention of the poet, but could not stop, some demon had taken hold of me; I had tried to make him jealous and had succeeded only too well. I tried to mitigate my offence. 'Come, come, Signor Benedick, let us be friends. You said to me once that I had bid you be a poet and a soldier. Come, tell me what my part shall be, as "woman"; I will study my lines, and speak my speech prettily.'

He stood still, and I stopped with him. We were now the still axis as the dancers revolved around us. 'Very well. A woman should not fire questions at a gentleman as if they were arrows. A woman should not dance alone. A woman should not fight in a man's attire. And she should not brawl first like a shrew. A woman should be mannerly, modest and sober.'

I stood still too, as if struck. Had Leonato spoken such words, when he married Innogen, and tamed her from a haggard to a household hawk? 'You do not think these things,' I said. 'Your new companions have put words in your mouth.' I was spitting with anger and did not mind who heard me. But before our dispute could be marked, the dance ended and it was time for us to make our reverences to each other.

He bowed and I curtsied, just as it should be. But beyond us, heedless that the music had ceased, I saw that Guglielma remained, dancing alone.

Act II scene vi

A rehearsal at the Greek theatre

Benedick: I had seen Lady Beatrice little in the few days that had elapsed since the wedding at Syracuse.

For one thing, I had been spending interminable hours in the service of Don Pedro at the viceroy's court in Palermo. There had been many comings and goings and meetings and colloquies, and a revolving cast of noble characters making their entrances and exits. The massive marble halls were worthy stage sets for noble and antique theatre, but sometimes it was more like a farce of the *commedia dell' Arte*. As one grandee left from one door, another, his mortal enemy, entered by another; all the time with neither one knowing their foe was in the palace at all.

So my duties kept me at Palermo, but when I was at Leonato's house, at dinner or at mass, I noted that Lady Beatrice studied to seat herself as far away from me as possible. A few times I thought I had seen her blond head from afar, as she wandered along the beach, or picked oranges with her cousin from the espaliers in the garden. But I had not been near enough to greet her, nor to tell her that I was sorry.

For I was sorry. I had been angry that night at Syracuse. I had not known that that night I would not be at my leisure, but would be at work for Don Pedro. While the grandees gathered on the Far it is true that I had little to do but watch and guard, but after that my pawn came into play. Don Pedro charged me to talk to Duke Egeon, with general friendliness and good humour, but all the time with the design of discovering the size and dispersal of his fleet. By the time I had leisure to join the couples on the dance floor, Beatrice was well entrenched with that young scribbler she'd met. I was jealous, and my tongue, unbidden, had spoken those bitter words to her that I did not mean.

I do not know whether I had been influenced by the archbishop's sermon, or whether I resented the freedom that her uncle and aunt allowed her – an indulgence in a niece that would not be allowed her as a daughter – a freedom that allowed her to form an intimacy with Signor Crollalanza on so short an acquaintance. A father's eyes, which would watch his daughter as a hawk watches a mouse, could wink at a niece who chooses to dress herself as a knight and fight in a tournament. It had not occurred to me then that the freedoms that allowed her to form a companionship with that poet were the same ones that had allowed her to form one with me. I too had been complicit in that freedom, for I had had my chance to expose her when she fought me in the tourney. I could have lifted her visor and left her to public denunciation and her uncle's wrath. My own inconsistencies were not a comfort to me.

At least, that evening, I had proved myself useful to Don Pedro in my conversation with Egeon. Apparently the duke had a vast fleet of ships, not only at Syracuse but, crucially, a good number of vessels at Marcellus' Road in the south of France. Added to his fleets he seemed to have an argosy in every port upon the map. Don Pedro then wanted me to find out whether his ships were for lease, and where his political sympathies lay. Some local lords, said Don Pedro, were no friends to the Spanish rule, and although their outward shows were friendly and they would have a regiment billeted on their house or invite the grandees to their son's wedding, they would, if given the chance, spring up at vespers with a knife to your throat, and return Sicily to the Sicilians.

At Palermo, as we waited for the Archbishop of Monreale in a vast room of porphyry and gold, Don Pedro asked me what I had gleaned from the Duke of Syracuse. I was able to tell him, with complete honesty, that I thought that the old man would be amenable to anything, and that now he had his sons back, and his wife too, he would listen with a sympathetic ear to any cause that was laid before him which would not require his sons to leave his side. In fact, I thought that, to speak frankly, he would be very much agreeable to the idea of letting his ships fatten his fortune while he stayed at home and enjoyed the society of his reunited family. Don Pedro commended me, but I felt a little shamed at accepting those thanks; for truly I had done little else but what I would always do at dinner, make myself agreeable to my host, crack a few jests and ask him about his business.

Today, however, Don Pedro had me on a mission that I would never usually come upon in the common way. I was charged, with the rest of the Aragonese, with the preparation of a great spectacle for a noble gathering. A Naumachia, a naval pageant, was to be held for the local nobility at the ancient Greek theatre in the town of Taormina. I did not see the purpose in the pageant, as there seemed to be a lot of time and trial given to what was essentially a piece of theatre, and it seemed from the dark hints dropped from Don Pedro's lips that there were weightier matters afoot. But I gave it my full attention for my friend's sake; truth to tell, my first interest in the whole affair was that I knew for a certainty that I would, at the very least, see the Lady Beatrice that night.

The theatre was a beautiful place, and if anything besides the prospect of seeing Beatrice could lift my spirits it would be this aspect. The stage sat in a pleasing natural bowl in the scorched hillside – ranks upon ranks of stone tiers rose in a heartbreaking curve, and beyond the hills, the omnipresent volcano rose out of blue shadow and gently belched white steam.

The stage itself, a vast flat paved hemicycle, was presenting a logistical problem for the Aragonese; Don Pedro had come up with a conceit that we were to recreate an old Roman sea battle between the provinces of Iberia and Albion. There were to be two actual fleets of wooden ships sailing on a baby ocean, but there seemed no easy way to flood the basin with water. Many barrels, drawn from the sea and pulled here by bad-tempered mules and worse-tempered muleteers, had been poured on to the stones only to disappear into the Sicilian sand. Even now, from my perch on the topmost tier of the stones, I could see the Spanish engineers pacing the stage below me, like fretful players who had forgotten their lines, stroking their beards and scratching their heads.

Don Pedro was to join us later, but without the water we could not rehearse and there would be nothing to show him, and the angelus chiming from nearby Taormina reminded me that time was shortening. The engineers had sent for some great seaman to join us to give us the benefit of his advice – a Venetian admiral, a local man who lived just outside Messina – I was to greet him when he arrived but there was no sign of him yet. Until he came I could, I supposed, take my ease.

I saw Claudio, sitting a few tiers down from me, also taking his ease, the wind blowing his curls back from his face. He looked very carefree, a boy today, not the stiff young man I had seen emerging in Syracuse and Palermo, a little statesman trying to understand the great affairs of which, it seemed, he was to be a part. Although I had delivered him safely to the stewardship of his uncle, and was no longer – Lady Beatrice's jibe returned to me – his nursemaid, I still kept an eye on the lad, and tried as much as I could to make him merry, and allow him, as much as I could, to be an ordinary young man.

I wanted him to cast off, sometimes, the purple that he wore and wear a different colour. A cassock of Florentine cloth had arrived for him and the seamstresses had been about him all week, clipping and sewing his finery for tonight, for he was to play a major part in this pageant. Tonight he must be a count, but today I'd found him a tunic of fustian and fashioned him a *fionda*, a catapult, such as I'd had when I was a boy, from a forked stick and a bootstrap. A small smile had crept across his face as I'd demonstrated how far the thing could fling a stone, and all morning the count had been wandering about the tiers, finding stones that the careless Greeks had dropped, and firing these ancient missiles at the unsuspecting gulls. I smiled to see him thus.

The sun was hot, a bee droned in the broom flowers and I felt my eyes begin to close. Moments or hours later I heard the scrape of a boot above me and felt a slab of shadow fall across me, cooling the sun. I opened my eyes, thinking this would be the admiral come, but it was not; a stranger apparition I have never seen.

The fellow was approximately fifty years old; his complexion weathered, his face gaunt. He wore armour that was stained with rust and covered with mildew, as if it had spent many long years stored and forgotten in a corner. He had evidently misplaced most of the helmet, though, for he had only a simple headpiece from the original hulme, but had compensated for it with his industry by fashioning a kind of half-helmet out of pasteboard which, when attached to the headpiece, gave the appearance of a full sallet. I took him for one of the players, already dressed in costume, for he had the bizarre appearance of an antique knight. The impression was assisted by the fact that he was deficient in the full complement of arms – he only had one. I closed my eyes again; but the apparition addressed me.

'Are you Signor Benedick of Padua?'

I squinted up at him. He had a thicker Spanish accent than Don Pedro, the archbishop and the viceroy put together, but I understood him well enough.

'Yes,' I said, but did not rise, for he was not of my rank. His years, though, secured my compassion and I asked him to sit and take his ease, for he breathed heavily, and his lungs made a strange wheezy music as if a mouse had chewed through a squeezebox.

He collapsed heavily beside me with a clatter of his accoutrements, and I could not help staring at the place where his left hand should be. He did not seem disposed to give his message, nor to leave, so I made conversation.

'It looks as though you have fought some bar brawls in your day, old-timer,' I said. It was meant for a joke, but the fellow bristled and skewed in his seat.

'*Qué?*' he queried, prickly at once.

'I meant no offence.' I held up my hands, then put them down again – I did not wish to be seen to be boasting that I had a pair. 'It is natural as a man gets old that he might sustain injuries such as his travails and scrapes might afford him. Do not take it amiss.'

'What I cannot help taking amiss,' said the old man, 'is that you charge me with being old and one-handed, as if it had been in my power to keep time from passing over me, or as if the loss of my hand had been brought about in some tavern, and not on the grandest occasion the past or present has seen, or the future can hope to see. I'll have you know that I sustained these injuries at the great battle of Lepanto, when the countries of the Holy League stood up against the infidel Turk.' He bristled, and sat a little taller, but the touchy knight ruined the dignity of his expression by scratching the sweaty hair under his makeshift helmet with his filthy nails. 'If my wounds have no beauty to your eye, they are, at least, honourable to those who know where they were received.'

It was my turn to stand now, for his rank exceeded mine, and respect was due; here was an honourable knight. I bowed. 'Forgive me. I took you for a brawling peasant, and it seems you are a hero.'

He smiled at me with his snaggle teeth, and waved me to be seated again. 'Perhaps I am both,' he said, 'many soldiers are.'

'You are the admiral, then, whom I have been told to greet?'

'I am not,' he said, 'but I can give you word of your admiral. He is not here, he is not coming; nor is he ever coming.'

'He is delayed?'

'In perpetuity. He is dead.'

I was shocked. 'You seem very sanguine about it.'

'It is not my habit to wear a sorrowful face. But believe me when I say that I am very sorry for it. For he was the best of men, and a veteran of that very battle of Lepanto I told you of. I fought beside him then, and in the Holy League since.'

'Well,' I said. 'I am sorry that the world has lost such a soldier. And now I do not know what to do, for he was to tell us where to put the ships, and form the battle, in as authentic a formation as possible.'

The strange knight clapped me on the shoulder. 'Your master Don Pedro sent for me to help instead. I settled on the island for a time, for I was in the hospital in Messina for some while after Lepanto.'

I looked down to the stage. 'Our greatest problem may be that we have not even a puddle, let alone a millpond.'

'They have solved it,' he said, clambering to his feet. 'They are running a conduit from the river, and are constructing a tank. Someone with sense told them that as water wants to run down and not up, it were better to divert the water from the river that runs off the volcano, than tax the poor mules further with emptying the sea, which has always seemed to me to be an impossible task.'

I stood too and headed slowly down the stone steps behind the strange knight, letting him set the leisurely pace.

'I imagine the Greeks had the idea first,' he said, 'for the muleteers found an existing conduit and an aqueduct beneath the column drums. Those Greeks seem to have had all the good ideas centuries before the rest of us.'

I gave him my hand down from the little wall into the cavea.

'But when the tank is full, I have been charged to help you with the formation, and besides this I have written a verse or two for the chorus to say. He is a windy actor, but for a theatre of this size, it is just as well. And what is your role in all of this?'

'When the ships meet, there is to be a mock battle, and I am to lead the charge and organise the fighting.' I knew it was my performance in the tourney which had bought me this role, for I had never been on a ship bigger than a gondola.

'A mock battle, eh? Ever been in a sea battle?'

I tired of this question. 'No.' I sighed. 'Nor a battle of any sort.'

'But you must be a pretty swordsman, I suppose?'

Pretty enough, as I had proven at the tournament, to put down any Spaniard, but I did not say as much. 'Just so much as to give the impression of the great sea wars of Albion and Iberia,' I replied carefully.

'Albion and Iberia, eh?' He kicked at the yellow sand of the arena with his ancient sabatons. 'Well; some will swallow it.' He looked about him, at the swarm of engineers filling the tanks, then to sea, volcano and stones, as if these elemental beings were eavesdropping. He lowered his voice. 'Do you know the true purpose of this pageant?'

I did not fully understand this enigmatical comment, but passed my instructions as I had received them to this strange little man. 'I know only that the forces of Albion are to appear to be utterly crushed, and I am to lead the battle and jump ship to ship, sword in hand.' The last thing I wanted was a wetting, in front of Beatrice; but I did not mention this foible, and merely said, 'I have been instructed to look heroic.'

'Aah.' It was a long, drawn-out syllable. 'To *look* heroic. Looking heroic is half of the battle. Do you think when a soldier leaps into the jaws of death, he is not terrified? His knees knock, his cod shrivels, and his bowels open. Every time, yes. But the *secret*,' he held one filthy finger up in front of his face, 'is to *look* valiant, to change your lamb's heart to the heart of lion.'

I think I understood him. 'Well, we will have some brave costumes – the prince's tailors have been about them all week.'

He shook his head. 'Your apparel, armour and finery, all of these are as nothing. You do not take my meaning. You could go to war with an old kettle as your hulme and a tin dish as your breastplate. Look at me.' He swept his one hand before his ancient armour with a flourish. 'You do not have to be striped like a tiger to imitate the action of a tiger. No, knighthood lives in *here*,' he banged his breastplate where his heart lived, 'and here.' He knocked at his shabby helmet till it clopped like a cowbell. 'Even if you fight in sackcloth, your imagination may aid you. Think of the weight of Italian chivalric history – your Marquis of Mantua, your Orlando Furioso. Embody them. In every bar brawl you have with a cheating landlord, who has taken two *reales* instead of one for a quart of beer, you are a knight suppressing a cheating castellan. Every stumbling whore you must set right upon her feet as if she is a *princesa*, and say, "How do you, lady, I hope you are not injured?" And you may do all this dressed in your everyday clothes.'

We stood together watching the tank fill, and the engineers pushed one of the prop ships on to the water. It looked troublingly rickety.

'When you stand on that nutshell made of cork and canvas tonight,' continued my new companion, 'imagine yourself at the head of a vast fleet in the Straits of Patras, as I was then, with the Turk ululating from their golden forecastles, waving their curved swords. Smell the acrid gunpowder in your nose,' he cried, drawing the gazes of the engineers as if he was an actor, 'feel the cannon boom in your ribs, hear the screaming timber as the ships crash together, and you know there is no way back but to draw your sword and leap.'

I turned to look at him, trying to imagine him in battle. 'What were you thinking, at Lepanto?' I asked.

He considered, the strange helmet shading the expression of his eyes from me. 'That the soldier shows to greater advantage dead in battle than alive in flight. When I jumped from a friendly ship to an enemy one, I did not think to ever come back.'

For the remainder of that hot afternoon we rehearsed painstakingly for the pageant that night. To say honestly, I did not truly understand the burden of the play, nor know any other part but my own – I was too concerned with the sea battle to concern myself with the rhetoric or allegory. I have never been a man for the classics – give me a good play at the *commedia dell'Arte* any day – good fun about a master and a servant or a Harlequin and his Columbine, not this antique posturing.

I did know, however, that there was a horse involved as well as a sea battle, for I saw a great white destrier cavorting around in the tunnels below the cavea, pulling his handlers around on his leading reins like puppets on strings. I knew too that Claudio had a greater part to play than I, and that the chorus who began the play seemed to be spouting nonsense, but was no wiser as to the drama we were to transmit to our audience.

The little ships, built in Taormina and pulled up the incline by mules, were set upon the lake and made a fine sight. Despite my initial fears they were sturdy things of wood and canvas, and held our weight admirably, though we had some to do to trim them and fight at the same time. The ships of Iberia were rendered in glossy varnished wood and silken scarlet sails, but the boats of Albion, while practically just as sturdy, had been given the appearance of rotten, old-fashioned vessels – here and there there was even a dragon prow such as were once in fashion with the northmen.

Claudio, it transpired, was to be the king of the Hispanic forces, and stand in the prow, but he was not to take part in the fighting. I was to o'erleap him and land on the wooden forecastle of the rickety flagship of Albion, painted in blue, in order to engage with the enemy forces, which seemed to be led by a red-headed Amazon queen. Again, I was not so troubled by the meaning of this allegory as the leap I was supposed to perform. A couple of times I had a wetting, when the ships were not close enough to jump the difference, and one time I was left clinging to a cannon, feet trailing in the makeshift sea, as my mentor, the ancient Spanish knight, laughed aloud. Pride bruised, I prayed that I should not fail so publicly in front of Beatrice.

As the sun began to sink it was time for me to transform myself into Benedick the Actor. I pulled on my light Roman armour of foil and canvas; not designed for close-up scrutiny but it would look brave enough from the tiers. Don Pedro's Aragonese were variously dressed as brave Iberians or dog-eared pagans or ruddy Moors, and there were even local women and children who had turned up at the promise of a few *reales*, to be dressed in particolours and to have their faces stained with the walnut.

Don Pedro's own barber passed among the principal actors, painting our eyes and faces. I blinked as he spat on a charcoal pad, and with a sable brush finer than the tail of a shrew, rimmed my eyes with charcoal, and ticklishly painted curling moustaches below my nose. A glance in the looking glass taught me that I resembled one of the puppets I had seen do battle on the little painted cart in Monreale, but I hoped that from many rows up in the theatre the effect would not be too ridiculous.

I looked at Claudio, his face pinched and serious, his complexion sallow with nerves. The barber painted him also – his eyes were ringed too, and a neat beard and moustache painted upon him to uncanny effect. He did not laugh now but looked into the distance, the dying sun turning his eyes yellow like a lion's. He was helped into his magnificent tabard – not purple today but Spanish scarlet, and the weight of it seemed to hang upon him like a burden. The device on the front, making the thing so heavy for it was worked in pearls and jewels of great price, was a cross. And something else marked him out from the rest of us. The dressers placed a heavy gold circlet on his head.

I felt a weight of foreboding resting on my chest where the bejewelled cross rested on his. What were we enacting here?

I felt a tap on my shoulder. It was the strange, ill-dressed Spaniard knight.

'I must go.' He held out his only hand, and I shook it, taken aback. He had spent the whole day arranging our battle formation, directing every sword stroke, and now all his actors were dressed he would leave before the first act? 'But we are about to begin!' I protested. 'You will not stay to see the spectacle?'

He shook his head and his eyes travelled past me to King Claudio.

I sensed he could tell me something I wanted to know. 'I suppose,' I hedged, 'that after what you have seen, it must seem trivial to you to see such a thing enacted for sport.'

He shrugged and his armour clanged together at the neck-guard. 'I like a play as much as any man, and I will laugh and clap in the gallery, munch my nuts and throw my cushions. But I will not stay tonight because this is not a show.' His eyes came back from the boy king to me. 'It is real.' And he turned and limped away before I could ask him what he meant.

As the sun lowered and set fire to the sea, I saw the old man in the helmet stumble away down the hill with a swift and rolling gait. As I watched he passed Don Pedro, come to watch our final rehearsal, and despite their rank the two embraced like brothers. I remembered how I had let Don Pedro dub me and dress me up for the night of the masque. I was more of a puppet then than now. My lamb's heart shrivelled within me. No wonder Lady Beatrice had laughed. I wondered then, when the two men met upon that road, whether the old man in the strange garb or the strapping prince in his scarlet and gold would be more of a tiger in the breach.

Don Pedro greeted me first of the company, as the greatest friend of his heart, even before Claudio. My chattering teeth stilled as my heart was warmed by his friendship, my qualms vanishing. 'How did you shift with Don Miguel?' he asked. 'He is a singular character, is he not?'

I thought for a moment, my eyes on the receding figure. 'A singular character indeed.' But what I really meant to say I did not want to speak out loud, so as not to offend my friend, which was that Miguel, if that was his name, had taught me more about knighthood in one afternoon than all Don Pedro's painted caballeros had taught me on the long road from Venice.

Act II scene vii

A Naumachia in the Greek theatre

Beatrice: As I climbed the steps of the Greek theatre, I marvelled at the place.

For a teller of stories this was a place that held my heart – for not only were the stones themselves a very reminder of the legends that I had heard in the schoolroom – and even struggled to read in the original Greek – I was pent up and excited by the notion of all the dramas that must have been played out upon this stage over the ages. I took my place among the toga-clad ghosts, and looked forward to the evening's entertainment; principally for the reason that, since this pageant was a brain-child of Don Pedro's, Benedick would surely be in the device somewhere, as he seemed to hang about the prince like a disease. I was anxious to see him, for something had gone badly awry when last we'd met. I needed to know whether he'd meant the bitter words he'd spoken at the wedding at Syracuse, or whether his sentiments had proceeded from misplaced jealousy. I wanted to return to our merry war, not this more serious conflict we'd embarked upon.

I followed my aunt and Hero up the stone steps to the very top tier, and was confronted with the glory of the vista. It was sunset, so the volcano was nothing more than a blue silhouette hunched over the town, the puff of smoke at the summit turned to coral and rose. The sky was saffron, and the sea was afire. Only my eagerness to lay my eyes on Signor Benedick could pull my eyes from the beauty, but I could not see him anywhere. I knew from Hero that her friend Claudio was appearing in the pageant in some capacity, but as I had had neither sight nor speech of Signor Benedick for above a week I did not know where he was likely to be.

I did note as I climbed that all the nobility of Messina seemed to be gathered here – I recognised many faces from the masque at my uncle's and the wedding at Syracuse too.

My aunt and I were directed to our seats by a local moppet dressed in a white toga with vine leaves in his curls. I noted that we were to be seated apart from my uncle; that he and Egeon were gathered about a golden throne set in a little balcony apart, which overlooked the finest views of the stage, where the antique emperors may have once sat. I thought the gilded chair was meant for the viceroy, but I saw that petty king sitting in between my uncle and the omnipresent Archbishop of Monreale. I smiled a little at the throne; I had suspected Don Pedro to be vainglorious, but thought that even he might not think it politic to sit in such a chair when the viceroy was present; but when the prince joined the grandees, he did not sit in the throne either. The golden chair sat empty, even when the torches in the auditorium were extinguished by the children in their wreaths and togas, and the pipers struck up, indicating that the performance was to begin.

Once the torches were lit about the cavea a marvel was revealed to us all. The stage was not stone, nor even wooden boards such as you may see at the *commedia*. It was water, a vast shallow tank filled to the brim, with curling white and blue waves painted on the front. The wood of the tank itself was painted blue so the water, lit by candles backed by shell-shaped mirrors, shimmered an azure hue. A narrator, dressed in a toga like my imagined ghosts, stepped into the waves, a hidden platform artfully making him appear as if he walked on water like the Christ.

The actor, a man of middle years with a scanty beard,

unfurled a scroll in his hands, and began to declaim in a loud voice that rolled around the tiers and echoed through the theatre. 'I am your chorus for the while; and pray your patience for my prologue, your attention for our play, and your kindly judgement for our epilogue. For although we will hear of great kings and venerable saints, and deeds long past, there is a chance for all of us to be a part of history in the days to come.'

After these portentous hints the chorus stepped forth from the water, and the play began. The azure pool sank into darkness as the cavea before it was lit with the mirrored lamps. A crowd of soldiers collected before the stage, chanting and singing in a strange tongue. As the lights warmed their faces I could see that their skin was stained as if with the juice of the walnut, and they had multicoloured turbans twisted about their heads. My skin chilled with foreboding despite the warm of the evening. They were Moors.

The narrator, back in his floating position on the pool, stood over the scene. 'In ancient Hispania, the good people of the region of Asturias were much troubled by the vile Moor. Then the brave king Ramiro gave battle but was surrounded.'

A figure in scarlet walked forth; it was Claudio. Dressed in blood red, with a jewel-encrusted cross on his breast and a crown on his head. Hero nudged me with her bony elbow fit to bruise my ribs. I squeezed her hand, as the Moors encircled him, their strange chants heavy with threat.

Claudio, now bathed in light, knelt and prayed for a miracle, his strong young voice reaching us even high in the arena where we sat. 'Blessed Saint James, descend to us now in our hour of need, and rid us of this pestilential horde, this viper in the bosom of Spain.'

I looked sideways at Hero, but she did not seem to understand the meaning of the words, just looked with warm admiration at her friend in his kingly garb. Claudio, his eyes tight shut and his mouth moving, really seemed to be praying.

And it worked – the miracle appeared. A path of light shone across the water while the Moors cowered and ceased their song. My skin prickled as I watched, for a white destrier appeared at the back of the stage and seemed to walk across the water. I knew that I was watching a trick; that there must be a concealed walkway just below the water's surface, but the effect was magical. The horse was carrying a rider dressed in the white robes of sanctity, his face covered by a white hood with only holes for eyes, giving an eerie impression. The rider wore a gold halo at the back of his head and wore a white tabard, with a device I had seen before. A red cross which resembled a dagger at its base; and a cockleshell floating above, the symbol of St James. In his hand the saint held an eerie wonder; a burning cross, artfully coated with flames that burned perpetually without damaging his gauntleted hand. The horse, despite the fire behind his head, walked carefully forth and stepped down from the tank to the delighted gasps of the audience. Then the creature stood obligingly still while the saint drew his sword and smote every Moor who stood before him. Each of the dusky actors must have concealed bladders of blood, for the gore flew around the pit and carmined both the horse's flanks and the snowy habit of the saint. Then, worse still, women and children wearing Moorish beads and bangles ran on to mourn their menfolk, and they were similarly cut down. By the time St James had finished, his white tabard had turned to red. The saint then handed his cross of fire to the thankful king, who received it upon his knees.

I was sickened. So this saint, this paragon and patron of the Spanish, was a Moor-slayer. This order of which Don Pedro was a member, this sacred brotherhood into which he had dubbed Signor Benedick, was the scourge of that fine man from the beach, that beautiful Moor. St James would have looked at Guglielma Crollalanza in the same way that the archbishop of Monreale had regarded her – looked at her broad nose and her amazing crinkled hair and her full mulberry lips and seen an animal, not a woman.

I had never questioned before when Hero had told me matter-of-factly of the expulsion of the Moors from Sicily. I assumed it had been necessary, military. But the play made me think differently. They had been expelled because they were *different*. I knew a woman who was half Moor, with a white husband and son. Could they be so different from us? And their expulsion had been blessed by St James. I felt sick. I had his fingerbone in the cabinet in my chamber.

The carnage over, the area in front of the tank was cast into darkness, and the blue sea was illuminated once more. The chorus appeared to stand upon the waves and declaimed again. I listened tensely, wondering what was coming, wondering whether anything could be worse. 'Given such a blessing by Saint James,' sing-songed the chorus, 'Ramiro vowed to continue his work to scourge the empire of the godless, and he set sail for Albion, to crush the red-haired witch Boudicca for her pagan beliefs.'

Now, I had studied Roman history and knew something was not right. 'This is singular,' I hissed to Hero, 'for Boudicca was born before Christ, and Ramiro after.' Hero flapped her hand at me, shushing my objections, and I held my peace. For fiction, as I well knew, is mutable, and many august writers have written of figures from history meeting in their imaginariums. I waited to see the drama unfold.

Before our eyes, a true spectacle appeared. Little ships, dozens of them – perhaps one-tenth of the size of a galleass but correct in every particular but scale – sailed upon the blue lake to gasps from the crowd. And the ships each had their seamen – an army crowded into each, bristling with weaponry and bent upon war. Chief of the forces of Albion was Boudicca; a man dressed as a lady, who had a breastplate crowned with two conical breasts, a leaden white face painted like a whore's, and a horned helmet atop a rippling mass of red hair. The hair – curled into tight ringlets – reminded me again, sharply, of Guglielma Crollalanza. I looked around the gathered grandees seated on the tiers, but it seemed that neither the lady nor her poet son were here tonight, and I was not surprised; the enmity that I had seen between her and the Archbishop of Monreale spoke of a formidable feud.

Claudio was to the fore again, as King Ramiro, at the helm of the Hispanic ships, now holding the cross of fire before his face. He was being blessed by a priest in a jewelled surplice who looked suspiciously like the Archbishop of Monreale. In the ships of Albion, pagans wearing fustian and sackcloth shook their bristling weapons and a Druid blessed Boudicca with a hazel switch, as a green man looked on. The red-headed queen seemed to writhe in ecstasy at her infidel blessing, waggling her tongue and rubbing her conical breasts most lasciviously. Despite the message the spectacle was wondrously well wrought, for the flotilla of Iberian ships and the pagan long-boats looked to be sailing convincingly towards each other on the sapphire lake. The timpani of the unseen musicians whipped up imaginary tempests and they described, with a clash of cymbals, the two fleets meeting together.

Then a heroic figure appeared in the prow – a tall figure; broad of shoulder and long of limb. He wore a centurion's helmet over his armour and there was a dark beard on his cheek, but his eyes were light beneath the face paint.

It was Benedick.

I was surprised to see him, for the story of the Moors had almost put him out of my mind for the first time since we'd met. Despite our argument I had to admit he cut an impressive figure in his scarlet and gold Roman garb. As he stood in the prow like a figurehead the audience held its breath and I tingled with anticipation. Then he leapt heroically an impossible distance across the water from one fleet to the other, and set about the pagans. I heard a yelp from Hero as I realised I'd been crushing her hand in mine, and that I was sitting so far forward in my seat I was nearly in the row before.

Now we saw proper swordplay as both sides drew and actual sparks flew from their blades. My eyes were always on Benedick as he twirled through the fray like a whirlwind – all his skill was on show as he crushed the enemy in his path. I knew it was theatre, but as I had seen him do likewise at the tournament, his part was given more veracity. Besides the fencing there was strategy too – the Spanish ships sailed around the fleet of Albion on three sides so that the pagan flotilla was forced back against its own paper coastline, where artfully painted paper rocks fell from great white cliffs which protruded from the sea. The victory was so complete that the red queen begged most piteously and knelt before Claudio-Ramiro. Benedick held his sword at her neck; but the king spoke up and said that she would be spared as long as she rendered up her treasure and accepted the One True God. The play ended with the queen accepting the cross of fire from Ramiro's hand and her cohorts covering their oppressors with pagan gold.

There was a moment of silence, and then, from behind us on the golden balcony, came the sound of one man clapping.

Every head turned towards him, and a hum of amazed murmurings rolled around the arena like broth in a pot.

Spare and elegant, no taller than Don Pedro, he had a neat beard covering a heavy Habsburg jaw and framing a stern mouth with one protruding lip. His curling black hair was combed severely back from his forehead. Even if he did not wear a crown, there could be no doubt among the crowd as to his identity – even to those of them who had not seen his likeness on a pamphlet or coin – for there was no other man in this world to whom the viceroy would cede his throne. This was Philip II of Spain, the Spanish king.

His scarlet doublet was embroidered with a heavy cross of

pearls and jewels, his stiff white ruff illumined his face, and, to put his identity beyond doubt, a golden circlet sat upon his noble brow. I thought with a jolt that he looked exactly like Claudio. Or rather, Claudio had been dressed to look exactly like him.

The king waved graciously at the company – unsmiling, as if such a benign expression was beneath him – before resuming his applause. The dukes and grandees too stood to applaud likewise, and the crowd soon followed. The king, once the crowd had begun to applaud and cheer, artfully stopped clapping and began to wave elegantly at the exalted crowd instead, thus appropriating our ovation for himself. I was slow to stand but Hero tugged at my arm till I rose reluctantly too.

But one person in that gathering did not rise – he sat three rows before me under the cover of a hooded cloak, but as the applause continued he got to his feet and climbed the tiers to leave unnoticed by the back way. As he passed me – did he nod or did I imagine it? – the wind lifted his cloak and I saw about his neck a quill and a crystal bottle with a black slick of ink within.

Then the king rose too, to a fanfare of trumpets, and walked down to the cavea to meet the actors. Far below I saw the toady archbishop, at his elbow, whisper to the king as he presented Claudio, and with his first sign of humanity the king touched the costume crown. Then he commended Signor Benedick, who stood a little behind Claudio, and as Benedick bowed briefly I tried and failed to read his expression.

Then the king was ushered from the theatre, while the Grecian-garbed stewards kept us in our places until he had gone.

Then a rising hubbub bubbled about me, and Hero chattered about the honour and spectacle of actually setting eyes on the Spanish king. I was as amazed as the rest but a new unease in my stomach added to the ill taste in my mouth left by the play. What was the king doing here? Why would he visit our tiny island, and not only watch this strange hotchpotch of a play, but promote to his underlords the message it contained?

As the actors left the stage too, I rose precipitately. I wanted to see Signor Benedick before he left. The king's appearance had made me quite forget our quarrel – there seemed to be bigger things at stake. Perhaps he, as one of the players, could shed some light upon the strange evening. As I followed my aunt and Hero as we made our way slowly down the stone steps, held up by the throng, fuming with impatience, I was trying so hard to see him over the bobbing heads of the crowd that I lost my footing on the treacherous crumbling steps. I tumbled down, sprawling on the ancient stones, and Hero gave an unmannerly shriek. But before she or my aunt could assist me a strong hand pulled me up and set me back on my feet.

My eyes, lowered in shame, took in every detail of my rescuer from bottom to top – gilded sabotons, oxblood leather breeches, a golden breastplate. A face bizarrely painted with red-rouged cheeks and eyes that were ringed in black and looked greener than ever even beneath the shade of a centurion's helmet. It was the centurion of Iberia, Signor Benedick.

I looked daggers at him – how timely that he should be my rescuer, when the last time he'd held me in hand we had been dancing a measure, and he insulted me most cruelly. But he only said, looking directly at me with those green eyes, 'How do you, lady? I hope you are not injured?'

I held my tongue and shook my head, for my fall had brought my aunt and Hero to my side, and I could not question him now, in my aunt's hearing; for whatever the king was doing here, my uncle was caught up in this coil. Besides, as Benedick turned to transfer my hand elegantly to my aunt's, and as he bowed to take his leave, I caught the glint of his medal of the military order of St James. He was bound up in it too.

ACT THREE

Act III scene i

The dunes before the Moor's house

Beatrice: The morning after the Naumachia I woke early from an uneasy sleep full of dreams and blood.

I walked along the shoreline to blow away the foreboding until I reached the harbour and found the friar and the fishermen playing *Scopa*. I joined them for a few rounds. My luck was in and as I held the *settebello* I thought about the card in my room, resting in my cabinet of curiosities with St James's finger. Both keepsakes had been given to me by Signor Benedick, for one victory and one defeat.

After I had fought with him I had been so happy; I thought he had respected me as an adversary. After I had danced with him I had been so sad; in his insults I thought I detected the influence of the Archbishop of Monreale and his other powerful new friends. And then yesterday, when he had picked me up as I stumbled down the ancient tiers of the theatre, he had spoken to me as if he did not know me, with perfect courtesy and propriety, like the very epitome of a knight errant. I preferred the insult, for to me no true respect lay behind such universal courtesy. I wondered whether his new military order had a code of behaviour to which he was striving to adhere. I wondered, too, if that was the case, whether the heart that beat beneath the medal of St James had altered for ever.

'Lady,' said the friar, for he never used my real name in this company, in case my little habit reached my uncle. 'The hand is yours.'

I realised I had not moved for some moments, and swept the cards into my hand from the back of the upturned boat. I shuffled them together, and said, '*Scopa.*' I had won the hand, and it was time to go. *Scopa* was all about knowing when to leave the game.

I refused the friar's kind offer to walk me back to my uncle's, for I needed the solitude of the beach. I remembered the last time I had walked here like this – one foot on sea and one on shore, the brine soaking my slipper. It was the day Benedick had come to the house. I had not even met him then. Then my heart had been full of the valiant Moor. But from that day to this it was Signor Benedick that was forever in my mind's eye. I had to admit to myself that at the tournament, and again the previous night at the Naumachia, he had overthrown more than his enemies. He had become to me the only man of Italy, the man that I would rather spend my time with than any other whether in dispute or accord. I would rather fight with him than be civil with any other man.

Yet to acknowledge the truth would avail me nothing. He had his brothers in arms, and Don Pedro, the friend of his heart. He had made his feelings about me, about all of my sex, as clear as day. I could never hope for the sweet bliss shared by the Moor and his lily-white love. I was passing their home now, and was suddenly struck; if he was an admiral and she a noblewoman, why had I not seen them since that day? Why had they not attended any of my uncle's many entertainments, if he was so regarded in military circles? Was it because the admiral was a Moor? I decided to climb the dunes to see whether I could spy the couple.

There was indeed a figure there on the sands by the Moor's house; but only one. He was hunched at the bottom of the dunes, facing the infinite sea, the wind lifting his thin hair. And round about him was a wonder – he had created a sea of his own. Hundreds of creamy pages were laid all about him, each one crammed with yard upon yard of spidery writing, and weighted down with a pebble to foil the wind. I watched him for a while; he was alternately scribbling on a page of paper resting on a hornbook, and raising his head to look out to sea, as if seeking inspiration. At length he would finish the page he was writing and hold it to the wind by two corners as if it was laundry. Then he turned my way to find a stone to anchor it. That's when he saw me. He was Michelangelo Crollalanza, the poet.

I was not sure whether to continue upon my way but he waved the sheet at me and I walked carefully over to him, stepping cautiously over the pages. I would have told him not to get up, but he made no move to rise in my presence and I suspected, as I had done before, that the expected courtesies of society held no importance for him; a trait, I guessed, that he inherited from his mother.

'What are you writing?'

'A wrong.' He smiled bitterly with one side of his mouth, as I had remembered him doing at the wedding at Syracuse.

'This is a singular place to write. Can you not write indoors?'

He shook his head. 'My father has the only study and has spread himself about it. My mother likes the outdoors. She says she never feels comfortable in a room.'

That I could understand – in the few encounters I'd had with her Guglielma Crollalanza always seemed to have something wild about her, as if she would be more at home in nature.

'His work is more important than mine, so I give up the space readily. He is righting wrongs too.'

'What wrongs?'

'The Spanish are bad stewards of his island. They have claimed the common land, they have trodden on the backs of the poor to build their great estates.'

Unbidden, I sat beside him. 'What do you mean?'

'Last night's pageant,' he argued, 'how much did it cost? One jewel from that player-king's tabard alone would feed a family for a year. And how many fine dishes have been paraded before you over the past many days? Honey of Ibla, and collyflowers and purslane? Do you know what the poor eat?' He did not wait for an answer. '*Maco*, a stew made of chickpeas. And if they can't get *maco*, they eat grass, like the kine.' He ripped a handful from the ground, and the sand whispered out of the roots. It looked dry and bitter, not something you would give even to a mule. 'Bread is so precious here that the Sicilians say that if you drop a crumb of bread on the ground you are condemned for eternity to try to pick it up with your eyelashes. But the viceroy himself said that the poor can sit and drink their own piss. Believe me, sometimes that happens. In Sperlinga, some of them live in caves, like beasts.'

I had never thought of such things, and felt ashamed, thinking of all the dishes I had left, at my uncle's house, at the wedding at Syracuse, because my belly was full, or because I had no appetite, so fattened was I with flirtation. 'Is that why your father came back?'

'Yes. He could not stand idly by. And we had word that he was in danger in the north.'

I remembered what Guglielma Crollalanza had said of her husband. *The sun grew too hot for him in the north.* And then I remembered something else. *He has a different religion to the archbishop and the intelligence to disseminate it.* After the play last night, such differences seemed dangerous. 'Because of his religion?'

'Yes. He follows the teachings of John Calvin.'

I knew a little of the to-do in Europe between the Protestants and Catholics, but it all seemed a long way away from Sicily. 'Do such things affect us here?'

Now he looked at me as if I was a stranger. 'Such matters affect all of us, everywhere.'

'Not I,' I said, thinking it true.

'And yet you watched a play about it, just last night.'

'So it was you, at the theatre!' The exclamation burst forth before I could stop it.

'Yes. And I did not like what I saw.'

I remembered he wrote plays as well as his poems. 'I suppose the subject matter *was* a little violent for an entertainment.'

He snorted. He seemed altogether more hostile than he had been when I had met him at dinner, more prickly, a good deal angrier. Had he changed too? I was sick of weathervane men, the shifting winds of their sex, and I would have left him to his scribblings, but I wanted to know more.

'The public love violence,' he said. 'There is always a bigger crowd at a hanging than a mass. As I said, the play was not about violence, but religion, and the two go hand in hand. Soon, very soon, we will all be cast in the drama, even to the very tiniest walk-on part.'

I struggled to understand; his mind seemed to jump about so. I missed again the sallies of Signor Benedick, for Michelangelo Crollalanza was not my equal in intellect, but my better. I was moved to display what little knowledge I had. 'But it was just an old tale; two old tales, if truth be told, for Ramiro and Boudicca never breathed the same air.'

'Exactly.' He waved his quill at me, as if pleased by my knowledge. 'It was an amalgam of legends, muddled together to fit *their* insidious theme. They were selling a commodity, like a hot pie at a pie stand, and we all gobbled it up.'

'Whose theme?'

'Wake up, Lady Beatrice. The Spanish.'

'But . . .' I stammered, feeling my way. 'It was just a play. A silly play.'

'Then why was the King of Spain there?'

He had made a point. 'So it was *not* a play?'

'It is all a play all right. All of it. Iberia is Spain, Albion is England. And they are all players – from Philip II himself to his player-king Claudio.'

'Claudio?'

'When I asked the count if he had seen *Pallas and the Centaur*, I did not just ask a fellow idly about a painting. The work hangs in the Medici Palace. He had seen the painting, he said, in his uncle's house. His uncle is a Medici.'

I watched a gull alight on a piece of driftwood. I was as much at sea as he. 'What does that signify?'

'Money, Lady Beatrice. It signifies money.'

I tried to put the pieces together. 'So Philip of Spain is planning the downfall of England, and he needs Medici money to achieve it.'

'And ships. That is why every nobleman in Sicily is being courted, and every merchant of note too.' He idly sucked the grass stalk he had picked, grimaced and spat. 'Philip also needs a harbour. That is why your uncle is Don Pedro's host. He has been given the honour in return for the deeps of Messina's harbour. It has the deepest sound in the seven seas, and Messina makes a good stop between Spain and England. Leonato can give Philip letters of marque – he is the Governor of Messina. When you have the thread you have the whole skein.'

I was aghast. When I had met him he had hardly known any of these men. Now he seemed to know everything, as if he could read their very mind's construction in their faces.

I had watched the play too, and listened and seen nothing. 'So Boudicca of Albion was Elizabeth of England.'

'A red-headed queen with an infidel religion. Yes.'

'And Ramiro of Asturias was Philip.'

'Yes. Young Claudio was almost his double, in appearance, dress, everything. Did you know that in Spain Philip has forbidden his image ever to be used in a play? But here, it was allowed, encouraged. Statecraft and stagecraft are not so different. They missed no detail, damn them.'

He was angry again, and I wondered why he took such a lofty plot so personally. Then I remembered. The part of the play that had shaken me the most, the part that had filled my dreams with blood. The Moors. His mother was part Moor. 'And what have the Moors to do with this coil?'

He did not seem to want to be drawn, but shook his head repeatedly, as if he could see the horror, until his English ruff bent like a gull's wing.

'That massacre, it was in Roman times. Centuries past.'

'Ah yes, the poor dead Moors. Ancient history.'

He seemed to agree with me, but his tone told me he did not. 'Or do you mean . . . is it . . .' The elements of the puzzle turned in my head for a moment like the planets in an orrery, and seemed to align; only to pass and separate. The conjunction of comprehension over, the darkness came again. 'Is it to do with the expulsion of the Moors from Sicily? But wasn't that years ago too – the first years of Spanish rule?'

'Years ago, yes,' he agreed, 'under the first viceroys. Or is it still going on, yes, even here in this very spot? The Spanish have always needed an enemy for the Sicilians, otherwise the Sicilians might ask themselves why they do not rise up and kick the Spanish into the sea. Just as they once did the French.' He threw the torn grass viciously towards the sea, and it blew back uselessly into his lap. 'Monreale thinks that if we can all be taught to hate the Moors then the Spanish may go about their enterprise against Elizabeth, the saviours of the island, and of the One True Religion.' He spat the words.

I did not fully understand this, but had one more question to ask. 'Why does Philip hate the English queen so?'

'He wanted to marry her, and she refused him. In his wife, he might have overlooked her religion. In a woman who scorned him, her faith is anathema to him. Hatred is a good horse – you can ride him all the way to England. And as you very well know, love is a very short step from hate. Nothing moves a man to bitter words more than a woman's scorn.'

Now he had performed his conjuror's trick on me; we had

moved from the political to the personal. 'Are you speaking of Signor Benedick?'

He clapped his hands together. 'Yes, let us talk of love. We have spoken of hate enough.'

I could feel my cheeks burn. 'Who said there was love in the case?'

'Love is often unspoken.'

I felt I could be honest with him. 'And looks to remain so.'

He regarded me. 'You are only in the middle of your story. Who knows how it will end? No one knows if they play in a comedy or a tragedy until the final curtain. The ending is the thing.'

I thought of the morning's card game. 'Like *Scopa*.' I expected to have to explain, but I had forgotten he was Sicilian born.

'Precisely. When you have the *settebello*, sweep the deck and leave.'

As if he suited the action to the words, he began to collect his papers, and as I helped him I read the fragment of a line.

She loved me for the dangers I had passed . . .

I felt a cold hand squeeze my heart. I looked up from the page. 'What is your play about?' The poet was ahead of me, climbing the dunes towards the house. I ran to catch up with him. It was suddenly crucial that I knew. 'Michelangelo! What is the play *about*?' I stumbled in the sand and nearly dropped the pages. The poet was opening the little wicket gate to the Moor's house. He must be acquainted with the admiral.

As I followed him to the little loggia of the house I glanced through the window, and paused at the sight. The walls were papered with writings; scribblings, diagrams and pamphlets were stuck up with pins from floor to ceiling. In the corner was a machine made of wood and metal, with rollers and clamps and some sort of press. A darkwood desk was set in the middle of the room, piled high with leather books on which were balanced, precariously, a globe and an orrery. A man sat at the desk in a black robe with a small white ruff, over which a grey beard flowed. He wore a close-fitting black cap upon his head, and was scratching over a paper with a quill. All this I saw in an instant, but did not note the half of it. All I could ask myself was: where was the Moor? And where was the lady? As if he felt himself watched, the old man stopped writing and looked up, straight at me.

I stepped back as if struck. Then there were footsteps; the poet came back to collect my pile of pages and saw my face.

'Who is that?' Hands full, I pointed my chin to the room.

'My father,' he said simply. 'Giovanni Florio Crollalanza.'

'Then you . . . you *live* here?'

'Yes. For a week now.'

I felt as if I were back in my dream. 'Then . . . where is the Moor?'

The angry look came back to the poet's face. He lifted the papers he carried to his chin. 'He lives only in these pages.'

'What do you mean?'

'He is dead.'

I sat down heavily in the groin of the roots of an olive tree. The leaves whispered above me, and their shadows passed across my skin like a shoal of dark fish.

The poet hunched beside me, as I had first found him, his eyes fixed on the horizon. 'I thought you knew,' he said, in a voice as flat as the yellow sands. 'Everyone knows. We took the house after it happened. It was your lady aunt who told my mother that the place was free.'

I tried to stand. Could not. 'She never told me,' I murmured. And there was no reason why she should have. My aunt knew nothing of my peeping and eavesdropping on the beach, of my stupid fantasy of the Moor and his wife. 'His poor, sweet lady,' I whispered. 'How will she live without him?'

The poet looked down at the infinite grains of sand. 'She does not have to. She is dead too, and by his hand. He strangled her for he thought her untrue.'

I put my head in my hands. How could they have come to this pass? The woman I had seen had eyes only for her Moor; how could he have lost trust in her? I felt, suddenly, unbearably bereft; not of the couple's company for I did not know them, but of the *idea* of them, of the *idea* of an idyllic marriage, built on true affection and forged on equal terms. They had seemed so happy, so in love!

The sun was climbing in the sky, and my aunt would scold me if I did not return. But I could not leave without knowing. The sea had a moonstone shimmer, and I thought of the lady sitting here, waiting for her husband's ship to come in. Now it never would. I could not bear the tragedy of it. 'What an ending.'

The poet rubbed the back of his neck with his hand, under his hair. 'Or a prelude to the final act.'

'What do you mean?'

He looked about him, as if the trees could listen as well as whisper.

'Tomorrow is Ascension Day, the day of the Vara and the Giganti in Messina. There you will see the climax of the play, I am sure of it. And a Moor will be at the centre of the stage. I told you, it is all about the ending.'

The Vara, I knew, was the Ascension Day parade in Messina, the climax of all our recent celebrations. Hero was to play an important role this year, as each year a young girl from a well-born family was chosen to act the role of the Virgin ascending, and it was a source of great pride and excitement to Hero that she had been chosen, a feeling augmented, I knew, by the strength of Claudio's faith. But I could not connect a local festival with this coil about the Moors. 'Is it not just a religious procession?' I asked.

'Ye-es,' he said slowly. 'But it has another element that the Church has been trying to excise for years. Two giant figures on horseback are conducted through the streets; Mata and Grifone. One is a white lady, and one a Moor.' My skin chilled.

'The legend says that long ago a gigantic Moor, whose name was Hassan Ibn Hammar, landed near Messina and plundered and sacked all around. One day, during a raid, he saw a girl whose name was Marta – which we Sicilians pronounce Mata – and fell in love with her. In the end, the cruel Saracen became a Christian, changed his name to Grifone and received baptism.'

I thought about the story. 'But it was a happy ending. A comedy, as you would say. The Moor converted, he married his love.'

He nodded. 'Yes. It is a story about conversion and the redeeming power of Christianity, and the Church could appropriate it; but since the expulsion of the Moors from Sicily our prelates – including our dear Archbishop of Monreale – denounced the celebration of a Moorish figure.'

'But,' I struggled to express my thoughts, 'the procession has nothing to do with the tragedy that was enacted in this house. The figures do not represent *this* Moor and his wife.'

'No,' he said. 'But I think tomorrow, they will.'

My head was beginning to ache, and I cared no more for the Spanish or their conniving. I thought about the Moor, of his nobility, his tenderness. When he'd looked at his lady as if only they existed in the world. How he caressed her cheeks and throat and kissed her most sweetly. How did he make the journey from that to placing his hands around her throat in hatred, and squeezing till he put out the light in her eyes, till the life he loved was gone? 'I cannot believe he killed her.'

'And what is more, he killed an idea, did he not?' said Michelangelo. He picked up a black pebble from the sand and rolled it in his fingers. 'Now you know of the Moor's history, two things are to be done. You may decide that the safest course is never to love.'

This seemed a bleak prospect indeed. 'And the second?'

'To take hold of love where you may.'

I looked out to sea, at the hundred different blues shifting on the surface of numberless fathoms. Would I be afraid all my life? Would I let the white lady's terrible end fright me? And yet, I had never been afraid. 'How would I take hold of it?'

Now he smiled, for the first time that day. 'Love, if not spoken, may yet be written.' He took his quill from the device at his neck, and put it in my hand, and spread a clean sheet of paper before me on the sand.

And I forgot my aunt, and the lateness of the hour. 'Show me how,' I said.

Act III scene ii

A procession in Messina

Benedick: Messina was a sea of white and blue.

Today was Ascension Day, the day to celebrate the Virgin's rise to heaven. I knew well that it was an important day in any town of Italy, but I dare swear that in all my life I had never seen such a to-do made of the day as in Messina.

On my way from my civilised home of Padua I had seen the Venetians go half mad on the Fat Tuesday of Carnevale, with their varnished faces and loose morals. I had seen the citizens of Rome return to their pagan ways as they ran around the city like demented savages at Lupercal. But I had never seen anything like the Vara.

I had been given what was, apparently, a great honour; I was to help to pull the Vara itself, the strange and vast machine that would lead the procession. The machine told the story of the Assumption of the Virgin Mary into heaven, by means of a complex apparatus created in the shape of a pyramid. At the base was a flat dun tombstone where the death of Mary was depicted, and, rising up from it, seven heavens represented by circular platforms in diminishing size through which the soul of the Virgin passed during her ascension. The universe was depicted by painted paper planets with the Earth at the centre of all; and the Sun, Moon and planets revolving around it. Crowning the structure stood the figure of Christ, who, with his right hand, raised the soul of the Virgin Mary to heaven. Some poor local maid would have to stand on Christ's wooden hand as the device rolled along the streets. I looked up doubtfully at the narrow platform, shaped for Christ's palm, and thanked God's son that I was not local, nor a maid. It seemed that whichever girl was selected could well end the day in heaven herself, not by ascension, but by tumbling from that height.

My role, by contrast, was easy. I was one of more than a thousand archers and rope pullers, dressed in white with blue waistbands, waiting to play our role. At the cry of 'Viva Maria' the Vara was to be dragged using two long hawsers. Sidesmen stood at the ready to leverage long shafts of wood and escort the cart along the correct path, preventing it from moving sideways. The roads had been wetted down by hundreds of water-carriers, to allow the Vara to slide along on steel skates.

As we awaited our signal I looked up at the vast apparatus. Each circular platform was large enough to support several local children, dressed as saints and apostles. There was Peter with his keys and James with his scallop, Thomas holding a real fish which was beginning to stink in the sun, all fidgeting and mewling as we waited. All single able-bodied men in the town were tied into the traces like fill-horses, either to push the thing forward with great oars or to pull on the great knotted ropes attached to the device, each one twisted as thick as a man's arm. I had left off my Spanish colours today for it was traditional that all those in the procession would wear the colours of the Virgin, so we were all in white, with blue waistbands and white and blue neckerchiefs about our throats.

We were all told, however, that we could wear rosaries or religious medals of our particular saint, so I had placed above my white and blue tabard the medal of St James, my symbol of knighthood. I spat upon the medallion, and rubbed it on my kerchief, then laid the roundel on my palm and examined it. Was it my imagination or had it lost a little lustre since the Naumachia? I recalled the scene of the massacre of the Moors uneasily – the blood had been very impressive, and the staging wondrously well wrought. The Moors themselves died a good death in battle, and it was not for me to question an apostle's thirst for Moorish blood. But watching the women and the children writhing in the gore had made me queasy. I thanked St James, where he sat in my palm, that we lived in more civilised days; then hung the Moor-slayer back around my neck.

My neighbour in the traces, a huge swarthy fellow with a neck as wide as his skull and a rosary tied around his forehead, made some remark in a dialect so thick I did not understand him. I smiled nervously and thankfully he smiled back, showing me a mouth with more gaps than teeth. Feeling he offered little opportunity for conversation to ease the wait, I looked about me for Lady Beatrice; but as none of the ladies was in evidence I assumed they would be joining us in the main procession from the harbour. The viceroy, Don Pedro and the other luminaries of the island were to meet by the golden statue of the Madonna of the Letter by the harbour, to be led to us, inevitably, by the archbishop. But the most important personage of the day was not the prince, nor the governor, nor even the viceroy, but the young girl who would be the Virgin of the Vara, for she was Queen of Messina for the day. Claudio, too, had some role in the procession, for there did not seem to be a day when he could be free of his uncle's designs.

We were in a beautiful square, the main piazza of the city, beneath a shining duomo with crenellated buttresses and a pointed campanile casting a merciful shadow over the sweating citizens. There was an elaborate fountain with tiers just like the Vara, and mythical beasts crouching about the base, enjoying the spray of the water. I envied them, and then my attention was caught.

A man stood by the fountain. Despite the heat of the day he wore black robes which fell to his feet, a small white stiff ruff in the Paduan style, and a black skullcap close to his head. He was the only slab of darkness in a sea of white and blue, and he looked as dour as the Virgin's tomb. He had a beard and wise eyes, and so resembled a natural philosopher, an apothecary or an attorney, someone with a serious profession. In his beringed hand a pile of creamy pamphlets fluttered – yet there was no breeze. It must be some tremor of his own, and I wondered whether he had an ague.

As if summoned by my glance he came forth to my line. 'Some reading matter while you wait, sirs?' His accent was Sicilian.

Grateful for the diversion, I thanked him and took a look at the thing as he passed down the line handing out the papers. I wished him well with his mission, for I would lay a wager that none of the fellows on my oar could read their own name, let alone some polemic.

I have never been a great one for letters but I read the writing easily, for the matter was printed in good blackletter. The first section seemed to be about religious toleration; 'All the children of the promise,' I read, 'reborn of God, who have obeyed the commands by faith working through love, have belonged to the New Covenant since the world began.' This did not speak to me, for I am the most tolerant fellow I know on these matters, and I skipped ahead. But at the bottom of the page the word 'Spanish' jumped out at me, and I here I read bitter accusations; of enclosure and cruelty to the Sicilian people, of Spanish landlords starving their Sicilian tenants, of the levy of ruinous tithes and taxes. The pamphlet ended by calling the Spanish overlords 'profane dogs who stupidly devour all the riches of the earth with their unrestrained cupidity'.

Foolishly the author had put his name to it; no title, but simply: 'Cardenio'.

I looked about me for the man in black, but he had vanished like the necromancer he resembled. If I could have speech with him again I would advise Signor Cardenio to be gone before the Spanish got here. Leonato's Watch were a pair of errant fools;

but Don Pedro's constables were a different matter – efficient, steel-clad professionals who would take him up as soon as look at him for one hundredth of the insults written here. I put the pamphlet in my tabard, for one can read a paper even on the ground, and I would not have an arrest on my conscience.

Despite my doubts it seemed that not only could some of my fellows in the traces read the pamphlet, but they seemed to be agreeing with the sentiments writ there. I heard the Sicilian for 'Spanish' rising above the hubbub a score of times, and I did not think they were expressing their love for their overlords. The atmosphere now had a strange charge to it, and my skin began to prickle. I prayed that we would soon begin pulling before these hotheads became more agitated, but still we waited for our sign to begin. I swear I could feel the trickle of childish urine splashing the runnels of the Vara, as one little saint found the wait just too long.

Then, from the direction of the harbour, along the way they call the Via Lepanto in memory of the great battle, I saw the procession coming. As soon as my eyes could see the individual figures my gaze settled on Lady Beatrice, looking remarkably well in the colours of the Virgin. Her blond curls were given great advantage by the white headdress and the colour of the gown matched her eyes. I was determined, in the freedom and confusion that such feast days and holidays as this afforded, that I would get some speech of her today, spend some time with her, and tell her how I truly felt. I would apologise for those words that were not mine, and substitute my own, heartfelt pledges.

Beatrice was walking with her aunt and uncle, behind Don Pedro and the viceroy. I could not, at first, see Hero; but then I realised she was between her parents, a small figure but a powerful one, for she was dressed as the Virgin. I understood then that Leonato's daughter had been given the honour of being the central figure of today's procession. With her sallow skin and dark hair she was Mary to the life, as if she had stepped down from a fresco from any church in this land. I sought the archbishop in the march, for I knew he would be at the centre of this coil, but I could not see him either, until I identified the figure far in front of the parade, followed by some sort of herald in red.

As the figure came closer what I saw almost made me forget Beatrice.

It was the archbishop, dressed in a brief plain robe of white cut short around his thighs. I had never seen him this way before – gone were the mitre and the chasuble, the cloth of gold and the crook. On his head he wore a humble crown of thorns, and as he came nearer I could see that the sharp barbs had pierced his bleeding brow. Worse, he had something in his hand with which he was repeatedly slapping his thighs and calves – the device must have been sharp for it pierced his skin so that the blood flowed freely – he left a trail behind him like a steer at the slaughterhouse.

In his path walked Claudio, his face pale as milk under his dark curls, also wearing a crown of thorns and a robe as red as his uncle's blood. In his hands he held a tall cross which cast its double shadow over his uncle.

The archbishop's legs looked flayed now, and as he approached the Vara I saw that his face was running with his trademark tears to mingle with the blood from the thorns. I did not pity him; he was in an ecstasy of his own piety. I was more concerned with Claudio, as the wooden cross he was carrying was wavering. I remembered how young he was, and that he had never seen battle; and I thought he would swoon from the blood.

As he reached the Vara the archbishop turned to Hero. Don Pedro and the viceroy kissed the little virgin's hand in turn, then the archbishop handed her to the burly fellows at the ropes, who lifted her from the tombstone to the first platform of the device. The people, who had been cowed into silence by such obvious devotion, suddenly began to cheer at Hero's ascension. The cries mounted and the pamphlets were dropped and forgotten, trodden in the dust and blood.

As all eyes watched Hero climb to the very top tier of the Vara, lifted on the rising volume of the crowd's cheers, I alone watched something else – Claudio falling to his knees in the dust. But there was a great firing of firecrackers, and our chief, from the top of the tombstone, gave the starting signal; everyone but me laid hold of the oars and heaved, and the machine jerked forward on its runners.

Buffeted in the back by the wooden levers, I was suddenly angry. Abandoning the honour afforded me, I dropped my oar and ran under the ropes as the Vara began to move. I grabbed Claudio by his upper arm, hauled him to his feet and out of the path of the machine, and marched him to the fountain. I snatched the thorns from his head, licked my thumb and wiped the drops of dried blood away. He was shivering, despite the searing heat of the day. 'It was a cork,' he said. 'My uncle held a broad cork in his palm with thirteen pieces of glass set in there. One for each apostle.' His teeth were chattering. 'It was not a miracle. And he made me walk in the blood.'

I helped him up, count though he was, and sat him on the side of the fountain. I washed his feet for him as if I was the Magdalene, until the bowl ran red. A shadow fell across us and the fellow in black with the pamphlets was suddenly there again. He stood over us like a sentinel and watched ahead, as if he was shielding Claudio from the eyes of his uncle. When I had done and looked for him to thank him, his pamphlets were scattered about the pavings and he was gone.

I turned to Claudio. 'At least your feet were on the floor,' I said. 'Your friend Hero is to be an angel of the skies.' He smiled a little at this, his colour returning, and we returned to the procession.

By now Hero was on her perilous perch on the very top of

the Vara device, standing precariously on the upstretched right hand of a plaster figurine of Christ. Her waving fingers touched the clouds.

The cries of *Viva Maria!* rang out from the crowds in a deafening chant. Archers with golden bows shot flowers at the tower and passed up a bunch of white roses to be conveyed all the way to Hero. The little maid looked more comely than I had ever seen her in her blue robe and white wimple with a chaplet of flowers about her forehead, her dark hair rippling below the headdress almost to her knees, roses blooming in her cheeks too. You could see, then, the promise to come. In her hand she held a red crystal heart, the Sacred Heart, I supposed, of Christ.

With the momentum great gilded wheels with the sun and moon set upon their axles began to turn. The ever-decreasing circular platforms of the whole contraption began to revolve sickeningly, contrariwise with the motion of the machine. The heavenly bodies and planets and stars revolved like an orrery and this complication of superstitious whirligigs rendered the poor little apostles squeamish. Some of them fell asleep, many of them puked most grievously, and some did still worse: but these unseemly emissions did not seem to affect the edification of the people. Little St James, who seemed to be the direst case, was simply passed down to his mother in the crowd.

I could not leave Claudio yet, and I could not have my talk with Beatrice with him at hand, but I manoeuvred us in the procession so I could keep her in sight. As we reached the harbour and curved round to the golden statue, following in the path of the archbishop's blood, we stopped at last and seemed to wait once more. For there was more to come.

As we watched, two giants rolled down the hill towards us. For one foolish moment I thought they were real; but then I saw that they were huge constructions on wheels – two horses as vast as the horse of Troy, one white, one black, carrying riders. Riders made of wood, painted and varnished.

The white horse carried a white lady, with a blue dress with gold curlicues on the stomacher and a white apron at the skirts. She had a crown made of the towers of a citadel on her head. The black horse carried a Moor in Roman armour with a scarlet cloak about his shoulders and a laurel wreath of victory upon his head. Their coming was eerie – they must have moved upon wheels but they seemed to float, the noise of their machinery inaudible above the hubbub of the crowd. It was as if two huge leviathans had forsaken their unsounded deeps to ride upon the sands.

As they drew closer the crowd grew quieter. I looked about me and drew Claudio nearer – there was an uneasy atmosphere once again, as the people of Messina looked upon the giants, the black man and the white lady staring forward with their varnished faces, implacable. Then someone shouted '*Matamoros!*' I looked around – I thought I recognised the voice; it belonged to an ensign in Don Pedro's company. Others took up the shout; all Spaniards, for the word they shouted was a Spanish word. I had heard it before; it was a name they had given as a badge of honour to their patron St James the Great. Matamoros; Kill the Moor.

From behind us the regiment began to throw missiles at the black rider. They arced over us like arrows; fallen lemons, sticks. And then stones.

'Let's go,' I hissed to Claudio, and pulled him back towards the church door. The archbishop, dressed now in his chasuble and finery, stood there in the duomo's porch watching the trouble, with eyes empty of tears and surprise. I knew in an instant he had done this. I thrust Claudio at him. 'Take him in,' I commanded, caring not for his rank. He nodded once and took his nephew under his arm. I waited till they all went within and barred the doors, as if they knew the storm was coming.

I dashed back to the fray with only one thought – Beatrice. Now people were screaming and running. There was an angry, seething crowd about the legs of the plaster Moor's wooden horse and still they were screaming the word *Matamoros!* The horse was rocking and would soon be toppled. I looked at the Vara beyond it; the children were already jumping down to safety in the arms of their mothers. I came face to face with Beatrice.

For a moment I held her in a beautiful firm embrace, as relief flooded me, and as we parted I read the same relief on her face, to be chased away by panic. 'Benedick,' she said, and my own name seemed the sweetest word in the lexicon at that moment. But she pointed. 'Hero!'

I turned; saw at once. The Vara was rocking precariously, the paper planets tumbling down as if the universe had ended. Hero, clinging to her perch, was losing her grip, her chaplet of roses awry and her cheeks streaked with tears. As if time had slowed, the painted Moor and his horse toppled over to be broken and trampled and spat upon by the Aragonese. Beatrice was still by my side but I thrust her away from me. 'Get out of this,' I said. 'I will find you.'

I did not expect her to obey and nor she did, but stood and watched in the screaming chaos as Hero toppled from the right hand of Christ and dropped like a stone. The girl landed in my arms, winding me, but Beatrice was there to fetch us up. I dragged them, one on each arm, to the cathedral porch and pounded at the studded doors. Hero was safely conveyed to her uncle and aunt, and I would have pressed Beatrice within too, but she tugged my hand.

Wordlessly, we went back into the fray. Hand in hand we walked through the chaos. The Moor was shattered into dust, the black plaster chipped from his face – he was now white. In opposition, as if to redress some balance of opposing forces, the sky darkened into dusk. The fireworks burst overhead, and I wondered what there was to celebrate. The Vara contraption lay on its side, and the townsfolk were cutting the great ropes into little pieces with their wicked knives and handing the hemp around to the pullers and bowmen. This may have been a custom with them but now it just seemed of a piece with the general anarchy. I followed Beatrice out of the madness and as I left the thoroughfare I felt a crunch underfoot.

The red crystal Sacred Heart lay shattered in the archbishop's congealed blood.

Act III scene iii

The dunes before the Moor's house

Beatrice: I could not stop the tears from sliding down my cheeks as I stumbled down the shoreline in the direction of the Moor's house.

I was certain that the poet and his family were in danger, that the mob I had just seen would not differentiate between past and present tenant and that the house had once been the home of the murderous Moor would be enough for them to burn the place to the ground.

I scrambled through the cacti and my dress tore a little; prickly fruits were knocked to the ground and I trod them underfoot, smelling their cloying sweet flesh. In my haste my hand had broken from Signor Benedick's but I knew he still followed me, for now and again he called my name. The word sounded so lovely on his lips it was snatched and blown away by the jealous zephyr. I tasted salt on my lips; my tears and the sea spray were one. The field of stars overhead made the night as bright as day, shining in their thousands like the crystals of Egyptian blue.

I blinked the tears away in an effort to see the house ahead; but it was all right, only the lamp burned in the study window. Giovanni Florio Crollalanza was no doubt at his pamphlets – no torches touched the timbers, no stones broke the quarrels, no angry citizens wielded their moonlight daggers. The silver sea was calm and flat as a looking glass, the tide whispered in in intervals, and the hubbub from the town sounded no louder here than the waves.

At the dunes I collapsed into the sand where I had sat yesterday disputing with the poet. Benedick knelt before me, and
touched one of the tears on my cheek. 'Lady Beatrice, have you
wept all this while?'

'Yes, and I have tears enough to rival the stars in number.'

'But your cousin is safe,' he assured me.

Yes, and he had saved her. 'How much might the man
deserve of me that righted her!' I clasped the finger that had
touched the teardrop. I could not explain the real reason for my
tears; the Moor's horse falling, the plaster Moor, his face stoved
in, blanched by violence, and let go of the finger. 'But there are
other wrongs here to be righted.'

'Is there any way to show such friendship?' His kneeling
posture turned him supplicant. 'May a man do it?'

I thought of the poet. 'It is a man's office, but not yours.'

He rose, so precipitately that sand flew into my skirts,
suddenly angry. 'Then whose? That scribbler?'

I sat under the benign stars, their light doubling and trebling
through the lens of my tears. They seemed to be falling. I did
not hear the danger in his voice. 'He knew. He knew how it
would be. He told me here, on this very spot, just yesterday.'

I looked at Benedick's angry, shuttered face, the angles of
it sharp in the moonlight. How could I explain that a fortnight earlier, I would have thrilled to sit here with him, back
when I had wanted, so much, a Moor of my own. That the
poet had been helping me to write a sonnet, for him, which
expressed exactly what I wanted to say? That I had wanted to
give it to him, here, tonight, on these dunes? But now it had
all turned sour, for the Moor's crime against nature
had shaken the constellations, and ruptured the ordained orbit
of my life too.

Yet if the poet was right this had all started well before, with
the massacre of Ramiro of Asturias centuries ago, with the
heavenly connivance of St James the Moor-slayer – St James

Matamoros – and the expulsion of the Moors from Spain and from Sicily. Now it was ended, this whole sorry history of the Moors in Sicily – the last living Moor had gone, slain by his own hand, and even the plaster Moor Grifone, that colossus of the Ascension parade, was utterly vanquished. The play was over; and it was a tragedy, defined by its ending. Sun and day and love had turned to night and dark and murder, and I wish the planets could be turned and we could revolve once again into day, but I did not know how that might be achieved.

I thought Benedick was the answer. I had brought him here because I had thought him, somehow, the key to this celestial reversal. I had once thought him a jester or a fool, the personification of mirth, but now he looked as furious as the mob. 'Who said these things?' He knelt again, but in dominance this time, not submission, and laid his hands upon my shoulders. 'You talked with a man, here, yesterday?'

I sighed – I owed him the truth, even though I knew it would anger him. 'It was the poet. Michelangelo Florio Crollalanza. His house is there.' I pointed to the light beyond the cacti.

He released my shoulders and turned to look at the window, as if he could not trust himself. 'And now, you were running to *him*? That is the right of it, isn't it?'

'No,' I protested. 'I mean, yes. But not like that. I wanted to warn him.'

'Warn him of what?'

I thought of all Michelangelo had said of the Spanish, of Benedick's friends. 'I cannot say.'

'You have your *secrets*, then,' he spat.

Worse and worse. 'Do not believe me; and yet, I do not lie . . .' I was babbling, but Benedick was so tied to the affair, so complicit in it all – bound to Don Pedro by those inexorable bonds of brotherhood and friendship, tied to St James the Moor-slayer by reason of the medal he still wore around his neck. What if I told him of the poet's suspicions and he ran back to his brother-prince? I thought speedily and told a half-truth. 'We spoke of love. What else do poets know?'

He came to me then, his eyes dark with something indefinable. I thought him angry, but then he took my hands. 'I may not have the simpering syllables of Monsieur Love,' he whispered fervently, 'I can only speak like an honest man and a soldier. But I can speak of love too.' He took a breath as if he would plunge into five fathoms. '*I do love nothing in the world so well as you.*'

There it was. He had done the impossible. He had turned the world around. I was suddenly shining in the firmament with the dayspring, overflowing with joy. 'Why, then, God forgive me!' I exclaimed. 'I was about to protest I loved you.'

Then suddenly his lips were on mine, our bodies pressed together. The fire in the sky was between us now, descended from the celestial to the mortal, it was burning in our hearts, twin coals. We kissed until we could not breathe, and collapsed on the sand, side by side, hands entwined. The stars glittered just for us. I blinked back at them, unable to believe such happiness; and saw then, brighter than them all, the crooked constellation that was most dear to me. I pointed. 'There, do you see? That group of five stars, shaped like a double V?'

He followed my finger with his gaze. 'Yes.'

'That is Cassiopeia's chair. And there is a sixth star, see, at the bottom.'

'I see it,' he said. 'It is smaller than the rest, and brighter.'

'That is because it is young – it is not even a score of years old.'

He leaned on his elbow, and looked at me indulgently. 'How do you know?'

'It is my star,' I said. 'It was born when I was born.'

He began to kiss my throat, small, fluttering kisses like butterflies, so sweet that they made it difficult to speak. 'Explain.'

'My mother bore me in her chamber, at the top of our castle's tower. As she laboured, she looked on the stars for comfort, and she told me that at the very second of my birth, that new star danced into being, lighting up like a candle flame. I always thought it her fancy, but claimed the star for my own. It was something we shared, even when she died.' The little kisses stopped; resumed again. 'Then I came here, and our own Friar Francis, who is something of an astronomer, told me she spoke truly; the star was a *stella nova*, born on November 11th just like me.' I sighed like the zephyr, happily now. Benedick was the first person save the friar I had told about the star. The star had been mine and my mother's; I had not told my father, nor yet my brother. But now, at last, I had someone to tell, someone who loved me. 'Its proper name is Tycho's Supernova, but I prefer to think of it as a diamond set into Cassiopeia's chair,' I smiled at the skies, 'a fitting ornament for the goddess who boasted of her unrivalled beauty.'

'She has a rival now,' said Benedick, and moved his mouth up to meet mine.

I was on the dunes, my back pressed into the giving sand, soft and hard at once, and moulding to my body. He was upon me, his lips so soft, his body hard, two states at once like the sand. Our garments, the white and blue, were twined and combined. My hands moved into his warm hair, and learned the shape of the back of his head. My eyes closed, my head twisted back and my throat arched with pleasure and fear. Then his lips moved downwards and my hands clawed and clasped the sand in my ecstasy. I felt the powder harden in my fist; then begin to slip, inevitably, out of my grasp, until I was holding nothing.

My eyes flew open. Benedick was above me, and the stars were gone. All was blackness; he had put out the light.

Put out the light.

I sat bolt upright, shoving him away with a strength I didn't know I had, my heart thudding.

Benedick lay back on the sand, laughing, uncertain. 'Beatrice? My love? What's amiss?'

How could I tell him? How could I explain to Benedick that I was not thinking of my chastity, or my reputation, or my maidenhead? I was not some Pope-holy poppet who would go so far then refuse to go farther. All I could think was that all such acts of love had the same sequel. The caress that turned to the death grip, love corroding to jealousy. I had seen the darkness in Benedick's eyes before, at the wedding at Syracuse, when he had spoken to me of the poet, and again tonight, when he thought I had run to Michelangelo Crollalanza, despite the fact that my heart had not even the smallest corner of space for him. Or if it did, only that region which held friendship, certainly not love; for all of my heart was occupied by the forces of one Knight of St James.

I looked down at Benedick beside me, breathing heavily, hoisting himself to his elbow. His hair tumbled, his clothes disarranged, he smiled tenderly but uncertainly. He had never looked more handsome, and I would have given anything to sink back down with him, and let the universe keep turning as it would. Then he reached up his hand to my throat, and I realised that my own fingers were there, squeezing, shielding. Gently he removed them, touching tenderly where I swallowed and breathed, as gently as he had kissed me there moments ago. Now his touch terrified me.

I flinched. 'I am gone, though I am here,' I croaked, hoarse as if I had been throttled in truth.

He laughed and put his arms about me again, to pull me down – I felt his strength, and saw again that darkness in his eyes. 'There is no love in you,' I hissed, 'nay, I pray you, let me go.' The last word was a shout.

I stumbled away through the sand, tripping and stumbling, shaking, turning and walking backward, fearful he would follow, half-hoping that he would.

'Tarry, sweet Beatrice!' He was half laughing, half concerned, as if I played some lover's game. But the game was my life.

I tried to regain composure. I brushed the sand from my gown and straightened myself. 'In faith, I will go.' And I ran towards the house on the dunes, thinking all the time that, just as I had watched the lovers in the sand a fortnight since, we too had been observed by spying eyes.

Act III scene iv

The *studiolo* in the Moor's house

Beatrice: I walked towards the light of the little window as if it were the light of the Bethlehem star.

It spelled sanctuary for me, for I knew that Benedick would look for me, and if he caught me I would acquiesce. I was not proof against him, not proof against my own feelings. I wanted nothing more than to run back into his arms, for I had not felt as safe nor as wanted since I was a child. I had felt, for one instant, the centre of the universe, the Earth in the orrery, that all the planets and heavenly bodies revolved around me. Around us. But so had the Moor's wife felt when the sun of the Moor's affection had shone upon her; and now she was cold in the ground.

I was at the window of the study now. I don't know whether I expected to see Giovanni Florio Crollalanza, working at his pamphlets, or even the poet himself, taking lease of his father's desk. But the person I saw was someone who did not, as I had once been told, look right in a room. It was Guglielma Crollalanza.

She was sitting at the desk, amid her husband's papers, with her chin on one hand and her black ringlets obscuring her face. She held the other hand outstretched to touch the orrery on the desk. The brass rings revolved at her touch and the little planets spun about the Earth at the centre. I noticed that despite the golden colour of her skin, her hand was dark skinned on the back and her palm and fingers were white below. I realised then with a jolt that there was one more Moor still left on the island.

She looked as if she had troubles of her own, but still I tapped on the window and saw her turn rapidly, as if expecting someone else. But she forced a smile, took her hand away from the planets and beckoned me in. I looked for a doorway and entered through the little loggia. I walked through the dark little house to the lit room. The lamp on the desk was the only light in the place.

Guglielma did not look as me as I entered the *studiolo*. Her white teeth chewed her mulberry lower lip. 'Giovanni has not returned from the Vara,' she said. 'Michelangelo has gone to seek him.'

I recognised a larger problem than my own and began to withdraw. 'I will go.'

'No,' she said. 'Stay. I need company.' Now she looked at me, with searching eyes. 'Were you looking for my son?'

I took the sonnet that only yesterday her son had helped me to write from my bodice. I had planned to put it in Benedick's hand tonight. Instead I put it in hers. 'He helped me write this,' I said.

'May I?'

I nodded, colouring a little, for the sentiment was raw and the construction faulty. As she unfolded the paper the *settebello* card, which had been nestling in my bodice with the sonnet, fell on to the leather topper of the desk, and I thought she had not noted it.

There was no sound but her breathing as she read. Her full lips moved a little as if she spoke the sonnet aloud. 'It is very beautiful.' She looked directly at me with her eyes black as sloes, and I blushed deeper. 'But it is not meant for Michelangelo, I think?'

'He is not the subject,' I said hurriedly, 'but he gave me the ink and the paper, and as the components are his, I am come to render them to him again.'

'But it is not the ink and the paper that have value. The value lies in the words, and they are yours.'

I strove to be fair. 'Michelangelo helped me.'

'No; I know his style. This is from *your* heart. This is your definition of love. The subject did not want these words?'

'I did not offer them to him.'

She set down the paper and saw the playing card. 'The *settebello*,' she said, as if she greeted an old friend. She turned it over in her pied fingers, and the seven coins on the face seemed to glitter. 'Was this for him too?'

I was shamefaced. 'Yes.'

'So he is the winner. And you were to be the prize.'

'Yes.'

'But not now?'

I paced the room, as I sought the words. 'I do not *want* it. I do not *want* to love him. I do not wish to be enslaved to this feeling.' I spun to face her. 'Is it possible to fall out of love?'

'Not for me. But in Sicily, it is, yes.'

Her answer seemed oddly worded.

She stood. 'Watch the window,' she charged me, 'for I am about to do something that should not be seen, and tell something that should not be overheard.'

She moved over to the device at the corner, the one I had seen from the window – was it only the previous day? – with the great iron rollers and wooden presses. She went to the wooden frame and began to pull some small iron blocks from it, disarranging them, changing one for the other, pulling some out of order entirely and throwing them in a receptacle on the floor. As I squinted in the lamplight I realised what she was doing – the thing was a printing press, one of the new-fangled machines that had put the scribes out of business, and by disarranging the blocks she was removing the evidence of the pamphlet her husband had printed. *What had it said?* I wondered. Had those dangerous little metal blocks combined to extol his love for John Calvin? Or his hatred of the Spaniards?

I would never know, for Guglielma worked fast, and talked of other things. I watched her quick, black hands and thought: 'She has had to do this before.' I was so mesmerised that for a moment I did not heed what she was saying. Then her musical accent broke through my thoughts. 'The ladies of the island perform a certain ritual tomorrow, the day after Ascension Day. It is a . . . dance, called the Tarantella.' She rolled the word around her tongue. 'It is named for a spider.' She held out her black hands and wiggled the fingers. 'I have danced it every year I have lived here, and my grandmothers did it too, and their grandmothers before them; all the Archirafi women. You can do it for fun, or in earnest.' She wiped the little blocks with a coarse cloth, removing the ink and the evidence together. 'I called the Tarantella a dance. At the least, that is what it is. At the most, it is an incantation in movement. A cure.'

'A cure for what?'

'For anything you want rid of. Including a man.'

'And does it work?'

She stopped, and looked up at me, the whites of her eyes very white, the pupils as black as her fingers. 'Oh yes.' Her deliberate destruction complete, she wiped her hands on her skirt. 'We women spend the day together, reach the hill at sundown, and dance on the side of the mountain.'

It seemed like a harmless way to pass a day. 'I will come,' I decided.

Guglielma said nothing at first. She began to shuffle the pamphlets together into a bundle. She took another lamp from the sconce on the wall and lit it with a taper from the first. She ushered me outside; the night was still warm, the stars back in their proper places.

'I can help you,' she whispered, and the dune grasses whispered back. 'But you have to be *sure* you want this. It is no little thing. We will be calling on an ancient primal power, from the crater of the volcano and the belly of the very island itself.' She kissed my cheek quickly and I noticed that her skin had a granular quality. 'If you are sure, come to the Via Catania outside your uncle's gate at dawn tomorrow. Tell your aunt you are pursuing a private penance to the Virgin – such things are common at the Ascension. And it is not the blackest lie – for Mary was the epitome of womanhood and it is with womanhood that we deal tomorrow.'

I was slightly shocked, for I had never heard the blessed Virgin named so, by her given name, as if she were a tiring maid or a laundress.

'If your aunt were not wed to Leonato Leonatus,' Guglielma went on, 'I would tell her the truth myself.' She shot me a look. 'If she were not married to Leonato Leonatus she would be coming herself, as she did once when she was first wed.'

My eyes widened. 'My aunt? My aunt danced the Tarantella?' I wondered, briefly, what demons my aunt had wanted rid of all those years ago. But Guglielma was looking about her as if pursued, and seemed in a hurry. She did not answer but dismissed me. 'And now, you must go to your business before your aunt worries, and I to mine.'

I looked at the sheaf of pamphlets in her hand. And it occurred to me that loving Giovanni Florio Crollalanza might, in its own way, be as lethal as loving the Moor. And yet, Michelangelo was easily twenty, so the unlikely pair had been devoted for a score of years at least. I looked at the stars and the sea; the sky was dark but Guglielma was darker, now a silhouette against the firmament. I could not see her eyes, so I had the courage to ask, 'Do you never wish yourself out of love?'

'No, I do not wish myself out of love. But it would be better if I did – for Giovanni is hurrying to his grave, and will take us all with him.' I could not see her expression; she was just a voice, a voice that meant every word. 'But I would rather die

with him than live with any other. That is *my* definition of love.'
Then she set off down the hill, leaving me behind and taking the
lamp, the taper and the sheaf of pamphlets to the shore. I turned
and trudged to the sea road, suddenly deathly tired.

Looking back some minutes later from the stony path, I
could see the light from the Moor's house had split into two;
there was the square of light in the window of the study and
there was a fire, on the beach, dancing merrily like a noon-day
Devil.

Act III scene v

Benedick's chamber in Leonato's house

Benedick: I sought out Don Pedro the very next morning.

After Lady Beatrice had run from me, I had walked back to Leonato's house along the shoreline, one foot on the sand and the other in the night-black water, and by the time I had gained the palazzo I had made up my mind.

I knew what was the matter with Beatrice. It was clear as day. I knew her own heart as well as my own – I had heard it beat, pressed to mine, as her lips flowered under my kiss. There was no doubt that she wanted me – we were meant to be together, we were two sides of the same heart.

She was not at fault – she showed the right measure of maiden modesty to run from me. I was to blame, and had let my passions rule my honour. It would have been wrong indeed if I had, upon the dunes, made defeat of her virginity. She was not to be tumbled like a Trastavere tart or a Venetian vixen. She was a princess of Villafranca and Leonato's niece and however lax he might be in allowing her freedoms, I could not, should not, dishonour her. I would make her my wife. Then, once we were betrothed, she could embrace me as a husband and extenuate the forehand sin.

I would resign my commission and offer her marriage. I had no wish, now, to be a knight errant – I had been playing a part these past several days. I had no desire to draw my sword and jump from ship to ship, with no knowledge of whether I would ever return. I could not agree with that ancient combatant Don

Miguel that the soldier shows to better advantage dead in battle than alive in flight; I wanted my life, and I wanted to live it with Beatrice. We would go north, away from the fierce gaze of the southern sun, and with her fortune and my . . . wits, we would shift very well. I might even find another profession, when I was done with soldiery.

I could not afford to go to war and return with hollow honours and striped with battle scars, for if I marched with Don Pedro in a fortnight Beatrice would be left here with Monsieur Love, and I was not about to lose her to that scribbling bard.

I asked to see Don Pedro straight after we had broken our fast, and he surprised me by following me to my chamber, as if he wanted to speak with me as much as I with him.

As soon as we were alone I blurted out my intentions. 'I wish to leave your service and marry,' I stated with no preamble.

He said nothing at first so I knelt and kissed his hand, lifted the medal of St James from my neck and hooked it over the fingers I had saluted. When it was gone from me I felt that a millstone had been lifted – now I knew I had not wanted to wear it since the night of the Naumachia, for from then on it had hung about my neck like a usurer's chain.

The thing dangled from his hand, winking in the morning light, the ribbon entwined in fingers baked dark gold by the Sicilian sun. His eyes were hooded. I wondered whether he was angry, for on the day I'd met him I'd assured him that I had no attachments of the heart. But he seemed to take the news quite equably – he walked to the window, and looked out of it, as if he could already see his ship sailing away. I waited, saying nothing, and at length he turned back. 'Which way do you look?'

'Upon the Lady Beatrice.'

His dark eyebrows shot up and I could see the expression in his eyes for an instant. No longer veiled, they were surprised into honesty, and for just a moment I saw naked envy. Then the eyes were hooded again, and I knew I had been mistaken. 'I congratulate you,' he said heartily. 'You played the seven of coins and won yourself a princess.' For the first time I wished I had not told him of my trick of giving out the *settebello* card to the ladies, and I cursed my damned impulse to make everybody laugh.

'Her wealth is nothing to me,' I said stiffly. 'As Your Highness knows, the Minolas of Padua are comfortable merchants. My prospects for the future are good, and I have chinks enough for now.'

He nodded, as if he had not heard me. 'And the lady feels the same way?'

'I think so.'

His smile grew wider, his eyes graver. 'Then I will say this. If you feel as you do now on the day we weigh anchor, then we will say goodbye with my blessing. If you change your mind, you will sail with me, to wherever the King's Enterprise will take us.'

It seemed a fair bargain; for I knew that nothing in this world could flout me out of my humour. 'Agreed.'

He turned back to the window. 'But since you are as yet in my employ, I will ask you to complete one last mission.'

'A mission?' I did not want to invite accusations of cowardice, but I did not wish to encounter any danger to my person, now that I had decided to hang up my barely worn soldier's coat.

'I misspoke,' he said hastily. 'It is more of a jest, or a wager; and I know how you love such sport. It is not dangerous. There will be no arms where you are bound, nor a single man to bear them.'

He turned his back to the window, and I could no longer see his expression. 'You see, I have accepted a wager from my friend the Archbishop of Monreale.'

I frowned, thinking of the bloodied creature I had seen only yesterday flaying his own flesh in the streets of Messina. He did not seem to me the kind of man to accept a wager. 'Do not his vows forbid him to gamble?'

'You are right,' he blustered. 'I meant the viceroy.'

I knew less of the viceroy, for although he had been at nearly every one of our many gatherings I had never heard him utter a word. I thought him, despite his titles, of no more mark than one of the mammets in the puppet theatre – bravely dressed, but mute until some puppetmaster put words into his mouth.

'I made a bet with him – the viceroy, that is – for we do not leave these shores till Monday next, and I told him that the time shall not go idly by us,' continued the prince. 'There is a ritual, a godless thing, that the womenfolk of Sicily practise on the evening after the Ascension.'

'Tonight?'

'Tonight. They come together to perform a pagan dance. No man is allowed to take part, nor even set eyes on it. I said I knew a man who would be able to observe it, and tell us what passed.'

I was silent, for I could not speak my thought; which was that this seemed an unworthy game for princes.

'If you succeed, I will give you one hundred golden *reales*.'

My jaw dropped open. One hundred golden *reales* would make a handsome start to my union with Beatrice. Despite my protestations there was no doubt that a princess of Villafranca had a greater fortune than a minor merchant of Padua, and a hundred gold *reales* was no small purse. I wondered what the principal sum of the bet was, if my part share could be so much. 'And how am I to penetrate such a gathering?'

'You could dress yourself as a woman.' He observed my dubious expression. 'The players do it. Two nights past we saw one of my own cavalry dressed as Boudicca.'

I remembered well, a wag called Juan who had donned the red wig and metal breastplate of the Britons' queen a little too readily. But Juan was small, and slight. I was as tall as a maypole. 'Why me?'

He clapped my shoulder with the hand that held the medal, and it kissed one of my buckles with a chink. 'My dear fellow, who better? Everyone knows you for a man of excellent humour. If you are discovered, everyone will take it for a jest.'

I narrowed my eyes. 'So what is it really?'

'Just that, dear fellow, just that.'

He was a bad liar, and I recalled for an instant the dark hints that Beatrice had spoken upon the dunes. But I cared no more for Spanish conniving – soon enough it would no longer be my affair. Whatever the reason for the wager, I saw no honour in it; but since the prince had given me my freedom, I owed him this in the name of friendship if not in the name of St James. It was a small price to pay – I might have to endure an evening without Lady Beatrice, but God and luck willing it would be my last one.

'Very well.' I kissed his hand again, with the medal of St James still twined around his fingers. The thing chinked against my teeth. He saw it. 'Once a Knight of Saint James,' he said, his brown eyes solemn, 'always a Knight of Saint James.'

He turned with a flourish to leave the room, and caught sight of a paper lying on the rushes. He stooped and picked the thing up. He was suddenly as still as a statue, frozen, reading silently. 'Where did you get this?'

I peered at the pamphlet. It was the polemic I'd been given on Ascension Day, by the fellow dressed as a magus or necromancer. Signor Cardenio.

'I was given it at the Vara,' I said uneasily. 'By an old man.'

Don Pedro's black eyes skimmed the blackletter print again, taking in, I was sure, every insult and epithet laid at the Spaniards' door. His tone, when he next spoke, was light, belying the expression in his eyes. 'Ah, the Vara. That was many days ago. And could you identify him if you saw him again?'

I did not like the way the interrogation tended. 'I could,' I said slowly, 'but I would not wish to if it would cause him any ill. For he did us a kindness, Claudio and me.' I remembered him shielding us like a shadow as I washed Claudio's feet; an action which, in that religious context, would have been taken as profane by his uncle. The archbishop seemed to want his nephew to be doused in blood, a literal show of their consanguinity.

'Your loyalty commends you. But you mistake me. I would not wish him ill. I welcome opposition, when it is so well expressed. His quarrel is lively and well argued. I might have some little commission for him for Spain, that is all.' Don Pedro paused lightly. 'And do I not deserve some loyalty also? We are brothers of Saint James.'

He had forgotten that I had returned my medal, but he made an excellent point. He was my friend, and I did him a disservice with my suspicion – I had confused him with his friend the archbishop. 'He was tall,' I said, 'and wore a stiff Padovani ruff and a black scholar's gown. He had a grey beard, deep-set eyes, and a black skullcap. When he spoke it was with a Sicilian accent, and his name was Cardenio.'

'You see,' he cried, clapping my shoulder. 'I said you would be an excellent spy. You will be missed in my company.'

I bowed, relieved that he seemed to have made his peace with my leaving him; but I had the feeling his mind had already gone from the room. He shortly followed it, absentmindedly pocketing the pamphlet as he left the chamber.

Act III scene vi

A night on the volcano

Beatrice: I rose at first light, and dressed by the mote of gilded light bleeding through the shutters.

Hero was sleeping peacefully, her long black lashes lying like spiders on her cheeks. I did not want to wake her. I told myself she had had a torrid time at the Vara and needed her rest, but the real reason was that if I told her that I was going on a pilgrimage to honour the Virgin she would beg to come, tired or no, for Mary was her personal goddess now, her touchstone and main-saint. She had gained from Claudio the virtue of . . . well, virtue.

My exit was a tricky business for I had to step carefully over Margherita, who slept curled on a mat by the door. I closed the door behind me soundlessly and tiptoed barefoot down the cool stone steps before putting on my soft leather slippers. The slip-pers were cross-gartered and took more time than I cared about to tie with my shaking hands. I thought at every minute that Orsola would find me on the stair, for Orsola was a tattle-tongue who minded everybody's business but her own. I was not discovered, though, and let myself out of the gate from the painted courtyard into the chapel cloister. On a whim I crossed the little green court to the chapel and found Friar Francis at the tabernacle, readying the host for prime.

'Lady Beatrice!' he said. 'You have risen early on this holy day.'

I looked at him guiltily through my lashes. 'I am spending the day at penance.'

He wiped his hands on his habit and came through the rood screen to regard me in the tinted light from the stained glass. 'What penance?' he said.

'Oh, a local pilgrimage,' I said airily. 'Local women of good character have invited me to walk up the hill. It is a representation of Christ's walk to Calvary.'

He scratched his scanty beard, and his eyes twinkled. 'Tell the goodwives from me that they are very early in their observances. Six months early,' he said pointedly, 'for such a pilgrimage would normally take place at Easter.'

'I mean, Mary's ascension into heaven,' I prattled. 'It is my scripture that is faulty, not theirs,' I assured him.

'Perhaps I should do better in my instruction,' he mused aloud, and I thought, on this point at least, he was being serious.

'I did not want to wake my aunt—'

'Very considerate of you—'

'So if she enquires after me, perhaps you would tell her that I am well and will be back by nightfall?'

He pursed his thin lips, worried now. 'God make it true.' His hazel eyes, normally mild and benign, bored into me like awls. I turned and walked down the nave before I told him everything.

'Lady Beatrice.'

I stopped but did not look back.

'All actions have consequences. Be sure of what you are doing.'

Guglielma Crollalanza had said the exact same thing. I carried on walking, but on my way out I sketched a cross guiltily in the direction of the statue of Mary. I considered, as I let myself out of the lychgate to the sea road, that I had caught the habit of thinking of the Virgin by her first name. Like a tiring maid. Like a laundress. Like a woman.

I met the company on the Via Catania, a merry bundle of

women of all ages from little maids who must still taste their first communion, to grandames. They were all dressed, as I was, in Sicilian dress; a red skirt as full as a circle, a white blouse with puffed sleeves, a tightly fitting black waistcoat and black slippers with cross-garters. I greeted Guglielma with a kiss, as seemed natural after our exchange of confidence; and I felt again the granular nature of her dark cheek. Like sand.

I climbed the hill beside her. She had brought a blackthorn stick with her and she flourished it at me like a sword, laughing. 'The way is hard,' she said.

I said, 'They make a joke about my family in Verona; they say the Scaligeri never have to trouble about a mountain, a staircase or the steps to a maiden's bed, for they always have a ladder with them.' I explained, 'The ladder is the emblem of our family arms, the Della Scala.'

She nodded up the hill, blowing hard. 'We may need your ladder later, for we go right to the summit. It is needful now, for secrecy; in days gone we used to dance our measure before the cathedral, in full view of the prelates of the town. But since the archbishop came, the ladies tell me, it is well to be secret. He does not like our rituals, would ban them if he could.' She winked at me – something I had never seen a woman do, and she did it well, closing one eye entirely, keeping the other wide, smiling all the while. 'But such things will not be easily suppressed. Sicilian women have danced the Tarantella since Sicily was part of Magna Graecia.'

I looked down to the port of Messina. The day was bright and the bay blue and the golden statue of Mary shone in the harbour like a beacon, as if blessing our enterprise. 'And do these women *all* wish to rid themselves of a man?'

She laughed again, carefree. 'No. The dance was a curative one originally, made to rid the body of a spider's bite. When the sweat pours from your flesh, and it will, it flushes out the venom of a spider bite or another malady. You give whatever you do not want back to the mountain. You will sweat your man out of you.' She struck at the path before her with her stick. 'I will be giving thanks that I got mine back.'

I stopped walking. 'Your husband is returned?'

'Yes. The Spanish questioned him as I feared, but there was nothing to connect him to the pamphlets he had distributed, for he signed them with an alias, and no man could be found who would positively identify him as the giver of these epistles. I had but to play my part at the house, and the evidence was gone.' She lowered her voice, for all that she was among friends, and I thought that somewhere in the last twenty years, secrecy had become a habit with her. 'Something once read cannot be forgotten, and his words had hit home. The men of the Vara were not disposed to tell what they knew, for Giovanni Florio is a Sicilian by birth and dialect and accent, and they look after their own.' She tapped the side of her broad nose with her finger, confidentially. 'Three score pamphlets were handed out that day, but not one was given up to the Inquisitors, nor found on the ground to be presented in evidence. The streets were as clean as on Palm Saturday.'

I was humbled by her courage, and her confidence, for she was sharing dangerous information with me.

'Giovanni was foolish, of course. But he cannot help himself when he sees a wrong done.' She breathed the thinning air and sighed it out again. 'I think we are not long for this island.'

I was sorry for it. I did not want to lose her, nor the companionship of her son. I wondered what it was like to be wed to a man for whom the eye of the sun grew too hot wherever he went. It seemed Guglielma and her household would be constantly moving. No wonder they had so few sticks of furniture – they would be better suited to a Romany's caravan, or to carry all on their backs like a tortoise.

The slope steepened, and silenced our talk for a while. The earth on the slopes of the volcano was evidently rich with minerals, for not only was it coloured in ochre stripes but it encouraged a burgeoning of growth. Contented bees circled our heads and yellow ginestra bloomed so high that the bushes were taller than we women, all except one. A lofty laundress kept her face covered – perhaps she had some malady of the skin which she wished to give back to the volcano.

We made our way through a thicket of golden chestnut trees, and beyond the treeline the fauna changed with the altitude. Grasses became parched, flowers became spare and there were blooms I did not recognise. A sulphurous smell permeated the air and the stones underfoot were black and porous. The sun lowered behind the hunchback hill, and even the smallest scree sent striped slabs of shadow from the summit. I could now see the very mouth of the volcano, a jagged chasm belching white and drifting steam.

At length we looked down into a dell which was nothing but a bare black crater. Unless someone was to undertake the arduous climb to the lip and look over, our activities would be shielded from all eyes.

Perhaps it was the smell of sulphur, but I began to be afraid; as if some nameless evil lived in this crater. I felt that we were to dance on the back of a great black sleeping dragon who would at any minute wake from his rumbling sleep, constrict us with his stony coils and consume us in his fiery breath. What was I doing here?

The musicians – all women – gathered a little above the crater. I saw a lady bearing a mandolin; another held a local instrument called a guitar. I spotted an accordion, flutes, fiddles, trumpets and clarinets, while those less skilled clutched tambourines. Guglielma took my hand and we half scrambled, half slid down the ashy slope and formed a circle with the other dancers at the bottom of the crater. And waited, breathing the acrid air.

The strange resonant sound of the Jew's harp giving time

twanged around the hillside, then the musicians began to play. Our circle of dancers began to revolve and my fear evaporated. What had I been afraid of? The music was infectious – my heart kept time with the driving rhythm, and my foot was tapping with the rest. To begin with I forgot why we were there – it was a joyous, happy occasion. Moreover I enjoyed, so much, the novelty of being at a dance where there were only women. There was no matter of concern about propriety, of trying to spy the man of your heart among the company. There was no worrying about your dress, or the correctness of your dancing steps, or remembering the order of each revolution of the measure. I was moving in every direction but the right one, and if I managed the correct step it was by accident. But helpful hands guided me, clasping mine and twirling me about, guiding me on my elbow or back. I made many friends that night; wordlessly, for dance was our conversation. I garnered smiles and nods from the girls of Hero's age as much as from the ancient widows hitching up their skirts to show their hairy shanks.

I saw Guglielma as I made the round. She clasped my arm and mouthed in my ear, 'Tell the music; tell the mountain what you want to rid yourself of. Her name is Etna,' she said. Then, as the music got faster and faster and louder and louder, the ladies began to sink to the floor. It was then I saw why the dance was named for a spider – they were all legs, rolling and crawling and even waggling every limb in the air while they lay on the ground in their transported state. The ash turned their clothes black, and in the half-light they resembled the Trinacria, the very emblem of their island, many legs and a woman's head.

Feeling foolish, now pulled out of the ecstasy of the moment, I sank to the ground and began to roll like the rest. Soon I was covered in ash, and the bitter smell rose to my nose, but I felt elated. I had not behaved so, grubbing on the floor, since I was a child. I was the music, the music was me; I was the mountain, the mountain was me. I laughed aloud. Guglielma, writhing next to me, shouted, 'You see?'

'Yes!' I cried. I was me. I did not need any man. I was Beatrice Della Scala, and I would rather hear a dog bark at a crow than a man swear he loved me. All around me I heard the women speak their prayers to the mountain. *Etna, let me not love the Dottore, for he is married . . . May I be rid of Angelo the drover . . . Let me not think of Salvatore any more . . .* 'Let me be free of him!' I cried, louder than all of them. 'Let me be free of Signor Benedick!'

As I spoke I saw a flare on the lip of the crater and I stopped; pulled out of my hysteria as if slapped. I sat up, frightened by what I had said; and wanting, like a guilty child, to take it back. Had my words ignited the volcano, woken the dragon from his slumber? Around me, the frenzy continued, the music getting ever louder, ever quicker. But I alone saw one flare become two, until the entire lip of the crater, all the way round, was lit by torches, each one illuminating the Spanish soldier that held it.

Then, up to the lip of the crater on a white horse like St James, rode the Archbishop of Monreale, as if he had planned his entrance as carefully as any actor. He looked down at the gathering, but his gaze settled on no one but Guglielma Crollalanza. The musicians faltered and stopped. In the sudden silence his order could be heard as clearly as if he were giving a sermon. 'Arrest the Moor,' he said.

Then all was confusion. Some of the women ran, some screamed, these powerful ladies turned into so many speckled hens by the appearance of such male authority. All but Guglielma, who stood dignified and silent, awaiting her fate at the axis of all; the still centre around which the chaos revolved. I tried to go to her, but was prevented. An iron grip on my arm.

I turned, ready to fight, for I thought my captor a soldier; but it was the tall laundress. 'Come out of this,' she hissed, in a deep and familiar voice. As she marched me up the crater, through the dark towards the ring of torches, garments flew above us like great shadowy birds, and by the time we were in the torchlight, the laundress had turned into Benedick.

My addled mind, even in the face of much greater trouble, could only ask itself how much he had heard.

'*Capitano* Escobar,' said Benedick to the nearest horseman. 'You know the Lady Beatrice. She led me to this place, and is guiltless in this coil. See her conveyed safely home.'

The captain dismounted, and offered me his arm. 'Such a friend of Spain may travel in the archbishop's carriage, for His Grace prefers to ride.' And he escorted me to the track, where the ladies in their Sicilian dress were scuttling back down the mountain into the night, before the Spanish could identify them. They could have been caught easily, but the cavalry let them go. The archbishop had the only spider he wanted.

I tried to protest, and turned in the captain's grip. 'Benedick!' I cried. He looked after us, impassive, but his gaze in the torchlight was as black as flint. He bowed curtly, and turned away, and I knew then that he had heard every one of my words.

All the way down the mountain in the archbishop's carriage I was racked with guilt and horror. My hands shook so that I had to clasp them together. I gave no thought to what trouble awaited me at home, my uncle's shame, my aunt's switch, and Hero's disappointment; but tortured myself only upon the subject of what Benedick had been doing at the Tarantella. Was he such a creature of Spain that he had spied on Guglielma for the archbishop? Or had he seen me quit the house and followed to protect me, for, once again, he had saved me? I did not know what to think.

The motion of the carriage was unbearable, and my stomach lurched, my throat retched. I was bathed in the sweat of the dance and the horror, not only at what I had spoken in front of Benedick, but of this dreadful twist in the tale; a play now swelling into a tragedy worthy of the legends of Magna Graecia. What hubris had my presence brought upon the head of Guglielma Crollalanza, allowing her nemesis the archbishop to catch her thus? She was the spider, but his was the web.

Act III scene vii

A courtroom in Messina

Benedick: A cold sense of foreboding sat in my chest like a stone, where my heart had once been.

Not a seat was left in the place as the good people of Messina gathered to see the trial of a Moorish witch by the Inquisition. It was a fine title for a playbill, and the crowds had come for their entertainment. I had never seen a church so full.

And yet, there was a priest presiding over the proceedings; the Archbishop of Monreale led the Tribunal of the Inquisition. He was seated behind an impossibly high oaken bench set upon a platform on a dais, flanked by the viceroy, brave in his gold and velvets. Shrouded in a humble habit like a monk, Leonato Leonatus, Governor of Messina, made a third. Above them the Spanish standard flew. There was no sign, now, of the Trinacria, the Sicilian flag.

Three days had passed since the night on the mountain and this, and more than a dozen times at Leonato's house, in his gardens, his chapel and his orchard walks I had been entreated by the Lady Beatrice. She had pressed notes upon me which I returned unread. She had slipped the *settebello* into my hand, but I had let it drop from my fingers. I did not want to hear more words from her. I had heard enough on the bare mountain. She had wanted rid of me, and she would get her wish.

I could see her now, across the courtroom beside her aunt. Her very frame seemed to have shrunk inside her blue gown, and her collarbones stood forth. Her skin was as white as an elephant's tooth. Her cheeks had sunk, and even her golden curls had dropped to smooth and sober waves. There were violet shadows beneath her eyes. As I looked upon her, as if bidden, she lifted her gaze to me; her eyes were a stormy tourmaline. I stifled any pity under a stony gaze.

I twitched on the polished wooden bench. I cared not for the Moorish dame, and had, thankfully, not been called as a witness. No. I had done my unwitting part when I had followed Beatrice to the mountaintop, like Don Pedro's faithful gazehound, and led the hunt to the stag at bay. They did not need me to describe what I saw, for there were more costly witnesses here – one of the tribunes himself. But I was here to mark the trial, for if the Lady Beatrice was implicated in any of the action I would have to step forth. No matter that she had denounced me, no matter that she had taken part in that godless dance, I still would see her saved from censure before I left this accursed island.

And I had ammunition in my arsenal. I had listened carefully over the last few weeks, closeted in the gorgeous golden chambers of Palermo and Monreale – I was not so green as I once was. While Beatrice and I were gaily passing back and forth the *settebello* in our lover's game (how I wished for those light times now!) a more weighty game of *Scopa* was being played in the viceroy's courts. Spain's king had a great scheme in hand, one that needed Leonato.

I peered keenly at Beatrice's uncle, the governor, where he sat on the tribune's bench. Leonato looked sick, as if he would rather be anywhere but here, and I knew, in an instant, why. My education of the last few weeks had served me well. I had learned to think, not in a straightforward course, but in the convoluted ways of the politician; a path that was as twisting as the constellation of Cassiopeia.

I knew that the archbishop had seen through my device. I had placed Beatrice in his carriage, told his captain that she had led me to the dance, in order to exonerate her. But the archbishop had known, somehow, that she had gone there on her own account. And now he had that knowledge to hold over Leonato. I knew, and he knew, that Leonato would do exactly as he was told, or else Beatrice could be charged too. Leonato was now the lapdog of Spain. Beatrice was safe. I could go. But I did not.

I looked to the public gallery where she sat, and there beside her sat one who looked even more white and pinched than Leonato, and more sleepless and tearful than Beatrice; her aunt the Lady Innogen. Only then did I recall that I had seen her at certain gatherings with the Moorish dame. They must be friends, for the lady looked sick with apprehension. I thought grimly that she was right to look so.

I knew few others in the gathering but I knew their type. They were those who would come to a hanging – the indignant, the curious, the bloodthirsty, the indifferent. In amongst them were two faces I was surprised to see; the poet known as Michelangelo, and beside him, as if they were friends, the pamphleteer Signor Cardenio. I wondered what their business was here; I imagined the poet sought drama, and if so he could not do better than this trial, and the magus would like to collect more evidence of the iniquities of the Spanish, but they both looked as if there was more to their presence. They looked, if possible, queasier than my lady Beatrice and her aunt.

Hero, being full young, had been spared the proceedings, but as for poor Claudio, witnessing summary justice was to be part of his education, it seemed. He sat two rows before me looking white and pinched and incredibly young.

Don Pedro sat before me amongst his cohorts, and his demeanour was singular. He seemed almost at pains to disassociate himself from the proceedings. He was solicitous and apologetic, but I felt, for the first time, as if he had used me. Although he had not revived his story of the wager he insisted that he had not known of this darker game that the archbishop played – to catch a spider in his trap. I wanted very much to believe him, for now I had no prospect of marriage it seemed as if I was destined to follow the prince's banner wherever it led. There was no question now of my paying court to the Lady Beatrice – I might as well go and get myself killed on whatever worldly enterprise the don and his king had dreamed up. Whatever Philip's 'Great Enterprise' was – always hinted at, but never explicitly spoken – I knew, with my newly whetted instinct, that this trial of a local Moorish woman, however small and humble, had something to do with that great design, as the little wheels in the belly of the Vara device turned the greater cogs.

But I did not really care. The nations of the world could blast themselves to smithereens, into as many different pieces as my heart. My chest felt hollow. I felt I had lost Beatrice, and become the dupe of my dearest friend. Had he ever liked me at all? Had she?

My expression must have fitted the doleful proceedings, for no one in the prince's company troubled me for a jest. I usually could be relied upon to lighten any situation, but not today. Indeed, everyone in the crowd wore their Monday face.

The only one in the room who seemed unmoved by the proceedings was the defendant herself. She stood impassive, her Sicilian traditional dress ruined from three days' wear in the cells. The red skirt was torn, the once white blouse soiled and the black waistcoat rent at the lacings. On her dusky wrists, tied in front of her, the cruel marks of the *strappado* told their terrible tale. I knew the ways of the Inquisition and guessed that she would have spent some hours suspended from the ceiling of her cell, her wrists twisted behind her. Her mouth was bruised and blood had settled at the corners of the full lips.

But despite these horrors, her stance was strong and her coal-black eyes looked unwaveringly at her accusers. Abruptly, unwillingly, I began to care about her fate.

The Archbishop of Monreale got to his feet, and the crowd quieted.

His eyes were veiled in his pasty face, and he licked his already moist purple lips as if he was about to break his fast. He read the Edict of Grace in rapid Latin, then switched to his accented Sicilian. Whatever the purpose of this drama, he wanted the citizens of Messina to understand every word.

'The following charges pertain to the Moorish woman known as Guglielma, whom you see before you here,' he began, pointing a skinny finger at the prisoner. I noted two things – that he called her a Moor without qualification, despite the fact that it was clear from her appearance that she had white blood in her too; and that he did not dignify her with a second name. A family name would humanise her; a Sicilian name would raise local loyalties.

'You must hear the charges before we proceed to judgement. Have you anything to say?'

Her gaze was unwavering, 'What judgement shall I fear, doing no wrong?' Her voice was musical and strong, with a song of the south in it.

The archbishop sniffed. 'You are charged that on the sixteenth night of August, in this year of Our Lord fifteen hundred and eighty-eight, you led a ritual on the slopes of Mount Etna to call forth the Devil.'

A murmur passed around the crowd, and my blood ran cold. This coil was much more serious than I had thought – I had expected them to make some sort of example of her, perhaps the stocks or a public whipping. But the stakes were at the highest – the dame was playing for her life. I hoped she had a good hand.

'You are charged that you did lead certain ladies of the town of Messina to the foothills of Mount Etna, and there in a dark and godless place you did begin your rituals. Music was played at a tempo forbidden by the church, and rose to an indecent climax. At that point you danced yourself into a heathen ecstasy, and fell to the floor, crawling and spinning about like a spider, a creature that all know to be the familiar of Satan. You then began to utter your spells and incantations, called upon the Lord to quit your body and the Devil to enter your flesh with his incubus of fire.'

I heard the Lady Beatrice utter a cry; and she half-rose as if to protest, to be pulled back sharply by her aunt, whose eyes were haunted and afraid. Before the archbishop's reptilian gaze could identify the source of the disturbance I scrambled to my feet.

All eyes were suddenly upon me – my mouth was as dry as a powder keg. 'It was not as you say,' I stammered. I could hear Don Pedro hissing at me to be seated, feel his hands upon me. I shrugged them off. 'They were performing a dance. A folk dance which became faster and faster. At length they did fall to the floor but it was an ecstasy of music' – I cursed myself for the use of the word *ecstasy* – 'not of devilry.' I turned to Don Pedro. 'The prince will tell you. Sire – you yourself spoke of an inno-cent folk dance.' He was silent, the muscles in his jaw pulsing rhythmically. 'Tell them. You said that if I witnessed it you would win a wager with the viceroy.'

The prince shifted in his golden chair, and a titter from the crowd showed him his escape. 'Benedick,' he said, mock reproving. 'Always jesting.' But his laugh was as uncomfortable as it was unconvincing.

I turned away in scorn. 'The dames were merely enjoying the music; I was *told*,' this for the prince, 'that it is a custom with them. And those "chants" were to do with nothing more than men's names,' I swallowed, 'to banish those men from their hearts.'

'What do you mean?' rapped out the archbishop.

I looked at Beatrice and she dropped her eyes.

'The ladies were naming those they no longer wished to love,' I stammered.

'Like Christ.'

'*No.*'

'I say *yes.*' The bishop thumped the bench before him for emphasis. 'It is indeed an exorcism, but of God and all the saints. Such rituals are performed so that Christ leaves the body and the Devil may make his home.'

'But . . .'

'*Signor* Benedick of Padua,' said the archbishop, speaking over me. 'We are grateful to you for your intelligence of this gathering, and you did an admirable job of leading Spain's forces to the mountaintop. But your testimony is not required. The requisite five-and-twenty witnesses, all cavalrymen of the order of Saint James, *and* myself, witnessed the calling forth of the Devil.'

I felt Beatrice's eyes on me still, and wanted to protest; but I could say no more than I had already spoken. Don Pedro tugged at my cope and I sank to my seat.

But as I sat another stood. 'I must speak,' he said, his tones ringing about the courtroom like those of an actor. Now everyone turned to look at the speaker, as if in a game at tennis, at Michelangelo Florio Crollalanza. The poet descended from his seat to the space before the prisoner and, with an expression which showed the assembly how much the gesture cost him, he knelt on the wooden boards.

'Now must the archbishop be merciful.'

'On what compulsion must I?' asked the prelate, unmoved. 'Tell me that?'

'There is a meet reason for each of the three of you.' The poet got to his feet and approached the bench, appealing first to the viceroy. 'You, my Lord Viceroy. Know that mercy becomes the throned monarch better than his crown.' He walked, like a man-at-law, to stand before Leonato. 'You, my Lord Governor. Know that mercy shows the force of temporal power.' Leonato would not raise his eyes, and Signor Crollalanza walked to stand before the archbishop. 'And you, my Lord Archbishop. Know that mercy is an attribute of God himself.'

The court was silent with admiration for some moments, before murmurings of agreement and approbation broke about my ears. I was amazed at the poet's appeal. Not just the eloquence, the erudition of it, but the heartfelt nature of the plea. It seemed that he was near tears. What was the lady to him, or he to the lady? Was he just a champion of social justice, a habit he had picked up from his friend the pamphleteer? But I had to admit, little as I liked the fellow, he made a fine appeal – better than I. Even the bishop admitted as much.

'Well spoken, Master Crollalanza,' said the prelate, 'but the law of Spain – of *Sicily*,' he corrected himself hurriedly, 'admits of no pardon for a crime as heinous as Devil-worship. But,' he held up a beringed hand against the murmuring of the court, 'the law is equitable. If you, Guglielma, can provide five-and-twenty witnesses to support the innocence of your claim, bring them forth, and you may go free.'

I held my breath; there were at least that number at the dance that night, and surely some of them were in this room. But I suspected a trick – if these women revealed themselves, they would be indicted too. The Lady Beatrice, as I knew she would, went to rise, and it was not the aunt but Guglielma herself who stayed her this time. 'No,' she said. 'The fault lies with me alone. No other ladies made the spider.'

The archbishop nodded, as if he had expected this answer. 'There is yet one path of salvation open to you.' He steepled his yellow fingers together, and fixed his gaze upon the defendant. 'This is an island of fishermen. Sometimes when a fisherman catches a little fish, and then catches a bigger, he lets the little one go. There is a worse heretic than you in Messina, who writes dreadful slanders against myself, the viceroy, and even the King of Spain himself. Do you know who that might be?'

Now I saw his evil purpose. He would trade a life for information, and who would be proof against such a trade? I looked to the crowd, where the black-clad pamphleteer sat. But the archbishop had reckoned without the courage of the lady. She shook her head. 'I know no one who writes lies about the Spanish,' she said.

The archbishop snorted. 'Not even your husband, Giovanni Florio Crollalanza? Or should I say *Cardenio*?'

The pieces fell abruptly into place. The pamphleteer in the black costume was her *husband*.

'My husband is only a poet, Your Grace.' There was a gentle irony in her use of his title. 'His greatest work is entitled *The Second Fruits*. I am sure Your Grace is well read enough to have perused it.'

'I am not in the habit of reading heresy.'

'Oh, but it is not heresy,' she corrected. 'It is a collection of Merry Proverbs, Witty Sentences and Golden Sayings. My husband preaches humour, not hate. And if you have evidence to the contrary, present it.'

I shifted uncomfortably, thinking of the pamphlet that Don Pedro had taken from my room. If they had not presented the paper in open court, then they had nothing to connect the pamphlet to the man. It seemed they could do as they wished with a Moorish woman, but to indict a white Sicilian man, of ancient name, they needed evidence. He – or his resourceful wife – must have covered his tracks admirably.

The archbishop was silent, but he was not defeated. The defendant's denials spurred him to spiteful vengeance, like a child deprived. He was still for a moment, then his eyes became glass, and shimmered as the tears fattened on his scanty lashes and dropped in crystal runnels down his cheeks. The court was still, mouths agape at the commonplace miracle. 'This is a sad day. I would be merciful but you have bound my hands as I have bound yours.' His tears, unfelt and involuntary, fell apace on his cope. 'The Church jurisdiction cannot take life. Only the state can do so and for that I must turn to the other tribunes.' He suited the action to the words. 'Viceroy. The penalty for Devil-worship is death by fire. What say you?'

Ludovico de Torres did not hesitate but got to his feet. 'Guilty as charged,' he said, in his reedy Spanish accent. It was the first time I had ever heard him speak. He would have sat again but the archbishop cleared his throat pointedly. 'But we Spaniards are but guests on this great island,' went on the viceroy hurriedly. 'In this matter both you and I, Archbishop, must defer to the local government.'

'Governor?' The archbishop turned to his right. Leonato looked grey and shrunken; as if contracted under the burden of incalculable age. He was as ashen as the dust of the volcano. Almost imperceptibly, without looking up, he nodded once.

The courtroom erupted. The poet began to shout, his voice drowned out by the cacophony of the chamber. Heads bobbed and boiled like lava. Certain of the women of the gallery, moved to action by the verdict, began to protest, and I wagered they had been there with the lady on that night. I began to shout too, but I know not what I said. I tried to push my way through to Beatrice, almost climbing on the backs of the crowd that impeded my way. Occasionally I had sight of her and could see that she was in the arms of her aunt. Above everything the archbishop brought his staff down on the dais with a resounding crash. As when Moses parted the waves, the crowd fell silent and parted to reveal the one still figure at its heart – the accused herself, chin high, black eyes still undefeated.

'Silence!' called the archbishop redundantly in ringing tones. 'I am to ask the condemned if she has anything to say.'

There was a deathly hush now as all eyes turned to the dark lady. The condemned woman looked directly at the Archbishop of Monreale, full in the eye. Her eyes burned like coals in the fire. She spoke, quite clearly and distinctly, and even through the layers of her strange accent all the assembled could hear what she said. '*Ti manciu 'u cori*,' she said. 'I will eat your heart.' Then she pointed her finger at the viceroy. '*Ti manciu 'u cori*,' she repeated.

I expected her, then, to turn the cursed finger on Leonato, the third of the tribunal, but she swung around like a weathervane and pointed into the crowd, in my direction. I thought for one heart-freezing moment that she pointed at me, but her eyes and finger fixed upon Don Pedro. '*Ti manciu 'u cori.*'

All now looked at the three men for their reaction to this dreadful curse. I saw the colour drain from Don Pedro's ruddy face, while the viceroy blustered and gobbled into his many chins like a turkey-cock. The archbishop's reaction might have been more expected, for tears fell anew from his eyes; but this time with a difference. They were real.

I knew, in that moment, that he was afraid of her. The great archbishop in the golden chasuble was afraid of the bound Moor in the torn gown. He whispered into the silence, 'Take her away.'

As the woman was bundled from the room, the crowd jostled, yammering and chattering, to the doorways, as if the sentence was to be carried out directly, as if they did not want to miss the flames. I made for the Lady Beatrice again; my anger gone, I wanted to explain that I had just been a fool, not a traitor.

But Don Pedro stayed me with a hand on my shoulder. He leaned forward and his whispering breath was warm in my ear. I thought he would seek reassurance in the face of such an evil curse, or at least censure me for my defence of the Moor; but he said something entirely different. 'The fellow that gave you the pamphlet at the Vara,' he said. 'Do you see him here today?'

I looked at the crowd – I could see the Moor's husband clearly – he was embracing the poet, who looked as if his heart was as broken as mine. The fellow's back was to me, but I still knew him, could have pointed him out to Don Pedro. But I thought of the woman Guglielma, and her bravery in the face of the horror to come, her refusal to implicate Beatrice or her own husband. I looked not into Don Pedro's eyes but steadfastly at the medal of St James where it hung over his heart. But I was thinking of St Peter as I made my three denials. 'No,' I said. 'I have not seen him. He is not here.' And I shrugged off the prince's hand and followed the rest into the cathedral square.

Act III scene viii

The cathedral square in Messina

Beatrice: I could not stay away from the cathedral square that dawn.

I had crept from my bed, donned my hooded cloak, and stepped over the sleeping Margherita, who was propped at the chamber door.

As I walked the silver shore my heart beat fast and painfully. I prayed that there was something I could do to save Guglielma Crollalanza. I wished I could have appealed to Benedick – after his clumsy impassioned defence of Guglielma at the trial I was sorrier than ever that I had repudiated him. I wanted the chance to explain, to beg forgiveness. I knew him now for the best of men, knew that he would help me this dawn if he could, but I could not risk going to fetch him from his quarters, lest I be caught and stopped.

I did not know why he had been at the Tarantella, nor how he had led the Spanish there; but his actions at the trial told me that his betrayal of us had been none of his choosing, and God knows he was no more culpable than I. It was true that the Tarantella would have taken place with or without me, but it was my folly that had brought Guglielma to book.

The morning was grey and leaden, the sky heavy with foreboding. The moon was still in the sky, though it was morning, a silver disc lurking behind scudding silver clouds; but the sun had not shown her face. The days were out of joint.

In the cathedral square the bells tolled dolefully and I felt their song in my chest. A press of people surrounded a dreadful new structure; a pyre of well-stacked faggots with a stake thrust into the centre. From the open door of the great cathedral drifted the last notes of the mass of the auto-da-fé.

The dignitaries filed out – the viceroy first, then the archbishop with Claudio in his wake. Such sights as the day promised were not meet for maids – Hero was at home with my aunt – but poor Claudio must witness the darkness. Lastly, my uncle appeared from the shadow of the doorway, but the shadow seemed to stay with him and dog him as closely as his own. He looked bowed down and defeated.

I pitied him, for I knew my own involvement in the Tarantella had forced his hand in the verdict. He was not a bad man, but a weak one, and to defy the Spanish would be to lose his governorship, his house, his fortune and Hero's too. I hoped Signor Crollalanza would not blame my uncle overmuch; but I did not see Michelangelo anywhere, nor his father. Good sense should have driven them from these shores already, but I knew that neither man would leave a beloved mother or wife to her fate without a fight, and I scanned the crowd, fearful that by the day's end they would be taken too.

I saw Guglielma then, surrounded by an impenetrable phalanx of soldiers. I could glimpse her through their brave scarlets. She was a small figure, barefoot, and dressed in a *sanbenito* of yellow sackcloth the colour of sunrays. Odd that the colour she had favoured in life was to be her shroud. On the sackcloth were painted crude black devils augmenting the red daubed flames that rose up towards her heart. Her face was serene, and upon her forehead was painted a red 'H' for heretic. She wore a rope noose around her neck and carried a yellow candle in her hand. My view was then obscured and for a time I could see only the candle, and it did not shake in her grasp even a little. I watched the taper as she walked to the pyre, and as far as I could see, it never trembled at all.

As she rose to the pyre she turned to face the assembly. Despite the crude garb she somehow looked more noble than her judges; her sackcloth more glorious than their cloth of gold, her noose more costly than their chains of office, her candle more weighty than their sceptres of power. The archbishop spoke the anathema over her, and her lips moved too in response. I knew what she said, her eyes fixed upon the archbishop. I could read her full lips. She repeated the curse that she'd spoken in the courtroom, a scourge as old as the island: *Ti manciu 'u cori*. I will eat your heart.

When the prayers were done the Spanish soldiers, those noble cavaliers of St James, jeered and shouted Moorish slurs. I heard the word '*Matamoros*' on their lips many times over.

It was then that two figures detached themselves from the crowd and rushed the ring of Spanish pikes. It was an impassioned, ill-advised rescue bid, and it did no good at all. I, perhaps alone of the crowd, knew the identities of the desperate father and son beneath the cowls.

'Arrest them,' said the archbishop, and before anyone could move a tall, armoured figure wearing the helm of St James took the two men in hand. Outnumbering their captor, they could have shaken him off; but he spoke rapidly to them, and besides, there was nowhere for them to go. The knight led them past the cordon, but through the numb horror I knew that they, at least, were safe. For I would know the bearing and carriage of Signor Benedick anywhere; even beneath a suit of armour.

But now there was no escape for Guglielma. I watched, dumb, as she was lashed to the stake. It seemed so cruel, so out of all proportion with common decency and sense. Was the archbishop so desperate to remove the last vestige of Moorish blood from the island? Her arms were tied tight from shoulder to elbow, and I saw, with sudden clarity, that with both her hands she had made the sign of the horns, the salute she had made to me at the tournament. She had never told me what it meant, but I thought I knew; it was not a sign of the Devil but a sign of defiance, a rejection of submission, a sign of women that confound men.

I waited for the people to rise up, for an angel to split the clouds, for a saint to ride over the volcano and slice her ropes with a fiery sword. Was there a celestial counterweight to St James Matamoros? Would St Zeno, the black saint of Verona, descend from the skies like an ebony-faced avenger and defend one of his own? But there was no intervention, earthly or heavenly. It seemed impossible, unbelievable, what was about to happen.

I don't know what I expected – that such a dreadful end would necessarily be slow; but as soon as the faggots were lit her gown caught almost at once and she was, instantly, a pall of flame. As the flames cleared I could see that her hands were still twisted into the gesture of the horns. She burned soundlessly, and the crowd were horribly silent too. I do not know when she died, but her body itself began to make strange corporeal sounds – crackling and whistlings as the air left her charred form. Worse, the burning flesh began to smell, and I heard, about me, many a stomach rumble, as the famished civilians smelled cooking meat. I remembered what Michelangelo had said to me on the dunes – that the people were starving.

I looked accusingly at the archbishop, with his trademark tears running down his face, then back at the faces around me. They were not looking at Guglielma any more. They were looking at him. I could not help but feel that his plan, whatever it was, had somehow misfired; that despite the jeers of the Spanish the citizens of Messina were not enjoying the spectacle that had been orchestrated for their benefit.

Perhaps it was the sight of one of their own burning, an Archirafi, a Crollalanza – a Sicilian. Perhaps the hunger in their bellies awakened their rebellion too late. But the air prickled with dissent; it floated about with Guglielma's ash, into every eye and every mouth, inescapable. I felt pressure at my back and realised that the crowd was surging forward to the cathedral. It was eerie, that wordless movement forward, the hundreds of hollow eyes, the relentless shuffling feet, moving forth in silent protest. The Knights of St James raised their pikes, shouted threats and warnings, but the crowd did not abate. It was a protest, an uprising.

The archbishop, the viceroy and my uncle rose hurriedly from their thrones and retreated back inside the cathedral, and the doors closed behind them with a hollow boom. I half expected the people to hammer the doors in, but if they did not respect the prelate himself they respected the sanctity of the church, and went no further.

The fire lost its fierceness as the sun rose, as if that burning orb had appropriated the heat of the fire. Now there was nothing but ash, the crowd began to disperse; drifting away across the square with the cinders of martyred flesh.

This, then, was the end of Guglielma's story. And Guglielma's play had been a tragedy, as had the entire history of the Moors in Sicily. I had thought, and Michelangelo had thought that day on the dunes, that the Vara would be the climax of the story; the iconoclasm of the Moor's image, the chaos of the crowd. We had both been wrong. The archbishop had given the drama a climax as surely as any great impresario, a climax which plumbed the very depths of horror.

But the story had an epilogue; for in that dreadful, ashy aftermath the women came, the women who had danced with Guglielma, the women whom her courage had saved from calumny. They crept silently from every corner of the square, black clad in mourning, stealthy; spiders themselves. They knelt in the cinders and began to gather the cooled ash in their hands. Wordlessly, I joined them, sifting the ash until my hands were as black as they had been the day I first saw the Moor, when Signor Benedick had kissed my inky fingers. At length the women found their grisly trophy – a hot and blackened skull, nothingness staring from empty orbs. Impossible that those burning eyes had now been extinguished, that another light had been put out.

The women handed the skull to a tall, hooded lady who held open a velvet-lined casket. Her cowl fell back a little to reveal alabaster skin and blue-grey eyes. It was my aunt.

I went to her and rested my head for an instant on her shoulder. I said nothing. There was nothing to say. I gathered the other bones with the rest to place in the casket, and then, powdered with ash like penitents, we followed my aunt as she led us from the square.

I bowed my head as we climbed, and my guilt mounted with the altitude. It was meet that I should wear ash upon my forehead, and if I could have changed my gown for sackcloth I would have done that too. Of all these penitents, these women who had not spoken up in time, I was the worst. I had drawn Benedick to the Tarantella, and so too the Spanish. My presence there had drawn my uncle's teeth at the trial, so he could do nothing else but convict Guglielma or expose me. That I, whose tongue would run away like a buckshee horse upon any other subject, could have stayed silent in that courtroom, restrained by my aunt's firm hand!

I looked ahead to the tall figure who led us up the slope. Did my aunt feel the burden of guilt as heavily as I? It was little comfort to tell myself that the courtroom appeals of both Guglielma's son and Signor Benedick had been to no avail. It was no use to assure myself that the archbishop, bent on destruction and the eradication of her race, would have convicted Guglielma even if God himself had intervened. I was as guilty as he.

We climbed the little hill from the Via Catania to a place I had heard of but never seen, the hilltop necropolis of the *Cimiterio Monumentale*, the family tomb of the Leonati. A small stone mausoleum crowned the hill, and a scar of dark flesh lay in the hillside. The watchman, standing beside a hillock of fresh earth with a spade in his hand, had dug a grave ready. My aunt placed the casket in the ground, and the old man dug it over as if he were burying a cur, without a thought for what he did.

We all gathered about the grave, and in the fierce heat of the sun my aunt took a scroll from her sleeve and read from it; a verse about the killing power of slanderous tongues. She placed the paper on the mound, and anchored it with a handful of earth.

The Sicilian ladies each threw a handful of earth on the paper eulogy in turn, until it was quite, quite gone, the words interred with the bones. It was fitting that words should share her grave; for words had killed her. Witch. Devil-worshipper. Heretic. The falsehoods had gone through and through her like a blade.

One by one, the women walked slowly down the hill, a sombre black procession, back the way they had come. I sat with my aunt on a warm tombstone, watching as Orsola gathered flowers a little way off. I felt suddenly deathly tired, as if grief and horror had drawn the strength from my limbs. I could only sit, numb. I did not speak; for once I had no words in me. But my aunt did. 'Her son wrote the eulogy,' she said.

Her son. I thought the beautiful, dolorous words bore Michelangelo's stamp, for no one could so well express the pain as he. I wondered what he had felt as he wrote them, knowing when they would be spoken. I wondered how I would face him, if I ever saw him more, knowing that I had brought his mother low. My aunt spoke again.

'I saw her last night, Beatrice. Guglielma gave me the paper, and she herself asked me to perform the ritual we undertook just now. She wanted to be here so she could always see the island. Her island.' She breathed out a long and wavering breath.

'You saw her?'

'Yes. They held her in the Palazzo Chiaramonte; she was

alone in a big whitewashed room. She did not give up, Beatrice. She'd found some charcoal and in three days of captivity she'd covered the walls with drawings; drawings of such skill, Niece, as you never saw.' Her blue-grey eyes looked like pebbles in a stream. 'Even the guards had given her colours and pigments. She drew ships, flowers, angels. And women; many, many women. She sent a message to *us*.'

I stole a glance at her profile, strong and sure, like a ship's figurehead. 'Does my uncle know you saw her?'

'No, and shall not. I was expressly forbidden to enter, even as the governor's wife. But Friar Francis was given leave to visit Guglielma for the last rites, and he gave me leave to go in his habit and his stead.'

My own eyes prickled, and I looked out to sea, impossibly moved. In the *extremis* of her friend, my aunt had become the Innogen of old.

'She was so brave, Beatrice, so brave. Her only concern was that her son and husband should get away to the north, and be safe. I went home and pleaded with your uncle, Beatrice, to lessen the sentence. I pleaded the hours around; until the sky lightened and it was time to leave for mass. He said if he intervened we would lose everything. But still I hoped, right until I saw her brought into the square.'

Her countenance crumbled, the ship now wrecked. How had I thought her strong and resolute?

'There is a gown they wear,' she went on, 'the heretics. When they have been pardoned, the flames point downwards. They are called *fuego repolto*. I prayed, Beatrice, that after mass she would be wearing such a gown; that she would have been pardoned. But I saw the flames first. They pointed up, towards her heart.' My aunt was dry eyed, but there was pain in every word. I thought of the archbishop's copious, meaningless tears and compared them to my aunt's dry but dreadful grief.

'She had such spirit, Beatrice. Such spirit. And now it is gone.'

I looked at her then, and tried to articulate a thought that had accompanied me up the hillside. 'Only gone if you let it go,' I said. 'Raise Hero like her. With courage, and freedom, and the chance to think and speak and breathe. Do not let her become the modest miss that her uncle would have her be,' I urged. 'Let her rather live in the image of Guglielma Crollalanza.'

My aunt said nothing, but I thought she was weighing my words.

I looked down to the shoreline again and Guglielma's house; the Moor's house, mindful of the dark lady's final wish. A new urgency entered my sombre repose. I must go there, find the Crollalanzas, make sure they quit the place before they were captured.

I took leave of my aunt, pressing a tender kiss to her temple, leaving her in the arms of Orsola, and set off down the hill. The heat was fierce and I threw back my cloak. It seemed so unfair that the sun should shine that day after all. It should have hidden its face, shamed by what wrongs its cousin fire had done.

When I reached the house on the beach, the little door was open.

I ran into the study and both father and son were there, gathering up papers. They turned like a couple of guilty things; their relief palpable when they saw me, their expressions strangely alike. The father I was not acquainted with, but it was no time for introductions. He looked grey, his eyes hollow like the hot skull we had buried. I could not give tongue to my condolences, did not know what to say. 'We sail tonight with the tide,' said Michelangelo.

I walked over to the printing press; to the innocent letter blocks Guglielma had jumbled out of their heretical lines. I pressed my fingertip into one of them, hard, hard enough to hurt me. I studied the fleshy pad and the mark upon it.

H for heretic. The same letter that had been branded on Guglielma's forehead.

'This is our last chance to talk,' I murmured, once again bereft that day.

'Go,' said the father to the son. 'I will finish here.'

Michelangelo and I sat on the dunes; in the place where he'd told me about the Moor, the place where I'd embraced Benedick. I wanted to make amends somehow, yet there was no way to atone for my crime.

But he made it easy for me. He began to weep, as he could not have wept before his father. Then I knew exactly what to do; I held the poet close, as if he were a child, as his mother would never hold him again.

Still in the embrace, I saw a figure ride across the dunes in the far distance, in the direction of Leonato's house. I recognised the horse before the rider, for it was the white royal destrier of Don Pedro.

Act III scene ix

Benedick's chamber in Leonato's house

Benedick: There was some sort of hurry.

The house was a ferment of preparation and packing. Horses were shod, the quartermaster dispatched to the cellars and larders, carts and haywains appropriated for our great movement. It seemed we would leave the next morning. While the lady burned at the stake, and all eyes were elsewhere, the Spanish ships had amassed, unseen, in the harbour.

It did not matter to me when they left. The sooner they quit the place the better. It seemed that the death of the last Moor had changed the people's perception of their overlords, and the Spanish felt that their days on the island were numbered. The Archbishop of Monreale had overplayed his hand.

But the death had changed me too. Life was short, and you had only one hand to play. I would rather spend the rest of my life being insulted by Beatrice than being given sweet compliments by any other lady. I returned to my room to collect my armour and take it to the armourer – I'd worn it to convey the poet and his pamphleteer friend safely home after their ill-advised attempt to free the Moorish dame, and now I would have no further need of it.

Don Pedro was there in my chamber, sitting in the embrasure, curled up and small, somehow diminished as I had never seen him. His velvets seemed duller, his hair less shiny, his golden skin sallow. I felt no pity for my friend – between him and his conspirators he had killed an innocent lady; no glory lies behind the back of such deeds. The medal of St James dangled from his hand, winking in the sun. He did not turn as I entered, but slipped something into the cushions of the window seat.

'You are resolute?' He spoke to the horizon.

'Yes,' I said. 'I must stay.' Everything seemed stripped away, and I felt it was the time for complete candour.

He uncurled himself from the embrasure, and stood before me, somehow more of my equal than he had ever been. 'Benedick,' he said, 'if you are staying to pay your court to the Lady Beatrice, do not be such a fool. For I am certain that I am in possession of some knowledge that will change your mind.'

My skin chilled. His eyes, though shadowed, were candid. 'Hear me,' he said. 'I am your dearest friend, whether you know it or not, and as such, will not go about to link my dear friend to a common stale.'

I laid my hand upon the sword I had not yet given up. 'If you speak of the Lady Beatrice I must entreat you to retract your words. Curst she may be, but chaste she certainly is.'

He shook his head. 'Lay not your hand upon your sword. I came here to tell you that, in short, the lady is disloyal.'

I was aghast. 'Who, Beatrice?'

'Even she; Leonato's Beatrice, your Beatrice, every man's Beatrice.'

'Disloyal?'

He looked genuinely unhappy. 'Go with me now, you shall see. If you love her then, tomorrow wed her; but it would better fit your honour to change your mind.' He faced me squarely, like an adversary. 'She has formed . . . an attachment, with the poet Michelangelo. I saw them, even now, embracing on the dunes, outside his house on the shore.'

Our dunes – the dunes where she had told me of her star? I would not believe it. He put a gentle hand on my shoulder in sympathy – I flung it off, and spun to the window, as if I could see her from there. 'I will not think it.'

'If you will follow me, I will show you enough. I will disparage her no farther till you are my witness.'

I pushed past him and down the stone stairs. He followed. We clattered down into the courtyard, where his destrier was still saddled and waiting in the hand of an ostler. Babieca, the big bay he had given me with my livery, stood beside the royal beast, waiting too, as if the prince had planned this. I mounted Babieca in one swift vault without the block.

As we whirled through the gateway and thundered down the coast road, I could feel Don Pedro at my elbow, his horse breathing at my sleeve. It had become a furious, foolish race, as if whoever reached Beatrice first would be right about her.

I won, but I lost. She was indeed there on the dunes, where I had embraced her that one wonderful time. She had her arms around the poet, and he was pressed into her body as if they were one, shuddering as she held him. She pulled him to her, so tightly that her knuckles were white and her eyes were pressed closed; she was crooning sweet words into his hair.

Don Pedro was beside me, breathing almost as heavily as the lovers. 'Come away,' he said softly, pulling at my riding cope.

I had seen enough, and now docile, allowed Babieca to be turned around. Don Pedro led me back beyond the dunes on a leading rein, for I had suddenly forgotten how to ride.

At the roadside shrine he put a hand to my face. 'I must away to the house, to make the preparations. Why not ride on for a little, clear your head. I will take care of all things needful in your chamber.'

I nodded, numb, and spurred my horse towards Messina, as the prince rode in the other direction back to Leonato's. I had no other thought than to put as many furlongs between me and the Lady Beatrice as I could.

Act III scene x

The courtyard in Leonato's house

Beatrice: I had to see him before he went.

I had to give him the *Scopa* card – to tell him he was the worthiest knight after all. The little colourful card was my dearest possession, but I would give it up gladly – it was more precious to me than the reliquary, than a thousand reliquaries. A unique touchstone of our love.

Yes, love! I said the silly single syllable to myself a thousand times as I skipped through the gardens, giddy as a top. I was sure, and to be sure felt so good. After I had comforted him on the beach Michelangelo had told me what he and his father owed Benedick, that he got them out of the cathedral square, and led them safely to the shore. He had not spoken a word, nor asked for thanks, but pressed his army pay into Michelangelo's hand for their passage to Naples. The poet had shown me the piece of eight, Benedick's bite marks still in the frill. I'd kissed the coin before handing it back. Dear Benedick; I had been listening to his words when all this time I should have been watching his actions. 'Now will you give him the sonnet you wrote?' Michelangelo had asked. I'd nodded, and today I would make good on the promise.

My words and the card were for Benedick and no other. I did not even know if he knew where his friend Don Pedro led him, if the king's Great Enterprise would lead him into the jaws of the English navy, a navy reputed to be the finest in the world. So he had to know what I felt before he left. I ran through the gardens – the day sparkled. With the departure of the Crollalanzas it was as if the darkness of Guglielma's death had been lifted. I would commemorate her life by living mine to the full; I would run towards love and embrace it. Embrace *him*.

The friendly sun sparkled on my uncle's fountains, sunbeams playing with the water sprays, disputing which was brighter. The fruit trees, pregnant with their summer burden, stretched out their espaliered branches like arms reaching wide for an embrace. I knew I would see Benedick tonight, for my uncle and aunt were holding a great farewell feast for the Spanish; the final event in their interminable calendar of entertainments. But I could not wait for tonight, could not wait an hour, nor even a single minute. I could not bear to think of him gone, could not bear to go back to the old life. I did not recognise the Beatrice of one month ago, living quietly as Hero's companion, my only excitement watching the doomed Moor and his wife on the beach. They were gone, the world was changed and I had changed too.

I ran to the stable block, for I knew the soldiers were preparing for their journey. I looked for Benedick's beloved Babieca, but the big bay was gone. Disappointed, I left the stables and cannoned into Don Pedro.

The prince set me back by my shoulders and regarded me with a quizzical eye. I had not become much acquainted with him in the month that was gone, but he had always been gallant to me; in fact once or twice at our various entertainments my vanity told me that he looked upon me with more than a soldier's eye.

Now he smiled as widely as ever, and kissed my hand. He had bought three magnificent destriers as a parting gift for Leonato, Hero and Innogen, and was leaving three of his best Spanish ostlers behind to settle them. I waited impatiently while he gabbled on about the quality of the horseflesh – for one did not interrupt a prince – but his gifts smacked to me of an unspoken guilt; he had broken something in his sojourn here, like a child with a toy, and was clumsily making amends. His gallantry was as much in evidence as ever, but his eyes were veiled and his expression guarded. Something was amiss. He looked, at the same moment, surprised, shifty and pent up by some scheme of his own, something that had nothing to do with destriers and ostlers. He paused in his paean and I grasped my chance. 'My Lord,' I gasped, for I was still in want of breath from careening through the pleasure gardens, 'have you seen Signor Benedick? I must speak with him.'

He looked about him, as if he had never heard of the gentleman. I could see a number of expressions process across his face, and his eyes told me that a number of answers marched through his brain likewise before he settled on one. 'I think he is in his chamber,' he said. 'Or if he is not, then he follows me hard upon from his errands.' He looked at me intently. 'There is a pleasant window seat in the embrasure of his room. You may wait there in comfort, and see him coming from the road.'

I thanked him, and he smiled at me; a genuine, brilliant smile this time, which left me feeling uneasy. It was the smile of a victor.

I climbed the stairs in the direction of the soldier's quarters. I had never been inside Benedick's room before, not even been alone in that wing of the house where the soldiers were billeted, for propriety would not allow a well-born maid to go tramping in the soldiers' quarters unchaperoned. I had gleaned, though, in the course of a month, the location of his room; oft-times looking up at his window from the gardens at night, trying to guess from that gold square of light whether he read or slept.

I located the door that I knew to be his; and as I turned the handle, saying his name, it did not once strike me as odd that Don Pedro, who had grown up with etiquette fed to him at his mother's dug, would suggest that it would be suitable to wait for a man alone in his bedchamber.

The room was empty, and just as untidy as I would have expected it to be. But it had the same pleasing aspect as my own and Hero's room, with a large arched window and a balcony looking directly out on to the sea road. Benedick was not here now, but Don Pedro had promised he would be here soon. I settled myself happily to wait.

I looked out at the sparkling bay, bit my lips and pinched my cheeks, but in truth my innards were roiling and my heart beating so wildly that I was likely rosy enough. I even arranged my bodice so that it fell becomingly, and patted my curls into place. What was happening to me? As I smoothed my stomacher a crackle of paper reminded me, and I drew out the sonnet I'd written for him. I flattened it out to read it over one last time before it became his, and something fell from the folds. The *settebello*.

I moved my position a little on the window seat cushion, and scrabbled for the card down its edges. From the gap between the casement and the padded seat, I drew out not one card, but a pack of *Scopa* cards in a little box. I opened them idly and fondly – this must be the pack from which he took the card to give to me. I fanned them out – frowned, then began, with shaking fingers, to deal them one by one into my lap, until they spilled and scattered to the floor.

Every one had seven coloured coins upon it, rendered in red and yellow and blue.

Every card, every single one, was the seven of coins, the *settebello*.

I turned over the box. The card-maker's legend said 'Treviso'. He had bought the cards in the north before he'd ever seen me. A cheat's pack.

My heart raced and my brain slowed. He had won my heart with false dice. How many women had he given the card to, from the courts of Padua to the stews of Venice? How many foolish maids had carried the thing around with them, as I had?

A touchstone for our love, my eye. I found my card and held it next to one of the pristine ones. My card was softened at the edges, one corner turned over, a little torn, the design a little scuffed. It was loved, and had been passed back and forth at dinners, wedding and tourneys, meaning in every exchange. But in fact, it meant nothing.

Cold now with anger, I rose with my ragged *settebello* in my hand, letting the rest fall to the floor, a shower of red and blue and yellow coins. I walked deliberately on the cards, leaving them scattered all over the floor, and I left the room.

Act III scene xi

A farewell feast at Leonato's house

Benedick: By the time I sat down to dinner, I was very drunk.

I had spent the afternoon in the Mermaid Tavern in Messina, among some of the shipmen who were loading the Spanish ships. I played at *Scopa* with the recklessness of one who did not care a jot if he lost the *settebello*, for I felt that particular card would burn my hand. But by some quirk of fate I began to win, and as I won more, I drank more.

I left the table once for a piss on the wharf, and actually saw the poet and the pamphleteer catching their boat to Naples, paying, no doubt, with the eight *reales* I'd given them. They both, as I'd seen all Sicilians do, touched the golden statue of the Virgin on the wharf for luck before embarking. As I watched they walked up the gangplank together, embraced at the bulwark; and then the younger man came back down to shore. The ship weighed anchor, and the poet waved to his friend till he'd sailed out of sight.

I spat inaccurately on the ground, hitting my boots a little. How ironic that I'd unknowingly saved Beatrice's love; if the Spanish had only fried him too I would have no rival for my affection. He had clearly stayed on the island to pay suit to her. I wondered how quickly he would run back to her – whether they would soon wed. It did not matter if they did or did not; she was lost to me now; fallen, an approved wanton, a rotten orange. I wanted to run at him, and punch him repeatedly until he fell into the sea, there to rest in the deeps until his poetic bones could become coral. But the damage had been done; and in my current state I did not trust my aim. I staggered back inside the tavern, resolved to drink my winnings.

I was rescued, ultimately, by a fellow at the card table, whom it took me a couple of rounds to remember in my fuddled state, despite the fact that he wore a simple habit of fustian. He was Friar Francis, the priest of Leonato's chapel. He squeezed his bulk between the barrels and the carolling sailors and yanked me out of the tavern into the fresh air. It was then, standing on the stoup, that I realised that the stars were turning around me as if I was the Earth itself, the dusty little planet at the centre of the orrery. Somewhere up there was Beatrice's star, and I struggled to focus on it, but it kept sliding away like a raindrop. The friar held me by the shoulders until the cosmos righted itself. His grip was surprisingly strong.

'Frailty,' I said, stumbling over the word, and waving my arm approximately at Cassiopeia's chair, 'thy name is woman.'

The friar sighed. 'So that's the way of it.' He put his arm about my shoulder and led me to my horse. I had neglected to tie Babieca up, but the bay was obligingly wandering among the barrels on the wharf. 'Once,' said the friar, grunting as he gave me a leg-up into my stirrups, 'I would have agreed with you. That is why I wear this habit.'

I looked at him, trying to focus, pointing a wavering finger in his face. 'There is no. Living. With. Them,' I said precisely.

'Perhaps. But there is no living at the bottom of a bottle either. Believe me, I have tried that too.'

I tried to shake my head, for the Rhenish wine had improved my afternoon immeasurably. But I nearly fell from my saddle, and decided to slump forward on Babieca's warm neck instead. The horse had listened patiently to my grievances upon the journey here, and cocked his ears back to receive more wisdom. 'Sleepy drinks,' I murmured into the soft nap of the pelt.

I felt the priest lift the reins over my head and lead Babieca along the shoreline. I may have slept, for the next thing I remembered was a cold plunge as he tipped me from the saddle into the little watering hole just round the corner from Leonato's house.

Sobered, I spluttered and surfaced. The water was warm on this summer's night and not unpleasant, but I had my *Scopa* winnings weighing me down and had to strike out for the edge, indignant. 'What was that for?'

He sat on a hillock, holding the reins as my horse cropped grass, impassive. 'You have a feast to go to.'

I pulled myself, dripping, from the drink. 'I do not wish to see *her*.'

He did not ask whom I meant. It seemed he already knew. 'It is your last chance.'

I remounted with as much dignity as I could muster, and he said no more till we passed through the gatehouse. The night was so warm I was almost dry as I entered the courtyard. The moon hung low and was the colour of Baltic amber, the orb as sick as I.

The first person I saw was the Lady Beatrice marching towards me between two rows of burning torches, her face like thunder. The priest melted away, with a cautionary word. 'No more sack,' he said.

Beatrice stopped in front of me and I regarded her coldly, perusing her face for changes. Would the construction of her face differ now that Monsieur Love had made defeat of her virginity? I did spy some marks of love in her, but no longer for me. She positively spat her message at me.

'Against my will, I am sent to bid you to come into dinner.'

'Fair Beatrice,' I said with heavy irony, for her face was hateful to me now, 'I thank you for your pains.'

She turned her back on me so fast that her slippers crunched on the mosaic underfoot. 'If it had been painful,' she retorted over her shoulder, 'I would not have come.'

I followed her to the great hall, where the cosmos continued its revenges upon me. For the first time in this whirligig of festivities I wanted to be nowhere near Beatrice; but I was seated right next to her. I reached for my cup at once. I was seated next to Claudio on my other side, and she next to Hero, as if in light of our imminent parting and the fact that our lives would be restored to the way they were before, a month ago. New friendships were to be forgotten and replaced by old, but this was an illusion.

The very atmosphere was different from one month ago. Then there had been hope, and laughter, and delicious anticipation of the summer's lease to come. Now there was the sour taste of disappointment, and the stench of the dark lady's death fires hung over the feast like a pall. Beatrice and I were forever estranged, and I would never know again the sweetness I had found with her in the dunes. She had made her choice, and was to be a poet's wife.

Leonato was a pawn of the Spanish – they had taken his money and his reputation and, I was sure, he could not wait for them to leave. The lion was reduced to a lamb. Meanwhile, his wife Innogen seemed as estranged to him as Beatrice was to me, for he had failed her too in the judicial murder of her friend.

The viceroy and the archbishop were absent from our gathering; and I would not have been surprised if they had already embarked, for in the month that they had been here Sicily's relations with her overlords had soured to the extent that they must have concluded that they had better not stay to hear another vespers bell.

Only Claudio and Hero, with the innocence of youth, had found a bosom friend in each other, and forged a companionship that might prevail through the years. But for their last night together they had the impediment of Beatrice and myself sitting between them, as cold and contrary as Scylla and Charybdis.

Frankly, I was surprised at Beatrice's hostility to me. I had seen *her* on the dunes, knew *her* dreadful secret, but really, she owed *me* no censure but rather thanks, for I had saved her lover and his friend from certain arrest. But it did not matter; her enmity made our parting easier, and before long we began to joust again; no snappings of courtship now. The tipguard was gone from the épée; these were the spits and thrusts of naked hostility.

'You will be glad to know,' I began, 'that Signor Cardenio caught the evening tide to Naples.'

'I am indeed glad for him,' said the lady coldly, 'but sad for Sicily; he was an honourable man.'

'Then allow me to lift your spirits; Monsieur Love, the poetic Signor Crollalanza, did *not* get on the boat.'

She seemed genuinely surprised. 'Michelangelo? Are you sure?'

'If I may believe my own eyes,' I said with heavy significance, 'and I believe I may.'

'But . . .' She stopped herself. 'Then I am glad for myself. For at least there is one man of honour left upon this island.'

I was stung. 'There are more men of honour than he upon this isle.'

She looked at me, her blue eyes luminous. 'And yet one of their number played me for a fool.'

I was intrigued. Had the poet already abandoned her, then? For it is sure I had never seen her as sad as I had that night. 'Were the stakes high?'

'At the highest. I played for my heart.'

'And lost it?'

'He won it of me with false dice. Or, rather, a cheat's deck. So you may well say I have lost it.'

I was grimly glad, but her desolation afforded me no comfort – I would not take another man's leavings.

'But I have gained something else,' she went on.

'And what is that?'

'Wisdom. I have learned never to trust a man, be he ever so noble.' She raised her goblet in the direction of Don Pedro and her uncle at the dais. I could see the prince regarding us carefully – he seemed preoccupied by our conversation. 'Princes and counties!' she snorted. 'Men are only turned into tongue, their mannerly appearance is everything, their actions set at naught.'

'That is not a man's vice,' I rejoined. 'It is the woman's part to lie and to deceive. It is a woman's tongue which flatters while her heart corrodes with disdain.' I was starting to shout as I listed her faults; or were they the faults of all women? 'Ambitions, covetings, slanders, mutability. All faults that Hell knows are hers.' I leaned close to her, and my head began to spin; I was near as close as when I had kissed her. But now I could think of her only in the poet's arms, kissing and crooning on the dunes. 'Yet even her vices cannot be relied upon,' I held up a wavering finger, 'but are changing still.'

She looked at me with a pity that riled me further. '*You* have changed.'

I looked at her – her face was undulating before my gaze and she seemed to have more than the usual complement of eyes. 'The salty winds of this island have brought about a difference,' I agreed, pouring another goblet imprecisely. 'It is amazing what foul winds puff along the shoreline, on the *dunes*, for example. You are right; I *have* suffered a sea-change. I have transformed from Benedick the Lover into Benedick the Soldier.' I waved my goblet at arm's length, encompassing the entire company as if making an announcement. 'I have exchanged the tabor and the pipe for the drum and the fife. I will trust my brothers in arms, and no woman shall come in my grace.' I jumped to my feet, and nearly pitched to the floor. I stood at attention and lifted my goblet above my head in a salute. 'Don Pedro!' I called. 'Prince, brother, friend!' The prince looked up at my toast and lifted his goblet in reply. I waxed even more lyrical, touched by his tribute, feeling Lady Beatrice's scornful eyes at my back. I began to make a heartfelt speech about our order of St James, our brotherhood of sol-diery. My sentiments were so beautiful they brought tears to my eyes, but my words just elicited laughter and catcalls from the regiment, who were used to my sallies. More than one ruffle of bread had hit me in the head before my speech brought Don Pedro to his feet and to my side. He bowed to Beatrice, who was regarding me with her habitual disdain.

'Forgive my friend,' he said. 'He is somewhat in his cups.'

'Cups, swords, clubs and coins,' she said enigmatically, naming the suits of the *Scopa* deck. 'Then, Highness, by all means sweep him away.'

He made a reverence again and bore me off to his table. I know he would have given me a chair if he'd had one to spare, but he allowed me to stand behind his, and I was proud to do so. I swayed gently and kept my gaze on Lady Beatrice, who had exchanged chairs with Hero to allow the little maid and Claudio to converse. My misery was complete when I recognised that I envied my young friend – his summer friendship was well planted and had blossomed over this past month, to grow strong roots for future regard – but mine and Lady Beatrice's friendship had become a canker in a hedge, something to regret; and forget.

As the pipers struck up to begin the dancing I noted that even they had been affected by the malaise of the evening; for they did not play a sink-a-pace or a Scotch jig, but a sedate pavane of fifty years before. Few couples took up the floor, and the mournful ostentation persisted.

But the lady Innogen stood up, quite suddenly. I thought she would lead her husband in the host's dance but she did not so much as glance at him. She walked forward to the very centre of the dance floor, looking neither left nor right.

All chatter stopped, every hand stilled on his trencher; all eyes looked at her. Even the musicians faltered in their playing, but she waved them on with an elegant gesture of her hand. Then she began to dance; alone. Slowly, elegantly, her arms moving in graceful arcs, her feet pointing to describe wide circles on the ground.

It was not at that moment improper, or scandalous, but curiously moving. Don Pedro looked on in disapproval, but said nothing; Leonato looked like the volcano, dark and glowering and about to explode, but could not reprimand his wife publicly.

I looked at Beatrice to see how she would take this extraordinary behaviour. She was smiling for the first time that night, her eyes shining with unshed tears. Suddenly kneed in the stomach with longing, I pushed my chair back and took my sorry self off to bed.

Act III scene xii

A courtyard in Leonato's house

Beatrice: The morning after the feast we were back in the courtyard where one month ago we had greeted the Spanish.

I stood on the same tiny jewelled tiles set into the mosaic floor, and watched the same cast of characters revolving under Medusa's eye. There were the same Spanish faces from the major characters – Don Pedro, Claudio – to the bit-part players – the skinny Conrad, the portly Borachio. Only the pennants were different. Now the red and gold Spanish standard took precedence everywhere; no longer did the Trinacria flag of Sicily flutter above the eaves. I was there under sufferance for I could not wait for the Spanish to leave and take their ensign with them.

Hero, though, was downcast – she took her friend Claudio's hand most sweetly, and kissed his cheek. I wandered away from them. The Spanish were brave in their scarlet as ever. They hurt my eyes. I could see no sign of Benedick among the throng.

Don Pedro took an affectionate leave of Leonato, who seemed much diminished from the man who had greeted the cavalcade a month ago. The prince was as charming as ever, but kept casting an eye to the skies, where the burning sun was already riding high among dandelion puffs of cloud. He glanced about him, shifted his feet and tapped his teeth with his gauntlet.

His deputy spoke in his ear and I was close enough to hear. 'Sire, we must be gone – the tide awaits.'

Don Pedro shook his head slightly. 'A moment longer, Captain. He will come.'

I was sure 'he' would; for no one who had heard Signor Benedick's impassioned speech the previous day at dinner could be in any doubt that his heart lay with this regiment. It was just that he had shipped enough sack yestereve to make him hug his mattress this morning. But I began, despite myself, to hope, with every moment that passed; would he stay?

The cavalry mounted, all excepting Don Pedro, and the watchman opened the great gates. As the light flooded the courtyard, picking out the gold in the mosaic, a figure came down the stairs.

He was tall, dressed *cap à pe* down to the last detail in the scarlet and gold uniform of a Knight of St James. His sword and rapier hung sheathed in his scabbard. His hair curled damply about his face, and his cheek was clean shaven. He was Signor Benedick.

In the sudden hush he walked forth to Don Pedro. Chatter began again and horses neighed, their shoes clopping on the ground, fresh dung dropping from beneath raised tails on the gilded mosaics. I edged closer to the prince and Benedick, and in the melee could easily overhear what was being said.

'Well, Benedick? Will you stay and marry the lady, or come to gather glory?'

I hid behind the broad fellow they called Borachio, my heart thumping.

'I would rather live in Hell than marry her. In fact, I am wondering what sin I may comfortably commit, so I may be sent there and away from her sight.'

'You are sure?' asked the prince gently enough.

'Indeed,' came the reply. 'For I would rather live quietly among Beelzebub and all his fiends than in her presence.'

I could not believe what I had done to deserve such censure. *I* was the wronged one; *I* was the one who had found his trick deck of *Scopa* cards. *I* was the one who had been falsely won, with a hoax that he must have used on every maid from Trento to Napoli.

Borachio shifted and Don Pedro caught sight of me. He smiled and looked a little sheepish, with the same expression I had caught upon him yesterday. Under his breath, he murmured to Benedick, 'Look, here she comes.'

I had no choice but to nonchalantly approach, as if I was coming to take my leave anyway.

But Benedick merely turned and looked upon me as if I was a stranger. His raised his voice, and addressed the prince with his eyes on me. 'Now I will sail with Your Highness to the world's end, on any voyage you may devise,' he was playing to the gallery now, 'rather than hear another word from this harpy. Tell me you have some employment for me?'

Don Pedro answered quietly, 'You know I have. Come away now.'

But Benedick had one more insult to hurl at me and said it right to my face. 'Willingly: for I cannot endure my Lady Tongue.'

I stood rooted to the spot, hot tears needling my throat, with every eye in that courtyard watching me, every ear hearing me mocked into air.

At this my aunt, understanding something of what had passed, swept forward. She was tall enough to look Signor Benedick in the eye, and I expected her to leap to my defence; but she was clearly in a different mind as to who was really responsible for the tribulations of the last month.

She looked down upon Don Pedro, with a disdain that belied their ranks. 'Prince. Leave this house now and do not come back into it while I am alive.'

Don Pedro stepped back as if struck. He actually put his hands up as if to ward off a blow. 'Lady . . .' he began, but could say nothing more. The Spanish were all as silent as errant schoolboys, and even Signor Benedick had halted his tongue.

I looked at my aunt's face – implacable, unafraid – and saw Guglielma Crollalanza staring out of her eyes. I suddenly knew that Hero would be all right.

Don Pedro, his face curiously set, mounted his horse without another word and Benedick did likewise. Then they spurred their mounts and moved off through the great arch, as close as two Templars, with the rest of the cavalry behind them. Claudio in his purple turned back and waved to a tearful Hero, but Benedick sat in his saddle, his broad back straight as a rod, and did not turn at all.

I clenched my fists in frustration. I had to have my reply.

I ran as fast as I could out of the gate, and over down the mountain path, prickly with cactuses, where there was a short cut to the corner with the shrine upon it. There I stood on a rocky outcrop high above the road. And the procession passed below me.

I did not know what I wanted to say, but knew I had to have the last word. I spied Signor Benedick's golden head and screamed like a fishwife. 'Aye. Go, then!' He looked up, and Babieca stumbled. 'For I promise to eat all of your killing!' But he turned his stony face to the road, and spurred his horse to catch up his sworn brother Don Pedro. He had made his choice.

I scrambled down to the shrine, and looked after the train until it was gone from my sight. Suddenly desolate, I brushed the dust from my skirts. I felt someone watching me and turned to the roadside icon of Mary. She regarded me from her almond eyes.

I straightened up, and raised my chin. I did not need a husband. I would live free, speak my mind, and henceforth I would dance alone.

ACT FOUR

Act IV scene i

El Escorial, Madrid

Benedick: I, Benedick, born of merchant stock in Padua, was sitting in the presence chamber of the man they called the most potent monarch in Christendom.

We had travelled directly from Messina to Madrid, and thence to El Escorial, a vast palace of creamy stone, with towers and domes and roofs of pewter-grey slate. Here, as the sun lowered behind the pollarded trees outside, we were to attend, with all Spanish nobles, the king's legendary *Junta de Noche*. The Colloquy of the Night.

It was an ironic title; for they said that His Spanish Majesty had a command so wide that in his lands the sun would neither rise nor set. It was always day somewhere in his empire; it was said he could command the sun. I hoped so. For from the hints I had gleaned along the way about the enterprise he planned here this night, he would need to command the sun, the moon and the four winds too.

I was sensible of the honour of attending such a conference, and was looking forward to serving so great a king. But I had been seated for hours now in the great chamber that looked on to the beauteous gardens, as the golden afternoon wore away. I'd sat through numerous separate colloquies on the subject of munitions, arms and armour, and the provision of ships. It seemed that every eventuality had to be covered, and I yawned discreetly through the endless talk. The chancellery legislators had even laid down the exact form of words which were to be followed should anyone happen upon treasure in the course of this mysterious mission. 'Let each man who finds a trove lay his hands upon it and say the following form of words . . . His Majesty shall vouchsafe a tithe share of the treasure to the finder, and ennoble him in the rolls of Spain.' I did not really listen, for such a provision seemed overly optimistic.

Nobles and princes were called up from the floor to give their opinions or information from their provinces, but I had nothing to contribute. I daydreamed through the collation of all these facts that were being gathered in preparation for the arrival of the king at dusk.

I was seated far from my prince and Claudio, for we were arranged in rank; and those that were highest born were nearest the empty throne. But I did not resent my position; in my backwater by the garden doors I could doze unseen. The sunrays gilded the glass, and the livery of my order was hot. I dreamed and drifted in that honeyed, stuffy chamber, fancying in my half-aware state that the glass had become molten and surrounded me, trapping me like a bee in seeping amber. I was woken only at sundown by a chamberlain barking the presence of the king.

I had seen Philip II before, of course, at the Naumachia at the antique theatre in Taormina. Then, he had been in scarlet, crusted with jewels, with black hair and ruddy skin. But as we stood and the king entered, I saw that from that day to this he had changed so much as to become unrecognisable. Now his complexion was sallow, his cheek sunken, and most of his teeth were gone. His pate was balding and his remaining hair was almost completely white. I wondered what tribulations had come to him in this month or two's space. I had heard many tales of the king in the short time I had been at El Escorial. I knew he had lost many royal children, and as many wars. Maybe these troubles had taken a toll upon his face, or perhaps it was his hatred of the English queen that had corroded his person.

Now, as he sat unsteadily in his gilded chair, he cut a dour figure. He was dressed from tip to toe in black, his Habsburg lip even more prominent than in the portraits that gazed down upon us. He was a king of contrasts. He was a greybeard, but he looked like a pouting child who could not get his own way. He was a great king, but insisted to all who spoke that he be addressed as *Señor*. He was engaged on the most serious business, and yet crouched at his feet sat a comic and grotesque figure.

She was a female dwarf; dressed, down to the last particular, as Elizabeth of England. Her damascene gown was the colour of flame, cross-embroidered with silver thread and studded with topaz. A rebato of filigree and pearl stood stiff behind her oversized head, and she was greedily consuming strawberries from a bowl. As the tiny hands crammed the fruits into the misshapen mouth, the pulp carmined her lips as if she devoured flesh. I had to look away.

The king dandled his long fingers on the dwarf's wiry red curls. The perspective must have pleased him; Elizabeth, diminutive and dwarfed at his feet like a lapdog. But he was agitated, and the fingers drummed on the dwarf's wig impatiently. Then Philip began to speak in reedy, sibilant accents; the Castilian he spoke was near enough to Italian for me to understand his words.

At long last I was to hear the meaning of those words 'The King's Great Enterprise'. I had heard them the whole summer long, but even on the road to Madrid was never told explicitly what they meant. Secrecy, it seemed, was uppermost in the king's mind too, as it was the first word that he uttered. 'Secrecy,' he began. 'Speed and secrecy.' The snaky S's hissed though his missing teeth. 'We must be quick, so that between tomorrow and Saturday we can reach the decision which I asked for the other day. Time is passing us by very fast; and time lost is never regained.' He glanced through the windows at the setting sun, then down at his buffoon. 'Magdalena is impatient too, aren't you, Magdalena?'

The dwarf, strawberry faced, nodded. The king patted the creature on the head. 'And be *secret*,' he continued. 'For danger may result from any slight carelessness, even by those who keep secrets well.' He spoke as if to his dwarf, but addressed the room. 'Begin,' he commanded, waving his beringed hand at his councillors. 'Tell me where we are. For I give you all notice, that I am so keen to achieve the consummation of this enterprise – I am so attached to it in my heart – that I cannot be dissuaded from putting it into operation. We will take England, from the sea, with a great armada.'

So now I knew; and all fell into place. The last time I'd seen the king the play we'd performed for him in the antique theatre had been a statement of his intent. And now, the play was to become a reality. The king's chief councillors, who sat before him around a long polished table, now had to make it happen.

Each gentleman introduced himself before he spoke. Don this, Don that, Don the other; they had the same names, the same clothes, the same voices. I could not differentiate between them, grouped as they were around the table, as if posing for a Dutchman's paintbrush. A black-clad murder of crows, brokering death for the simple sailors of England. They all talked over each other, and numbers were all I heard.

'. . . one million ducats . . .'

'. . . seventeen thousand veteran troops . . .'

'. . . five hundred and sixty ships and ninety-four thousand men . . .'

'. . . one hundred and thirty ships and thirty-three thousand men . . .'

The king silenced them with a wave. 'But we have the fruits of the Americas,' he protested. 'Over a million ducats annually from Peru alone.'

'Yes, Señor,' agreed one of the councillors. 'Gold we have

aplenty. But ships and men are another matter. I say again: we cannot proceed at this juncture.'

At this the king actually got up from his seat, and the dwarf dropped her bowl of strawberries with a clatter. 'Am I to be made a motley by the whore of England? Her creature Drake has spent the summer sailing up and down the Azores, harrying my ships and stealing my gold. They say he singed my beard.' He tugged furiously at his scanty whiskers.

There was a terrible silence, broken only by the dwarf Magdalena, who grubbed about on the floor for her strawberries, her silks whispering on the pavings, the bowl spinning and clattering to a stop. The king, breathing heavily, took his seat again, and the dwarf settled herself at his feet, eating the dirty strawberries she'd recovered with the same relish as before.

'Don Pedro of Aragon,' called the king into the silence, satisfied that no one would have the temerity to speak first. 'What of your summer in Sicily?'

I swallowed. In truth I never wished to think of Sicily again, let alone set foot on that poisonous island. I wondered whether the lady Beatrice had wed her poet yet. The notion of her as a wedded dame hurt so much that I pushed the thought away and I exerted myself to mark Don Pedro's answer. War thoughts must drive all memories of Beatrice from my mind. I was in the service of a prince, who was in the service of a king, and I had pledged my allegiance. I owed him that.

'How many ships?' asked the king.

Don Pedro stood, and the lowering light struck his medal of St James. He looked, in his livery, like the very flower of Spanish nobility 'Two hundred, Señor,' he said, to an audible gasp of admiration from the collective, 'from the Governor of Messina, the viceroy in Palermo and Duke Egeon of Syracuse.' He went on to itemise the men and guns in the muster and I listened proudly to his strong, articulate tones, suddenly sure I had been right to follow his banner. 'May I also present my young friend

Count Claudio Casadei, who has assured us an additional fleet from the Grand Duke of Tuscany.'

Claudio stood now, blushing, prominent among the crows in his Florentine purple. He looked as anxious as a man giving his neck verse. 'It is so, Sacred Catholic Majesty,' he concurred, his voice breaking slightly with nerves. 'I mean, S-Señor.' He stammered to a standstill.

Don Pedro came to his rescue. 'Claudio's worthy uncle has the honour to offer you three score of puissant ships from the city of Florence, well appointed with cannon, culverin and other great pieces of brass ordnance. The flagship the *Florencia*, which I will have the honour to command, is a marvel of modern shipping,' he added smoothly. I admired the prince greatly at that moment, and pondered the difference between those bred to nobility and those ennobled by trade. Claudio was a count, yet he was from merchant stock, a banking family. But Don Pedro seemed to have nobility bred into the very sinew of him; hundreds of years of the purest breeding.

'We thank you most graciously,' said the king. 'There, Medina Sidonia, do you care to adjust your judgement?'

The man he addressed stood, his ruff working at his scrawny neck as he swallowed nervously. 'I am sorry, Señor, but even with these most valuable additions my answer has to be no.'

There was another gasp in the room, this time in wonder at a fellow who would defy a king. 'In order for your Great Enterprise to be successful,' Medina Sidonia went on, 'the numbers have to be so much in our favour as to make us invincible. I am sensible of the contribution of our Prince of Aragon and Count Claudio, but even these fleets assembled, although they are a remarkable demonstration of Spanish power, are not sufficient to *guarantee* success.'

The king glowered and bit at his fingers as his councillors began to argue amongst themselves. He spoke suddenly, and they were silent at once. 'What if . . .' he mused aloud, 'we do not *directly* attack England. We have above seventeen thousand veteran troops in the Netherlands, under the command of the Duke of Parma. They are already recruited and trained and equipped. If our armada can reach the coast of Flanders, it can escort the veterans across the channel. If our two forces can but *meet*,' he brought his two hands together and clasped them as if in prayer, 'we *will* be invincible.'

The councillors exchanged glances. The brave one, Medina Sidonia, spoke up. 'And what then, Señor?'

'*Then* the redoubtable Parma will strike up though Kent and take London, with Elizabeth and her ministers in it. You take the apple and the worm comes too.' He paused for the sycophantic laughter. 'Then her enemies in the north and west and Ireland will rise against her. Our agents are already at work in those regions.'

I admired the king for the first time since I had seen him in the theatre. He might no longer have the outward show of majesty, but his intelligence was formidable, and such a scheme had every chance of success. I caught Don Pedro's eye across the room. He smiled and nodded very slightly. *You see?* he seemed to say. I did see.

Medina Sidonia spoke again. 'We will have to employ extremely precise navigation, Señor,' he said, 'and to that end, I have brought someone to meet you.' He looked into the collective, over our heads, and beckoned. 'This is Martín Cortés de Albacar, one of our foremost astronomers.'

A man in long dark robes and the square felt hat of a scholar stumbled forward hurriedly, bearing a book that was almost as big as he. The astronomer knelt before the king and proffered the enormous tome. Its shadow completely enshrouded the dwarf and she began to complain until the king smartly slapped her face. He perused the pages. 'What is this?'

'The *Arte de Navigar*, Señor, a book of my own making; astronomical charts to guide your ships.'

I craned around the beruffed nobleman in front of me in an attempt to see the charts – I could vaguely make out the fine black lines, the gilded constellations, the spidery annotations. The thing was a work of art.

'Señor, these are representations of the stars in the northern hemisphere.' The astronomer pointed. 'Here you can see the principal stars that will be visible after the spring equinox in the *Mare Brittanicus*. With the correct instruments, your ships will find the coast of Flanders and then the coast of England with ease.'

'But what is its *purpose?*'

The astronomer, confused, began to bluster. 'Such navigation frees you from the coasts. Large ships such as Your Majesty has at his disposal can run into trouble in the shallows – there is a risk of grounding. But with astronomical navigation, there is no necessity to hug the coasts and follow terrestrial maps.'

'Let me see.' The king raised the book to his face as if to study the charts more closely. Then, with utter calm, he tore a page out of the book. It seemed that no one in the room breathed. The king tore the next page, and the next. The dwarf giggled and clapped, catching the beautiful charts as they fell and balling them up between her tiny fists. The astronomer stood, mouth agape, as he saw his life's work crumpled before his eyes.

When the king was done, and just the spine and cover of the book remained, Philip spoke pleasantly to the devastated scientist. 'I thank you for your pains,' he said courteously. 'But, you see, I already have a navigator.' He pointed skywards. '*God.*'

He kicked the dwarf with his finely shod foot; and, taking her cue, she knelt. The astronomer, bemused and devastated, knelt too. Then every knight and prince in the place fell to his knees, with a great scraping and clattering of chair legs upon the floor.

'I have had a divine revelation that I am charged to regain England for the Faith,' proclaimed the king in ringing tones, 'and I am so convinced that God the Saviour must embrace it as his own cause, that he alone will lead the way.' He looked down at his kneeling councillors. 'Get on, then, and do your part. I must away to mass.' He stepped over the sea charts that he had let fall on the floor. 'Oh, *Magdalena*,' he said to his dwarf, with an admonitory shake of the head, as if it were she who had rent the book. He took her hand and the odd pair walked from the room.

I felt a sudden misgiving as I got to my feet. I had been from one edge of the map to the other on shipboard, and navigation by the stars was now becoming commonplace. What good was a commendable plan without the science to achieve it?

With the king gone I thought I could now go too, and discreetly let myself out through one of the crystal-paned doors leading to the garden. It was entirely dark outside, so, whatever they said, the sun had set upon Spain.

I gulped the cool air and tipped back my head to the jewelled sky, counting the useless stars that a king had rejected. I wandered the pleached alleys, shaking the hours of talk from my head and the abacus of numbers from my ears. I took long breaths as though I had spent the day underwater. I headed determinedly away from the palace, of a mind to get myself lost. I walked well beyond the manicured gardens and sought out unlit alleys, plunged into thickets of blackthorn, and unworked meadows.

But soon the melancholy magic of my own company began to work upon me. I waxed dolorous and became weighed down with pessimistic thoughts. My growing impression that none of the Spanish crows – save one – knew what they were talking about hardened about me like the amber of my afternoon metaphor. Philip was walking into the dark as much as I.

I was truly lost when I all but tripped over a figure who seemed to be crouching on the grass, his forehead pressed into the ground. 'Hoy!' I exclaimed in shocked surprise, and dragged the fellow to his feet. It was little wonder I had not noted him, for not only was he clad in dark robes that fell to his feet, but only his teeth and the balls of his eyes could be seen. His hair clung in crisp black curls to his head. He was a Moor.

I remembered the king's exhortation to secrecy, and as I held the struggling boy I was certain I had caught a spy. 'What are you doing here?'

'I work for the king.'

'Very likely. What are you about? Tell me quick and plain, before I take you to the guards.' I spoke in Italian, he in Castilian, but he seemed to understand me well enough.

He shrugged. 'Take me if you like, señor, for the guards know me well.'

I was still not convinced. 'What is your business?' I felt foolish asking the question, for he could not be more than fifteen years old. 'I told you, señor, I work for the king.'

'I don't believe you. You are a Moor. The king would never employ your kind.'

'He does when we know things that his own people do not.'

This seemed to me an extremely suspicious statement. I began to walk the boy towards the house, with the happy thought that the capture of a Moorish spy would be an auspicious beginning to my service for the king. The boy came along quite willingly, and my resolve faltered a little – could he be telling the truth? 'What things do you know?'

'How to find water,' the boy replied calmly.

'Water?'

'For the gardens. His Majesty has plans to build a watercourse, and a lake, and more fountains. But we have to find sources.'

I turned him about by the shoulders. He had no divining rods, no instruments.

'What is your name?'

'Faruq Sikkandar.'

'Well, Faruq Sikkandar, supposing you speak the truth. How do you find the water?'

He shrugged his narrow shoulders. 'I just know where it is. I hear it.'

'You hear the torrents and streams below ground?'

'No. Not that. I sense where it is. I *feel* it. It is a gift. My father Faruq had it too.'

I looked about the vast and ghostly gardens, as silver-green as an olive leaf in the moonlight. There was another Moor here? My skin began to prickle. 'Where is your father?'

'He's gone.' The shoulders drooped.

'Dead?' I asked gently.

'As good as. He was taken for the armada.'

This, I knew, was indeed a death sentence – as a sea-slave this boy's father had less chance of returning from the enterprise than any of us. It was kinder to speak of the water. 'How long will it take you to find the sources that the king needs?'

He slid his eyes to me in a sidewards glance. 'As long as possible without trying his patience. For when my work is done . . .'

I understood. He had to be of use to the king for as long as possible; for after that, he would be sent to the ships too. I no longer thought him a spy. We walked on in a strangely companionable silence. At the postern a guard shouted from his post. 'Still here, Faruq?'

'The water speaks louder at night, señor.'

I had the assurance I needed. Feeling foolish, I let go of the boy's shoulder and patted his robe straight where my grip had crushed it. But I felt curiously reluctant to take my leave of him. 'When I met you, you were praying, weren't you?'

I could not see his expression, but darkness is the parent of truth. 'Yes.'

We stopped walking and faced each other. We had come to the parting of our ways. '*Buona fortuna,*' I said.

'*As-salam alaykum,*' he replied. And his teeth flashed briefly in the moonlight as he turned away.

I watched the water-diviner go. We were both in the employ of the capricious king, and our lives were as straw to him. I turned back to the palace, guided by the light of the stars. Perhaps everything would be well; perhaps Medina Sidonia, the one Spaniard who seemed to speak more sense than folly, had something of this Moorish boy's gift – perhaps he could divine a way forward without knowing it for sure. And yet, foreboding sat upon my chest like a cold stone.

My only comfort, if comfort it was, was that the Lady Beatrice was safe in the peaceful backwater that was Sicily.

Act IV *scene ii*

A courtyard in Leonato's house, Messina

Beatrice: I woke in the middle of the night without knowing why.

I turned over in my bed, groaning gently. This was the first night since Benedick had ridden away that I had fallen asleep as soon as my head had sunk into the pillow. For four weeks now I'd twisted and tossed, and not fallen to sleep until grey dawn and cockcrow. In the daytime I had stuck to my resolution, to live and speak freely, and to scorn the company of men. But every night my treacherous mind had recalled every word and gesture of my month's acquaintance with Benedick. As if at a play I had watched, again and again in my mind's eye, every jocular exchange, every time we'd laughed, our declaration of love on the beach. I could still feel the imprint of his kiss on my lips, the weight of him on my body, pressing me into the dunes. But next on the playbill, I had to watch another drama – a tragic sequel to the comedy. His final, bitter repudiation of me. The sight of him riding down the coast road. In my dreams he turned his head. In reality, I knew he had not.

I had no one to confide in. My pride and my new resolution of independence would not allow me to admit how much I suffered; and Hero, my one remaining companion, was preoccupied with her own heartbreak at the loss of Claudio. There was another I might have confided in, but Michelangelo Florio Crollalanza had never returned. Whatever Benedick had maintained he must have fled the island with his father.

So I suffered alone, and tonight I had thought the spell broken. I had thought that at last I could close my eyes without seeing Benedick's face burned into the back of my lids, like the imprimatur of a letterpress. So it was particularly galling to be woken.

I hunched beneath the coverlet, inviting sleep again. But a sudden, unidentifiable sound made me sit bolt upright, with the absolute certainty that there was someone in the courtyard.

I padded to the window, my feet chilling on the floor slabs, taking the coverlet with me like a cloak. I peered from the window into the courtyard. There, in the middle of the mosaic, was a figure holding a flaming torch. At first I found his form familiar. My foolish heart thumped, telling me it was Benedick, returned to claim me. But the next heartbeat told me it was not.

The torch threw a warm circle around its bearer, animating the mosaics in the ring favoured by the light. The sight would have been beautiful, but fire held no comfort for me now. Flames did not speak of hearth and home any more, but of the fire that had taken Guglielma Crollalanza. I could not see the torch-bearer's face, but he stood very still and he seemed to be looking directly up at me. Suddenly I was soaked in a cold sweat. He did not move, and nor did I; only his flame wavered, a horrid reminder of the torches that once lit the faggots of faith.

As I watched the torch described an arc in the night, and touched another brand. A second flame flared to life, illuminating a second bearer, and that torch touched a third. Soon a circle of men stood in the courtyard, and all the dolphins and mermaids and sea monsters beneath their feet were lit blue, as if the brandsmen walked on water, with the great head of Medusa in the centre of all. In fact, Medusa's face was the only one in the company I could see, and her eyes, made up of tiny jetty tiles, seemed to hold a warning.

Without moving my feet, nor taking my eyes from the men below, I bent my knees, reached down and shook Hero awake where she lay in her bed below the window. I did not want to alarm her, but I knew we must go. As she sat, grumbling, my aunt burst into the room.

'Come!' she urged in a fierce whisper. 'There are intruders in the court. Come at once!'

She gathered Hero up, blankets and all, as if she was still a child. My heart racing, I followed. I knew we could not quit the house, for the torchmen held the courtyard, from which radiated all the doors and gates to the outside world. 'The rose tower,' commanded my aunt, and I followed her to the little winding stair of the pink crenellated tower.

I remembered as I climbed my father's words about the Della Scala family name. *Stairs are power. Stairs are wealth; they elevate us from the poor. Stairs keep us separate.* Now I thought: *Stairs are safety.* Those lords of San Gimignano who built a hundred spindly towers had somewhere to hide from marauders. Our own castle in Villafranca had the redstone stair for the same reason. *I am Beatrice of the Stairs*, I thought. *If I can climb to the rose tower, I will be safe.*

With extraordinary strength my aunt carried Hero like a babe up the hundred stairs. The girl's dark silken hair was so long it swept the stone steps before me. We climbed high to the little bell chamber, which was bare except for an animal skin on the floorboards and a bronze bell hanging above. There was a single arched window open to the air and the wind whistled through the opening, turning the tower to a stone flute. The eerie sound did nothing to calm our spirits.

My aunt answered Hero's staccato whispers, and one question could be heard above the others: *What do they want?* 'I do not know. But they will be gone soon, sweeting,' soothed my aunt; crooning, again, as if to a child. I leaned from the window. The wind snatched and lifted my hair, and I craned my neck to look down. The ring of torch-bearers was still there, unmoving, and the light of the firebrands made crazy spindly shadows on the sundial below the tower's window. It was all times, and no time.

The house below me was dark, but watchful. There was a charged silence and I was convinced that every person in the place was now awake, and watching the torch-bearers from every dark casement. But no one called from the windows; no one challenged the intruders. I wondered, at every moment, why my uncle did not come out to challenge the brigands; but no arrows were let fly, no daggers dropped from the quarrels. The torchmen, strangely, seemed to hold absolute power. I wondered why, for the intruders were lobsters in a pot; my uncle's men-at-arms could fall upon them here, massacre them in the courtyard.

I saw, then, why. The palace gates were thrown open, and beyond the walls there were more of them. A broader band of torch-bearers passed a flame from one to the other. I leaned farther out to see; they were in the pleasure gardens, the fruit walks, by the fountains, in a wider circle. The circle in the court-yard was just the axis – we were enclosed by a wagon-wheel of fire.

I was suddenly terribly sure that we had made a mistake in climbing the tower. *We* were the lobsters in the pot. We were all to be immolated in this house; we all faced a death like Guglielma's. I swallowed, and thought for a terrible moment that I must choose between being cooked like meat or breaking every bone in my body as I jumped from this tower. But as I watched, the circle in the courtyard miraculously broke.

Silently, the torch-bearers began to process from the court-yard. 'They are going,' I said, incredulous. My aunt and Hero joined me at the tiny embrasure, and we watched, silent, as the light-bearers walked through the gatehouse. Outside, the other torchmen converged from all about the house, and joined their brothers. The torches were now one conflagration. *Now*, I thought, *now they are without the walls they will cast their torches* into the courtyard, and the whole house will go up like firewood. Unprompted, a thought burned in my brain; Benedick's image flickered there. *I will never see you again.*

But the flames outside moved again and a wavering golden dragon made its way down the hill on the Via Catania in the direction of Messina.

It seemed we waited an age; I stared at the diminishing light, disbelieving, my eyes watering until the light was a wavering pinprick, was gone. Clutching each other, the three of us stumbled down the stairs and met my uncle dashing up. 'Are you well, my lady, my daughter, Beatrice?'

Innogen cupped his cheek and kissed him, the most intimacy I had ever seen them share. 'Quite well, my lord. And the household?' she asked in an undertone.

'No one injured, it seems,'

'Why did they come, *papino*?' said Hero, taking refuge in childish words.

'Just a mummer's play, *cara mia*,' said her father, but Leonato's voice shook.

We followed him to the courtyard, could hear the household calling to each other. *Lorenzo? Here, master! Margherita? Here, Mother!* Like password and counterword, they all assured themselves of their loved ones and underlings.

I was steeped in warm relief until Hero wandered to the centre of the mosaic where the Medusa's head was rendered. At first I thought a body was sprawled across the gorgon, some servant taking his ease in relief. But as I came closer I saw the dreadful truth – three human legs, neatly severed at the hip, were arranged around the mosaic head in a perfect recreation of the Sicilian flag.

The blood rushed in my ears, and as though underwater I heard Hero say, in a curiously high voice: 'Oh! The Trinacria! What does it mean?' Then, as she realised what she saw, she began to scream and scream.

My uncle was among us like a whirlwind. 'Inside!' he shouted in our faces. 'Get inside!' The courtyard emptied at his word. My aunt and Hero fled to the house, but in the darkness and confusion I found myself among the menfolk outside the gates, who were arming themselves with pikes and pitchforks. I was glad of my error. I could not be idle – I had to help, I had to know what had happened.

Now a terrible search ensued until the victims were found. I found myself walking the midnight gardens by the side of Friar Francis. He carried a switch and cut savagely at the plants as he passed. He seemed much less indulgent of my presence than he usually was, and was short with my questions. 'You should go back home, Lady Beatrice,' he said shortly. 'No one can sustain such a wound and survive. These are not cuts to be knit with cobwebs. We are looking for three dead men.'

His pronouncement chilled me and my footsteps stuttered on the dewy grass. But I trudged on, stubbornly. I nodded to the vintner's boys who had joined the search from the vinehouse; twins, with barely a whisker between them. 'There is no reason why a woman may not endure such sights, if boys such as these can.'

The friar turned to me and took my arm, roughly. His eyes were black in the gloaming. 'Lady Beatrice, take it from one who has been to war. Some sights, once seen, cannot be unseen.' I was rigid with shock – he had never spoken to me in this manner before. He jabbed his finger towards the search party. 'These fellows are in your uncle's pay, and I must attend these poor souls as my duty to a higher paymaster.' He looked to heaven and crossed his fustian rapidly. 'But a person who *invites* such images into their mind through senseless bravado, whether man *or* woman, is a fool.'

I stopped in my tracks then, and stood still to be left behind while he and the other menfolk walked on. I turned back to the house, and, for the first time since Benedick had left, felt tears pricking the backs of my eyes. Then I heard an ear-splitting scream, not the girlish screams of Hero but the screams of boys who were not ready to be men.

The vintner's twins.

Running now from what they must have seen, I scrambled up the stone steps to Hero's room and hid under the coverlet, just as I had done as a child, as if the coverlet could defend me from the demons and devils that I had seen on the walls of our church.

Sleep did not come to me again that night. I saw again and again the three severed legs; but, almost more frightening, the man with the torch who had just looked at me and looked at me and would not look away. I could not shake the feeling that the brand-bearer had been Michelangelo Florio Crollalanza.

In the morning I had the news from Orsola; the three Spanish ostlers left behind by their prince had been found in the stables. Each one had been hog-tied to a beam and their left leg taken while they still lived. They'd bled out on to the hay like pigs, and one was still alive when they found him. He did not live long. Not a drop of *Sicilian* blood had been spilt, said Orsola, and the last of the Spanish had gone from the island. It was spoken with a certain emphasis that set me wondering. I watched my uncle Leonato as he went about the house like a spectre, grey and hollow. His hair had whitened overnight.

I sought out the friar in the little chapel where he was determinedly preparing for mass as if nothing had happened. I sat in the cool front pew. 'What did it mean?'

He was at the tabernacle, with his back to me; he did not turn, nor did he trifle with me by asking me what *I* meant.

'Your uncle would no longer fly the Trinacria. So the brigands brought it to him in his very house. It was a warning,' he said, 'something the Sicilians do remarkably effectively.'

I considered this. 'Because of Guglielma Crollalanza?'

'Yes. Lord Leonato sentenced a Sicilian woman to death; he

went against his own. Not just any Sicilian, but an Archirafi. Signora Crollalanza's family is as old as time, nobles and brigands both. They are serious enemies to make.' He poured the wine into the chalice and I had to look away. To me it was the ostlers' blood. 'Your uncle flew the Aragonese standard above the Sicilian flag. He threw in his lot with the Spanish, and now they are not here to protect him.' He put down the bread and the silver cup, and sat beside me on the pew. 'Lady Beatrice.' He touched my arm again, with his rough fingers with the short square nails. Under the silk was the bruise he had made the previous night. He was my friend again, his eyes hazel again instead of black, the lines radiating from their edges, the wages of a lifetime of smiles. But he did not smile now. 'You should go home,' he said.

It was the same exhortation as the night before, but today I thought I divined a different meaning. I frowned. 'Back into the house?'

'No. *All* the way home, to Verona.'

I was dumbstruck. I thought of Sicily as my home now. I said nothing, but shook my head. Foolishly, I identified the island with Benedick. In my heart, I was waiting for him to return.

The friar sighed, and the smile was back. 'I did not expect you to easily acquiesce,' he said. 'But perhaps there is *one* in this world who may command you.'

Within the day the friar had done his work. He spoke to my aunt, who wrote to my father. And within the week I was holding a letter in my hand from the one man I may not gainsay. '*Daughter*,' it began. Endearments were not my father's style. '*I desire and command you to return home with all possible haste.*'

Act IV scene iii

The *Florencia*: Calais, the French coast

Benedick: The Spanish ruled the waves.

Kings, we sailed forth from Lisbon. Our mission was to take our armada to Gravelines on the Flemish coast, there to join with the Duke of Parma, and another myriad of ships to swell our force into invincibility. It was to be a simple undertaking, a walk in the piazza.

Especially in a ship such as this. The *Florencia* was a wondrous vessel, every ordnance the last word in modern maritime warfare. On the first day at sea the prince, Claudio and I were conducted over the whole ship by the boatswain. We admired the luxurious officers' quarters complete with darkwood box beds and feather mattresses, the spacious dormitories with neat swinging hammocks of canvas the colour of cream, the sparkling gun deck with the neat ranks of guns with shining brass muzzles. There were no oarsmen, for the boatswain explained that Lepanto was the last of the oared battles – now the innumerable sails and the latest steering systems could take us anywhere on the map.

The fellow named every sail for us, both square and triangle, and every rope too, but I did not remember a single term. The names were most poetical, musical, even. It was a different language, this language of the sea; I heard the new words, and looked at the tangle of ropes and sails with detached interest but no curiosity. I was happy to be ignorant – I would fight when called upon, but did not need to know how the ship worked.

That was the business of my betters and my inferiors. I was Benedick the Soldier; Benedick the Sailor could go by.

The deck crew had been seafaring for Claudio's uncle upon merchant routes before the ship was recommissioned for military service in Sicily. The captain was a Genoese named Lorenzo Bartoli, a bluff and capable man to whom I warmed immediately. He worked closely with a skilled Portuguese pilot named Gaspar da Sousa, and under them the crew were an efficient unit. Each man did his part with skill and dispatch; but on the King's Great Enterprise the chain of command would be somewhat different to the common way. Captain Bartoli was the maritime captain, but Don Pedro was the military captain and had ultimate command of the ship. Nothing could happen without the prince's sanction.

We officers were made most comfortable aboard ship. Our night cabins were well appointed and cosy, and our nightly dinners raucous and generous. We enjoyed mess of venison, chops of beef and mutton stew nightly, washed down with sack, port and Rhenish. We were drunk on the adventure as much as the wine. The sea was as flat as a mirror, there was not even enough swell to shift the silver candlesticks upon the table, and as I weaved back to my night cabin, it was the drink that took my feet from under me, not the motion of the ship.

Thanks to the investment of the Grand Duke, the *Florencia* boasted fifty-two brass guns, which shone bravely in the eternal sunshine that blessed our voyage. They seemed innocent and decorative, their beauty belying their purpose. The captain urged Don Pedro to perform gun exercises; he would have the prince do them every day. Don Pedro teased the captain charmingly as he delayed. Each day he promised to carry out such exercises, but each day the sun rose at starboard and set at larboard, and the guns had not once left their holes. On the one day the prince made good upon his promise I watched the gunners roll out the guns on their two-wheeled carriages – turn them, load them, turn them back, roll them forth and fire – all without forethought. It was a ballet of brass, something to be enjoyed and admired. It seemed purely ceremonial, and even the ear-splitting practice blasts seemed more for the observance than the breach. Don Pedro pronounced himself satisfied, and between Lisbon and Calais he did not trouble the gunners to practise again.

Our voyage seemed a jaunt, an exploit. I did not think of the future, but enjoyed every sparkling day at sea. I would do my part, and I trusted Medina Sidonia, with whom I had had the pleasure to become better acquainted on the way to Lisbon. We were in his fleet, the Portugal fleet, and I felt comfortable to be under his ultimate command. After the first few days of a queasy cod – due, said the captain, to the motion of the ship – I became used to the sea, and walked about the great vessel with ease.

Above all, I trusted Don Pedro. The prince carried all before him. He was an irresistible force. He shone like the sun. He was a glorious leader but had the common touch; he had a word for everyone from his captain to the humblest powder-monkey. I knew this in him of old, for although he was my prince he was my friend – had he not gone out of his way to warn me of the Lady Beatrice? He had taken an interest in my personal affairs, even though I was merely a gentleman of Padua. Had he not, I might even now be married to a fallen woman.

At times Don Pedro would sit on the very prow of the ship, the bowsprit between his legs like a great phallus, as the *Florencia* forged through the waves. The other ships, some near enough to spit upon, some mere specks on the horizon, would wave at him and ring their ship's bells, salute him and sing him macaroons. He, more than the decrepit king, seemed to embody Spain. He was the future; he was what they were all fighting for. There was already a hero of this expedition, and it was he. In the friendly rivalry between fleets, the best was the Portugal, and in the friendly rivalry between the vessels of the Portugal the *Florencia* won hands down. The best ship; the handsomest, most charismatic leader. We all adored the prince – his dazzling smile, his confidence. Claudio and I were happy to follow him. We knew he had been bred for this battle and would know, both instinctively, and strategically, what to do. We could not lose.

Don Pedro and I became even closer on the voyage. We talked the day away, and laughed all night. We spoke of what glories would meet him upon his return, of how the king might reward him. His lands in Aragon (administered in his absence by his faithful brother Don John) would be augmented, his fortunes swollen. He even spoke of returning to Sicily (here I fell silent) as viceroy.

Often he would rebuff a request for an audience from the captain himself, in order to carry on his discourse with me. At night he made me the star of dinners in his cabin; he encouraged me in my jokes and stories. The best laughs always came at the expense of the English queen; I had only to question her parentage, or suggest that Elizabeth spent her nights working in the notorious London stews of Southwark, to have the table roaring. At night in my bed I would sometimes squirm with guilt; sometimes think of the lady I maligned, who was, famously, a virgin. But the next night, I would tell the jokes again, craving the laughter of my royal friend.

Don Pedro did not stint us at dinner; when the captain attempted to curb his generosity, with some trifling concerns about rationing, Don Pedro waved him fondly away. 'We will be dining on Kentish beef and drinking English March beer on the way home,' he maintained. 'There is no need to make provision.' We loved him for his confidence.

One evening, at last, the lookout spied the havens of Calais, and in the shallows we dropped anchor for the night, knowing that tomorrow we would meet with our sister force, and, most likely, engage with the English. Don Pedro stood on the forecastle in the warm evening, and gathered the crew with the ship's bell.

We all watched him. The sun was behind his head, a sorrowing red disc; the beautiful French coast was beyond his shoulder, but we all watched him. The sun turned his helm to gold, his teeth to pearls, his hair to jet. He was glorious. And then he spoke. 'I have spent my life pitying my brother, Don John,' he began, softly. 'He is a bastard, and a cripple, born of the Bar Sinister from an indiscretion of my father's. For my love of him I have dedicated my life to lessening his tribulation, and mitigating the stain of his birth. But I pity him tonight most of all. For while he is at home in Aragon, safe in his bed, tonight we will begin our assault upon England, and the infidel queen.' He jumped lightly down from the forecastle and walked among the men, chucking a cheek here, pulling upon an earlobe there. 'Whether you were born in a palace or a whorehouse, whether in wedlock or without, today you are all trueborn princes. In the name of God, the king and Santiago!'

The answering roar near put wind in the sails. 'In the name of God, the king and Santiago!'

I shouted louder than most and applauded louder than any, and felt a thickening in my throat. Don Pedro leapt up on to the foredeck, lithe as a leopard. In a moment I was at his side. 'My lord, you were . . .' I had no words.

He embraced me, and said, as he broke away: 'I have something for you, in return for your loyal service. You once gave me this. Now I think it is time to return it to you, for tomorrow, we must wear our livery.'

He clasped my hand, and when he pulled his away there was a cool little disc in my palm. My medal of St James. 'Our livery?' I asked, a break in my voice.

'Yes,' he said, low voiced. And smiled. 'Once a Knight of Saint James, always a Knight of Saint James.'

From the time of Don Pedro's speech onwards Santiago was with us on the ship. His name was invoked that evening more than the Lord's, and I formed a habit of clasping the medal at my throat, to assure myself that it was there. I was a Knight of St James once more, but now not just in name; tomorrow I would do honour to that name. I wished, for a moment, that Lady Beatrice could see us, could see me, about to fulfil my soldier's destiny. Would she regret her choice if she could see what I had become?

We had the most raucous dinner of all that evening in Don Pedro's luxurious night cabin. We drank a keg dry toasting our special saint, as if our libations could bribe him to save our skins.

In the morning we had clammy skin, slack cods and hollow eyes. We did no credit to the livery of St James, which we all donned for the first time since shore. The ship's bell roused us at dawn, and by first light we were all assembled on deck. As if to reflect the mood the weather had changed completely. It was cold enough for us to be grateful for Santiago's velvets and boiled leather, the sea was a leaden grey and the ship pitched alarmingly. There was no knowing whether the sun had survived the night, for a thick white fog blocked out the light like a funeral pall. Spain, Sicily and the summer seemed worlds away. It felt as if we were in different, darker waters; as if dreary, damp England had dominion over the weather here.

We waited in near-silence, until the lookout's shout sent our hearts speeding; but he only heralded a harbinger from Medina Sidonia, who rowed to larboard in a fast pinnace. An officer wearing the duke's colours scrambled aboard to issue final orders, and give us the fleet's watchwords.

'Sunday is Jesus,' he began in a lisping monotone. 'Monday, Holy Ghost. Tuesday, Most Holy Trinity. Wednesday, Santiago. Thursday, The Angels. Friday, All Saints. Saturday, Our Lady.'

I had lost track of the days upon our adventure. 'What's today?' I asked.

'Wednesday,' supplied Captain Bartoli curtly. 'Santiago.'

'There,' I said to the prince, 'an omen.'

Don Pedro did not return my smile. He looked a different man to the one we'd seen at the forecastle last night. He was grey and fidgety, his olive-black eyes darting about if he was hunted. He seemed to have shrunk overnight, his clothes visibly loose upon his frame. I hoped he was not sick, for I knew how anxious he was to get into the fray and prove his steel. I expected that he was suffering from the wine, as we all were.

We watched the harbinger rowing his pinnace away and the fog swallowed him almost at once – I hoped he would find his way back to the flagship once his messages were given. Once he was safely clear, we weighed anchor and hoisted the sails. This was always an exciting happening, and never more so than today, when we were sailing to join battle. The whistles blew and the bells rang and the sail crew swarmed over the ratlines like so many Barbary monkeys, lifting creamy sheets into the force of the wind. Today the breeze was strong, and the canvas snapped and cracked as the sails bellied and filled, and the ship lurched forth at a brisk speed. But because of the fog we could not see above a man's length before us; even the figurehead disappeared. Ship's bells rang all around us out of the fog like plague tolls.

For three days we sailed, blindly, into the fog. There was no knowing where we went, for there were no stars at night, and no instruments nor charts aboard that would help us, having been declared heretical by His Catholic Majesty. We knew of the passage of the days only because we would near another ship of the fleet, narrowly avoiding collision, and the boatswains would exchange watchwords from helm to helm. The Angels, All Saints and Our Lady passed, with the English dancing around us, refusing to engage, leading us God knew where.

We did not sail with quiet minds. There were ghosts in the darkness. From time to time, in ragged holes torn in the fog, we would glimpse, in a moment of clarity, angles and fragments of enormous and dreadful shapes. A mast as tall as an oak. The corner of a vast sail. An English ensign. Sometimes it seemed that we were surrounded, and the enemy forces would fall upon us. At other times these ghost fleets entirely disappeared. We were constantly upon the watch, with crew stationed all around the bulwarks from larboard to starboard, fore to aft. The officers' nerves were shredded and the crew were all of a jitter.

The hours of darkness were worse. Then there would be a great clamour from the fog, as if pots and pans were beaten, at the hour of darkest night and deepest sleep; or a ghostly English carol, sung in plainsong, would sound out of the dark, so near us as to make the most seasoned sailor jump out of his skin and begin babbling about mermaids. In the grey dawn we might see tantalising glances of a hellish coastline, black rocks standing upright like needles, treacherous cliffs and steely lakes and inlets of dead water. At such times we steered as hard away from the coastline, and the very real risk of running aground, as we could. Sometimes we had no such warnings, but the ship's stem would grate along the rocks of the shallows, with such a groaning and screaming of timbers that we thought we were lost. These incidents rudely woke the sleeping and unnerved the wakeful.

After a day of such tribulations Don Pedro went to his cabin and did not come out again. 'Shall we keep you informed, Highness?' called the captain, as the prince left the helm. Don Pedro did not reply, but disappeared into the fog like a spirit.

One by one the grandees followed him; until all that were left on deck were myself, Captain Bartoli and the regular crew, and, to my surprise, Claudio. The young Florentine took paper and charcoal and began to record such glimpses of coastline as we could make out, designing a putative sea chart, so that at least we could see if we repeated our navigational errors.

In those three days I learned more about shipboard than in

the three weeks previous. With our vision robbed from us our eyes turned inwards – maintaining the ship became of the upmost importance. I began to understand the terminology, to know my jib from my flying jib, my topmast from my topgallant, my mizzen from my mainsail. The universe had shrunk down to this ship, and the *Florencia* was now our little world. We could see nothing else, so our vessel was our east and our west, our north and south.

On the dank morning of the third day the insubstantial fear crystallised into terror. It was Claudio, at the end of two watches, who first spotted the glow. The fog had ignited somewhere in its murky centre like a coal at the heart of a fire, and a flickering golden sprite could be seen, frosted and dispersed, like a flame under ice.

Claudio shouted. In a trice I was with him. Captain Bartoli, who moved fast for a burly man, was at my shoulder. Now I could hear a crackling like a midsummer bonfire, and the golden sprite was joined by another, and another. I would have thought that I imagined these fire sprites of the ocean, that this was some legend of the high seas that I had failed to read about in the schoolroom. But now I could see sails and masts burning, the crosstrees afire like a forest of flame. I sensed now what the Moors of Asturias must have felt when they saw the burning cross of St James – they knew they were dead men.

'Fire ships,' said the captain. In an icy sweat, we counted eight of them. They were either sailing inexorably toward us, or we were sailing towards them. In this nightmarish, topsy-turvy universe I could not tell.

I set my chin, and laid my hand on my sword. If this was death, it had to be faced. 'Should we engage?' I asked the captain.

'No one to engage with,' he said bluntly. 'These ships are not manned. They are old hulls, smeared with wildfire pitch and rosin, and set alight.'

'What devilry,' Claudio breathed.

'Devilry is right,' said Bartoli grimly. 'They are full of brimstone. If you boarded, you would be in Hell indeed.'

'What is to be done?'

'Fire ships can be diverted using smaller oared vessels, and the *Florencia* has two such, lashed to the gunwales. We would need two pilots for them.'

'I'll make one,' I said.

'And I another,' volunteered Claudio.

'Medina Sidonia may also launch some such, but we have had no signal. My last orders from the flagship were that the vessels of the Portugal fleet should hold to our crescent formation at all costs.'

'Then we will fry like pancetta,' said I. The eight crosses were getting ever closer. 'Captain, what do you suggest?'

'I suggest you ask the prince to sanction the launch of our pinnaces with all possible speed,' he barked, his Genoese accent much more marked in these testing times. 'Only he can amend an existing order from High Command.'

I ran for Don Pedro, and hammered on the door of his day cabin. 'Prince! There is danger ahead; we need your orders.'

No reply. I hammered louder. 'For God's sake, sire, we must have your orders.'

I could hear him moving around within – shuffling footsteps, the scrape of a chair leg. 'Prince, open up here.' I tried a last desperate appeal. 'In Santiago's name.'

The door opened a crack and his royal eye appeared. I put my foot in the door and took the prince's arm. 'There is something you must see.' I could feel him pulling back with reluctance. I looked at him hard, for whatever ailed him he must not shame himself in front of the crew. I marched Don Pedro to the larboard side where Claudio and the captain were waiting, and showed him the eight burning crosses.

He sank to his knees. 'God be praised!' he cried. 'We are

saved. The burning crosses of Saint James! Santiago has come to our aid.'

I looked at him with horror – had the prince lost his wits? I helped him to his feet, gently, as if he were an invalid. 'They are English fire ships, sire,' I said. 'The captain here wants to know what your orders are.'

Don Pedro looked at each of us with eyes wide, his full lips working. His skin had a grey sheen of fear. I could see the captain was disconcerted by the prince's reaction.

'In order to maintain our formation in the fleet as we were ordered,' Bartoli said, clearly but urgently, 'we must launch the pinnaces and try to divert the fire ships.' I was already undoing my buckles, belts and baldrics, and removing my doublet in expectation of some hard rowing. Claudio did likewise, also anticipating the mere formality of the order. But the order never came; Don Pedro was silent, staring, with crosses of fire in his eyes.

'Sire,' barked the captain. 'Do we have your permission to launch the pinnaces?'

'No.' It was almost a whisper. 'I think it better that we sail away as fast as we may, and return to Spain.'

My mouth fell open as wide as Claudio's. Contempt fought with deference in Bartoli's weathered face. It was down to me to question the prince, for the captain could not.

'But what of our formation? And the rest of the fleet?'

'To Hell with the rest of the fleet! Turn about,' he spat.

I told the prince what I'd learned in the last three days. 'We cannot turn about, sire,' I said patiently, 'for we have sails, not oars. We go where the wind tells us.'

'Besides,' put in Claudio, 'my charts tell me that we are close to the coast – it could be the English coast. The fire-fleet may push us into the shallows.'

Don Pedro looked hunted – he looked from Claudio to myself, to the captain, trapped. 'Then what do we do?' His voice was a pleading bleat, so different to the smooth and low tones in which he'd addressed the crew just the other night.

'Can we outrun them?' I asked Bartoli.

'Yes,' said the captain. 'If we act *now*. Our best chance is to hoist all sails and ditch any ballast we can spare.'

'What of the horses?' I said, dreading the answer. The hold was full of horseflesh, from my dear destrier Babieca to the humblest mule; but if we were not to go ashore, what need had we of them? The captain thought for no longer than a heartbeat. 'No,' he said. 'The horses stay. Our rations are depleted. We may need food.' Bartoli followed this dreadful statement with another; he looked to Claudio, for the *Florencia* was his uncle's ship. 'We must ditch the guns, though. The battle is over.'

This was a dreadful sacrifice, for the newly cast guns had never fired a shot. Claudio nodded. 'I'll see to it,' he said, and I admired him very much at that moment.

'Not until the prince gives the order, Count,' said the captain, every word paining him, for now, I could see, he had his measure of Don Pedro. He turned to the prince. 'Sire, I beg you, we have little time. Give the order. Our anchor is dragging us, and the fire ships are faster for they do not have crew or cargo. They may catch us whatever we try.'

'Give the order,' I said, quietly.

Don Pedro was now visibly shaking. 'We run,' he said. 'See it done.'

'Aye-aye,' said the captain, those two syllables communicating a world of scorn.

There was little time to reflect on what had passed. Claudio and I ran with the captain and crew, all rank abandoned as the order was given to raise the sails. I tugged on a slippery rope till my muscles screamed, not knowing what I did, fighting the wind at all times for the rope ragged and snapped like a whip. Agonisingly slowly I felt the ship answer and we pulled away, gradually, from the dreadful burning crosses. I could see Claudio calmly supervising the ditching of the guns, as the wheeled carriages were untethered and two-and-fifty of the brass beauties rolled into the sea. I lost sight of the prince and knew, with a sinking heart, that he had gone back to skulk in his cabin.

But I was wrong.

Amid the swinging booms and whipping ropes I saw him, upon the bulwark of the stern, doused with sea spray and chopping at something with his father's sword. I thought he'd taken leave of his senses, and was tilting at phantoms. But as I dropped my rope and ran to him I saw that he was hacking at the anchor rope, a twisted cord as thick as a man's arm. He was halfway through it.

'Prince!' I screamed over the protesting caulking. 'This is madness! Without the anchor we are at the mercy of the wind.'

He looked at me for a moment with the visage of a soul in Hell – I could see that in that moment he did not even know me. I knew then with a certainty like a stone in my stomach that Don Pedro was a coward.

Then Claudio was at my elbow. 'What's amiss?' he yelled.

'He's cutting the anchor!' I shouted back. 'Get the captain!'

Don Pedro's sword had cut almost through the rope now, the fibres snapping and fraying as they gave way. I tried to stop the prince's slashes but nearly lost my arm. 'Help me,' I shouted to some nearby sailors, but no one dared gainsay a prince.

The captain heaved into sight. 'Sire!' he shouted. 'If we lose the anchor we are dead men!' But it was too late. Don Pedro brought down his sword one last time like an executioner; the rope split, spun, sliced through, and the ship leapt forward.

The dreadful fiery crosses receded; but we were now at the mercy of the sea.

Act IV scene iv

The Castello Scaligero, Villafranca di Verona

Beatrice: There was no one there to meet the carriage when I arrived at Villafranca di Verona.

The driver halted the horses at the Mastio tower, by the great red arch of the city gate. The sun was at its height, so it must be noon, the appointed time for my arrival; but there was no one in my father's livery to be seen. I had expected to see Ventimiglia, my father's major-domo, or one of the keep-stewards at the very least.

I leaned forward and tapped the driver on his hunched shoulder. 'Could you help me carry my box to the castello?' I pointed under the arch to where the castle stood, with tooth-some crenellated towers and shredded banners streaming into the noonday sky. The vast red fort dominated the countryside; the little town, which had sprung up in the shadow of the talus like a clump of mushrooms, was no more than an afterthought. The castle was so big I'd had my eyes on it for above an hour upon the road. Like all Della Scala edifices it had red brick above with a stripe of white marble below. The Castello Scaligero was the landmark of the region. It was also my home.

The driver considered my request, then muttered something through his snaggle teeth. It sounded like 'Why should I?'

I sat a little straighter. 'Because I am Beatrice Della Scala.'

He sounded like a Florentine. His accent was a peasant version of Claudio's. That explained it. Only a foreigner would not know my father, whose long reach extended all through the Veneto.

'What's that to me? You got coin, I carry box. No coin, no box.'

The truth was, I didn't have coin. I'd expected Ventimiglia to meet the carriage with a purse, for my aunt had sent a harbinger.

I sighed. 'I am a Scaligeri.' I gave the colloquial name for my family, in case such a yokel did not know the more formal form of Della Scala.

'So?'

'Well, let's see,' I said patiently. I pointed to the stone tower looming above us. 'You see that little ladder on the architrave? That is my family's blazon. That castle is the Castello Scaligero. I am Beatrice Scaligeri. My family *own* this town.'

The simpleton shrugged, and tipped my strongbox off the carriage. It landed on the pavings with a crash. I followed it down precipitately, for the carriage took off with a lurch as the yokel touched the horses with his whip. Cursing like a man, I picked myself up and humped the box on to my back. Luckily, it contained very little; a reliquary of St James, a playing card and a single gown.

I knew that I had a chamber full of silk dresses at home in the castello so I'd left my Sicily wardrobe where it hung. The sole gown I had brought with me was the one I'd worn at the wedding at Syracuse. I called it my starlight dress; the one with the graduating skirts of differing blues and the constellation of diamonds on the bodice. I told myself I had brought it with me because my aunt had it made for me, but I knew in truth I had brought that one because Benedick had told me that I looked well in it. And nestling under the folds of the gown was the single *Scopa* card, the *settebello*. I did not know why I had brought it; I should have left it with the rest of Benedick's trick deck on his chamber floor, or cast it into the sea as I sailed to

Naples. But through accident or sentiment, I had brought it; and there it lay, next to St James's fingerbone, cradled in blue silk.

Still, the box itself was heavy; strong oak with brass bounds. I huffed and puffed at the weight as I trudged under the gate that bore my arms.

Villafranca looked just the same, and I remembered running up this very street as a child, with my brother Tebaldo chasing me with a wooden sword. I had another memory too, of me chasing him back the other way, once my swordplay had begun to match his own. We had never liked each other, my brother and I, and we fought like cat and cur every day. We even dubbed each other with certain names; I called him Prince of Cats and he called me Queen of Curs, and we would battle for supremacy for all the hours we were not in the schoolroom. I wondered whether we would be amiable now we were grown.

My footsteps were heavy, and not just because of the weight of the box. The truth was I had no great wish to be home. I loved Villafranca well enough, the little town with the great castle. It was far enough from Verona for my father to remain above the squabbles of Montecchi and Capuletti – the two great families of the town – but near enough to mediate. Yet my brother disliked me, and my father thought of nothing but his beloved heir, and his own importance in the role of Prince Escalus. I should not, really, have been surprised that my father had not sent a servant to meet the coach. He had never even noted me, let alone loved me. I was that rare thing; a daughter who could not even be of use as a marriage prize.

I wondered now whether he and Tebaldo had shaped my character, for I was raised in the great red-stone tower of a castle full of men. My mother died as soon as I began to grow and question. Just as I became a woman she ceased to be one, taking a fever and dying in the space of a single summer, the same summer I started to bleed.

I'd not known what to do, or how to stem the flow. There

was nobody to ask. I'd wandered about the castle, crying for my mother, the blood running unchecked down my legs for four days. My father, displaying no great concern, dispassionately called a physician, telling him, in my hearing, that he thought I might be dying too. After the male physician had, rather distastefully, explained to me about my women's courses, and outlined the nature of the problem to the Prince Escalus, my father had gone back to ignoring me.

From then on I had become harder, and more outspoken. I would not be weak again. And now I had to readjust, after a summer in the company of women. Hero had been the nearest thing to a sister I had ever known; in my aunt I had seen my mother again, and in Guglielma Crollalanza I had found – and lost – a role model. And yet, even with these female paragons about me, I'd still sought male company this summer; perhaps I had sought out Benedick because I missed Tebaldo's sparring. Would the company of my brother, now, in any way fill the void left by Benedick's defection?

I was across the bridge now, and in the heart of the town. There, on my left, was the little church of the Disciplina where I had been christened and confirmed. And on the right, the Serraglio walls with their defensive towers overlooking the river.

Now in the main thoroughfare, I knew I would find someone to help me with my box – I had not changed so much in a brace of months that the Villafranchese would not know me – they were my father's people born and bred. I shook my riding hood from my hair so they would see the Della Scala curls, the same barley-blond as my father's. The blazon painted on the lid of my strongbox bore the same arms that I'd shown the driver, the same arms as the flag that now flew from the red-stone tower of the castle – the ladder of the Scaligeri. *Stairs elevate us from the poor. Stairs keep us separate. Stairs keep us safe.*

But something was wrong.

Instead of feeling the safety and security of home, I felt danger, prickling under the curls at my nape.

There was no one in the street, not a soul.

Every house was shuttered, every door closed, as if a storm was coming. Yet the day was bright and sparkling, and in my childhood I had known every door to be open, and every citizen to call a greeting. In one alleyway I saw a little moppet with curls like my own – I called to her, but a hand shot out from a dark door and pulled her within.

I carried on to the castle, and my skin cooled with foreboding as I entered the long shadow of the clock tower. The familiar blue and gold clock watched me like a warning eye – for here, too, something was amiss. There were no guards at the postern; only the dark cypress trees stood sentinel at the curtain wall. The great gate was wide open like a gaping mouth.

My heart started to beat fast and painfully – I was reminded of the night intruders at Leonato's palace, and thought for one dreadful, foolish moment that the Sicilian brigands had followed me here. Then my foot hit something with a clang. I looked down. It was a bloody rapier.

I set down the lockbox and knelt to examine the weapon. It was a fine blade, the haft finely chased and set with rubies, the handle wrapped with supple dog leather. But the blade was carmined to halfway with bright blood.

Suddenly I was back in the castle courtyard of my childhood, watching Tebaldo's morning swordplay lesson. 'Halfway,' said Signor Archangeli, my father's master-at-arms. 'If you have occasion to kill, pass the blade through your opponent's body to halfway, then claim it back. Any further, and if the fellow falls, he'll take your sword with him.'

I picked up the blade from the ground and weighed it in my hand. I touched the edge; the blood was still liquid, not tacky. Someone had been run through with this sword, and recently. I looked to the pavings again and saw a ruby had dropped from its setting in the skirmish; and a little farther along, another. The truth thumped in my ears. Not rubies; blood.

There was a trail of red up the drawbridge and into the castle. I unfastened my cloak from my shoulders and let it drop over the box, and left both outside the barbican. But I took the sword with me.

In the shadow of the gatehouse I was suddenly cold. But ahead in the sunlit courtyard I could see why the town was empty. All the citizens were here. There were scores of them, but curiously silent, all jostling to see something in the middle of the circle. I was in the north now, so the citizens were as tall as I, and I couldn't see anything. But a fellow turned and noted me. 'Let her through,' he said, 'she's the sister.'

She's the sister. It seemed a singular way to describe me. I did not know what the fellow meant by it, but walked forth anyway. The crowd parted respectfully and I walked as if in a dream, still clutching the sword.

There, in the centre of the courtyard, was the great fountain, and lying on the basin of it, my brother was sleeping. My father, the blond giant, stood over him, waiting for him to wake. Tebaldo was always a slug-a-bed, so I went right up to him and shook him, as I had so often as a child. His midriff fell open like a shirt and I could see ruby snakes clustered within his chest. The water of the fountain ran red.

'The future is over,' said my father. 'Tebaldo is dead.'

Act IV scene v

The *Florencia*: open sea

Benedick: It was bitterly cold.

We forged onwards through the grey seas, whipped by the wind and harried daily by English gunships. We could not fire back, for our guns were at the bottom of the sound. There was no stopping nor turning in our onward rush for we had no anchor. Bartoli and Da Sousa did what they could with the ship's wheel and the sails, but we were like a leaf in the current. The wind had whipped the sea up into angry grey mountains, and sometimes we were so low in the cleft of a pewter valley that we could not see the sky. Our wondrous ship the *Florencia*, the vessel that had ruled the waves from Lisbon to Calais, had no sway in the English Channel. We were bound in a nutshell, caught in a mill race.

My hours on deck were spent clinging to ropes or skating on planks as slippery as glass. My short hours in the cabin were spent rolling around in my cot, sleepless, like a pea on a drum.

Each day I would go down into the hold to see my loyal horse Babieca. He was held in place, like all the destriers, by four crossed ropes. His flanks were glassy with sweat and his eyes rolled to show the whites. Ordure ran down his back legs, matting the velvet skin. The smell of manure was terrible. I stroked him and sang to him, and in comforting him found comfort myself.

For all was confusion on board. The camaraderie that had characterised the first part of our voyage had entirely disappeared. We were cold and afraid. Santiago was no longer our battle cry – but the word 'Parma' was now passed around like a prayer. The Duke of Parma was coming with the veterans from the Low Countries. Thousands of men. Countless fleets. I heard a rosary of numbers again, as I had in El Escorial, and the amen of *Parma, Parma*. We did not trust in saints any more; but an earthly saviour, Parma, would come. Parma would save us.

Don Pedro kept to his cabin. The prince would accept food from a deckhand thrice a day, but would speak to no one. Having dealt the voyage its death blow with his father's sword, he retreated completely.

Bartoli, Claudio and I met in the captain's cabin at the dawn of each day. We spoke the watchword every morning so we could keep track of the passage of time. I told my own rosary day by day; Jesus, Our Lady, Holy Ghost. When Santiago came around again I knew it had been a week since the fire ships at Calais. We knew, too, that Parma was not coming.

It was time for action, and we managed the ship as best we could. We set the redundant powder-monkeys down to ostle the horses. We surveyed the gun damage we'd sustained and gave orders to the carpenter for repair. We divided up the watches, so that lookouts could be kept the whole day around. For as often as we glimpsed another limping ship of the armada, we saw an English gunship with the ensign of Drake or Effingham or Howard.

I came to know the colours of our enemy, and the ships too. I went from blissful ignorance to unquiet knowledge. There was another rosary to learn, a rosary painted in gold on the gunwale of each enemy vessel; *Victory, Elizabeth, Golden Lion, Mary Rose, Dreadnought* and *Swallow*. Although we always took evasive action against attack, in truth we were fish in a barrel, waiting for the telltale boom of the guns, powerless to fire back, able only to lick our wounds after the fact, and hope that we would not be holed below the waterline.

We saw Medina Sidonia's flagship once, and the captain took out his spyglass to read the orders from the signaller. I squinted to watch the remote figure waving his coloured flags, without a clue as to what they signified. When Bartoli lowered his glass there was a red ring around his eye but his face was white.

He looked at Claudio and me, and jerked his head towards his cabin. We followed him.

Bartoli walked across the little room to the bottled window. Claudio and I clung to the walls and placed ourselves in two chairs. The captain looked from the casement for a moment, without speaking, at the roiling sea. He never needed to hold on to anything – I never saw him support himself in all our time on the *Florencia*. On the captain's little desk an orrery revolved and spun with the motion of the ship. Ironic, I thought, to have such an instrument when we were not permitted to steer by the stars. The captain spoke at last. 'We are to go north about,' he said.

Claudio and I looked at each other.

'North about?' I asked.

The captain turned, and would not quite meet my eyes. He crossed to his desk, jerked open a drawer and pulled out a chart. He spread it before us and placed his grubby finger on the map. 'We are here . . . or hereabouts,' he said ruefully. 'We are commanded to go north, around the tip of Scotland and the west coast of Ireland, and back to Spain via the Atlantic.' The finger travelled the route, and we followed it with wide eyes. It seemed impossible. To turn and go back to Spain, if we had an anchor, would take the three weeks it had taken us to get here. But to go this route would take months, if we even lasted so long. This map would be no help to us, for although Spain and Portugal were painstakingly described, England and her islands were no more than insubstantial blobs.

I looked up at the captain. 'Can it be achieved?' I asked.

He rubbed the back of his neck, under his ruff. 'We would struggle to return even to Spain on the food we have. Your prince – my captain – was . . . generous with our supplies on our way here.' Ever correct with respect to his chain of command, he stopped short, as he always did, of criticising his superior. 'But to go this route . . .' He tailed off expressively. 'Well.' He dusted his hands together. 'We have our orders,' he said. 'I will tell the crew.'

Claudio, the captain and I spent the rest of the day in the hold, making an inventory of our supplies. No member of the crew was admitted to our conference, not even the quartermaster, for the captain feared for morale. 'Let us apprise ourselves of the situation first,' he said.

I was always stupid at figures, but Claudio proved to have a mind like an abacus, and as he had a better fist than I he wrote down our calculations. The horses would do well for now, for their feed was more plentiful than ours, but our supplies were already troublingly low. Our stomachs growled audibly at the pile of food. There were dried meats, ship's biscuits, cheeses and sausages, even a barrel of preserved oranges for the officers. Claudio fished one out, a sunny, fragrant orb; but his thumb went right through it. 'Rotten,' he pronounced.

We divided our supplies into three, for each month that we might be at sea, and then divided each pile into four for each week, then seven for each day. Then we did the same for the barrels of sack and Rhenish and small beer. Our conclusion was that each man would have a meal the size of a walnut once a day, with half a cup of wine or beer, and the same of water, to wash it down. None of us spoke our thought – that no man could live on so little let alone maintain the strength to sail a ship of this size. We were doomed.

I cursed Don Pedro's extravagant feasts on the voyage from Lisbon to Calais, and the nights when I had drained a keg of Rhenish on my own. 'Sleep with your daggers tonight,' said the captain, as he lifted the trapdoor to go back on deck. 'The men will not be happy.'

I held the ladder for him. 'They are loyal, are they not?'

'To a point,' said the captain. 'But the farthest they have sailed before today is from Livorno to Ragusa and back. Every man has his limits.'

I followed him back to deck in silence. I took his meaning, for I knew at least one man on board who had reached his.

Three days later, on the day of Jesus, we once again had sight of the *San Martin*, Medina Sidonia's vessel and the flagship of the Portugal fleet. We took another signal from the miniature flagman who waved our fate to us. My innards, already contracting with hunger, lurched; for I had lost all faith in our officers and wondered what new lunacy was to be handed down.

The captain lowered his spyglass. 'We are to ditch the horses and mules,' he said, shaking his head as if from a blow. He was conditioned to accept all orders, but his mouth worked and his choler rose.

'For what reason?'

'Speed,' he said. 'If we do not lose the weight we will not get home on our rations.'

I spoke back to him the dreadful words he'd uttered when we fled from the fire ships. 'But . . . you said yourself . . . that . . . the horses could be . . . food.'

'Not any more, it seems,' he said; and I knew I would not get him to gainsay Medina Sidonia, whatever his private feelings.

I stumbled to Don Pedro's cabin, in the eye of the wind. As before I knocked at his door but could not hear a reply. Then I had a notion, and put on my best Florentine accent. 'Your dinner, sire.'

The door opened a crack, and as I'd done once before, I put my foot in it. The prince retreated swiftly to a shadow, and I nearly fell through the door. After the brightness of topside I could not see him at once but then I spied him, hunched in a chair by the bottle-glass window. I approached him and knelt.

Now I could see him a little. His hair was unkempt, his linens soiled. The neat shape of his beard was blurred with an ashy stubble. 'Well?' he said. 'Where is my dinner?'

I looked at him askance, as if he made a jest. 'It is I,' I said gently, 'Benedick.' My heart began to thud in my throat. Had he lost his wits?

'Yes,' he said patiently. 'You may bring me my dinner now.'

I chose my words carefully. 'There is no dinner,' I said. 'Our commanders have elected that we return to Spain via the northern route, and to do this we will suffer extreme privation. And now,' I continued when he did not react, 'Medina Sidonia commands that we dump the horses and mules in the sea.'

Silence.

'The fact is, Highness, that in the days to come, those creatures may be the difference between life and death. If you could send a signal ... intercede, for no one but of your rank could hold sway with Medina Sidonia.'

He leant forward. Now I could see his eyes, still as black as olives, but even they had changed; they were glittering, fanatical. 'Let me be clear. I, Don Pedro, Prince of Aragon and Duke of Castile, am to send word to Medina Sidonia, Duke of Niebla of the House of Olivares, to beg that I am to be allowed to eat a *mule*? A prince,' he said, 'does not eat a mule. Now *bring me my dinner.*'

My heart sank. I knew it was no good to protest, but I heard myself doing so. 'But Prince, think of your men,' I said. 'We will all starve.'

He looked at me as if I were a stranger. 'I care not,' he said. 'Leave me be.'

Realisation dawned upon me, and a dreadful knowledge swelled in my chest as I understood what he was saying. I retreated from him as if I had been struck, and scrambled from that terrible room – I could not wait to quit his presence.

The act was to be carried out at sunset, when the sea grew calm. The powder-monkeys turned stableboys wept openly as they untied the mules and horses one by one. I led Babieca myself, for I could not give such an office to another. The big bay followed me trustingly, as he always had, delighted to be freed from his dank prison, his nostrils flaring at the fresh air. His hooves stuttered and stumbled on the slippery planks of the deck as he danced delightedly. He nudged the pit of my arm as he'd done so often on the road, asking me, I knew, what new adventure we would embark upon together.

In truth the next adventure was his last and he was to go alone – it was a broad ramp, roped to the open bulwark and leading nowhere. Each horse before us reared and skittered at the edge, foam-flecked and desperately protesting, before being pushed into the brine with a colossal splash. One horse ahead of us, Don Pedro's grey, kicked out as he was forced into the sea and laid low one of the powder-monkeys. The boy lay on the deck, prone and green, the purple imprint of a perfect horseshoe on his face. He was thrown in after the horse; the only difference that he was afforded a brief prayer.

Now it was Babieca's turn. I'd been given him in Sicily, by Don Pedro, on the day I'd been dubbed a Knight of St James. The horse had been with me in the happiest of times; even borne Beatrice and me on his back when we'd rode down the beach like Templars. And in the worst of times, when I'd lost her, I'd whispered my misery into his velvet ear.

As I led him to the open bulwark I pressed my lips to his silky cheek. Now I was glad of the sea spray to douse my face. I took off his head collar and slapped his rump, but it took myself and three others to shove him forward. He screamed as he fell. I had not known that a horse could scream. But I knew I would never forget the sound.

The setting sun turned the sea to blood. I watched, listening to the terrible screams of the horses and mules. The sea was churning with horses, not just of our fleet but of all the others too – the order had been given to the entire northbound armada. Hundreds, thousands of horses and mules swam desperately until they sank; hooves flailing, eyes rolling, mouths choking with the brine. I watched Babieca until I could no longer see his creamy head – he had turned into the white horses that rode the waves.

Wakeful in my bed that night I thought of all that had been lost. Beatrice. Babieca. And Don Pedro, my friend; that shining prince I'd met on the steps of Monreale cathedral. I should have left him there that day; greeted him as his rank demanded, and moved along. Then he would always have remained a prince to me. For of all the horrors I had seen this day, worse than the boy on the deck, worse than the horses in the sea, was the look in Don Pedro's eye as he'd said '*I care not*,' and dismissed me from his cabin.

Act IV scene vi

The Castello Scaligero, Villafranca di Verona

Beatrice: My father's anger at Tebaldo's death was greater than his grief.

Various accounts from the townspeople all told the same tale; Tebaldo had become embroiled in a street fight in Verona, and had slain a Montecchi swordsman. Not one detail of this story surprised me; but the sequel was more singular. For the Montecchi's dearest friend and kinsman had ridden all the way to Villafranca to challenge Tebaldo for his transgression; fought him, and killed him. And it was this, this breach of Prince Escalus' citadel, this violation of the peace of the place they called 'Old Freetown', that incensed my father almost as much as his son's death.

He took, at once, a dozen men-at arms, and rode in a whirl-wind to Verona, there, I was sure, to knock down Montecchi doors until he found the villain who had slain his heir.

So on the night of Tebaldo's murder I was alone in charge of the castle, and I could not sleep. As if angered by the crime the day had committed, the night weather had broken and a rain-storm raged around the turret of the red-stone tower. This room had been my mother's, and I had been born in it; she'd told me many times how she looked through the single arched window at the stars.

I was transported back to that night, long ago, when my mother had taken me to the turret and shown me my star, right by Cassiopeia's chair. We were so high that the stars were brought low – so low that I reached out my chubby hands to grab at them, and the reremice that flapped about the turret on their leather wings batted, startled, into my grasp. 'I laboured the night long with you,' my mother had said. 'It went harder with you than with Tebaldo. So all the time I looked at the stars, to take me from this earth, to take me away from the pain. And at the very *instant* you were born, *this* star was born too.'

She pointed, and I followed her long white finger to the heavens. There it was, a shining diamond prominence, young, and vital and sharp, not like the duller ageing stars.

'When you came out of me,' said my mother, kissing the top of my head, 'that new star danced for joy.'

I sat up now; tried to remember my mother's face, could not. My father did not go in for portraiture. I peered out of the arched window in search of my star but the sky was crammed with sullen violet clouds, and there were no constellations to be seen.

I sank back down again, coaxing sleep, but it was no use. Long past midnight I was still awake, listening to the bells edging the time in quarter-hour increments towards dawn. I had a book by my bed – as I'd always had ever since I could read – but no light. I threw a cloak about me and padded down to the kitchens for a flame for my candle.

On my way back from the fire I was passing the great doors of the red-stone tower when I heard a knocking. Thinking my father had returned, I lifted the great iron latch without waiting for a servant.

I saw there a young man, his hair and clothes black with rain, his face pale, his shoes so soaked that water ran in at the heels and out at the toes. Behind him a dark horse danced, tethered to a ring set into the talus.

'I am the Montecchi you seek,' he said, in a rush. 'I took Tebaldo's life.'

If my father had been at home, those would have been the last words he uttered. Prince Escalus would, in his rage, have struck him down there and then, and beaten him to death in the red fort. Even if Ventimiglia the major-domo had opened the door, this boy would have found himself in the dungeons, contemplating the rack and the scold's bridle and all the other outdated instruments of torture. But they had not answered the door; I had. And I could deal with this young man as I saw fit. I took him by the arm, and bore him off stealthily to the kitchens, shoving him into a chair beside the fire at which I'd just lit my candle.

There was no one there save the fool who was employed to keep the fire in. He was so simple in the head he could only say the word 'fire' and so would not be able to repeat our conference. But just to be safe, I sent him to get Ventimiglia. 'Fire,' he said in acquiescence, and went.

Once we were alone the young man spoke. 'This is better treatment, lady, than I have any right to expect.'

I was impressed, once again, by how he expressed himself. This was no street-brawling hothead. I ladled him a cup of small beer from the barrel in the squarestone. 'Do not thank me yet,' I said, 'for I have not yet decided what to do.'

'What to do?'

'With you,' I said. 'For I am the lady of the house.'

He knelt before me. 'Then it is your forgiveness I must crave. I attacked your brother in defence of a friend whom he had slain in turn.'

I was not to be mollified by fine words. 'I know the fable. Save your explanation for your trial.'

His cup hovered halfway to his lips. 'If I am to be tried, I must even now enter a plea for mercy,' he said, hope flaring with the firelight in his eyes. 'For there is a lady in Verona to whom I have pledged my affections, a maid by the name of—'

'Shhhh.' My mind was racing. 'Let me *think*.' Three times of late the Montecchi and Capuletti had brawled openly in the streets, and my father had decreed that anyone offering violence would be immediately put to death. But I knew there would be no benefit in taking this young man's life. I would rather stop the bloodshed. If I sentenced this young man to death, then another Capuletti would be taken in revenge; on and on, an eye for an eye until the whole of Verona was blind. Yet if this Montecchi boy was still here in the morning, he was dead; of that there could be no doubt. I had to act tonight.

The fire-fool gambolled back into the room, and Ventimiglia followed him, bustling in his nightgown, looking less dignified than I had ever seen him. 'My lady? Is your father returned?' He did not, at once, see the young man in the chimney-corner.

'Not yet. But I have something to ask of you. When my brother lived, if some . . . business pertaining to the estate made itself known while my father was from home, what would come to pass?'

Ventimiglia looked confused. 'Well, should such a set of cir-cumstances arise, your lord brother would take the mantle of Escalus in your father's stead.'

'And he could pass certain decrees, make judgements in the moot?'

'Why, yes.'

'And such decrees did not have to wait to be ratified by my father's seal?'

'Well, no, my lady; in such cases, your brother's ring served well enough.'

I rose. 'In that case, I, Princess Beatrice della Scala, in the absence of my father Prince Bartolomeo della Scala, call the moot court of the Freetown of Villafranca di Verona into session, to try the murderer of Tebaldo della Scala.' I pointed to the shadows. 'This is the miscreant – put him in chains.'

The Montecchi boy calmly put down his cup, and rose to stand beside Ventimiglia. His dignity did him great credit. Ventimiglia looked from the young man to me.

'But, my lady, it is impossible. Would it not be better to wait till morning, and your father's return?'

'Ventimiglia, *I* am in command here. Find me the requisite three judges and dozen witnesses.'

'From whence, my lady?'

'The mayor, the priest, the aldermen – drag them from their beds if need be. We will meet in the red-stone tower at matins.'

Ventimiglia hesitated. I drew myself up to my full height and looked him dead in the eye. 'Do it.' For the first time, I hoped that my eyes resembled my father's. They must have, for suddenly I was alone with the fool and the flames.

'Fire,' said the simpleton.

'Yes,' I agreed; and left him to it.

The castle was all of a clamour and I went downstairs to the chapel unnoticed. More stairs down and I was in the crypt, where Tebaldo lay on a great stone table, his candles kept burning night and day as assiduously as the fool's fire. His face was beginning to fall in, his flesh to soften, and he wore a more benign expression than he'd ever done in life. I lifted the shroud above his right hand. It was easy to slip the seal ring from his finger, as death had already nipped the flesh from his bones. I tucked him in again, as if he slept, and climbed the steps out of the underworld. The seal ring, with the little ladder blazon upon it, now rode upon my finger.

I presided over the candlelit moot court with precision but in haste, at every moment expecting the thunder of my father riding back over the drawbridge.

I heard the evidence from the Montecchi and the burghers of Villafranca, and made my judgement. I wrote the order, dripped the wax and sealed it with Tebaldo's ring; my ring.

I took the guilty man to the door myself. The Montecchi kneeled and kissed the sealstone, still warm from the wax.

'You have a horse?' I asked him.

'Tethered outside.'

'Then go.' And I remembered; 'and do not take the Verona road.'

By the time my father returned it was dawn, and the sky was the colour of his eyes. I was waiting for him, in the red-stone tower, seated in his wooden chair carved with ladders.

'Beatrice.'

I stood, my body heavy with fatigue and dread.

'Father, Tebaldo's murderer came here to give himself up.'

'He's here?'

'Not any more,' I said. 'Tried and dispatched. By me.'

Murder flared in his eyes. 'Dead?'

I could have lied. I so *wanted* to lie, but it would have been a futile untruth, and I would be safe from my father's wrath only for the time it took for him to hear the full story from Ventimiglia.

'Banished. To Mantua, never to return.'

I began to explain my reasoning, but his pale eyes blazed again, his hand shot out and he struck me, backhanded, to the floor.

In the morning I had a little ladder mark from his ring upon on my cheek.

My father's anger dissipated with that blow, but now his grief remained. He was diminished and listless. He did not even send to Mantua, to petition for the return of the fugitive. I think he knew by then it would make no difference. Tebaldo would still be dead, sleeping upon that slab downstairs in our crypt, now wearing once again the ring that I'd stolen for a night.

My father's purpose in life, the role of the Della Scala, had now gone. For centuries Prince Escalus had been a mediator. It was as if the balance of the Montecchi and the Capuletti, those opposing forces, had kept him upright like two whips laying upon a top – now the balance was gone, the spinning top faltered and fell. He sat in his great wooden chair, carved with the ladders of his blazon, and would neither eat nor sleep. He did not seem inclined to take up the business of the castle, so I continued to preside over the moot. He watched me with his pale blue eyes and barely moved; and he spoke never a word.

Each night we dined together at the great table in the redstone tower, and I felt as if I was back in time. The Castello Scaligero had always seemed of another era, but now it fossilised with grief. The red stone was cold, the fires barely stayed lit. There were animal skins on the floor in place of rugs, and animal heads and antlers on the walls in place of tapestries. Musicians played discreetly from the gallery on instruments of the region that had not changed for hundreds of years, and the meats that were ranked upon the table were not butchered but complete with lights and offal and lacking only the heads that stared from the walls and the skins that lay upon the floors.

For days we dined in silence, and I had begun to forget what my father's voice was like, to forget that he even had the power of speech. So when one evening he passed a remark, it was as if one of the animals' masks upon the wall had assumed life and spoken to me.

'Tebaldo danced with death every day. He was in love with her. He sought her out,' he said.

I nodded, acknowledging the wisdom of this remark; and having begun to talk, he did not cease.

As the weeks passed and Tebaldo's death drew farther away like a gallows by the roadside, I detected a sea-change in my father. He seemed to exert himself to be pleasant to me, and his stern demeanour was leavened by an unaccustomed good humour. He would make conversation, talk of the matters of the day, occasionally pass comment on a fine haunch of meat that we were enjoying.

Sometimes after dinner we would even play *Scopa* together. My father did not really approve of women playing a man's game: 'A woman should hold a fan before her face,' he'd say, 'not a fan of cards.' He was surprised that I knew the rules; but once he'd accepted that I had some skill at the game I sensed he found it comforting, for I knew that he used to play with Tebaldo of an evening. I made sure he always won – sometimes I let him, sometimes he bested me, and sometimes he even smiled. Even touching the deck was bittersweet for me – for the cards were the exact same type as that which Benedick had given me, even down to the back-pattern and the maker's mark from Treviso. Proof positive that Benedick had bought his cards in the north, and dealt his cheat's deck to every comely woman from Bolzano to Naples.

I tried not to think of Benedick; but in truth I was hungry for news of Spain, of England, of whatever worldly enterprise had taken Benedick from me in the company of the Aragonese. But my father's interests did not even reach as far as Milan or Florence; he was bounded in his little world of the Veneto, a world that seemed no bigger than a nutshell.

So he talked to me instead of the politics of Verona, the origins of the dispute between the Montecchi and the Capuletti, and of how they were more than just warring families but political factions. He spoke of the history of the mediating princes of Escalus, and the neutral status of Villafranca as a freetown.

He was telling me things I already knew, for I had grown hearing him instruct Tebaldo at table; but then I realised that my father had not been aware of my presence on any of those nights. He'd thought, then, of nothing but Tebaldo; I might as well not have been there. Now our acquaintance was beginning again, as if I had just been born, as if my mother had just brought me down, swaddled, from that starlit chamber.

I think I knew why. I began to realise that, much as he had loved Tebaldo, he had loved him less as a person and more as an heir. My father now had no successor. Could it be that, in the past weeks, I had proved myself to him? When I had been the chatelaine of his castle and had presided over his moot court, had he recognised that I, though a woman, had the faculties to run the place once he was gone? I could be *Princess Escalus*, and keep the peace; I could claim the ring from Tebaldo's hand, and balance the sword and the scales in his stead. My heart quickened. Could *this* be my destiny? Could a woman really rule here? What would a man like Benedick matter to Princess Escalus of Villafranca?

One night I determined to raise the matter with my father but he beat me to the lists. He clasped my hand across the table; something he had never done. 'Beatrice, I am so glad you are home. For with your brother gone, you are to assume an important new role.'

My heart warmed to him for the first time. I returned the pressure. 'Dear father.' I smiled. 'I grieve for the son and brother we lost in Tebaldo. But I most gladly accept the mantle you have vouchsafed me. I will be a worthy heir.'

He gave a bark of laughter. 'A mere woman! Heir to the principality and mediator of Verona? No, my dear.'

My heart sank, but I persisted. 'But . . . you have heard me. In court, in conclave.'

He shook his head. 'I was not listening. I have not heard a word. I have been *watching* you. You have grown into a beautiful and noble woman. That summer in Sicily put colour in your cheeks and life in your eyes; you have a good figure, fine hips.' He patted my hand, then removed his. 'You will never be my heir, but you shall *bear* my heir. Now the issue is to get you married, and get a male child in your belly as soon as may be.'

Act IV scene vii

The *Florencia,* open sea

Benedick: The Angels. All Saints. Our Lady. Jesus. Holy Ghost. Most Holy Trinity. Santiago.

The weeks went by, and we repeated the seven watchwords until we had forgotten the proper names for the days of the week. Some days we felt that we were alone on this lonely sea, trapped in a drear grey vortex, doomed to sail for ever on our ship of fools without seeing another sail. On other days we would see another ship on the horizon, and the captain would raise his spyglass and read the ensign. '*San Juan de Sicilia,*' he'd say, 'from the Levantine fleet,' or: '*La Asuncion,* from the Castilian ships.' Sometimes the sea fog would lift to show us ten or twenty such vessels and I realised there were many more of us in misfortune's flotilla. And some were not as lucky as we – when the *San Juan* went away from us on a rogue wind, I saw she had a red wake. She was sailing wounded, and I wondered what terrible injuries had befallen the crew, that their lifeblood could dye the very seas.

The weather was dire, even though it was high summer, and I wondered how the English survived from one year's end to the next without seeing the sun. We shivered in our ragged silks, for no one had thought to don furs in July. We were battered day and night by howling winds, driving rain and even hailstones.

Water was never in shortage, for in this grim weather our rainbutts were ever full. The greatest privation was the lack of food. I had never been hungry in my life before this week. Though my family were but gentlemen stock in Padua we always had a groaning board, and I always had a reputation as a trencherman. Tall and broad as I was, starvation took a cruel toll upon my frame. My stomach was constantly growling from hunger, my mouth dry as dust; and it was difficult to ignore my twisting innards long enough to sleep. My dreams in the first week were of Leonato's feasting table – even the strange dishes of Sicily seemed as manna to me now. In the second week I dreamed of roasting a spit of Babieca over an open fire, and of eating my faithful horse's haunches till the juices ran down my chin. In the third week I dreamed dreadful dark dreams that made me wake with shame, dreams which I would speak of to no one, dreams of tearing my fellow sailors limb from limb and eating their flesh raw.

I had my comforts. Sicily now became the place I went to in my mind. Once I had thought I never wished to go back there, that I never even wanted to hear tell of the place. But now I spent my days there. I would volunteer to guard the rations for the quartermaster, and would sit atop the trapdoor to the hold. Deprived of sleep at night, I would doze in the daytime with my back to the mainmast, huddled in sackcloth against the wind, thinking of the sun, always the sun. Now the summer in Messina assumed a golden haze to me. And dancing through those days, I saw Beatrice, always Beatrice, twirling in her starlight dress, the sun glinting in her tumbling blond curls. It seemed not to matter now that I dreamed of another man's wife. In my dreams, she was mine. These were fantasies, insubstantial reveries. No one would know how I comforted myself. It seemed likely that I would die on this ship. We would all die. My memories were all I had.

My recollections of Sicily led me to thoughts of the prince, too. I had not seen Don Pedro since the day we drowned the horses. I knew he lived, for I made sure he had double rations each day, but I charged one of the crew to serve him; I had no wish to see him, and he did not emerge even once.

I began to think of our times in Messina. Had he always been beyond reproach? I recalled the time that he had duped me into spying on Beatrice and the lady Guglielma at the Tarantella, a 'jape' that had led to the dark lady's death. And if he was wrong then, could he have been mistaken about Beatrice? No; for I had seen her in the poet's arms right on the very spot where she had once embraced me. Surely I could trust my own eyes? I could not lay every sin at the prince's door.

And yet, there was little doubt that, through his cutting of the anchor – an act of panic and, yes, cowardice – he had put our lives in very great peril. He was not the prince I had thought him. He was a puppet, just as I had seen in Sicily, all shiny armour and wind and roar, but no substance. I thought then of the strange Spanish knight who had prepared us for the Naumachia. He had tried to tell me that true honour did not live in the outward show. And yet I had tied my banner to an empty kettle. Such thoughts kept me wakeful as much as my hunger.

At night I now escaped my tortured bed and I began to sit out on deck in the very same place that I spent my days. I would wrap myself in sackcloth and look at the skies. The moon was untrustworthy, shifting every night, waxing and waning, serving only to tell me of the passage of time, of the rations that were fast running out. It was Santiago today; by next Santiago we would have even less to eat. Would we then turn on each other, as savages did in the Africas, as we had in my nightmare, and devour the flesh from each other's limbs?

I looked at my fellow sailors, who were using those very limbs to play a desultory game of *Scopa* on the moonlit deck. I had not the heart to join in. I could not hold the *settebello* in my hand – the card would burn me. I had given my best card to one woman, and one woman alone – I could not hand it to a scruffy sailor. I missed Beatrice with a dreadful pang at that moment, and decided to look for her in the stars.

I sought the constellation she had shown me, that wonderful, terrible night on the dunes. I tilted my head back to rest on the mainmast. I stared up at the stars studding the night until my eyes watered. I had thought, before this night, that the stars were uniform, regular diamonds sprinkled across the heavens. That night I learned that some twinkled and glimmered, some did not. Some were diamonds indeed, but some were yellow, some red, some green. The sky was a treasure house.

At last among the gems I found Cassiopeia's chair just above the fighting top upon the mast. I remembered the story of the vain queen seated in her silver throne, who was enamoured of her own beauty. By the foot of the chair sparkled Beatrice's star, the *stella nova* that had appeared at the hour of her birth. It seemed to shine bright and constant. But if the moon was tricky, unfaithful, were the stars to be trusted? Could I rely on Beatrice's star?

I went back to the cabin and gathered writing materials. I had expected to use these instruments to write blithe letters home, or even to Beatrice, to tell her of my magnificent exploits. Now I took them on deck with a hurricane lamp and by its light I wrote our course, the watchword of the day, and a picture of Cassiopeia's constellation riding directly above the mast. I annotated my charts with our speed and wind direction. If the heavens *were* fixed, perhaps, this way, the constant stars could guide us home. '*Constant stars . . .*' I scribbled, '*in them I read such art . . .*' I scribbled till the small hours, but somehow in the darkest part of the night, when the stars were brightest and biggest, somewhere in my scribblings science turned to poetry and my sextant to a sestet. Before I knew it, in the marginalia of my almanac were the beginnings of a sonnet. I woke at dawn, stiff in the sacking, and read over my words in the grey dawnlight; my writings seemed to be more about Beatrice than the stars, and I could see where the pen had trailed away and I had finally slept. But at least I *had* slept, untroubled by hunger-fuelled nightmares.

But on that next morning of The Angels, we found another man dead. Hunger had already taken a dozen of the crew, and this one, like them, was thrown from the bows without even a prayer to follow him into the water. We were too weak to even observe his passing.

We who were left were a sorry collection of knights. Our hair and beards grew long and unkempt, and we could not wash our persons or our clothes unless we wished to clamber into the icy sea. This was a perilous undertaking, for it was necessary to cling on to the ropes, for which we had no strength. And if the waves did not take you, you would almost certainly catch a chill; shivering through the night in wet attire. Disease was rife aboard ship, and we had had to cast as many corpses overboard in the last month from the fever as from starvation. Our ship's surgeon, with little regard for his obligations, was one of the first to die; and those that lived suffered greatly – weeping sores, hacking coughs and buckled limbs were commonplace. It was not unusual to see a tooth lying upon the deck where it had fallen from diseased gums. It was as if, having no food to chew upon, our incisors had become redundant.

As we neared Scotland there was no more leisure to daydream. Because of the poor quality of our charts we were compelled to hug the coasts, so there was the constant fear of running aground. The Scottish shoreline seemed an infinity of the same sooty cliffs, the same rocky beaches, the same alien seabirds which mocked us with their screeching cries day and night but never stooped low enough for us to catch them for food. Sometimes strange peoples, savages in fur and plaid, would wade into the sea and hurl missiles at us. Fortunately no one in Scotland seemed to own an arquebus or a cannon, so we were never in any real danger; but although the missiles never reached us the force of their hatred did, and I was forced for the first time to question Philip's conception of the loyalties in the north.

Claudio, the captain and I had discussed, many times, the notion of appealing for supplies in Scotland, for the king had maintained that in those lands the natives were more loyal to the true religion than the red-haired queen. But these fire-eyed savages were openly hostile, and looked as if they were more likely to worship a tree or a rock than the Catholic God. And yet; I wondered how we looked to them, almost as savage, I'd warrant. I myself had not prayed since I asked God to shift us from the fire ships. And the crew were a godless lot; the chaplain had followed the surgeon into a briny grave in short order, and thus our souls as well as our bodies were forfeit. I had not heard mass said once upon the ship. I wondered whether the Spanish were really any more godly than the inhabitants of this beleaguered island.

Claudio was the one devout on this heretic ship. I often caught him at prayer when I knocked at his cabin, and he would always finish his devotions unashamedly and cross himself before he rose to greet me. As the men became less observant he became more so; and, perhaps as a reaction to the savages and the dark and hellish crags, he began to say mass on deck every morning and night with the zeal of a missionary. Some men came along to hear him and prayed fervently, eyes squeezed tight shut, as they asked God and Santiago for deliverance. Some came along for the familiarity of the words – the balm of acquaintance took them, for that brief half-hour, home again to their village church or their family chapel. Some came along, as I did myself, to make a landmark in their day; to relieve the unknowable tedium of those hours on a cold grey sea, to differentiate between the hour that had gone before and the hour that was to come. Claudio cut a noble figure – he was as bearded and as long haired as the rest of us; but on him the state of keen hunger gave new planes to his face, and he assumed the air of a religious ascetic. He officiated well, and I remembered with a jolt he was the nephew of an archbishop.

Claudio and I took to meeting each night, now that it was too cold to go upon deck, in his cabin or mine. We invited the captain but each time he demurred until we stopped asking him. I suspected that, with his strict adherence to rank, Bartoli thought that he should not mix with officers. I thought that we had sailed past such conventions; besides, Claudio and I were not so noble. I was of a gentleman's family, and Claudio was a count of commerce, ennobled by trade and moneylending, a baron of the banknote. But the captain clung to the chain of command as if it were a rescue rope that would save him from the deeps. I wondered whether it had become his comfort, as Sicily and Beatrice were mine; if he let it go, he would be lost.

So Claudio and I now spent every evening in each other's company. We each made efforts with our appearance before our 'dinner', tidying our hair and straightening our clothes; comforted by such conventions. We sat at the board together, with empty plates before us, and toyed with wine glasses with nothing in them. As we had nothing to eat nor drink, we talked.

In a short space I knew everything about him; more than I had learned in the preceding months in Venice, on the road and in Sicily. I heard of a childhood spent in Florence, educated by monks. Of a mother who left his father for another. Of an elder brother who died at twenty. Of a father who spent his time administering the Medici coffers and thought more of his banking tables than of his sons. I heard the minutiae too – I saw the scar on Claudio's knee where he'd fallen from his horse at the age of ten, I heard of the leather knight his father once brought him from Lombardy, with a detachable helm, the only present his father ever gave him. I talked too; of my riverside house in Padua and my loving parents, of my friend Sebastian. Of how, as a child, I'd made the noble boys laugh and they'd let me share the swordfighting lessons my father couldn't afford.

And at length, inevitably, we spoke of Sicily. That night of the mass, I asked him the question that had been in my mind since I'd heard him intone the paternoster, and seen comfort steal over the faces of the starving sailors.

'If we ever quit this ship,' I began, which was the manner in which we began all conversations about the future, 'will you enter the Church?'

He spun the fine crystal goblet between his fingers. 'No.' He smiled. 'I thought of it once, before my brother died. But now I will be expected to enter the bank.' He sounded wistful.

'You don't mind?'

He looked surprised. 'Not at all. My father's plans are in accord with my own, for he wishes me to marry a well-born woman, and have children.'

And so, in that manner, our conversation returned to Sicily, as if it had never left. 'Hero?' I asked.

'Yes. You know how much I liked her before we went to wars. If we ever quit this ship, I will go directly to Sicily, and claim her if she is still free.'

My heart gave a lurch. 'I am sure that she will wait. For it seemed to me that the two of you formed an attachment which had already grown into a mountain of affection before we left her father's house.'

I tried to be happy for him; I *was* happy for him, but felt a pang below my heart that was nothing to do with hunger.

Claudio looked at me keenly. 'The prince told me what passed between you and the Lady Beatrice. I am heartily sorry that the lady was untrue.'

It was a shock to hear her name; a shock to hear her termed so. *Untrue.*

In my private thoughts Beatrice had been flawless, and mine. But now in conversation with my friend my daydreams of Sicily receded and showed themselves for what they were; insubstantial, airy dreams, golden bubbles pricked and burst by the reality of sharp words. Unspoken, my reveries were boundlessly comforting to me; but once they were articulated, I had to accept the bare facts. Beatrice was untrue.

Unthinking, I raised my empty glass to my lips to purchase time, a reflex that had been a lifetime in the making. Now, I had not spoken a word of Beatrice's transgression to Claudio. I had no wish to besmirch her reputation if she did not wed her poet, and if they did wed, it would extenuate the forehand sin. I would not have expected the prince to tattle about such matters like a washerwoman; once again, he had let me down. I looked at Claudio over the glass. We had not mentioned Don Pedro either since his cowardly act had sent us upon this fool's voyage; perhaps, in this intimate moment, it was time.

'I had thought . . .' I began, then abandoned caution. What did it matter what I said? The chances of ever getting home were vanishingly small. 'I have been wondering if my lord prince was mistaken. About Lady Beatrice.'

'In what way?'

'I do not rightly know. But I recognise now that he is not . . . infallible.'

Claudio lowered his eyes. I could see that his breeding fought with his desire to mention Don Pedro's dishonour. 'I accept that the prince has made certain . . . errors on this voyage. But in the case of the lady, I believed it to be the case that you saw her transgression with your own eyes?'

'Yes.'

'What exactly did you see?'

'I saw her embrace a man upon the beach.'

'A man with whom she was acquainted?'

'Yes.'

'And he himself was free? And of an age and class to pay suit to her?'

'Yes.'

'And there is no chance that he was her brother or any other relation by blood?'

'No. He was the poet who attended a number of Leonato's entertainments, by the name of Michelangelo Florio Crollalanza.'

Claudio let forth a sigh. 'Then I am afraid, my friend, that her actions are unforgivable. If I saw a woman of whom I was enamoured embracing a man thus, she would be dead to me. A woman must be beyond reproach, but, furthermore, beyond *suspicion*. The slightest lightness of conduct must place her beneath your notice. The conclusion must be that if she went on to wed this gentleman then she is guiltless, but married. And if she did not, then she is just as lost to you, for such behaviour cannot be overlooked.' He leaned forward and the candlelight struck the lean angles of his face. 'Think of it; in a year, two years, you would be wearing the cuckold's horns upon your forehead. You would question the parentage of your children. You would be wed to unquietness all your life.'

Sometimes it was hard to recall that Claudio was younger than I. He had a certain wisdom beyond his years. I had been ready to forgive; but I knew he was right; I put down the glass. 'Then I will hereby swear never to marry; and will beseech you in this empty glass to toast and join me.' I borrowed a smile from somewhere. 'But as I know you will not, if we ever quit this ship I will help you to this honourable sacrament with the lady Hero, for at least we know that *she* is very well worthy.'

Under a mask of jollity I clinked my crystal goblet with Claudio's, and we talked of other things.

After that evening my spirits sank even lower. Now I could not even think of Beatrice with impunity – Claudio was right; married or not she was lost to me. Shivering in my sacking one grey noon I dolefully watched the inhospitable coast. Now I saw crags and sea-lochs, and strange slug-grey creatures draped over the rocks, whiskered like a dog and as big as a man. The creatures eyed me back, and as the ship passed they made their ungainly way down the shingle to the sea. Once in the water they suddenly became as lithe as mermaids; and I wondered whether they were sailors who had become enchanted, for there was not a soul to be seen on the shingle, for mile upon nautical mile.

And then, as I watched, I did see someone.

There, on the rocky coast, was a body; emaciated, wearing what had once been a Spanish sailor's livery and very, very dead. Next to him lay another. And another.

My legs as lead-heavy as my heart, I quietly fetched the captain and Claudio, and pointed to the graveyard upon the shingle.

'Can we distract the men somehow? Get them below?' For I knew what this sight would do to morale.

'I will batten down all hands, all but the watch-standers,' agreed the captain, but before he could send for the drummer, Claudio said, 'Too late.' He nodded aft, to where the men were shouting and gathering.

There was nothing to do but watch, together, as we made our slow progress past the scores of bodies.

'We should count them,' said Claudio with great presence of mind, and got out his tables.

I do not know what had befallen these men on the beach, but they were tangled together anyhow, limbs interwoven in a terrible casual embrace. Blank eyes stared at the skies and reflected the blue. There was not a wound among them, nor a drop of blood to be seen. Had they starved? Drowned? Or just given up and lain down together?

'One thousand souls, or thereabouts,' said Claudio, once we'd passed the next cove and the grisly view was out of our sight. As I settled back in place under the mainmast I could not help thinking that, by some awful prescience, we had seen our own deaths; that the men on the beach were the crew of the *Florencia.*

Act IV scene viii

The Castello Scaligero, Villafranca di Verona

Beatrice: I stood behind my father's great chair and watched him write my name on the *impalmamento*, the marriage contract.

The slick black ink dried under his hand, sealing my fate. I was trapped by those words; those black spidery lines were threads fit to bind me like Ariadne. The name of the gentleman hardly mattered, but I watched my father inscribe it below mine. *PARIS*.

My father told me little of this man, this word on a contract who was now to be my future. Paris was a young count of Verona; he had a good fortune and much land, not just in Italy but in the Germanic Habsburg lands, where his bloodline had originated. But what marked him out in eligibility was that he was related to the Capuletti, and staunchly of that party. Now my father had abandoned his impartiality, he would move against the Montecchi with swift decisiveness.

My father had been away from the castle for a brace of days, as he had travelled to Verona to meet with my intended for the *sponsalia*, a meeting of the male members of the marrying families. No women were admitted to such conventions, not even the bride. I had never been acquainted with Paris, despite being raised in the very best of Veronese society, for he had been at the university when I had lived at home. So I was reduced to finding out snippets about my future husband from the servants who had accompanied my father. But all I ever heard tell of the gentleman, in the kitchens and courts, was that he was a 'man of wax'; so perfect a specimen of a man, in form and person, that he might have been fashioned of tallow. I tried to console myself that, however little I knew about him, he was reputed so; but in truth I did not like the sound of a waxen husband. Wax was changeable, wax could wane, wax could melt and be broken like a seal. But I had no say whatsoever in the matter. I was trapped, so I did not know why my father had summoned me from my chamber to watch him write. He signed the *impalmamento* with a flourish, daubed wax by his name and made his imprimatur with his seal ring. The ladder of the Della Scala congealed within the wax, trapped too.

'Signed and sealed.' I sneered, with the barely veiled insolence I had employed since I'd heard my fate. I'd pleaded, cajoled and scolded at first, but my father was implacable. I was to be married, and that was that, so now I'd settled upon scorn. 'May I go now?'

'No.' My father set the parchment by to dry.

'But that is all? The business is complete?'

'Not quite.'

He pointed his quill to the studded door. As if bidden by the gesture the door opened, and eight figures filed in. They were robed in scarlet, and all wore white gloves. All except one – the fellow that led them wore a surgeon's cap, and his hands were bare.

My skin chilled. 'Who are they?'

My father was silent.

'Father, who are these gentlemen?'

'You were in Sicily for the summer. We have to make sure that some knave did not take your maidenhead.'

I laughed, hollowly, and the sound rolled around the keep. I thought he was jesting. Then I thought of Benedick, of the night in the dunes, of how close I came. 'Is my word not enough?'

He looked at me then, his light eyes veiled. 'The Count Paris is a powerful man. The union of our lands will vanquish the Montecchi for ever. We cannot give him,' he said precisely, 'a rotten orange.'

'But I am a princess of Villafranca,' I protested. But the red figures encircled me. Red had always been a colour of comfort, red meant our pennant, red stone meant the Della Scala castle. Now it was the colour of fear. 'No,' I cried in a panic, as the figures grew closer. 'Please, Father. Don't let them.'

My father waved his long fingers at the fellow in the close cap, the fellow without the gloves. 'Baldi is a surgeon, and these others are men of medicine; the seven requisite witnesses to your virginity. Lie down.'

'But Father . . .'

'*Lie down.*' He did not shout – my father never shouted. Even at the death of Tebaldo I had never heard him cry out. But his quiet voice cut like a blade, and I was afraid of him. The kites screeched from the rafters, as if they mocked me.

Hopelessly, I lay down on the great table where we ate our dinner every night. Baldi, the surgeon, carefully turned up my skirts from the knee; once, twice, as if he made a bed.

I had expected the shame, but I had not expected it to hurt so much. His hands were cold, hard. He touched me where no one had ever touched, where *I* had not even touched.

I looked fixedly at the rafters of the red-stone tower, and saw the shadows of the kites flitting from their conical nests. I took my mind away, to Sicily, to Syracuse, where a sparrow had fallen dead at the feet of the Archbishop of Monreale. Anything to take my mind away from the dreadful probing.

Silent tears ran from my eyes and into my ears. The dreadful irony was not lost on me – in order to ensure that I was untouched by a man's hand, this man, this *stranger*, could prod and probe in my most intimate woman's parts. After an age the terrible fingers withdrew, out of me, away from me, and the skirts were folded down again.

'She is *intacta.*'

The others nodded in corroboration. I was innocent. But they were wrong – I was not, not any more. Not after this. And forever more, this man, Baldi, sometime surgeon of Prince Escalus, would be the first man to touch me intimately. Whatever the future held, whomever I married, he would be the first. I did not even know his given name.

My father took up his pen again, and passed it to the surgeon, to the hand which had touched me. Baldi laid down more ink in my cause; a confirmation of my virginity. This time my father sealed the words with sand, then blew the sand away. This document had to be dried well; for the covenant of virginity was to be conveyed to Verona, and placed in the hand of my future husband. More ink to bind me. And in a week, I would follow that trail of ink, in person, to be betrothed to Count Paris.

The medical men filed out, until there was just my father and me in the room, and the kites screeching in the rafters. I clambered down, gingerly, from the table, my insides aching. I stood straight, and walked unsteadily to him.

'What would you have done?'

My father had a trick of staring with his light blue eyes, unblinking, like a gazehound. He looked at me that way now, and stroked his long, noble nose with his forefinger.

'What would you have done if I had not been found a maid?'

He looked at me, still unblinking. 'Then I would have been childless.'

I took his meaning – if a woman was not chaste, she might as well be dead.

I was suddenly angry with him, furious. I was no longer afraid of him. He would not strike at my life now I was proved virtuous. But my fury was impotent. I needed a plan, an escape.

'Tell me something of him. Of Paris.'

My father did not look up from his writing. 'He is a man of wax.'

'A man of wax!' I parroted back. 'I have heard him called so all about this castle from dungeon to turret. I need more.'

Still my father wrote his record of my maidenhead.

I put my hand on the parchment, before his pen, halting the wet black thread. 'Tell me something else of him. You *owe* me that, after what I've just endured.'

He looked up at me then, speculatively, with his pale eyes. 'He is very learned. He likes his books.' He lifted my hand from the page, and continued his writing. There was ink on my hand, as there had been the day I'd met Benedick, and he had kissed it away. My father said no more, and did not look up again, but he had said enough. I knew what I must do.

I climbed the winding stair set in the wall of the red-stone tower, the tallest stair in the Veneto. As I climbed farther and farther from the table, and the scene of that dreadful examination, I felt more confident. I looked at the Della Scala red stone, and climbed each stair with my father's words in my ears. *Stairs divide us from the poor, stairs keep us safe*, and then, at the next turn, *He is learned, he loves his books*. I began to see a way forward, to formulate a plan.

In the library I turned around and around, perusing the books that lined the walls all the way up to the conical turret. Despite the castle's old-world aspect, my father had always been beyond reproach in the respect of his book collection. I passed by his histories of the Veneto, then thought better of it, backtracked and picked out his favourite volume. Then I selected Catullus, most famous son of Verona. Then Dante's *Vita Nuova*. Then Bandello's *Stories*, Ovid's *Ars Amoria*, Boccaccio's *Decameron*. Machiavelli's *Il Principe*. These would be a good start.

I opened the first book, the Catullus. Friendly ink. Words that were not about me, or my dowry or my maidenhead.

Pages where my name was not writ once. Ink had imprisoned me, now ink would set me free. I began to read, and on the hard library stool my poor loins still felt tender from the reach of probing fingers.

Act IV scene ix

The *Florencia,* open sea

Benedick: The sight of the thousand bodies affected the crew profoundly.

Claudio and I attempted to raise morale. The count said mass daily but his congregation dwindled. Some were too weak to attend, some too sick at heart; but some began to question, openly, a God that would so smite their enterprise to leave a thousand Spanish bodies on a beach like seaweed. I would tell jokes that barely raised a smile, as if the men had forgotten how; I carried on, regardless, but my forced humour was an irritant even to myself. Because the length of the voyage had exceeded our early expectations we had been forced to cut rations again, and our daily portions would not, now, keep a ship's rat alive. Men were dying, daily, of starvation.

Now when I sat by the masthead to navigate, a fat gull would settle on the bulwark to peer at me with his hard little agate eyes. I had not even the strength to grab at him, but if I could have, I would have eaten him whole, feathers, beak and all. I knew now that the men on the beach had not drowned, but starved.

I had left something else on that beach with those men. My good humour had gone, my eternal optimism was quashed. The tribulations of the summer, the loss of the one woman ordained by the heavens to stand up with me, seemed as nothing. Now I knew what it was to be a soldier – to see death at close hand.

In this battle I had joined I had not once drawn my sword, nor fired a shot. The two-and-fifty fancy brass guns of the *Florencia* now sat at the bottom of the English Channel, wreathed in seaweed, a playground for fishes. I recalled my conversations with Beatrice, my happy acceptance of the medal of St James, as if being a soldier was no more than wearing a uniform. I shrivelled inside to think of the night I had come to Leonato's masque dressed as a dandy soldier, the night when I'd bandied words at dinner and called a knight an empty kettle. Of the night when I'd performed in the Naumachia like a Barbary monkey. Now I knew I had left my boyhood on the beach of the thousand bodies. I knew, now, the wages of soldiery. All of the thousand men had worn a coat just like mine. Still, I gazed at Beatrice's star every night, and in my brief dreams still saw her face – I vowed that if I ever saw her again, she should know a different Benedick.

The weather matched the mood of the men. It was now, by my calculations, November, and I had never known such cold. Rain, hail and driving snow the like of which I had never seen. On one day – The Angels – our lookout fell from the crow's nest, stiff and dead. When we lifted him to drop him over the stern, his limbs remained taut and frozen, until we threw him into the leaden seas and the salt waters melted him.

It was perhaps fortunate that we had not the leisure to give rein to our doleful thoughts, for we entered a channel that was fiendishly difficult to navigate. We were beset on all sides by myriad rocky islands, a deadly archipelago which threatened at every moment to run us aground. Barely a quarter-hour passed without the dreadful sound of planking screaming against underwater crags, and our hearts would leap as we waited for the whole ship to splinter. Captain Bartoli had the thankless choice of taking down the sails to slow us down, in which case our rations would never see us back to Spain, or continuing at our current speed at the constant risk of foundering. The order was given – all but the topsails were lowered; but what we gained in safety we lost in speed, leading to mutterings among the crew. I did not like their unhappy looks, nor the way their discontent united them. They had gone from being hangdogs to a pack of wolves.

On the morning of Trinity a shout went up. The rocky islands had opened up to a broad sound and a wide bay like a bite taken out of the coast. Small cots huddled about the edge of the shore, and smoke wreathed the little chimneys. A castle stood sentinel over the bay, and black mountains rolled away into the distance. But it was neither the mountains nor the houses that claimed our attention. For in the bay nestled a ship.

Captain Bartoli whipped out his spyglass. 'Spanish,' he said at once, easing our troubled minds. 'The *San Juan de Sicilia*.'

I recalled the ship from the muster; one of Duke Egeon's vessels, built at Ragusa. And I'd heard the name since; I remembered we'd seen the ship pulling away from us in the Channel, also heading 'north about', trailing a red wake like an injured hind dragged home from hunting.

Claudio joined us at the helm. 'Did she put in for supplies?' he wondered.

'I do not know,' replied the captain.

The men had all left their posts and were crowding to the starboard side, all gabbling about warm fires, and food, and shelter. 'If another ship has put in for supplies, why mayn't we?' asked the pilot. My mouth began to water involuntarily.

The captain's quarterdeck voice rose above all. 'It is our duty to go back to Spain. Those were our orders from Medina Sidonia, and they have not been countermanded. We have no way of knowing if these northern peoples are loyal to their queen. If they are, we are all dead men.'

This gave the men pause, but the pilot, Da Sousa, spoke up again. 'But if we stay aboard, we are dead anyway. How can we survive another week, another day?'

The captain had an answer to this. 'But the *San Juan* has an anchor, we do not. How do you propose that we make our halt?'

'We can cut the mizzenmast,' said Da Sousa, sensing victory for his position, 'then the lateen sail will trail into the sea. This will create enough drag to halt us in the bay; I have seen it done, once, in the Azores. It is low tide now; we will sit on the sandbar till high tide, then refloat. Then we hoist all sails, and run for Spain.'

'All sails, save one.' Bartoli shook his grizzled head. 'We cannot sacrifice a sail, for the sake of provisions we may not even be able to gather. It is highly unlikely that we will reach Spain on our current ration even with full sail – without the lateen you may add a week to the journey. No, Señor da Sousa,' he said decidedly. 'We must go by. Full sail.'

Da Sousa did not move. There was utter, utter silence on deck.

Bartoli had clearly never had to repeat an order in his life. '*Full sail*, I said.'

The men dispersed insolently slowly, and the captain returned to the helm. I settled myself by the mast, waiting for the well-remembered surge at my back as the sails caught the wind. At least I could look forward to some shelter, for the bellying canvas was as good as a battle tent for keeping off the rain. But something was wrong. The steady, mizzling rain fell unimpeded on my head. I looked up to see slack ratlines and naked crosstrees. The sails had not been raised.

I turned my head to call the captain, and that is when the blow fell.

Act IV scene x

The Palazzo Maffei, Verona

Beatrice: I travelled to Verona alone, and of this I was glad; for I could not carry forth my plan under my father's eye.

I was to sit for my wedding portrait, feast with the Capuletti, and my father was to join me in a week for the wedding on the steps of the Basilica. But I swore such a day would never come. I could not defy my father; I would take my steps in the wedding dance – but only as far as the church door. I could not refuse the Count Paris, but I could make him refuse me. I had just one short week to make it clear to him that I was not the bride for him.

My only company in the carriage was my *cassone*, my dowry chest. The thing was enormous, and left no room for even a maid for me. Its contents were so precious that two armed guards travelled beside the driver, and outriders in the Della Scala colours rode behind. The chest bumped against my feet, bruising my toes in my fancy jewelled boots. Plain and unadorned, the casket reminded me of a coffin. The *cassone* should symbolise a beginning, but it seemed an ending.

As the carriage bounced along the road the contents of the chest bumped about like a wakened body. It was our family treasure knocking to get out – priceless tapestries, garters, jewels, cloth-of-gold. Brass lamps from Byzantium, mirrors from Venice, spices from the Indies, all brought from the four corners of the world to be entombed in this casket. My dowry, my bride price. The thing made me a little afraid.

My heart speeded to keep time with the horses' hoofbeats, for we were near the city walls. I could see the grove of syca- mores near the Porta Palio, and beyond the walls, the looming theatre of the Romans like a great stone 'O'. Once we'd passed below the shadow of the gate I looked for comfort in the famil- iar buildings, for, as at home, the Della Scala were everywhere, writ in red stone. There was the Ponte Scaligeri, with the broad- est arch of any bridge in the world. There was our family church of Santa Maria della Antica; the Scaligeri tombs, with their ornate canopies, crowded in the little courtyard. I'd used to love coming here, to hear the tales of my ancestors; Cangrande I Della Scala, known as the 'big dog' and the first Della Scala ruler of Verona; Cansignorio Della Scala, Mastino II Della Scala. The names were music to me; they made me feel as if I owned the place. Even as a child, the notion that I would one day die and rest here did not trouble me at all. Now, with every red brick I saw, with every ladder blazon wrought in iron or stone, I was reminded of how valuable I was. What a prize. I was not the contents of the *cassone*. I was not myself. I was this city. *Verona* was my dowry. Who would not want to annex such a place? It might be harder to dissuade Paris from my hand than I realised. For as we drew into the Palazzo Erbe, with the beauti- ful frescoes growing on the façades like creeping vines, I realised that the Della Scala ancestral home, the red-stone Casa dei Mercanti, was cheek by jowl with the white Palazzo Maffei, Paris's home. Our union was literally set in stone.

At the gates, one of my father's men handed me down, but it took three of them to carry the *cassone* into the courtyard. The Palazzo Maffei was the last word in elegance, and seemed cen- turies away from the red-stone castle that was my home. It had many modern improvements made to its elegant, filigree façade; three galleries of creamy stone with an elegant balcony over each arcade, fluted semi-columns and large ornamental plaster masks between the snowy tympani. Indoors the elegance continued; marble columns rose to frescoed ceilings, and porphyry floors were polished like glass. In the atrium a vast marble staircase rose in a helix to the upper floors, twisting in on itself like a nautilus. It made my home's rough stone and animal skins look primitive and crude.

I was shown to my chamber – a riot of gilt and glass with cherubs on every cornice – by a smooth maidservant, and there on the coverlet I found a white gown cunningly fashioned into a hundred tiny pleats. There was a girdle of gold vine leaves and a coronet of the same gilded foliage for my hair. The maidservant begged me to change at once, for the wedding portrait was to be taken this very afternoon. Journey-tired but compliant, I slipped into the gown and let the maid loose my curls. I followed her back down the grand white stair to the salon, a great frescoed chamber. It seemed odd to meet one's betrothed for the first time with an artist looking on; but I did not mind for I had no intention of marrying Paris.

There was no one in the room save the artist, who was scratching around with his palettes. But my *cassone* had beaten me here, and was already elevated on a wooden arrangement like an elongated easel, the plain coffer waiting to be decorated with the traditional spousal portrait of the bride and groom. The thought of such a pictorial statement of intent made me nervous but – I raised my chin – placing Paris and me in a picture no more joined us in matrimony than all those lines of ink I'd witnessed. Contracts could be torn; bonds could be rendered void, wooden chests painted over. I knocked on the casket and it boomed hollow. So the treasure had already been taken, inventoried, signed for. More ink.

I walked around the arrangements that had been placed in the middle of the room – there were plants and Romanesque pillars set together like the scenery of a play, hung about with garlands of flowers and arranged like a whimsical rural fantasia from antique times. I put out a finger and touched one of the plaster pillars – it rocked, for it was hollow; just for outward show.

'You like the scene?' It was the artist who spoke, a tall fellow, well favoured for an artisan and dressed in a rustic smock. He was poking at the colours that had been arranged at his easel with a brush; a series of oyster shells, each with a different puddle of colour in the bottom. All the colours that were present in the rainbow, and some that were not.

I turned to him, haughtily; surprised that he should presume to address a princess. 'Well enough. What is the tableau to be?'

'The *Judgement of Paris*, of course,' said he.

I snorted. The count was clearly an egotist; in most cases the *cassone* was decorated with some antique allegory, and usually one to do with a wedding – the story of Esther was very popular. But rarely did the groom choose a subject so self-congratulatory, nor with such a direct reference to his name.

'And now that I have seen you, I cannot imagine anyone else playing the choice of his heart; Helen, the most beautiful woman in the world.' I ignored the compliment, for it did not seem to me that he was quite of the rank to offer it.

'And who will pose for the two goddesses he rejects?'

'Two young Capuletti cousins – Rosaline and Giulietta. But they are stars to your sun; in your presence there could be no other choice.' His brown eyes raked me appreciatively.

This was too much. 'You are saucy, sir. You do not know me.' I backed away. 'Sometimes our outward shows do not correspond with our inner parts. The most beautiful vessel can be hollow,' I said, thinking of the pillar. 'Had Paris actually *conversed* with Helen of Troy before they wed, he might have found her wanting. He might have wished he had chosen another prize.'

'I do not think so.' He came from behind the easel, took my hand, and kissed it. 'This Paris is very happy with his choice.'

Then I knew. This was the count himself, and my intended. I

cursed that I had been caught so off guard. This was a fine start to our counter-courtship. I attempted to recover my poise. 'My lord! Forgive me.'

'There is nothing to forgive, for I was at fault. I took advantage of your misprision. I was amusing myself, and I am sorry. In truth I am a keen painter – though with no great skill – and Signor Cagliari, our esteemed artist, indulges me in my interest in his pigments. Ah, here is Cagliari, and he brings the ladies with him.'

A man wearing a velvet biretta entered the room, hung about with cloths and bottles and bristling with brushes. Behind him came two young ladies, dressed in white flowing gowns like myself, with their arms wreathed around each other's waists as if by sticking together they could combat their timidity.

'Perhaps I can make amends by making proper introductions this time? May I present Rosaline Capuletti-Maffei, a cousin of mine. And of course, you know Giulietta Capuletti – a fair cousin of yours I believe.'

I might have used the word fair to describe his cousin, but not mine; Giulietta, whom I'd known as a girl, had grown into a plain, sallow little thing, with such a dolorous expression that it seemed she might burst into tears at any moment. However, on seeing me, she broke from Rosaline's arms and favoured me with such a fervent embrace that she nearly squeezed the breath out of me. I was surprised at such a heartfelt greeting, for I'd never known her well; she'd been too young to be my playmate, and I was always more of a child for a sword than a sampler. But Paris drew me aside solicitously. 'I'm afraid she has taken the death of your brother Tebaldo very much to heart, and grieves most piteously for her cousin.'

Again, I was taken aback – Giulietta had had even less to do with Tebaldo than with me. And yet – I caught my breath – I had been away for some time; perhaps they had formed an understanding? Perhaps there was to be another wedding before that young Montecchi had taken Tebaldo's life and got himself banished for his crime. I looked kindly on the little maid – her grief would certainly add conviction to her portrayal of a woman rejected.

For the rest of the afternoon we all stood as still as we could, while the artist painted our likenesses on the broad front panel of the *cassone*. Paris himself, now clothed in an ochre cloak, reclined in a golden chair and held out a glossy green apple to me. I stood slightly before Rosaline and Giulietta, smiling down on him till my cheeks ached. It was not the most restful afternoon I have ever spent, for Signor Cagliari had me balance my weight on one foot and slightly point the other in a Grecian attitude, and of course I had to reach out one hand to the apple. But happily, Paris and I could converse with each other through the course of the afternoon – if through rigid jaws – and I thought I knew how to begin my assault.

The irony was not lost upon me; I was to play the exact opposite part to my goddess in the tableau. My task was to urge Paris *not* to choose me.

I had thought long and hard about how to achieve this. I could not risk my reputation by pretending to be loose of morals, besides which, my humiliating examination in the red-stone tower had put my chastity beyond doubt. And I could not pretend to be a *religieuse* – a Pope-holy dame longing for the nunnery – for a simple enquiry to my father would give the lie to that charade. No; I had to be myself, but even more myself, in brighter, bolder colours like stained glass after the rain. I had always been clever, I had always been outspoken, I had always been well read; I just had to be that. My plan was simple. My notion was that no man wanted a wife who was cleverer than him, and spoke boldly enough to show the world that she was. To this end I had read every book in my father's library, new texts and old. And one of the stories I'd read repeatedly – in Homer, in Ovid, in Lucian – was this one. The Judgement of Paris.

'My lord,' I began, 'I'm afraid I must begin our acquaintance by correcting you.'

The two Capuletti maids gave a gasp – the first and last sound I heard them utter for the whole afternoon – as if shocked that I would speak so to their noble cousin. Even the artist paused with his brush in the air poised between palette and *cassone*.

'Then please,' replied Paris tightly, 'tell me how I've erred.'

'You spoke just now of Helen of Troy,' I said through my teeth, smiling fixedly for the benefit of Signor Cagliari, 'but Helen was *not* one of the ladies offered to Paris. There were three goddesses only, Hera, Athena and Aphrodite.

'The judgement we depict took place at the marriage of Peleus and Thetis, parents of Achilles.' I looked down at the count, long limbed and easy in his Grecian smock and sandals. 'Eris, goddess of discord, was excluded from the gathering, and in revenge she threw an apple into the company, inscribed τη καλλίστη; which – I am sure you know – means "for the fairest one". The goddesses disputed who was the fairest, and asked Zeus to judge them, but Zeus gave the honour to your name-sake Paris.' His smile began to waver. 'The goddesses attempted to bribe Paris, and Athena offered him Helen of Troy, considered to be the world's most beautiful woman. Paris chose Athena, and she was granted the apple. And so you see, although I appreciate your compliment greatly, its provenance was quite faulty.' I had to take a breath.

'I see,' replied Paris rigidly. 'Forgive me.'

'Do not trouble yourself,' I said kindly. 'It is a popular misconception.'

I let a silence fall, just long enough for the models to relax, and assume that my extraordinary lecture was over. But I was not done.

'A very little study of Collothus or Apuleius would furnish you with the details. I think it is Apuleius who writes: "There and then the Phrygian youth spontaneously awarded the girl the golden apple in his hand, which signalled the vote for victory.""

'I am obliged to you,' said Paris. 'I will certainly study the passage.'

The apple that he held out to me was beginning to shiver, but whether with the natural tremors of fatigue or annoyance I could not tell.

'Of course,' I said pleasantly, 'strictly speaking, the apple should not be green.'

Only Paris's evident breeding could mask the sigh in his voice. 'Why not?'

'The apple came from the Garden of the Hesperides, Hera's own orchard. The apples, which conferred immortality, were coloured gold.'

'Well, let us hope that Signor Cagliari has the wit to change one colour for another.'

A further silence.

'And some say that the fruit may not even have been an apple.'

This time my intended had no reply.

'Such "golden apples" were most probably oranges. But in ancient times there was no knowledge of the orange outside of Levantine and Eastern lands, so there may have been a mistranslation.'

I was even annoying myself, and I made a pleasing contrast to our two cousins; silent as the grave, eyes downcast, they were the perfect example of maidenly modesty.

'I am afraid, at this rate,' said Paris, 'that the *cassone* portrait will be a sad disappointment to you, Lady Beatrice.' And the count was silent for the rest of the sitting.

I held my peace too, but inside I was singing. My plan was working.

When the sun began to lower outside, Cagliari put up his brushes and Paris released us from our poses. 'I thank you, ladies,' he said. 'Please, take your ease until we feast tonight.'

I thought for a triumphant moment that he was going to leave with no further courtesies, but he turned to me at the last. 'Oh, and I believe this is rightfully yours, *Athena*.' He put the apple in my hand, smooth and round and heavy. I looked at him, and he winked, the ghost of a smile about his mouth.

I stood amongst the false flowers and hollow pillars long after everyone had gone, clutching the fruit, and biting my lip.

I had amused him, not annoyed him.

This was going to be harder than I'd imagined.

Act IV scene xi

The *Florencia*, Tobermory Bay

Benedick: I woke with a headache.

I located the centre of the pain just above my right eyebrow, and a sticky ooze dripped into the corner of my eye, turning my vision red.

I tried to raise my hand to wipe the blood away; could not. I was tied to the mast and the same hempen rope bound Claudio and the captain. Bartoli was still unconscious, but Claudio was wakeful, his pate broken too. 'They are doing it,' he said, 'they are felling the tree.'

For a moment I thought him light headed from the blow, then I craned aft to see Da Sousa and the others, armed with ship's axes, chopping at the mizzenmast. As we watched the timber gave and the great trunk fell – the creamy canvas crashed into the sea like a whale's tail, sending an enormous splash of salt spray high. The lateen sail settled and trailed in the sea, bellying with water as it had once filled with wind. I felt that, as the mast fell, all our hope of getting to Spain and the sun were dashed.

The pilot ran past us without a guilty glance and took the wheel, spinning it under his hand like a cartwheel, turning it hard to starboard into the bay. It was the work of a moment, and we felt the bump and drag of the deadwood upon sand, and a great lurch as the ship ran aground. The timbers screamed, the ropes lashed and snapped and the *Florencia* lurched perilously before rolling to a standstill. For a moment there was an awful silence, while the ship gently rocked with the wash of the tide, suspended on its sandbar. Then there was a flurry of activity as the mutineers let down the ship's boats, and, battling the tide, began to row to shore.

'And now,' said Claudio, 'we will see if the Scots are armed.'

But only women and children clustered at the shoreline; the children pointing, the women hiding their infants in their skirts, for I'd heard tell that Elizabeth had told her subjects that the Spanish devour babes. I assumed the men of the village were off fishing, or working in the fields, and I feared for these simple Scots. I wondered at their menfolk leaving them so vulnerable, for there was already a Spanish galliass in the bay. Perhaps the men of the *San Juan de Sicilia* had already vanquished the local fellows; but I remembered the red wake, thought of our own sorry state of near-starvation, and thought it more likely the Scots would have had the better of the Spaniards.

With the crew gone, we attempted to free ourselves, but in vain. Claudio and I could not reach our daggers, nor each other's. The captain was still unconscious, and unarmed. I smashed a nearby hurricane lamp with my foot, and desperately tried to reach the shards of glass, but they were just out of my grasp. We tried frantically to wriggle out of the ropes but ended up chafing our hands till they bled, for there was nothing we could do against the captain's bulk, slumped forward over the ropes. We were trapped, tied like mules, a little trinity alone on this massive hull, with the ship shifting and creaking. If the *Florencia* had been holed on impact, we would go down with it, and if the crew were not back by high tide, we would be carried away wherever the wind took us, until we starved.

There was nothing to do but watch and wait. I looked first to the shoreline.

In the distant bay our sailors were causing havoc in the little village. One house was on fire. I heard the screams of women, and babes, and the barking of dogs. I saw one sailor chasing a goat down the beach, as hen's eggs dropped from his pockets and a link of sausages flew from his belt like a pennant. It would have been comical were it not an action so utterly devoid of honour. I could not see that any of them would live out the night; and they were endangering us as much as them, for they were engendering hatred for every soldier of Spain.

Then I looked to the other ship, the *San Juan de Sicilia*. It looked black against the dull sky, as if it had been burned, and the shifting mists parted to show shredded sails. It was a galliass of our own class, slightly smaller than the *Florencia*. It looked ghostly, an impression assisted by the fact that there did not seem to be a living soul aboard. By moving my body until the ropes cut, I could just see at least one of the ship's boats still lashed to the side; a small pinnace, such as those in which our mutineers had rowed to shore. I had a sudden notion.

'Is Bartoli dead?' I mouthed to Claudio. Unaccountably, I felt that we must whisper.

'I cannot tell,' said Claudio, low voiced too. 'If he wakes, together we may be able to get free. But what then? We cannot get to shore. They have taken the boats.'

'We can get to the other ship. They have their boats still.'

'How?'

'A bosun's chair,' said an unsteady voice. It was Bartoli, sitting upright now.

We lost no time. With the three of us conscious we could lift the ropes; but by the movement of the pale disc of sun beyond pewter clouds it still took us above an hour to shift the first loop over our shoulders. Then it was easy; we were free in an instant, and stood unsteadily, joints creaking, broken heads pounding, limbs paining us as the blood and vital humours rushed back into deprived regions.

Bartoli set about rigging a bosun's chair. On our starboard side he tossed a rope on a grappling hook to the other ship, and Claudio, as the slightest, shinned across. The rope was looped round the balustrade of the *San Juan* and the hook tossed back, and a small stool attached to slide across on a pulley.

Bartoli, who was more injured and elderly than we, stayed with the ship, as he had sworn. He would receive and discipline any mutineers who were minded to reboard, and operate the bosun's chair for us if we needed it to return. Only when I was dangling over the open water with the golden chased lettering of the *San Juan de Sicilia* drawing ever closer did I wonder what we would find on this ship of ghosts.

There was no one on deck, and no sign of life whatsoever. Behind the mainmast I lifted the hatch I knew must lead to the hold, for the ship was a mirror of our own; but something was wrong here. I suddenly felt, holding open the hatch, as I had felt when I saw the thousand bodies. A dread foreboding crept over my flesh, and I felt that a nameless evil was emanating from the hold.

I dropped down into the dark, landing lightly on my feet, and held my lantern high. What I saw there reminded me of nothing so much as the fresco in the church of Santa Maria della Carmine in Padua, which I'd perused, round eyed, as a child at mass. Terrible, skeletal twisted souls, eyes open, unable to escape their fate. I could see, here and there, the livery of St James, the same colours I wore. Their saint had abandoned them. Worst of all, I saw gnawed limbs and bite marks, where men had tried to chew upon their own or others' flesh.

I had to pull my chemise over my mouth, for the stench was terrible. I did not fear contagion, for I thought I knew what had taken these men. It was another premonition for the men of the *Florencia*. They had starved.

'They are all dead,' I yelled to Claudio, my own voice a strange comfort to me. 'That is why they did not go ashore.'

'Any provisions?'

I did not even have to look; no man would devour another

while there were even the meanest victuals left. 'No.' I turned to go, but something caught my eye.

In the bilge were a pile of chests with brass boundings. I put down my lantern, forced one open with my dagger and saw a dull gleam. I put my hand in the chest, and countless coins slid through my fingers. I carried one to the hatch and held up the coin. A gold *real*. I turned about, the bodies all but forgotten.

Treasure.

A hundred chests of it. Terrible, inedible treasure. Chests of gold that, at the end, any one of these men would have happily traded for a single loaf of bread. Useless, priceless ballast which slowed down their voyage so that they could not make it even this far.

'Claudio!' I called, softly now. It did not occur to me to keep the find to myself as some men would. Claudio dropped down, and recoiled from the dead men, but I led him to the corner. His eye widened. 'How much?'

'A fortune.'

He turned to me. 'Say the words.'

I looked at him in confusion.

'Say the words. Claim it.'

'What about you?' I asked. 'You found it alongside me.'

'Dear Benedick,' he said. 'If I spent a bag of gold every hour from now till the day of my death, the Medici would still have chinks to spare. But this gold could be the making of you; could elevate you from gentleman to prince. If you claim it, by the laws of trove the king must give you a share. Say the words,' he urged again. 'For nobility can be bought as well as bred; who knows that better than I?'

Suddenly I was back in El Escorial, that dreaming, amber afternoon. I could hear the injunction of the chancellery legislators. 'Let each man who finds a trove lay his hands upon it and say the following form of words . . . His Majesty shall vouchsafe a tithe share of the treasure to the finder, and ennoble him in the rolls of Spain.'

I put my hands on the cold, inedible treasure and spoke the words. 'I, Benedick Minola of Padua, claim this treasure for Philip of Spain.' By the termination of the sentence, I was rich.

We laboriously lifted each chest to the deck, one by one, our weakened muscles protesting, our puny limbs barely able to lift the heavy caskets.

At last we were done, but as we shifted the last chest, a figure lurched out of the dark as though the treasure had birthed him. Two white eyes peered at us, and Claudio and I recoiled as one with a cry. A blade flashed too, but I caught at the hand that held it, and disarmed the fiend as easily as if he were a child. He collapsed in my grip and began to weep like a babe.

We dragged him to the light, but he gave me no resistance; he was all bone and skin, as light as a bird. We pulled him up on deck and he was not even as weighty as one of the chests of treasure. The drear daylight gave relief to his features but could not illuminate his skin. He was a Moor.

I spoke to him in Italian, and Spanish. Claudio had a little English, and less French. But the Moor just rolled his eyes and waggled his tongue; that silent member was as dry as cured meat and whiter than his skin. Then I remembered the last Moor I had met, and the farewell the water-diviner had bid me in the gardens of El Escorial. *'As-salaam alaykum.'*

As if in a dream, he replied to me. *'Wa' alaykum.'*

I sat, so that I could be at his level, for I did not think he could stand. Claudio stood over us, unsure of the dark creature we had found. And no wonder, for he was near as hellish a thing as the corpses below. The whites of his eyes were yellow, his orbs wept from the sudden light and I shuddered to think of how long he had been in the dark. His skin was an ashy grey, not the ebony black of the water-diviner, and hung from his bones like boiled leather. The tight wiry curls of his hair and beard had turned a powdery white, an incongruous contrast with his dusky skin.

'Can you speak Catalan?' I asked him in halting accents.

'Yes, and Italian and French.'

'What happened here?' I said in my own tongue.

'All starved,' he replied in passable Tuscan.

'How came the treasure to be here?'

'It is the king's.'

'Did the ship capture it?'

'No,' he said, struggling with his dry tongue. He tried to sit. 'It belongs to His Majesty King Philip II of Spain.'

Jesu, the fellow was loyal; even after his tribulations.

'Yes, and we will return it to him,' I said patiently. I showed him my medal. 'See, I am a knight of Saint James. I will see it done.'

He seemed to collapse then, as if at the end of a long labour, as if his responsibilities were somehow over.

'Pay chests,' he said, sounding short of breath.

I saw then. These were the wages for the victorious knights of the glorious armada.

We left him there to recover while we loaded the chests into the ship's boats, all the time conducting a whispered conversation about what we should do with this strange survivor.

'Leave him,' said Claudio. 'We have no food for him.'

I nodded to the shore. 'And yet we have lost a score of mouths today. We might need an able seaman to replace those defectors.'

Claudio looked at the figure hunched upon the deck. 'If he *is* an able seaman. He looks like a savage.'

'Well, only he can tell us. Been at sea long?' I called to our prisoner.

I could barely hear him. 'Seventeen years. Since Lepanto.'

I turned to Claudio. 'He might be useful,' I said.

Now there was an urgency to our enterprise, for the ship was rocking as the tide came in. Soon the *Florencia* would be afloat again. We cut free the bosun's chair, lowered the fast boats and rowed one each, with fifty chests each aboard and the Moor in my craft. By the time we'd gained the deck of the *Florencia*, eleven of the mutineers had returned with provisions, and were shamefacedly making themselves busy about the ship, having been promised a flogging for the morrow. But there was no sign of the other boat and we were neither willing nor inclined to wait for the remaining mutineers. At sundown the ship lifted from the shore. 'Cut the lateen sail free!' commanded the captain, and the men set about the ropes with their axes. The canvas and rigging of the mizzenmast swirled and darkened in the water, till they sank into the deeps.

As we sailed away torches descended from the hills into the bay like falling stars. The crofters had returned from the fields at the end of the day, and there was just enough light left to see them cut down the remaining mutineers of the *Florencia* – every last man – and leave the bodies lying on the beach.

Act IV scene xii

The Palazzo Maffei, Verona

Beatrice: Over the next week, I got to know Paris well.

In the mornings we would pose for our portrait on the *cassone*, and I would admire the scene that sprung to life under Signor Cagliari's talented hand. In the afternoons, after Paris had spent some hours administering his estates, we would go out, at the hour of *passeggiata*. Then we would mingle among the smart citizens of Verona processing along the beautiful streets in their finery. Always I was chaperoned by the young Capuletti cousins Giulietta and Rosaline.

Paris designed brave entertainments for his womenfolk – he would take us into private houses to see a holy relic, into a secret walled garden to admire a particularly decorative fountain, or a little chapel to see a fine fresco. We were taken to a private menagerie at a villa at Sant'Ambrogio, to see a camelopard; a vast, gentle creature chequered like a harlequin, with a neck so improbably long that I wondered that he could hold up his head. On another day we were taken to see the cabinet of curiosities belonging to one of Paris's German uncles. Peering into the *wunderkammer* we saw fleas dancing on a tiny stage, and fitted with an orchestra of minute instruments. So the count showed us wonders of every scale as if they were *his* dowry.

Once we took a golden barge upon the river and ate our dinner under my family bridge, the Ponte Scaligeri, as musicians played from the arches and fireflies danced in time. Paris made sure I never wanted for anything – he would press delicacies upon me at every turn – succulent shrimps, fat olives, delicate little cakes. I was full to bursting constantly, and when my stomacher began to pain me I started to conceal these foods in my skirt and discreetly drop them on the street or in the river.

And all the time, I talked. It was exhausting. I corrected the poor count relentlessly, even in the matter of works of art that he actually owned. In our tour of the city I regurgitated all that I had read in my father's books about Verona's history and civic politics, pre-empting Paris every time he attempted to tell us about a certain building or landmark.

In the Castello Scaligero in Villafranca there was a dark, dank dungeon. When I was a little girl Tebaldo used to drag me down there and make me scream by showing me various instruments of torture left there to rust since barbarian times. The most dreadful thing of all to me – worse than the instruments that would pierce flesh or tear limbs – was a scold's bridle, wrought of black iron, designed to silence a woman. Once Tebaldo managed to get the thing on me, and I ran around the castle with the bridle on my head, unable to scream, bashing my head against the walls like a fly in a bottle, until my nurse took it off. For days I could taste the metallic tang of iron and blood in my mouth, feel the corrugated metal tongue of the bridle squeezing my own.

If I'd had such a scold's bridle now, I would have donned it myself and strapped the buckle with my own hand. For my voice had become a rattle, and I began to appreciate, for the first time, the objections to being shackled to an unquiet woman.

But the patient Paris bore my corrections admirably, and seemed happy to be instructed in matters of music, literature, architecture and art. I ground my teeth. My plan was not working.

Increasingly desperate, I added to my repertoire of unquietness by always being too hot or too cold, asking for my cloak to be brought to me and taken away, asking for my fan to be fetched and then folded, sending his runners for iced sherbets or warmed wine. I was as contrary as I could be. Again, my intended husband indulged me in every particular, without a word of demurral.

As a matter of fact, despite myself, I began to like him. And on more than one occasion I wished, most heartily, that I had met him before Benedick. For that gentleman, even in his absence, continued to be a thorn in my side, for he troubled me to make constant comparisons between himself and Paris. Paris was tall, but not as tall as Benedick. He was amusing, but nowhere near such a wit. He had fine eyes, and a pleasing countenance, but his features could not compare to that one face that I missed. The only particular in which he would be a superior husband to Benedick was that his taste in diversions and pursuits marched with mine. He loved reading, art and music, whereas Benedick never picked up a book, looked on a picture or could tolerate a tune. Paris was what they said of him; he was a man of wax, a man that appeared to be so perfectly correct in every particular that he himself should stand in a cabinet of curiosity. But he was no more than that.

Giulietta and Rosaline were with me constantly, jealous guardians of my honour. Every night they were my bedfellows, every day they would follow a few steps behind Paris and me as we went about the city. They rarely talked, and if they did it was in a murmur so low I could barely hear them. I spoke about a thousand words for every one that they uttered. They made fine foils for my own runaway tongue, but all the same I longed for the vivacious company of my aunt or poor Guglielma Crollalanza. For Giulietta struggled daily with some secret sorrow, and Rosaline, a devout girl, was ever at her prayers. Her knees were worn from hours at the prie-dieu, and her fingers were always tangled in the beads of her rosary.

I learned little of these young women. I canvassed, once, their opinions of marriage; Rosaline, unsurprisingly, stated her intention to enter a nunnery, and Giulietta, with a faraway look, answered dreamily that marriage was the highest estate to which a man and a woman could aspire.

Too soon, my week in Verona was at an end, and I knew that night's betrothal feast would be my last chance to repel my groom. The next day my father would come for the marriage ceremony, to be held on the steps of the Basilica, and under his eye I could not behave as I had been.

As the young ladies and I readied ourselves for the revelry I was almost as silent as my handmaids, for I had much to think about. Rosaline and Giulietta, as befitted their youth and virginity, were clothed in white; Rosaline wore a girdle of olive leaves to recall Noah's dove, and Giulietta's gown was cunningly wrought of overlapping feathers, to resemble the plumage of a swan.

I pulled my starlight gown from my bed chest. The young maids helped me to dress, and I was glad to note that, despite my gluttony of the past week, the gown fitted as well as it ever had. I smoothed down the midnight-silk bodice with its constellation of diamonds, and traced Cassiopeia's chair with my finger. The waterfall of skirts fell to the floor, cunningly contrived of circles of fine silk in graduating colours of blue – the duck egg of midday for the underskirt, then an overskirt of afternoon, then evening blue, darkening through twilight to the bodice. Even my silent attendants exclaimed at the beauty of the gown. According to tradition, my hair would be worn loose until my wedding, and the young cousins brushed and burnished my hair till it fell in a spun gold skein to my shoulderblades. I pushed my feet into a pair of shoes with silver points, and, as if such shoes invited me to dance, I turned about until the skirts flew out in a circle.

From the folds, along with the damask and sprigs of lavender placed there by Paris's servants, fell the *settebello* card, and the sonnet that I'd written for Benedick, that day on the beach with

Michelangelo Crollalanza. I put the card in my bodice, more from habit than will, but the sonnet I set aside, unread, before the others could see it. I was ashamed of it now. The thought of those words, so passionate they near burned the paper, brought crimson to my cheeks. In the looking glass I saw, with annoyance, how becoming the flush was to me – perversely, the memory of Benedick had made me more comely for Paris. I wished I could hide my blush with a mask, but Paris had decreed that his guests, though they might be inventive in the matter of attire, should be unmasked. Perhaps the man of wax thought his features too fine to be hid. Ready, I led the maids down the staircase, a falling star.

The great hall looked as I had never seen it. In honour of the Capuletti, and in a neat play upon their family name, the solar had been given the air of a chapel. A thousand candles were lit in every niche and alcove, and, by some art, were suspended from the ceiling at differing heights, lighting the gloom of the cross-ribbed vaults with candle-flame constellations. The wax dripped upon the guests, riming them with white droppings to rival those of the kites that lived in our red-stone tower at home. There was no doubt, now, that the Capuletti were gods.

The best of Veronese society was in evidence, all with a Capuletti connection. My father did not like society, but his role as mediator had meant that he must attend family gatherings of both the Montecchi and Capuletti, so I'd known most of the assembly since childhood. There was Signor Martino and his wife and daughters; Count Anselme and his beautiful sisters; Vitravio's widow; Signor Placentio and his lovely nieces, Livia, Lucia and the lively Helena. I spied my uncle Capuletti and his wife, Giulietta's parents, seated beside each other at the high table in a pair of golden chairs. Tall and spare, they looked down their long noses at the company. They might have been brother and sister as they drank from chalice-like cups in tandem, and took no part in the merriment about them. They greeted me most courteously, but their smiles did not quite reach their flinty eyes. They looked at me as if I had taken a prize that, a year or two hence, they would have played their daughter for.

I seated myself beside Paris, with no appetite for the riches paraded before me. I had to make the breach, and make it tonight. But, unusually, I had a deal of trouble to claim Paris's attention. He could barely greet me for he was seated among the ranks of Capuletti uncles, who all seemed to be shouting the same story down the board at him; some news from England. Grinding my teeth with impatience, I knew I must wait. Giulietta was on my left, and I turned to speak to her, without much hope of conversation. But she seemed, for once, anxious to talk.

'I have been waiting to speak to you, cousin,' she said, low voiced, 'but Rosaline is always with us, and she is too devout to hear what I would tell. I must thank you.'

'Thank me?' I had not expected such a tribute. 'For what?'

She looked about her, cautiously. 'You saved someone's life. By your mercy you pardoned one who is the best of men.'

I was at sea, and not in the mood for riddles. I had too much to think about on my own account. 'I am not sure . . .'

'You banished a . . . young man, to Mantua. Your father would have sentenced him to die.'

Now she had my full attention. I remembered the young Montecchi; well spoken, handsome, and – most beguiling of all – utterly forbidden fruit to a Capuletti girl. 'Giulietta. Had you formed an understanding with this man?'

Now her silence spoke volumes. It was not the silence I had heard from her all week; the silence of a pliant maid. It was a stubborn silence of obstinate assent. I had been wrong about her – she had not formed an attachment to Tebaldo, but to his killer and a Montecchi at that. This boy would buy her death and despair. If he so much as set foot in Verona again, my father would have his head. I hardened my heart. 'You must be ruled by your father. He will choose your husband for you. Forget the Montecchi boy.' The words near choked me, for I knew better than any how hard it was to forget the heart's choice.

Giulietta looked at me. The gratitude was still there in her dark eyes, but tempered with disappointment. She had looked for an ally, and I had told her what she did not want to hear. I fell silent. Who was I to give her advice – I had doled out counsel that I would not take myself. My father had chosen Paris for me, a fitting match both in our ranks and temperaments, and I was set to refuse him. What was I about?

I looked around at the sumptuous Palazzo Maffei, at the fine mouldings, the beautiful frescoes on the walls. I looked at Paris, handsome in blue velvet to match my gown. I pulled on the count's sleeve. I had something to tell him. My decision did not make me happy, but now I thought it for the best.

I was ready to give in.

Paris was a good man, a kind one, and he had seen the worst of me in this last week. I had no illusions – a man may better tolerate contrary behaviours in a woman he is courting than one who is his wife; but from what I had seen I thought he would be a kind and considerate husband. If I did not accept him, what then? Go to a nunnery as Rosaline intended? I had never been one for religion, never done more than dutifully attend chapel, say the mass by rote and flatly sing the responses. I had lost my one chance at love in a game of *Scopa*. The losing card rode in my bodice. Benedick was off fighting a war for a king who was not his own, and even if he sat beside me now he was as lost to me as if he was in the Indies, for he had played me for a fool and rejected me cruelly when last we spoke. If I rejected Paris in my turn, my father would find me another husband now that he was fixed upon that course. Likely he would find a worse one; perhaps old or cruel, one deaf to art and music and books and the things that I loved. And if I was Countess of Verona and Princess of Villafranca I would have power, of a sort. My father could not live for ever. It was time to accept my fate.

When I addressed Paris at last he laid a hand on my arm to stay me, and did not take it away. I was to wait patiently until the menfolk had finished talking. I studied the hand that laid upon my arm, at the ring with Paris's arms upon it, the ring that, by the end of tonight, would ride upon my hand. Then I heard one word.

Armada.

There was much laughing and merriment – I could not hear more. The strange word bobbed and sunk and rose again upon the tempest of chatter. I craned close to Paris and he patted my arm with his ring hand. *In a moment, dearest, be patient. Men are talking.* Then one of my uncles, spitting chicken bones as he spoke, shouted down the others. He had just returned from Norwich, where this 'armada' was the talk of the countryside. Philip of Spain had moved against Elizabeth of England with a mighty fleet of ships.

My hand tightened on Paris's arm. *This* was the king's Great Enterprise, the plot of which Michelangelo Crollalanza and I had once spoken on a Sicilian beach. I sharpened my ears to hear more, for this was the first time I had heard the affairs of other nations spoken of in this little world of Verona – something must be badly awry.

And so it proved. 'Philip's ships were caught in a maelstrom, and the English guns shot them to bits. The Duke of Parma was too cowardly to come to their aid, and the fleets were scattered like *Scopa* cards.'

'They turned tail?' asked Paris.

'Couldn't,' spat my uncle. 'Signor Howard blocked the

channel. Any ships still afloat were sent scuttling north, around the frozen highlands.' He took a gulp of wine. 'They'll be dead by now; even if the rocks don't get 'em, or the sea-monsters, they only had rations for a month. There've been bodies washing up on the Scottish shores like cockleshells.' My uncle's face creased with mirth. 'The Spanish King's "Great Enterprise", blown to buggery by English wind.' He stuck out his tongue and blew a vulgar rasp from his lips.

Paris roared with laughter.

And I knew then I could not marry him.

I rose and stumbled from the room. He did not notice.

Act IV scene xiii

The Basilica of Saint Zeno, Verona

Beatrice: I wandered through the streets of Verona, under the stars.

The moon was a silver galleon sailing though an archipelago of indigo clouds. I looked up for my star at the foot of Cassiopeia's chair, and it blurred in my tears as it had done once before; the night when I was with Benedick on the dunes, the night he had embraced me. And now he was likely dead.

I imagined his lifeless face, eyes upturned and white as he sank down beneath the waves. These stars were likely the last things he saw. I could look at them no more and stumbled into a vast dark doorway. Inside all was marble, striped in black and white like a winter tiger. The Duomo.

The black tiles led me forth like footprints to the crypt, where a much older church nestled within the newer one. This was St Zeno's own Basilica, the early Christian church upon which the cathedral had been built. I knelt at the saint's shrine, and gazed up at the painting of Zeno with the holy family which hung above the little altar. As I looked at his black face, lambent with candlelight, all the events of the summer came back to me in a rush – the Moor, the masque, the wedding, the poet, the Naumachia, the fire, the Vara. And Benedick. Benedick at dinner, Benedick in the dunes, and now Benedick in the sea.

I remembered him on the day of the tourney, as Signor Mountanto. He was so self-possessed then, so wondrous at swordplay, so confident at beating anyone who stepped forth. I had always thought, unquestioningly, that he would return from whatever little skirmish he might encounter. I was confident that he was immortal. He may not have been mine, but somehow it was enough that he would always be somewhere on this earth, devil-may-care, talking his way out of trouble. I searched my heart for the smallest hope, but feared that Benedick had at last met with an enemy he could not vanquish with a word or a sword. For what could he do against the elements themselves? He could not gull the winds, he could not charm the seas.

St Zeno watched me dispassionately as I agonised, waiting patiently for the moment of my supplication. I screwed my eyes tight shut and clasped my hands, kneeling on the cold stone. The crystals on my midnight skirts cracked beneath my knees as I brought to mind the saint's legend, told to me as a child. St Zeno had once calmed the waters of the Adige when a horse and cart had bolted, parting the waves like Moses. He had magically kept the flood waters of the Veneto plains away from the cathedral door. Surely he could save one wretched, irritating man?

I did not know the Saint of Padua, I just knew *my* saint, a Moor who'd come all the way from the Africas to build this Basilica with his own hands. In the name of St Zeno every Moor was granted safe passage on Verona's streets by law – here they did not suffer the persecutions meted out by other communes (Messina, oh, Messina!). Zeno was from so far away, but he had become as parochial as my father. Every fisherman in Verona had his medal hanging from their rod, every cordwainer stamped his symbol into the shoes they made. So, for the first time, I prayed to Verona's saint as if I meant what I said. 'Saint Zeno,' I pleaded, looking up into his black face, polished ebony reflecting the light of the votive candles, 'please save him. Save Benedick.'

He looked at me with eyes as black and white as the marble

walls. His impassivity was somehow a comfort. He would help me, or he would not, with the casual dispatch of the divine. I had done all I could. I staggered to my feet, left through the great doors and paused on the steps. Tomorrow I would have stood here and become Beatrice Maffei. How curious the night was – it had switched around, as it had done once before for me in Benedick's presence, that night on the dunes. The skies had changed, like the dial on a verge clock or one hemisphere to another. Before dinner, Benedick might still have been alive, and I had been considering marriage to Paris. After dinner, I was as good as sure Benedick was dead; but now I knew that if I could not marry him, I could not marry anyone. If there was the smallest hope that he would return, I would wait.

Back at the Palazzo Maffei I climbed the great white spiral and went directly to my room. I rifled my bed chest until I found what I sought, grabbing at the piece of forgotten parchment. I flattened out the sonnet on my coverlet and read it through. Now every word had meaning, and my tears fell on the ink.

I dried my eyes – straightened the starlight dress and descended the spiral stair once more. The merriment in the great hall had become even more raucous, and after the quiet and cool of the night the noise broke over me like a wave.

The first person I saw was Giulietta, dreaming as usual, and she gave me an idea. She too had loved and lost – perhaps I could save her *and* myself? I passed her chair, laid aside her cap and pulled her dark hair about her shoulders so that it fell to her white bosom. 'It looks better this way, sweets,' I said. She gave me a shy smile.

I sat beside Paris once again, and at once – as if I had not been absent for an hour – his ring hand was back on my arm. I saw a different meaning to the gesture now – it was proprietorial. I waited for my moment to tell him that I could not marry him. There were to be no more games now, just a flat refusal. I would deal with my father later. But the male talk was unceasing; all still of England and of King Philip's failed attack. Of Parma, of a counter-attack, of what the queen would do, what the Pope would do, what the Lombard merchants would do.

'Their precious Saint John neglected to protect his knights,' Paris gloated.

I spoke up, idly, without agenda, without thinking. 'Saint James,' I said. 'The Knights of Saint John are French, and the Knights of the Garter English. Saint James is the patron saint of Spain.' By some strange accident of the conversational ebb and flow, I had spoken into a quiet lull, and my voice could be heard clearly from one end of the board to the other.

There was a short, strained silence, and then my kinsmen laughed. 'Have a care, Count,' called one. 'Lady Beatrice may give better instruction in the schoolroom than the bedroom.' The Capuletti menfolk laughed again.

Paris smiled, but a little muscle jumped in his cheek. He turned to me and spoke low voiced, his jaw as rigid as it had been when he had been posing for his portrait. But his blazing eyes more than conveyed his meaning.

'Do not *ever*,' he spat, 'presume to correct me in front of my kinsmen again. You may prattle as much as you please in private but never, *never* make me look a fool in front of my court.'

I lowered my eyes so he should not see the triumph there. The man of wax had cracked, at last, like the seal on a letter. And the answer had been so simple; he'd accepted my corrections in good grace when we'd been alone, but as soon as I'd corrected him in company – the company of men – I had taken a step too far. I looked about at the couples ranged around the board. How many of those wives outfaced their husbands at home, only to be silent in public? Was this the only way that a woman could rule, this private, domestic power?

If I had been Paris's wife in truth his outburst would have silenced me, but I was so close now, I would not be quieted. My heart beat so that I thought he must see it at my throat. 'Forgive me, my lord,' I said meekly. 'My tongue has ever been my fault. But I have always been of the opinion that it is much better to be a talker with decided opinions which one can readily share with one's husband, than one who is a dumb show. Who would want a modest maid who has nothing to say for herself, not a word to gainsay her husband? Who is as dumb as a block, and meekly agrees with every word her lord says.' I nodded down the board. 'Look at my cousin there, so still like an image, saying nothing. I swear I have not heard her utter one word from last week to this.' Paris followed my gaze, looking past me as if he could no longer see me.

Giulietta sat there beyond me; she had not heard the dispute; her dark eyes looked far away, through the walls and over the dark fields to Mantua. She looked remarkably well tonight, no longer the sallow maid I'd seen when I had come here, and I knew she was thinking of her love. Just as my memory of Benedick had done for me, her remembrances brought a becoming bloom to her cheek as where the sun touches a creamy magnolia petal with rose. Her white neck was long and elegant, her bosom high and white. Most becoming of all to the count, I was sure, was her modest silence – she sat quietly without a murmur, mute as a swan.

Paris rose, and spoke a word in the ear of my uncle Capuletti, Giulietta's father. The two men went for a private conference in the moonlit courtyard. And when they returned, I knew from Capuletti's expression of quiet triumph that I was free.

Act IV scene xiv

The *Florencia*, open sea

Benedick: With every league we put between the doomed *San Juan de Sicilia* and ourselves our spirits were elevated.

Because we were now so few, our rations, though still not enough to satisfy, seemed a king's feast. All the mutineers had brought supplies from the bay, and because of this, and for the sake of morale, Claudio and I had persuaded the captain to spare the miscreants a flogging. It was the only time at sea that I had known Bartoli deviate from his strict code of command.

In truth we were glad of the return of pilot Da Sousa, for we needed the experienced navigator to lead us through the tricky sounds. Our errant pilot had brought a goat aboard, an animal sacrifice to atone for his transgression, and we all benefited from her creamy milk and looked forward to her meat from slaughter. The wind blew and cracked his cheeks for us, filling our remaining sails, and as we sailed ever southwards the climate became more forgiving, the water more open. We still had the problem of navigation, but thanks to Beatrice's star, which I tracked and charted every night, I could at least inform the captain, with some confidence, that we were going due south.

Claudio and the captain pored over our inadequate charts daily, and finally we recognised landfall. A long spit of land reached into the sea; Claudio pronounced it to be Cornwall. Strong crosswinds buffeted us and the captain gave the order to trim our sails – we were once again in the English Channel.

We were not, of course, out of danger; as we broached the Channel again we kept an eye to the spyglass for English ships. But despite the spectacular failure of the armada it seemed the English had lost their nerve; we saw a merchant sloop here, a fishing smack there, but never a warship at all. We began to believe, for the first time since Scotland, that we could really get home.

Every man knew his new quarters, and I could at last give my attention to our newest crew member. I gave the Moor the surgeon's cabin, and for a week he could do naught but lie down. I doubted very much whether he would live, but I rifled the medicine chests of the dead doctor to find relief for his many ailments. As it transpired the Moor knew more of the compounds than I. He waved away the jars of undulating grey leeches and slippery silver mercury and pointed to the vials of arrowroot and cinnabar.

I noted as I treated the sores on his flesh that his arms were covered in some manner of black writing, but no amount of sponging would take it off – it had a faintly blue tinge and looked as if the ink had been trapped beneath the skin. I did not recognise the strange letters from any alphabet I had ever learned, and wondered from what alien lexicon those words originated. It did not seem, for a time, as if I would ever get the chance to ask him. His recovery was hampered by the fact that he could not sleep – and if he closed his eyes for an instant would wake with a cry. I knew that when he slept he was back on the *San Juan de Sicilia*.

But despite my fears, the Moor's health gradually improved, and as he gained strength I learned more of his history. His story would draw tears from a stone. He had been a boy slave from the northern Africas, given to the king's father Carlos as a gift. 'I had a talent of finding water' – at this my ears pricked like a cur's – 'and worked for the king at the Pardo, and later at El Escorial. But with the birth of my son the gift left me,' he said, dry mouthed, 'as if I had passed it to him.' Having failed to complete the water gardens for the king, he had been transferred to the galleys, and rowed to Lepanto and back. And now, in this age of ships with no oars, he had been taken for the short boats and pledged his allegiance to the king once more. And still he served; he had stayed with the treasure, had not abandoned the enterprise. By my calculation, and by my recall of the watchwords, he had been in the bay, on that ship of the dead, for a week before we'd arrived. I could not imagine the horror of what he'd encountered. 'And no one came for the treasure?' I asked, sitting on the end of his cot. 'Did not the Scots attempt to board the boat?'

'Only once,' he said. 'I saw them come. I put on a sea cloak, and lit a hurricane lamp. I went to the deck and stood on a barrel to make me tall. When they came close I threw back the hood and stretched out my arms like this, so they could see the writing.' He put out his arms in a cruciform, so I could see the inscription, but he was too weak to keep them there. 'It was dusk,' he said. 'I was lit from below. When they saw me thus they turned tail and never came back.'

I was not surprised. I had seen many Moors in my life, for there were many at the university in my home town of Padua. But this one had frighted me to the quick when he had risen from the dark in the hold of the *San Juan*; I could only imagine the impact his appearance had had on those simple Scottish peasants. I looked at his arms. 'What is writ there?'

'A prayer,' he said. 'A prayer in flesh. If it is written *on* you, it is written *in* you.' I thought of the devotion that he had shown to his king, and the devotion he had shown to his God, to have His word written in his flesh. This man, so lowly, had been the most faithful of servants, and had shown loyalty and courage that would well become a prince.

'Did you never wish to escape? To take one of the pinnaces and row to the bay?' He looked surprised, as if such a notion had never occurred. 'But I owe my king my allegiance till my last breath. For while I was in the galleys he took in my son as his ward.'

It was time to tell him what I knew. 'If his name is Faruq Sikkander, I have seen him; he is still there, at El Escorial.'

He sat up for the first time, eyes shining. 'Yes,' he said. 'Yes. He is my son, he bears my name; I am Faruq Sikkander too.'

I told him of my meeting with the water-diviner. 'He is well, and a fine young man.'

He made me tell the tale over and again, and as I strained to recall every detail, and invented what I could not remember, he slept for the first time since he'd left the *San Juan*.

After a few days on normal rations Faruq was able to work about the ship, and within a week became the strongest and most able seaman on the *Florencia*. I noticed that the crew accepted him readily, and even deferred to his experience; they were well used to sailors of all colours and nations, and they did not fear him. Faruq was fastidious, and brought up a bucket of seawater daily to wash himself, and would kneel in prayer a handful of times, with his head touching the deck. No one made comment.

The only person on board who treated Faruq with suspicion was Claudio. Now, when he said mass, he would choose the texts of St James, and speak of heretics and savages with his eyes on the Moor. I was surprised, for he was from Florence, a crucible of all nations and races, and had never, in Sicily, joined in the general censure of the Moors. Now, when I saw him looking at Faruq, I recalled the day when he had played the boy king Ramon of Asturias in the Naumachia and had called down St James upon the Moors. Yet only once in my hearing did Claudio make reference to his feelings. 'We should have left him on the *San Juan*,' he said.

'Why?'

Claudio's eyes followed Faruq as he pulled competently on the ratlines.

'Ask him,' he said. 'Ask him why he was the only one to survive.'

I did not fully understand Claudio's hostility. But nor did I ask the question, and after that exchange I left the Moor to his business and I kept to mine. And I kept my dagger close.

That night a storm blew up from nowhere, ragging the cordage and sending the ship from side to side with a stomach-wrenching lurch. I took to my bed instead of my usual stargazing, for I would have been swept off deck. In my cot I had much ado to coax sleep, for it seemed that just as we were within reach of home, a storm might take us where starvation had failed.

I must have slept eventually, for I woke suddenly, to the unmistakable creak of metal against metal. In the moonlight I saw the brass handle of my door begin to turn, and took my dagger from beneath my pillow. It had lived below the feathers ever since we had divided the rations. A figure crept into the room, hugging the panelling against the pitch and roll of the ship; bearded, emaciated, it could have been any of the crew. But the intruder had no blade – he sat unsteadily on my bed. 'Is it you, Faruq Sikkander?' I whispered to the weight.

'Greetings, Benedick.'

It was Don Pedro.

I had forgotten that he was even with us. Through all our tribulations he had kept his cabin; isolated in his rank, forgotten. When the mutiny had broken we could have called upon him to suppress it. When the mizzen had been cut, it must have crashed down upon his very cabin. When we'd been tied to the mast he could have freed us. But in our misery and preoccupation we had forgotten the most important personage on the ship; and the least.

I sat, unsure how to address him. Was he still my lord?

'I had a vision,' he said. 'A Moor was at my window in the middle of the storm; a terrible, sunken face with burning eyes. He spoke words over me, strange words, but in my dreams I understood them. He told me to right my wrongs.'

I did not know what to say. I knew it had only been Faruq who had looked in upon him; no vision, but a man of flesh and blood. But if the prince was having some sort of Damascene remorse, I did not want to discourage his atonement.

'Benedick,' he said again. 'Will we reach Spain?'

'I cannot tell,' I said, for it did not seem like the moment to lie. 'But I think – yes.'

He looked from the bottled windows out to sea, and the lightning found the hollows in his cheeks. I thought then of how much he must have suffered in his own way – he had been alone in his state, starving as we starved, but without the balm of company. Each body that was thrown into the sea would have fallen past his window, each toll of the ship's passing bell helping him to keep score of the deaths he had caused.

And there was another ending for him to endure; the demise of his own honour. Each day he had to live with the knowledge that he had placed us in this pass, and that, following the catastrophic loss of the anchor, he had not taken the lead of his men. That role had fallen to others – a sea captain, a banker, a gentleman. And a Moor. The prince's nobility had dwindled with his flesh.

'No one must know,' he said. 'No one must know what has passed upon this ship. Swear to me, upon your allegiance.'

I thought upon the word. Allegiance. I had put on the livery of St James, worn his medal, followed his flag. And this useless prince of Aragon was still my liege lord. I had been wrong about him. He had not been repenting, there in his lonely prison. Whatever natural shock the appearance of the Moor at his window had given him, his remorse had quickly given way to self-preservation. Now it seemed likely that we would get back to Spain alive, he had to reconcile how this new Don Pedro could live in the world. He had been debating how to keep his transgressions from general knowledge, to cover up what a paper prince he was. And he had found his answer in that one word: allegiance. I was his bondsman, and if he wanted my silence, he could command it.

'On my allegiance,' I agreed, having no other choice. My oath was like a sigh.

He pressed his hands together as if he prayed. *Relief*, I thought, *not contrition*. He bowed his head. 'In return, I must make a confession.'

I clasped my knees. Nothing he could say could interest me now; my stomach twisted with unease and something akin to shame. He had my oath; I wanted him to go.

'It concerns the Lady Beatrice.'

I sat up abruptly. 'Beatrice Della Scala?' It was the first time her name had been upon my lips since I had discussed her with Claudio.

'Yes.' He was silent for so long I thought he had changed his mind. Then he took a breath, as if he was about to plunge into the sea. 'The lady was not false. *I* parted you.'

'But . . . but . . . I saw her. With the poet.'

'You did not know what you saw.' Don Pedro shifted slightly. 'It was his mother who died in the fire. Her name was Guglielma Crollalanza.'

The woman I'd followed to the Tarantella. 'The Moorish lady was the poet's *mother*?'

'Yes. Beatrice embraced him in sympathy; and chastity.'

I thought back to that dread day when the prince had had me follow Beatrice to the dunes. I remembered every gesture and touch that passed between Beatrice and the poet, played it over in my head like an act from a play. Now I'd been furnished with the facts I forced myself to acknowledge the truth – he was a grieving son, bereaved in a most terrible way. There was nothing in the embrace, now that I considered the gesture in this new light, which could suggest anything other than a sisterly regard, and chaste comfort. I clenched my fists.

'And there is more. I knew you had given her the *settebello*; I had a pack of them made, and left them for her to find in your room.'

I only had one question, one word. 'Why?'

'I wanted a companion for this adventure. I wanted a brother.' But neither rang true, and this was the time for truth. I said nothing, said everything.

'Very well,' he said, in answer to the question unspoken. 'I did not want you to have her, when I could not.'

I could not speak, my senses reeling, the universe wheeling about my head.

He spoke instead. 'You have sworn your allegiance to me,' he reminded me.

I knew then why he'd had me swear first, before he'd spilled his story. I hated him at that moment. 'Oh, you shall have it,' I said tightly, with as much scorn as I could pack into five words.

'And in return, you shall have mine.' He laid his hand on my shoulder. 'If we reach home, I shall see you rewarded, you and Claudio too. And our first venture shall be to Sicily, to make all things right that went awry. A pair of brides for you and the count, hey?'

He sounded unnaturally hearty. I could not trust myself to answer him, and after a moment he went away; but I could still feel the place where his hand had rested on my shoulder.

It burned like a brand.

Act IV scene xv

The Castello Scaligero, Villafranca di Verona

Beatrice: When I returned home to the Castello Scaligero as a single woman, I was not greeted by a warm rapier and the jewels of my brother's blood. This time I was greeted by a trail of treasure.

On the drawbridge were two brass lamps from Byzantium, dented where they'd been hurled. Under the gatehouse was a surcoat of damascene silk, rent from top to toe. In the courtyard was a Venetian mirror shattered into a million glittering shards that spat back the sun. The stairs to the red-stone tower were slippery with spilled incense. I climbed the steps; stairs to safety were now stairs to danger.

My father stood in the middle of the keep, on a pile of the autumn leaves that often blew into the great hall, holding two letters in his hands. His arms were outstretched like scales, as if the two missives balanced him, as if he had reverted to his old mediating role of Justice.

By way of greeting he brought one of the letters before his face, and read it to me. 'To Bartolomeo Della Scala, Prince Escalus and Lord of the Freetown of Villafranca di Verona. My Esteemed Prince and Right Noble Kinsman, know by this that I may no longer offer matrimony to the Lady Beatrice, Princess of Villafranca. Please be assured that I mean no offence to your esteemed daughter, or yourself, and envy the man that claims such a prize. I must only plead that, however assiduously fond fathers make their plans, we cannot know where Cupid's arrows will fall; and love is a master that will not be gainsaid. I console myself that my new union will still bring us to closer kinship. I will marry your niece the lady Giulietta Capuletti at Saint Peter's church on Thursday next, and cordially invite you to attend the ceremony and afterward the feast. I have the honour to return the Lady Beatrice's dowry with this letter. Yours *et cetera*, Count Paris Maffei.'

I said nothing.

'And I cannot afford to slight him,' said my father, 'for I have now shunned the Montecchi; if I lose the Capuletti too, I lose all the Della Scala power. So now I, and you, must attend this wedding and smile and smile while that little Capuletti bitch claims the prize that should have been yours. Fourteen,' he cried. 'She is fourteen. Barely old enough to keep a babe in her cradle bones.' He looked at me in disgust. 'You have *utterly* failed me.'

I looked down, mock-hangdog. ''Tis not my fault,' I wheedled. 'I was utterly rejected. How do you think *I* feel, to be refused for one who is five summers younger than me? To have one's greatest hopes ruined by one's own cousin?' I wiped a tear that was not there.

It was too much; I'd gone too far and my father knew it at once. He crossed the rushes in an instant and took my chin in his hand, hard, hurting. He forced my gaze up to meet his.

'How now, my Headstrong!' he growled. '*What did you do?*'

'Nothing,' I protested, bleating like a butchered mutton. 'He made his judgement, and he chose another.'

He dropped my chin and the first letter at the same time. The missive fluttered to the leaf-strewn floor, and I saw then that he stood not upon leaves but on papers. I could make out the wording of my marriage contract, in flowing secretary hand, torn into a thousand halfpence. By the table stood a humble crate stuffed with sheep's flock, and the rest of my dowry peeped out of the wool. So Paris had sent everything back but the *cassone* – he had kept the precious wedding chest, with its fine painted panel, and sent my treasure back in a cheap olive-wood box. I could picture them now, all posing in the great solar of the Palazzo Maffei as the *Judgement of Paris*, with Giulietta now playing the role of Athena. I could imagine another little Capuletti cousin taking Giulietta's part, and Signor Cagliari, the artist, at the *cassone*, painstakingly painting Giulietta's face over mine.

I thought I had done my cousin a kindness. I did not question, then, the wisdom of assigning to Giulietta a fate I had rejected myself; I thought that I had bought her a kind and wealthy husband who would keep her safe. I did not ask myself what would happen if Giulietta, as I had, decided to wait for an insubstantial dream, instead of a solid reality. I was more concerned with my own fate, and I watched my father closely.

He sat heavily in his wooden throne, propped up by the wooden ladders of his name, in a brooding silence. The second letter was crumpled in his hand. I was reminded. 'And the other letter?'

He looked up, his eyelids heavy, his gaze hostile. 'What?'

'The other letter? Not more ill news?'

'What news could be worse?' he asked, balefully.

'Glad tidings, then?' My voice brightened unnaturally.

'Something that matters not to me at all,' he said. 'Your aunt is dead.'

I was confused for a moment, for I had many aunts, and most of them had been at the masque the previous night.

'Your mother's sister, Innogen. In Sicily.' As if it was nothing, he threw the second letter at me. I caught it and fled.

The courtyard was hot, but I was cold with shock. I sat on the fountain bowl that I'd once seen filled with Tebaldo's blood, and read the letter over and over.

It was in Leonato's hand, and told a sorry story; that my aunt had taken a fever and died within a week. Her body was to be laid in the *Cimiterio Monumentale*, in the family tomb.

All of a sudden I was back in Sicily, on the mountainside the day of the Moor's death, burying Guglielma Crollalanza's ashes in the plot where my aunt would now lie. I thought of Innogen, the only personification of my mother's line that I had left, and of Hero. How would my cousin shift now without Innogen to teach her that she could be independent, and strong willed? Who would now teach her that she could dance alone?

I went back into the keep; my father, it seemed, had not moved at all.

'Father, I must speak with you.'

He regarded me, unblinking, from his pale eyes.

'I wish to return to Sicily to pay my duty to my aunt.'

He took a long breath in through his nose. 'She will already be interred. The letter will have taken a week to reach us. Corpses stink in the south.'

I did not like his saying, but could not reproach him. 'It is a matter of respect for our family.' I thought this would persuade him – I was wrong.

'When I let you go before, I had an heir. And you were in your aunt's care. Now your aunt is gone, and I had to call you home once before because of the dangers that befell your uncle's house. I cannot lose you.'

There was no affection in this last, no emotion; just political expediency. I was a bride prize. 'So I might have died *last* summer with no inconvenience to you, but not *this*.'

'Since you express it so; yes.'

This rejoinder quenched me like a cold douse of water. I was so astonished that I was silenced.

But I was not silent for long. For the next week and more I petitioned him. I had learned much from my sojourn in Verona with Paris, and knew well how to make myself unbearable. So I nagged, scolded, pleaded and cajoled. I thought sometimes he would strike me again, but he never did. He just refused me steadfastly. In desperation I tried a different tack; I tried to be diffident, obedient and humble. I made myself good society in the evening, talking to him of his favourite subject of Verona and her environs. We even took up our *Scopa* games once more, and I watched him find small satisfaction in my inevitable defeats.

And then I had the idea. I took the *Scopa* deck down to dinner one night and played my last desperate card.

'Father,' I said, once the meats had been cleared away and the servants had left the room, 'tonight I will play you for a stake. If I win, I want you to let me go to Sicily to pay my respects to my aunt.'

He opened his mouth to refuse me once again, but I held up my hand. 'If you allow this, I will be back in one month, and then I will marry whomever you please.'

He stroked his nose. 'With no clever schemes or devices to make a man refuse you?'

I met his eyes, and knew then that he had divined exactly what happened with Paris. 'None,' I promised firmly.

'And if I refuse the wager?'

I took a deep breath. 'Then I will enter a nunnery, and your line will die with you.'

He was silent for a time; I could not tell whether his silence proceeded from anger or grudging admiration. Then: 'And if I win?'

'I will never gainsay you again. And I will take a husband tomorrow.'

I had put the cards upon the table. But my father liked courage and honesty.

'Then deal,' he said; with the slightest shrug, and the slightest smile. And I did, as I had done so many times before.

I shuffled the cards, and asked my father to cut the pack. I dealt three cards for him, three for me. Then I turned four cards face up, placing them in the middle of the table. The remaining pile I kept close to my elbow. And we began to play *Scopa*. Just my father and I, in that great keep, before the fire.

There was nothing here of the modern world. Nothing to remind us that we did not live in a world of cups and swords and clubs and coins, a world of knaves and kings and queens. I could feel the ghosts crowding me; lords and ladies of the past thronging to my shoulder to read my hand, as I held my cards high before my face like a fan. Turn by turn, my father and I played, trying to 'capture' the deal cards – a nine for a nine, a knave for a knave. We imprisoned our captures in crossways tricks at our right hands. My father was ahead, then we were even, then he was ahead again. All might have been lost, but I was not worried. At the final deal I made my move, the imperceptible shake of my sleeve, which I had been practising in my chamber. The *settebello*, Benedick's *settebello*, slipped silently from my cuff to the table.

I kept my eyes on my father – in the flickering firelight, he had not noticed. I played the rogue card. '*Scopa*,' I said, quietly but firmly.

My father looked at the card, then at me. For a moment I could not breathe, and it seemed that my heart had stopped. Would he divine what I had done? The card itself was still crisp and uncreased, its edges only a little blurred by its travels; not enough, I hoped, to mark it out from the rest of the pack in a dingy, firelit keep. For an eternal moment my father did not move. Then he stood and swept the cards from the board, and they scattered to the rushes. He pointed a long finger at me.

'One month,' said my father, 'not a day more.'

And he stalked from the room. I stooped to pick up the cards and put the *settebello*, Benedick's *settebello*, back in my bodice, where it belonged.

Act IV scene xvi

The *Florencia*, open sea

Benedick: The morning after my meeting with Don Pedro, the maelstrom of my mind had settled; I could see the way ahead.

The weather and my mind were in accord. The wind had dropped and the sea was becalmed and broad and blue. I could see little windmills on the cliffs to starboard – Da Sousa, who had been this way before, said they sat upon the shores of Brittany. We were off the coast of France.

Henceforward I paid a daily visit to Don Pedro, to apprise him of our progress as was fitting to my liege lord. Each day now he was up, dressed and sitting at his desk – he seemed to be writing letters, and was, in every particular, a prince again. He still did not leave his cabin, but now sent messages to the captain and wrote letters to his brother Don John, the custodian of his estates in Aragon, to be sent upon landing. He also wrote to the king.

I informed the captain that the prince's rations should be increased, and he merely nodded. I discovered later that Bartoli, correct in every particular, had ensured that the prince had had his rations every day since we'd sailed, except the day of the mutiny, and he'd failed then only because he had been bound.

As the crew filled every sail and Da Sousa turned the wheel for Santander, I decided upon my own course. My prince was still my prince, no matter what his actions upon the *Florencia*. If we reached Spain I would collect my reward – God knows I'd earned it. I had no illusions about Beatrice, who might very well be wed by now. To serve the prince was the first matter; to get home was the second. But at night, under Beatrice's star, nothing could bind my hopes, nor tether my dreams.

Faruq Sikkander worked efficiently and silently. I did not ask him about the night he'd looked in upon Don Pedro but I wondered whether he could divine sin as he had once divined water. I watched the Moor at his ablutions and prayers, looked at the writing on his forearms as he sluiced them with seawater, and thought, as I had once before of him, that some things were better left alone.

And then, on the day of Santiago, we sighted Santander, to a great cheer from all the men.

My warmest embrace was for Claudio, for he was now so much more than a friend to me. When we parted his eyes were wet, and mine too. 'I have a brother,' he said.

'And I.' We made no vows, nor mingled our blood as the Spanish did. Our clasped hands were enough, a gesture that bound us for ever.

Ravenously we finished the rest of the rations, joyously we followed our captain's orders to swab the ship, polish the brackets and make the sorry hull as fine as she could be for the inevitable celebrations.

Only when we made landfall did the prince come on deck, dressed as neatly as he could be, to wave to the expected assembly. But our homecoming was shameful – no trumpets, nor cheering crowds, just a wounded dragon of a ship limping into shore. Da Sousa did his best, without an anchor, to slow our landing, but we still crashed into the jetty at such speed that we holed our bow. As we clambered off the ship in Don Pedro's wake we all fell to the ground like babes, for we had forgotten how to walk. While I was down there I kissed the sweet soil.

I do not know how a returning ship was usually received, but there was little that day to cheer us. No representatives of the Crown were present in the port so we left the men in the tavern and the Moor outside, and walked to find the mayor of the town. In the sunlit whitewashed streets children cheered us ironically and pelted us with rotten vegetables. Only a day or two earlier I would have caught and eaten, thankfully, what they threw. Only the sheer joy of being alive and walking unsteadily on *terra firma* mitigated the shame of our homecoming. The mayor could not meet us but his registrar told us the sorry truth – that battered ships had been arriving back piecemeal since October, and the people had long since ceased to commemorate such sights. Our orders were to report to the king at El Escorial, as soon as we might.

We bought mules in the port, and arranged for the transport of my treasure, and in the week it took us to reach El Escorial, the world had righted itself. The ground was the ground again, the days of the week had their proper names, but it was many years before I could prevent myself from calling Wednesday Santiago.

And there, at the king's palace again many months after I had left it, I was happy to undertake the only task of which I felt proud in the whole affair. I reunited Faruq Sikkander with his son of the same name. They embraced in the gardens under an arc of water that they had found.

I left them to it and went to the chapel of St James for a thanksgiving mass, where I sat between Don Pedro and Claudio. Captain Bartoli was not with us – he had died in the portside inn in Santander, the day after we'd docked. His duty done at last, he'd slept and never woke. His last ship, the *Florencia* – pride of the Duke of Tuscany – had to be scrapped.

Don Pedro sat and listened to the mass, a beatific smile on his face. I had heard from Claudio upon the road that the prince had elicited the same vow from the count that he had from me; that nothing should be spoken of what had passed on board the *Florencia*. Claudio, as a nod to his uncle the Grand Duke and compensation for the loss of his ship, was to be hailed as the hero of the expedition. With our silence pledged and the captain dead, Don Pedro was safe to be a prince again; glorious, handsome, well dressed and fed. His face exhibited a glowing sheen as if he'd been varnished, like the lambent saints all about us. I glanced up at the spandrels where a roundel of St James sat between the pillars. St James the Great – *Matamoros*. I turned away from the image. I had nothing to thank him for.

I had no expectations, now, that Don Pedro would keep any promise, but he made good on the vows that he had made on that stormy night in my cabin. He reported my deeds to the king, and Philip gave me a tithe of the treasure recovered from the *San Juan de Sicilia*. I discovered that it would have been no small shame if the armada pay chests had been claimed by Elizabeth, so the king's gratitude for their recovery knew no bounds. He ennobled me as Duke of Leon, the previous duke having conveniently perished on the armada. I was now a nobleman and, which was more, a rich one.

In addition to this, Don Pedro reiterated his intention to return to Sicily via his estates in Aragon, for it seemed that some new circumstance had paved the way for another visit to Leonato's palace. 'The Lady Hero's mother bid me never to return,' he said with arch good humour as if the voyage had never happened, 'but I have received word that she lately took a fever and passed away, so our welcome is assured.'

I did not appreciate either his sentiments or the news, for I had liked the Lady Innogen well; but I was reconciled to this new Don Pedro, for I had made the discovery that one does not have to like a man to serve him.

On the day we were to leave for Sicily I sought out Faruq Sikkander to give him one of the treasure chests. I had plenty to spare and I thought it his due; but he just looked at the casket where it lay in my hands, as if it might burn him.

'If you will not accept my money,' I said, 'may I offer you some advice?'

He nodded, with a ghost of a smile.

'Take your son and go to Verona. There, they revere a black saint and protect the lives of Moors in his name.'

I knew that the Moors could expect new dangers in Spain, for Philip had had it decreed this day from El Escorial that the armada had failed because the king had taken too long to expel the Moors from Granada. So with the first *real* I spent from my hoard I bought father and son a mule each and set them on their way. As I watched Faruq wind along the northern road with his son he looked forward, ever forward, and missed my wave. I could not blame him. If I had seen what he had seen, I would not want to lay eyes on anyone who had been on board the *San Juan de Sicilia* ever again.

For now I knew the answer to Claudio's question. I knew how he'd survived on board that fell ship. He'd had to do what they said of him. He'd had to personify the dreadful seafarers' tales of dark savages that devour unwary sailors, and cook them in great cauldrons like pottage. He'd had to do what he did alone, and in the desperate dark, and it would haunt him for ever.

'Benedick,' called Claudio haltingly. 'Are you coming? Sicily awaits.'

Sicily. And now I could think of Beatrice, and unleash those hopes at last. I was under no illusions – she might have married the poet after all, as I had rejected and abandoned her and cast her in his way. Or she might have gone home to Verona and found some young sprig there. I could only hope against hope that she might be in Sicily to pay her respects to her aunt, and was still free.

And then? Then I would know how to act. I would not simper nor posture, nor sigh like a lover. I was done with dandy clothes and fancy airs. I would be myself, be the Benedick I had learned to be. And we would battle in our old way, and I would pray that the blows might turn to kisses, as they had once before.

I turned my horse to walk alongside Claudio's, and we met the prince at the gatehouse of El Escorial. Don Pedro spurred his horse ahead of his company, his pennant streaming forth. And as I had done a year ago, I followed the prince, Claudio and the sun; to Sicily.

ACT FIVE

Sicily: Summer 1589

Act V scene i

Leonato's palace, Messina, Sicily

Beatrice: I should not have come, for now I was in Sicily Benedick was everywhere; and nowhere.

I had done no more than leave my trunk at my uncle's house and greet my grieving cousin before I had gone at once, even in the midday sun, to climb the mount to my aunt's tomb. And on that journey, short as it was, the memories of Benedick assailed me. The ebb and flow of the tide sounded like his voice, and the temperate winds whispered his name. The scamels sung his favourite air from the oleanders, and the crickets imitated his laughter from the dunes.

I kept my eyes ahead as I climbed to the hilltop necropolis of the *Cimiterio Monumentale*. I resisted the peerless view that was whispering at my back. I did not want to look, yet, at this land of absolutes – the place where I laughed the most, and cried the most. The place where I found love and lost it. The place where I had given Benedick use for my heart. I knew now he'd abandoned it here when he'd left. And now I'd come back to claim it, it was worthless; a single heart instead of a double one.

At last I reached the Leonatus family tomb, where the dead Leonati huddled in their chilly mausoleums to overlook their living relatives below. It was hard to think that my aunt Innogen, mother's sister to me, was now inside that pale stone. I twined my fingers in the curlicues of the wrought-iron gates, gates that represented the portal between the living and the dead, from which, once passed, no traveller returns. Bumbling bees buzzed around the floral tributes twined into the wrought iron, but determinedly did not pass through the grille. Even such lowly insects knew that to enter a tomb meant no coming out again. 'Greetings, Aunt,' I said, and took a crust from my sleeve.

I had come to perform a rite. A rite that once seemed strange to me as a northerner – I found it odd that in Sicily you would remember the dead not with floral tributes and prayers and solemn hymns, but instead bring your children and your curs and your grandmothers and a picnic, and feast upon the tomb of an old friend. I wondered whether the camaraderie continued under the ground; if beneath the stone memorials and mournful epitaphs whole families embraced in a companionable jumble of bones, to dispute over whose knucklebones were whose.

As I broke my bread at the gates, I remembered with a jolt that in this particular tomb, two women lay. My aunt was interred here by family right and rite; but Guglielma Crollalanza, a handful of secret cinders, had been buried here too a year past.

My appetite was gone. I threw the last morsel of my bread through the gates to the dead and brushed the crumbs from my lap with an air of finality. Everything ends. You could not begin again. I had paid my respects, and now I would go. Hero would have to shift for herself; she had no need of me. I would collect my unopened trunk and head to the port, to buy passage on a ship to take me home again to my father. Sicily had changed beyond measure. For Benedick was not here, and without him, things could not be as they were a year earlier.

The buzz of the bees turned to the distant rasp of a trumpet.

As if I had summoned a vision, I looked below and saw a procession of soldiers winding along the sea road from the port. Their armour sparkled, their scarlet pennants streamed in the warm southern winds. I could not, at this distance, make out the device on the standard, but my heart recognised it with a jolt before my eyes did. The processional pennants of the royal house of Aragon.

Was the scene real? Or had my memory of a year ago, of a cavalcade just like this one, conjured it? For that procession had first brought Benedick to me. And all else was forgotten as I saw, as I had a year ago amongst the muster, a golden head bobbing on a horse. This horse was a grey, though; Benedick's beloved mount, Babieca, had been a bay. If the horse was different, was the rider too?

I had to be sure. Heart thudding, I set off down the incline, scattering a murrain flock of scrawny sheep who stopped and turned at a safe distance to watch me, before dipping their polls again to snatch at the bitter grass.

At the foot of the hill I hurried down the Via Catania to Leonato's house.

I ducked under the pleached bower, past the fountains and through the pleasure gardens. The fruit trees, pollarded and pruned, stood in a neat quincunx. They looked like soldiers. I felt a sudden foreboding; why had the regiment come back to Messina? Was there to be more fighting?

I hastened to the coloured courtyard where I found my uncle, in his black silken robes of mourning. He was in the centre of the Roman mosaic, standing upon the very face of Medusa. With one of his hands he held a letter close to his old eyes, with the other he stroked his silver beard. A messenger in scarlet livery knelt at his feet, keeping his eyes respectfully on the mosaic. My uncle looked up at my approach and waved the letter at me.

'It seems you are not to be our only visitor, Niece,' he said. 'I learn in this letter that Don Pedro of Aragon comes to Messina. Claudio is returned too, having done great service in these wars.'

I felt a squeeze of my hand, and Hero was beside me. I had not seen her enter the courtyard, nor even noted her till now. I understood just how well she had learned to hug the shadows in these last days, and stand in sober silence, just as my uncle wished. I glanced at her. Her mourning apparel did not become her, for dark colours drained her sallow complexion and grief had made new hollows in her cheeks. But now she looked as if she was lit from within; coral flamed in her pale cheeks, and her eyes were as bright as a gull's. Claudio's name had been enough to illuminate her like this.

My uncle spoke again. 'Claudio's uncle will be very glad of his return. I must send a missive by fast rider.'

So the Archbishop of Monreale still lived, I thought, with a curl of my lip. I had hoped he had died in the interim, but dismissed the prelate from my mind. I cared not for the prince or Claudio, or the county's evil uncle. I cared only for news of one man; but now it came to it, I could not say the words. 'Tell me, Uncle . . .' I thought quickly, pretending that I did not recall *his* name. 'Is Signor Mountanto returned from the wars?'

My uncle looked puzzled, as well he might. 'Who is it that you ask for, Niece?'

'My cousin means Signor Benedick of Padua,' supplied Hero hesitantly, as if she feared to speak in company.

My uncle chuckled, a sound at odds with his melancholy garb. 'Oh, he's returned; and will no doubt take up the cudgels with you for a bout.'

Warm relief washed me like the Messina tide. Then a tucket sounded and my heart leaped to my mouth. The cavalcade approached.

The soldiers rode in a phalanx, behind the standard-bearer, with the dark Don Pedro at their head, just as they had a year ago. They were all in the livery of St James, with their medals clanking against their half-armour as they trotted, but I had no difficulty in picking one knight out from the rest. It was

Benedick, really, truly he; breathing in and breathing out, and rising and falling in his saddle. It was the loveliest single moment of my life; the first time in a year I had proof positive – the most incontrovertible proof of all, the proof of my own eyes – that he was alive.

He was much changed. His skin was ruddy like a sailor's, tanned by the winds. His hair was longer and sun-gilded about his face with streaks as blond as winter wheat. And he was much thinner; as thin as a cursitor. I breathed in, cursing Paris for fattening me up like a Christmas goose. Benedick's slim frame made him seem taller, and his shoulders broader. The horse he rode was not his old horse Babieca, and I wondered what had happened to his favoured mount. There was no sign, either, of the easy smile that I remembered, but my breath quickened as he rode closer, and the breeze lifted the locks from his forehead. Now I saw that his eyes were greener than ever in a complexion tanned by travel. I could not look away. He had vitality in every inch of him.

Don Pedro dismounted on the Roman pavement and greeted my uncle. 'Good Signor Leonato,' said the prince, embracing the older man fondly, 'and so we must trouble you for your hospitality once more.'

'Trouble never came to my house in Your Grace's company,' babbled my uncle. Now this was far from true, for I recalled the events of the previous summer. I bobbed about upon the balls of my feet, trying to see Benedick, but there were more introductions to make. An ill-favoured and miserable-looking fellow stepped forth and was introduced as Don John, Don Pedro's brother. There seemed to have been some sort of schism between the brothers, lately reconciled, but I had no patience with their affairs. Hero stepped forth, and the prince warmly kissed her hand, but above his bowed head she and Claudio mingled eyes, and I recall that the count liked her before he went to war. Suddenly I realised why the cavalcade was here;

they were not here to wage war but to woo; and so their hearts were in just as much jeopardy as a year before.

Then the crowd divided like the Red Sea, and I saw Benedick clear at the same instant he saw me. He smiled, a smile of such sweetness and joy that the clouds parted and the angels surged forward. I smiled too, and we hurried, half running, towards each other, overwhelmed by the rightness of it. I truly think we would have embraced, but my uncle intervened, fetching him a slap on the back fit to knock him over. 'Good Signor Benedick, here is one who asked most particularly for news of you. I'll warrant she'll ask you to choose your weapon to continue the bout you began a year ago, and I'll wager you'll choose the same one as she; your tongue.'

The crowd waited, listening, smiling with anticipation like those who came to see a bear course. They fully expected a spectacle, and my plan to greet Benedick with private and affectionate courtesies now had to be changed. I wiped the joyful smile from my face and squared my shoulders like a pugilist.

'I, Uncle? I require nothing of Signor Benedick save for the same office I would require from my cook; that is, to find out what is for dinner.'

The household tittered, and Benedick frowned, his dark brows almost touching in the way I remembered.

'Lady Beatrice, I am glad to find you yet living; and so unchanged. But I have not the pleasure of understanding you.'

'Then you are the one who is unchanged, for you never could keep up.'

'Not with your tongue, it is true; for your waggling member would leave even Babieca . . .' he faltered, 'even the swiftest horse standing. For you speak all mirth and no matter, as you always did; for I am not a cook but a soldier.'

'I only speak mirth if oaths and promises do not matter. And I am glad indeed to hear you call yourself a soldier, for I wished to enquire how many you had killed in these wars. If you recall,

I promised to eat all of your killing; and *I* like to keep *my* promises. And to say truly, I missed my breakfast so that I may be hungry for my dinner.'

He blanched as white as ocean spray. And I was sorry at once when I saw what a sea-change my mention of killing had wrought in him. Had he killed a score of men at the armada; a hundred? Had the sights he had seen scarred him and suppressed his merry nature? Appalled, I wanted to apologise, but I could no more retract my misfired wit than he could have called back the shot from his ship's gunfire. But he recovered himself in a trice, and put up his defences.

'Well, my dear Lady Disdain, I release you from your vow; and pray that you will maintain a tolerable health without such a macabre dinner.'

I smiled sweetly, a parody of the smile I'd wanted to bestow upon him. 'I thank you; but I think my disdain will prosper now it has its favoured meat; a fine haunch of Signor Benedick.'

The crowd laughed, sickening me. I took no pleasure in this false bout.

'Well, lady, I fear your disdain will hunger too, for I will trespass on your presence no more, nor put you to the trouble of speaking such fine courtesies to me. For courtesy is a turncoat, and not the *first* I have known.' Here, he seemed to shoot a meaningful glance at the prince, who was conversing with his brother and missed the jest, if jest it was.

Claudio saw it, though, and took Benedick by the sleeve. 'Come away,' he said, as if the conversation had taken a dangerous turn. 'We must all prepare ourselves for dinner. Ladies.' Claudio bowed, Benedick did not, and they followed their master from the courtyard.

It was a masterstroke, a perfect strategy. Just as he used to do a year before, Benedick had stopped suddenly like a hurtling destrier and sent me toppling over the reins. The household had begun to mill about and talk among themselves, now my opponent had left the lists. Alone, now, in the centre of the courtyard, I looked after Benedick and mouthed to the ether.

My uncle clapped his hands. 'Tonight we will feast and have a masque in the prince's honour, just as we did a year past. And in the cause of merriment I decree that we shall all leave off our mourning.'

I looked sharply at Hero, to see how she would take this disrespect to her mother. My aunt Innogen had barely been in the ground for a week; at this rate the funeral baked meats could practically furnish the banqueting tables. But Hero took the news equably, and looking at her I suddenly knew that she was the reason that Leonato had decreed that mourning apparel should be cast off. I was not the only one who had seen the longing glances flit about the courtyard. Leonato had felt it best to get his daughter out of black, and into her finery; for a bird of paradise was better to spring a trap upon a noble husband than a plain country blackbird.

'Come, Cousin, let us prepare.' I let Hero drag me away for there would be much ado to make ourselves ready for sundown. I followed her across the coloured tiles, my heart beating fast from the reunion. Now I had Benedick safely back from the seas, now I knew I was to meet him that night and the next day and go on meeting for as many days and nights as we stayed here, I had to force myself to admit the truth. I may have learned to love him in the year's interim, but that did not mean that he had come to love a woman he had once rejected so bitterly. How much did that sunburst of a smile when first he saw me really mean? I remembered well the bitter words he had spoken of me when last we stood together in this courtyard. He had begged Don Pedro to take him away from me. *I cannot abide my Lady Tongue.* And now he had trotted after Claudio from the courtyard, leaving me mouthing my rejoinders to the fresh air. A jade's trick, and one I knew of old.

As I followed Hero up the stone stair to her chamber my happiness tempered a little. Benedick had a horse of a different colour and a new sworn brother. I very much feared that he had become the Knight of the Mirror, with an armour wrought of looking glass, to reflect any companion he stood beside.

Act V scene ii

A masque in Leonato's gardens

Benedick: I could not wait to see Beatrice at the masque that night.

It seemed almost a miracle that she was here, and I had seen something in her first smile that led me to hope. After that, we'd been playing a part and she had put me thoroughly out of countenance by her first utterance. Her innocent jest about killing and eating soldiers had taken me straight back to the *San Juan de Sicilia*, to the fate of Faruq Sikkander, and those dreadful chewed bodies. All were victims upon that boat and a jest that had been harmless the previous year now had the power to cut me to the bone. Beatrice's year-old promise to eat all of my killing took on a new significance, as if she'd had a prophetic soul and had foreseen the horrors ahead. But tonight, if I could only get her alone, I prayed that we might begin anew.

It was almost a year to the day since we'd danced in this very garden lit by the same torches, the same fireflies. Then, I'd arrived in my livery of St James. Today, I had come as Benedick of Padua. I might still wear the saint's livery but it did not wear me. I had chosen for my mask the face of a dolphin, for I had seen many of the friendly creatures at sea, and they had leavened my leaden days with their perpetual smiles. I could have worn damask and jewels and a golden garter in my new guise as the Duke of Leon, but I could not bring myself to wear the robes nor use the title of my new rank.

Some of my fellow actors were the same – Don Pedro and

Claudio went about love's business; their henchmen the thin Conrad and the fat Borachio were at their leisure to drink as much as they might. There was Hero, who looked as different to the plain girl who had met us in the courtyard as a parrot does to a sparrow. A coral gown now warmed her skin, her dark hair was wrapped in gilded thread and dressed in coils about her head, and she wore above fifty fine golden chains about her slender neck. Leonato, who had also abandoned his black, was lecturing her upon some serious subject. I heard a snippet of his sermon: 'If the prince *does* address you upon that subject, you know your answer.'

Some of the players had changed – there was no dark lady, and no Lady Innogen. I wondered whether their ghosts conversed together in the myrtle hedges, heads together, as they had been in life. The poet was also absent, thank God, and I had reason to hope anew that Lady Beatrice was unmarried.

Some actors were new to the drama; Margherita, the tiring maid who had seemed a child last summer, was now a young lady; similar in height and colouring to her mistress Hero, she had a saucy look in her eye and a round promise to her figure. A year ago I would have troubled her for a dance. But this year there was only one lady I sought.

I glimpsed Beatrice in the throng, in that gown of many blues that I remembered well, the gown she wore to the wedding at Syracuse. I would have known her bearing and her figure anywhere, but in any case her mask gave her away. It was a beauteous thing; a visor in the shape of a star, with eyeholes set in two of the five points, and rimed with crystals and pearls.

Like a star she kept disappearing behind clouds; one moment she would be lost in the multitude, only to appear again elsewhere in the galaxy of guests. I noted through narrowed, jealous eyes that she was dancing; but soon realised that she danced alone, with no gentleman upon her arm. She whirled through the company, spinning and spinning till her cerulean skirts flew about her in a circle, and the diamond constellations on her bodice wheeled about like a sparkling orrery. She was captivating, and I did not interrupt her sport. I knew where she was at all times, I could sense her shining presence, like the constellation which had guided us home. I was content – she and I were on the same path, in the same orbit. We would meet sooner or later alone; it was ordained.

In the meantime, I found an unlikely companion in Don John, Don Pedro's brother. He was an unprepossessing gentleman; a miller's thumb of a man, with a large head atop a skinny body and a wasted foot that made him limp. I had some sympathy for his predicament; he had mismanaged Don Pedro's estates in the past year, leading to considerable losses to the family fortune. He had been publicly scourged in the town square at Zaragoza, then newly taken into Don Pedro's grace. He was a prisoner dressed in silk, and resentment and respect did battle in his countenance.

In all particulars he seemed as commonplace as his brother seemed noble, and I knew he was a bastard, an illegitimate child of Don Pedro's father. The fact that he had been raised – not just tolerated but cultivated – at the prince's side throughout childhood and adulthood said a great deal about their father's character. Observing the two brothers, one might have thought that nobility had a physical manifestation; Don Pedro, of true blood and the union of two noble strains, was as handsome as his brother was ill favoured; but I knew now that nobility had nothing to do with appearance. Nobility was not carried in birth or breeding but was something more tangible. Nobility was not an airy gilded cloud but something harder – bred in the bone, the sinew, the beating heart. Nobility was not the wave of a white hand, nor a favour easily given; it was tough, difficult, it was a trial to the body and the soul. With this in mind, I greeted Don John courteously. All my information about his disgrace and his pardon had come to my ear from Don Pedro's tongue, and I had learned not to trust so easily. I decided the fellow deserved a chance.

I nodded at him in a friendly fashion and my courtesy drew him to my side, with Conrad and Borachio in his wake.

'Are you not Signor Benedick?'

Don John cut an odd figure in his silks and samites – like a peasant dressed up for mumming.

I bowed. 'You know me well.'

Don John looked about him. 'You are close in love to my brother, are you not?'

'I have that honour,' I said drily.

Don John drew close, and I could smell his wine-soaked breath at my ear. 'He is in love with Hero, our host's daughter, and woos her even as we speak. If you are his true friend, dissuade him from the match. She is no equal for his birth.'

The night was warm, but I was suddenly cold. Don Pedro was supposed to be furthering Claudio's cause; *could* he be wooing Hero for himself?

'Are you sure?' I had learned, in a year, to doubt the word of princes; even though this bastard don seemed to bear all the outward shows of honesty.

'I heard him swear his affection.'

'I too,' said Conrad, volunteering an opinion for which he had not been asked.

'And I,' confirmed Borachio. 'I heard he would marry her tonight.'

I looked from one to the other – all three had pushed their visors to the top of their heads, but all wore the same solemn expression beneath. I had only just met Don John, but Borachio and Conrad I had known the previous year, men from Don Pedro's Aragonese estates. They drank too much, but they were honest fellows. And even on so short an acquaintance, I had already more inclination to trust Don John than his brother.

Now the snippet of conversation I had heard when I'd passed Leonato and his daughter made sense. *If the prince does address you upon that subject, you know your answer.* Leonato had tried to catch the prince for Hero last year; now he could make good upon the bargain. Recently bereaved and anxious to secure his line, how was he to know that we had already parcelled up his daughter aboard ship, and chosen her mate for her? Claudio had a prodigious fortune, it was true, but at bottom he was a banker's son. Don Pedro was royalty, and besides there had been whispers – rilling, silvery whispers that rippled all the way from El Escorial to Messina – that the prince would soon be made Viceroy of Sicily, as a just reward for his bravery at the armada. As the wife of the viceroy, Hero would settle in nearby Palermo, but if she married Claudio Leonato would lose his daughter to Florence.

And as for the prince? Yes, on board ship he had sworn to get Hero for Claudio, and make all well between the Lady Beatrice and myself. But things had changed. He had, by his own admission, now lost the better part of his fortune through his brother's bad management while he was at sea. What better for him than an heiress, with coffers to match his lands?

I must have been silent for some time, for Don John, his warning given, bowed and disappeared, taking Conrad and Borachio with him.

I watched the prince; if Beatrice was a star then he was once again the sun, charming all before him, gilding the guests with flattery, flashing his teeth. Don Pedro might have been last year's prince; he was even wearing the same mask, the knave of the *Scopa* pack. Only I could see, behind the eyes, where his sheen had worn away. I observed the prince deep in conversation with Hero, holding her white hand in his brown one, now and again carrying it to his lips. I began to feel uneasy.

All of a sudden Beatrice was at my shoulder. I had been charting her course all night, and then she had appeared out of the dark like a *stella nova*. 'Did you feast on oranges only when you were in Spain, Signor Benedick? Your expression would turn the milk.'

I gave myself a little shake, and smiled at her. 'Do you seek me, lady?'

Her eyes glittered through the mask. 'Now, why on earth would I be seeking you? I am looking for your new sworn brother, Count Claudio, at the behest of the prince.'

I snorted. 'You will find him hiding under the sedges, like a hurt fowl.'

'Why?'

'The prince has got his Hero.'

'Yes,' she said patiently, as if to a child. 'He has wooed her in Claudio's name.'

I was silent.

'You think not?'

Still I said nothing. I could not voice my suspicions and was dumb with frustration. I had wanted to speak to her all night, and now I had her in my company she had touched upon the very subject on which I was sworn to silence.

'Well,' she exclaimed, 'I am not at my leisure to converse with a post. Fare you well.'

I went to the prince, full of foreboding, for he had linked his arm in Hero's as if they were at the church door, and she was laughing up into his face. A pox on this wooing by proxy; every man should negotiate for himself, for in the face of Hero's beauty Don Pedro's promises had clearly melted away.

The prince started at my approach, and looked a little guilty. His eyes flickered. 'Ah, Benedick – where's the count, did you see him?'

I decided to speak in defence of my friend. I had sworn allegiance to Don Pedro but I had sworn brotherhood to Claudio. 'He went in the direction of the willow, my lord. Perhaps to find a switch fit for his whipping.'

He laughed merrily. 'A count whipped like a schoolboy! This is a night of misrule indeed.'

'Indeed,' I said heavily. 'It is a night when counts can be schoolboys and princes can be knaves. His fault was that of a schoolboy, not a count. He found a bird's nest, told his friend and his friend stole it.'

Hero smiled bemusedly, looking from the prince to myself; happily, she could not follow our discourse. But Don Pedro's eyes were flint. 'I only teach his bird to sing, and return it to the owner. It is not a crime to entrust an office to a friend.'

'But it is a crime to *break* that trust.'

Then Beatrice approached with Claudio in tow, and broke the spell. 'By my troth, there are some sour-faced gentlemen abroad tonight! Surely wooing is not so serious a subject; you all look so tartly.'

Claudio looked askance at me, then at the prince, who had his arm entwined in Hero's.

'The prince and I were just talking of *allegiance*,' I said pointedly.

The prince looked at Claudio, Claudio looked at the prince. Somehow, in that moment, we were back on the *Florencia*. I hoped I had made my feeling plain. If the prince reneged on his promise to get him Hero, Claudio could tell the world what Don Pedro really was.

'Here, Claudio,' said Don Pedro. 'I have wooed in your name, and Hero is won. Name the day of marriage, and God give you joy.' But he held on to her arm a little too long – she had to pull away and almost stumbled into Claudio's arms.

All the assembly clapped and cheered; Claudio and Hero were wreathed in smiles. 'You see, Benedick,' Don Pedro said low voiced, his expression naked for once. 'You can put your trust in princes.'

I bowed and turned away, and nearly ran into Beatrice.

She fell into step with me. 'Did you really think the prince would have betrayed Count Claudio so? He is an honourable man, is he not?' She asked the question seriously, as if it really mattered to her.

'Oh yes,' I said with an ironic tone. 'He is the very best of men.'

She took the compliment at face value. 'And even were he the worst of men, he would be better than the best of women? After all' – her eyes glittered through her mask – 'you chose him once before, over another. Or is it Count Claudio who commands your loyalty now?'

I was once more silent, powerless to explain.

'Ah, you are as dumb as a songless bird, but your plumage proclaims for you. I see you are still wearing the livery of the prince's order. And now Claudio is to be wed, and taken from your company. What a shame there is not enough cloth in your doublet to cut you a kirtle. For then you could marry the prince, and God would give *you* joy. A double wedding for the single men.' She stalked ahead into the midnight garden, but turned back halfway up the lawn. 'Perhaps you could give him the *settebello*; I'm sure you have a card or two to spare.' And she strode away into the dark.

'Beatrice . . . wait!'

She did not turn again, and it was just as well, for there was nothing that I could say. Her glittering skirts swept the grass, her hem darkening with dew.

I kicked the same grass savagely as I walked back to the pink and torchlit house. I cursed my vow to Don Pedro, my oath upon an allegiance I no longer felt. At that rate, how could I tell Beatrice how he had parted us, how could I explain that it was the prince who had led me to discover her in the poet's embrace, he who he had left the *Scopa* cards for her to find in my chamber?

It was no use – I must labour for her favour with these innocent sins still at my door, for there could be no explanation without breaking my vow. I must rely on the prince to make all good; like Claudio before me I must trust him to woo for me. But after what I had seen tonight – even though all had ended happily – I did not know if I could do so.

Don Pedro had recreated himself as the shining hero; he was Knight Roland from the puppet show once more. I wondered how he remembered the voyage of the *Florencia* in his own head, until someone reminded him of the reality as I had done tonight. I wondered whether, in his memory, he *had* done great deeds, not cowered in his cabin. In his new image of himself, perfect and pristine, how likely was he to admit to the littleness of his subterfuge, or own that he was a man who had parted two lovers with a pack of lies and a pack of cards?

Act V scene iii

Leonato's gardens

Beatrice: It was the day before Hero's wedding, and I wandered the gardens watching the preparations.

The arrangements for the wedding were taking over both the interior and the exterior of the house, but the provisions were very different within and without the walls. In the house, soft and delicate transformations were taking place – fronds of flowers, wisps of coloured tissue, ribbons and confetti. But about the walls, a rosary of security; Leonato had redoubled his guard at the gates and around the perimeter of the house. And between these burly professionals stood dozens of Messinese peasants whom Leonato had recruited for the Watch. The constables were having a devil of a time pressing these new recruits into shape; the lame, the hobbled, the young, the old, the stupid. Incredibly, this makeshift Watch had orders to stay the prince himself if need be.

The only decorations outside the house were flags, hanging above the heads of these dolts. Dozens upon dozens of Trinacria flags, determinedly demonstrating Leonato's Sicilian allegiance, three bended legs wreathed around Medusa's head. There were no Aragonese flags to be seen, no ensigns of Spain or blazons of St James. Since the affair of the Spanish ostlers, there had been no more overt attacks on the house; but with the return of the Spanish the fear had returned too. I thought my uncle was right to be afraid – for more than once over the last week I had felt a pricking in my thumbs as if I was being observed, and had turned too late to see the watcher in the shadows. The previous night, at the masque, I had had the feeling again; but this time I had glimpsed a hooded figure wearing the mask of a crow. He had watched the assembly like a black raptor, before disappearing into the crowd.

I dismissed the spectre from my mind and I wandered down the rose walk to trail my hand in the fountain. Yet again I must watch a younger cousin beat me to the altar. I watched the bustle of the gardeners with studied indifference; not for worlds would I admit that I was hankering after just such a wedding. I had given Paris to Giulietta without a pang, but now to see such lanterns hung and flowers strewn pained me, for now I had the right groom back, I wanted the wedding.

I loved Hero well, and on my return we had resumed our close friendship as if we had never been parted. I was happy for her that she had the man of her dreams; yet even to Hero I could not admit my feelings for Benedick. But I think she guessed; for every time I happened upon Hero and Margherita, or Hero and Orsola, they were talking, loudly, of how worthy a gentleman Benedick was, and that he was not the unhopefullest husband they knew. But I could not let go of my persona of Beatrice the bachelor, Beatrice the wit, Beatrice the maid who would rather hear a dog bark at a crow than a man swear he loved her. If that Beatrice left me, who would I be? I had to be sure of Benedick – losing him once was the most difficult thing I'd had to endure; losing him again would kill me. Once again he'd come to Messina starstruck by his exalted company; last year it had been the prince, this year the count. And still there was the problem of his bitter words to me when we'd last parted, and the *Scopa* cards I'd found in his room the previous summer. Neither had been explained, although I had given him ample chance when I chid him about the *settebello* only the night before.

We had spoken so many words to each other over the past few days, always in public, always in conflict. I wonder whether he knew as well as I that we were performing, that we were unable to let go of the perception that we were at war. What I wanted more than anything was time alone with him, when I could ask him, with a sad countenance, what had caused him to leave me here. I had given my father my word that I would be back in Villafranca in a month – half of that time had now gone. So while I watched and wandered in the gardens I hoped, as I always did, that I would chance upon Benedick.

But it seemed I was destined to meet everyone in our party but him. In the pleached alley I came upon the prince's brother Don John and his henchmen Conrad and Borachio – they were deep in conversation about something, but when they saw me, ended their discourse abruptly and bowed politely. I greeted them, retraced my steps and went the other way. By the espaliered peach trees I saw Hero and Claudio, whispering to each other like billing doves. And, in an old straw hat and smock, Leonato bustled about, directing operations. At last I saw a lone man in the colours of St James come towards me, and my heart stuttered. But it was not he; as the figure rounded the alley of lemon trees I could see that it was Don Pedro. I arranged my disappointed expression into one of deferential greeting. I had always liked the prince well enough; he seemed noble and I knew him to be honourable. I was fair enough not to blame him that Benedick had chosen his service over my company.

'Lady Beatrice.' The prince bowed, and when he righted himself his face was flushed in a way that could not wholly be explained by him stooping so. He breathed as though he had been running. The day was punishingly hot, so perhaps that explained his discomfiture. 'Lady Beatrice,' he began again, more hesitantly than I had ever heard him speak, 'I have something to ask, and something to tell.'

'Shall we take shelter?' I indicated the Roman baths, beyond the rose walk, shady green pools as flat as mirrors, sheltered by a loggia of cool stone pillars. We walked and sat by the water, on stones older than the house. My aunt had once told me that the young single men of the house would wash here and take their sport, so it always pleased me to sit in a place where, centuries before, I would not have been allowed to venture.

Now we were here, the prince seemed in no hurry to begin. Bees drunkenly weaved in and out of the columns, dragonflies were a blue flash darting between lily pads. We watched the servants weaving willow switches into arches over the knot garden before the chapel.

At last the prince spoke. 'Your cousin's wedding is tomorrow, I think?' he asked.

'Yes,' I said with a windy sigh, making a jest of it. 'So goes every other soul into the world, except for you and I, Prince. We must sit and watch from this basin of bachelors.' As soon as I had said the words, I regretted them; for realisation struck me just as they left my lips. Now I understood the way Don Pedro was looking at me, that curious, intent expression. I understood the flushed cheeks, the laboured breathing. I looked at my ringless hands in my lap. '*That* was to be your question.'

'Yes,' he said. 'Will you have me, lady?'

And there and then, on the lip of those Roman baths, I was being offered that wedding I'd wanted. Just for a heartbeat I imagined my father's face if I returned to Villafranca with Don Pedro in tow. But I did not hesitate. I had refused a count of Verona, I could refuse a prince of Aragon. I looked into his dark eyes – affecting diffidence, but with a plea at their dark centre. Could it be that even a prince could feel what I had felt this morning, that all the world processed in pairs into the shady church, while we bachelors were left to burn in the sun?

His eyes were so serious that I felt I must jest. 'Prince, I fear you have been on a boat so long that you think all creatures must go aboard two by two. My cousin marries your friend, and now we must all take our partners for Hymen's dance? No, my lord, I thank you.'

Now it was the prince's turn to study his hands, and I saw there the yellow and red enamelled blazon of Aragon on his seal ring, a ring which, had my answer been different, would now have adorned my own hand. 'Could you give me a reason?'

I could not. I was silent, my mind racing. 'Then I will supply the objection,' he said, his lips twisted in a bitter smile. 'You love Benedick.' My instinct was to lie, to jest, to make denial. But I felt I owed him the truth. 'Yes.' The relief was enormous.

He saw it. 'You feel unburdened?'

I nodded. 'You are the first soul to know of it.' Then I remembered. 'Except . . . there was one . . . last summer.'

He nodded. 'The poet. Michelangelo Florio Crollalanza.' He spoke the name as if it was verse.

'How did you . . . ?' Then I recalled. The horseman on the beach. It had been the prince. I fell silent, suddenly toad cold. 'You said you had something to ask and something to tell.' My voice sounded curiously high and flat. 'What is it?'

He took in a deep breath. 'It pertains to that very man,' he said. 'Last summer, I led Benedick to believe that you were enamoured of that poet. I brought him to see where you two embraced upon the beach. I knew you consoled him for the loss of his mother. Benedick did not. *That* is why he rejected you.'

I stared, unseeing, at the dragonflies. *Benedick* had been there. He had seen us. Now I understood his strange behaviour at the farewell feast, his bitter and public repudiation of me in the coloured courtyard before he rode away. I needed space and quiet to order my thoughts, but I was not to be granted it, for Don Pedro spoke again.

'And the *Scopa* cards in his room – the trick deck – they were mine, left there so you should find them. The card he gave you was no cheat's hand. It was true.'

The bee's song hummed in my ears with my blood. 'Why did you do this?' My voice was no more than a whisper.

'I wanted him to come with me, to fulfil his obligations to his knight's vow, and to blessed Saint James.'

'But what of his vow to *me*?' The foolish words spilled out before I could prevent them.

'What vow?'

Now it was my turn to be silent. There had been no vow. There was no pre-contract, no ink set down to bind us. Benedick had broken no indenture. Only the vow made between lip and lip, that night upon the dunes; between body upon body, signed by stars and sealed in sand. I could not speak of this, so instead I asked the prince the question that burned into my mind. 'Why did you not tell me this first? Before you offered me marriage?'

He looked at me directly. 'Would you have considered me then?'

I did not have to reply. My answer was in the fall of my gaze from his. 'And if I had accepted your proposal? Would you have ever told me of these other things?' I looked at him again, and this time his eyes dropped first, and I knew. I would have been the Princess of Aragon, but I would have gone to my grave thinking Benedick untrue.

I gazed upon the calm Roman pools, my mind in turmoil. I did not know what to think. Whether to be gleeful and thankful that Benedick and I had been gulled, or to be angry that we had been parted with such a fool's trick. Whether to censure Don Pedro for his ignoble actions of a year ago, or commend him for his belated honesty. Whether to grieve for the year Benedick and I had lost, or to rejoice in the time ahead.

But before I could speak, a fast rider skidded to the gates, reining his horse in a cloud of dust. As the messenger attempted to argue his way past the guards, Don Pedro stood and hurried to the postern. 'What is your business?' he called to the rider.

'A message for the master of the house, my lord.'

I stood and followed the prince, full of foreboding. 'I am the

Prince of Aragon,' said Don Pedro. 'You may give the message to me.'

The messenger looked the prince up and down, and made his choice. 'Very well, Highness.' He knelt and held out a scroll. 'The Archbishop of Monreale was murdered last night in his bed, sire. Poisoned.'

Now that there was no bar to our union I would have sought out Benedick at once, but the goddess Fate – with cruel irony and little sympathy for a fellow female – decided that he would be absent for the rest of the day.

He had accompanied the prince and the count to Monreale, to discover the particulars of the untimely death of Claudio's uncle. Don John, the prince's brother, was most solicitous in their absence, assisting Leonato with the matters of the morrow. It did not seem to occur to my uncle to postpone the nuptials – in fact he seemed, if anything, more anxious to speed the business; and Don John was the man to help him. No detail was too trivial for the don; he even wished to know where everyone in the wedding party would be sleeping, and asked me which was Hero's window, as he desired to arrange for musicians to serenade her. I was surprised that he was such a good steward, for I had heard that he had been such a poor custodian of Don Pedro's estates that his mismanagement had placed the bad blood between them that his birth had not.

I am sorry to say that the archbishop's passing troubled we ladies not at all, and did not cast the slightest shadow upon the forthcoming wedding. If I gave the prelate a thought it was to reflect grimly that a debt had been paid for the life of Guglielma Crollalanza. Even Hero, who was a true devout, merely remarked mildly that she hoped Claudio would not mourn so grievously for his kinsman's passing as to temper his nuptial joy.

In the afternoon I helped Hero and Margherita with the final touches to Hero's wedding gown, but could barely sit still. I was hot and cold all at once, and alternately rushed to the window to gulp at the breeze, and shivered on my sewing stool. I had no patience for their womanly chatter about the Duchess of Milan's latest gown, or which rebato would be better with the wedding dress. When I caught my reflection behind Hero's in the looking glass I could see my cheeks were hectic, my lips rosy and full and my eyes burning blue. It was little wonder that my companions began to fear for my health.

'Are you sick, Beatrice?' asked Hero.

Had she been alone, I might have told her all; of how everything had been explained and all could now end well between Benedick and me. But I did not wholly trust Margherita, who could be a sly little thing; so I agreed that I suffered most grievously. 'I am exceeding ill,' I announced. 'I think it is a head-cold.' I held my cousin's eyes with my own, to prevent her turning to the beautiful day outside. I had once told her that I never suffered from head-colds as I was raised in a draughty castle, so would be hard put to explain why I had caught such a malady in the burning sun. I spent the rest of the afternoon counterfeiting to sneeze, and pretending I could not smell the exquisite perfume of the wedding gloves Claudio had sent for Hero. I hugged to myself the knowledge that I might soon receive a pair of gloves of my own.

'Perhaps you are in need of a tonic,' said Margherita innocently. 'I have heard it said that *Carduus benedictus* is a powerful remedy.'

I quelled her with a look, but she spoke no more than the truth; Benedick was my cure. As the afternoon wore on I began to worry that he would not return – that the archbishop's assassin would dispatch him too, that his horse would tread in a divot on the road and throw him, that brigands would rob and stab him on the road. That brief afternoon held more agony for me than the year Benedick had spent on board ship.

The menfolk were not back by dinner, so after we had supped there was nothing for it but to go to bed. As maid of honour I was to share a bed with Hero, as was the tradition on the wedding eve. I did not expect to sleep, for it was too hot to even tolerate a coverlet, even without thoughts of Benedick to keep my heart racing. But I must have slept, for I dreamed of rain – blessed heavy drops falling on my face and body. I woke to the warm night, Hero sleeping peacefully beside me. Then a little pebble landed on the pavings and skittered along the floor; another landed on the coverlet.

I went to the window and out on to the balcony. A figure resolved out of the darkness below and for a moment I felt a jag of fear – in just such a manner I had once seen an intruder with a torch, on the night the Spanish ostlers were dismembered. But in an instant my fear was replaced with relief. It was Benedick down there; even his silhouette was familiar to me. 'Lady Beatrice,' he called softly. 'The stars are out. Come down.'

I leaned over the balustrade. 'I cannot,' I whispered, my voice keen with disappointment. 'Margherita sleeps at the door.'

He pounded fist into palm, frustrated.

'I have waited a year,' he said, 'but now I cannot wait for another dawn.'

'Stay,' I said. I tiptoed back into Hero's room, and crept to the door. I had hoodwinked Margherita once, the night that I had stolen from the house to see the Tarantella. I slipped back the bolt and lifted the latch silently; as the door creaked open I could see Margherita's mat beyond, but no Margherita. Where had the little cate gone?

It mattered not; her defection made my flight easy. In an instant I was down in the courtyard beside Benedick. He held out his hand; I took it.

We flitted through the gardens on silent feet – I trod the very paths and alleys I had trodden that day, as happy now as I had been pensive then. Benedick led me to the Roman baths, to the exact spot where I had been with Don Pedro that morning. 'Look,' said Benedick. And there I saw the wonder.

The limpid green pool of that morning had been transformed into a starfield. It was a map of treasure, a sparkling Turkey carpet of stars which had been captured and brought to earth, reflected perfectly in the rectangular bath. Night had been distilled into a looking glass. Benedick had laid these jewels down before me, like the conquistadors who went to the Americas and dazzled the poor natives with their bounty. He had sailed many miles to come all the way here to this island, to me. I was his haven, and he had brought me treasure.

But he returned to me that which was my own; for there, in the middle of the constellations, was Cassiopeia's chair, and my star beneath. I could have sworn that I could have stepped out and walked upon the carpet, as if I was walking in the sky, could seat myself in that silver chair and converse with Cassiopeia and the rest of the deities of the heavens.

We sat on the stone basin, just where I'd sat with the prince; but we faced the other way, into the pool and not the garden. For Benedick had once again altered everything; he had changed one sky for another and tipped the universe. The stone was still warm from the day and we dangled our feet above the water, careful not to touch that sacred surface. For the smallest ripple would create a celestial maelstrom, and now the stars were aligned I was afraid to disturb them.

Benedick made as if to speak but I put my finger to his lips. I had to tell all, to wipe the schoolroom slate and begin again.

'Don Pedro told me how he tricked you, a year past.'

'Don Pedro did?' I had astonished him. 'He told you all?'

'Of how he brought you to the beach, and concealed the cheat's deck of *Scopa* cards in your room.'

He was silent for so long I thought him angry with his friend, and tried to mitigate the prince's crime. 'The sequel makes amends for the original offence. He is an honest man and a brave one too – it took great courage for him to tell me what he did.'

He smiled tightly. I thought him jealous then. How much more jealous would he be if he knew what I had left out? That the prince had offered me marriage first?

'Enough of other men and their good qualities,' said Benedick, the laughter back in his voice. He squeezed my hand, for he'd never let it go. 'For which of my fine attributes did you first fall in love with me?'

I smiled at him. 'Who said that I loved you?'

He looked at me in a way that made me shiver. 'Your eyes say it, for they are brighter than any of these brave stars.'

I'd admitted to a prince here that day that I loved Benedick; I could not counterfeit to the man himself. 'I will not deny you.'

'So come. Which of my good qualities caught at your heart?'

'Nothing which other men would name so.'

He feigned distress. 'Then, for which of my *bad* parts did you first fall in love with me?'

I looked at him, mock-earnest. 'That is easier to answer. Your foolishness, your garrulousness, your vanity, your gullibility, your facile nature.' I paused for breath. 'And for which of my good parts did you first fall in love with me?'

'I cannot think of any qualities that you possess.'

I smiled. 'Then which of my faults drew your notice?'

'Ah, that is simple. Your conceit, your disdainfulness, your wilful pride, your stubborn nature, your runaway tongue.' He smiled too.

I would rather hear such insults from his tongue than a thousand compliments from any other. 'We will never be civil to each other, will we?'

'Never,' he said. 'And in that cause we will ask the friar tomorrow to bind us when he binds my brother and your cousin. Then we can be unpleasant to each other every day for the rest of our lives.'

It was the second proposal I'd received that day upon this spot, and I knew, this time, that everything was as it was meant to be. Benedick had righted the skies again. Hero's wedding would be mine too, just as I had wished. '*Yes*,' I said, and that single frugal syllable was worth more than all my spendthrift wit. My happiness was complete. I could have nestled against him for ever.

Much, much later, I was struck by a thought. 'You call Claudio your brother?'

He breathed in and out again audibly. 'It is an oath we took on board ship,' he answered, his chest rising and falling beneath my cheek, 'once we knew we would live.'

I wriggled out of his arm so I could look at him. 'What happened out there?'

He avoided my gaze but looked up, now, at the stars in the sky; as if he did not want to look upon water. 'Deeds that should stay there, where we left them. All I can tell you is that there was little glory in the action, nor nobility nor bravery. But I did find nobility in Claudio and courage too. True courage.' Again, he did not mention the prince. 'Claudio and I held each other up, above the water.'

'And he brought you back?'

'No,' he replied. 'You did.' He pointed to Cassiopeia's chair. 'You once showed me a little star, and told me that you were born in the same hour. For when everything else went awry, that star stayed true, as true as I now know you to be; for the prince admitted all to me too.'

A little cloud passed over my happiness; for should he not have trusted me for myself? Should he have needed to be told of my innocence by his patron? Then he laid his hand on my cheek and I forgot my doubts. 'Your star was my guide. I kept my eyes on it from dusk to dawn, each night from Scotland to Santander.'

'I am glad,' I said. 'So glad I could do you such an office. I would have stowed on the ship if I could, then I could have been with you.'

'You were with me every day,' he said. 'And now there will be no more sailing by the star.' He took my face in his hands. 'I am home.'

It seemed that we kissed for hours, and the dark pool turned paler, bluer, like the layers of my starlight dress. Now the stars were not diamonds upon velvet, but milky pearls on Mary's cloak. 'I have to go back,' I said, regretfully. 'Hero will go to church in a few hours, and I have barely slept.'

We walked back through the night gardens and in the coloured courtyard I kissed him. 'One last time as a bachelor,' he said. He had been wrong; *his* eyes were the brightest stars of all.

I passed Borachio on the stairs – on another night I would have questioned his presence, for that stair led only to Hero's chamber. But that night my heart was full of Benedick and me. When I climbed the stairs Margherita was curled upon her mat once more – her cheeks flushed, her eyes screwed tight, her breathing even, feigning slumber.

I hesitated, standing over her. She had clearly been about some mischief for she was no more asleep than I. But if I allowed her counterfeit, she could ask me no saucy questions. Striding over her confidently into Hero's chamber, I let her lie.

Act V scene iv

Leonato's house

Benedick: As Claudio's groomsman I was charged with getting the count ready for his wedding.

Claudio stood naked in a pool of sunlight in the middle of his chamber, his brows stern, his face thoughtful. I joked with him, employing those timeworn jests that men have broken against grooms since antique times – but he did not respond. I was in tearing spirits myself; after my night among the stars with Beatrice, the future seemed paved with diamonds. I had not slept, but I was bursting with joy. I wanted to confide in Claudio, but his demeanour was so forbidding that I left him to his thoughts. I imagined that he was not just apprehensive of the ceremony ahead, but that his spirits were much depressed by our trip to Monreale to visit his uncle's corpse.

When we'd arrived at the beautiful hilltop town the day before, we had been invited to view the archbishop's body, for the constables had charged that it not be moved. So we trooped into the vast, sand-coloured palace and entered the prelate's velvet-draped chamber.

The archbishop lay with his eyes open, a black trickle falling from his mouth and his accustomed tears still standing in each eye. I had no love for the man, could not forget how he had condemned the dark lady to the fire; but I knew it must have been a rude shock for Claudio to see his kinsman so. He had planned, I know, to come here to ask the archbishop to officiate at his wedding; now he must arrange for his uncle's burial.

The sergeant-at-arms of the archbishop's palace gave us a cup of Rhenish in the gatehouse before we rode. ''T'was a lone assassin,' he said, 'a hooded man. He was dressed in the habit of a monk, but scaled the walls like a monkey.'

He grunted at his own jest, then straightened his face at Claudio's stern glance. 'We have heard tell of a hooded assassin who goes by the name of Cardenio, the Ragged One. In the last year his legend has grown.' The name jolted me; for that had been the signature upon the pamphlets I'd seen at the Vara. 'The poison is Mantuan – most parts mercury. Have a care, gentlemen,' he said as we drained our stirrup cups. 'And tell Lord Leonato to do the same at his daughter's wedding. These brigands are getting bolder.'

I had forgotten the warning on the road, for by then the stars were kindling and my thoughts were only of Beatrice. But now I guessed that the archbishop's murder, and the threat of some disruption to the day, hung heavily on Claudio's mind. For indeed, he did not resemble a man on his wedding morn.

The groom of the stool guided me through the elaborate dressing process, for I had never performed such an office before. I chafed Claudio's body with a linen rubber – gentle on the breast and back, then vigorously on the limbs until a ruddy blush stood forth upon the skin. Then I held out the little vials of perfume and the pomades to sweeten his scent and he took them and applied them as if in a trance. I helped him into his suit of clothes; the purple that he always wore, the purple of the Medici. This attire was a statement of wealth woven in cloth, for a year earlier, when he was more of a boastful boy than a man, he'd told me it took thirty thousand whelks to make the dye for just one ounce of this cloth. He wore his inheritance on his back, and when he was dressed I looked at him with pride; my new brother was a comely fellow; if only he would smile. I coaxed him to grin once, so that I could pick at his teeth with a tooth-pick made of the quill of a feather, and polish them with a toothcloth of stripped linen. But his smile was more of a grimace. Lastly I held a silver basin while he swilled his mouth with white wine, and gave him a handful of cumin seeds to chew. 'Must keep your breath sweet for Hero's kisses,' I said. He snorted; not the reaction I had expected to such a jest. I led him down the stair and through the courtyard as if he sleepwalked.

The little chapel was packed with a press of people and was dressed in its best for a feast day. The pews were bright and brave with ginestra blossom, the pillars hung about with garlands. Likewise, the stained windows transformed the workaday sunlight into a rainbow of colours, the panes dazzling prisms splitting the light. Even those of the congregation who had come in their simple fustians were painted such brave colours they might have been wearing velvet.

At the altar stood the bride in cloth-of-gold, a veil of gilded filigree thrown over her face. And by her side, a vision that eclipsed her as fully as May does December: Beatrice, in silver tissue, with diamond stars pinned in her blond curls. Natural order was inverted, as Beatrice's stars eclipsed Hero's sun. My heart raced – for these good people who ranked the pews thought they had come to see one wedding, but they had come to see two. By the time I left this holy place, I would be Benedick the Married Man.

In my role as groomsman I walked beside Claudio, who was as silent as a stone. I jostled him slightly and smiled, but his face was stern. No matter – when the formalities were done, we would raise a cup together, husbands both. A wake for our bachelor days.

Don Pedro walked before us and stood next to his brother Don John. Today the prince looked as tartly as his brother did, and said just as little. I thought that I could better interpret *his* moody silence; he must watch his protégé take a prize which might have been his. And yet today I had reason to love Don Pedro. Despite my misgivings he had kept his word; he had told Beatrice of her misprision, and wed her to me in all but law. Opposite the dons stood Leonato and his brother Antonio, two noble greybeards mirroring the princes, and showing them their futures in old age.

Friar Francis stood forth. I had not seen Father Francisco Maurolyco since the night he had dragged me out of the Mermaid tavern in Messina and brought me home; the eve of my departure a year hence. Then he had listened to me rail against Beatrice. Today he would hear me swear to love her unto death.

The friar raised his book, and began to speak the Latin of the wedding mass, but Leonato, as if an assassin were at his very gates, hurried him along. 'The plain form, the plain form, Father,' he urged, mopping his perspiring brow with a silken kerchief. 'You may recount their particular duties later.'

I might have thought him rude and peremptory on any other day; I might have thought him indelicate to disrupt his daughter's moment. But today his haste pleased me; it chimed well with my own impatience to complete Claudio's nuptial so that we might proceed to mine and have the business speeded as soon as we might.

'Very well,' said the friar, his disapproval just audible in his voice. 'But you know, sire, that the law requires a certain form of words.'

'Yes, yes.' Leonato waved his handkerchief at the friar. 'Proceed.'

The friar cleared his throat. 'Who giveth this woman to this man?'

'That do I,' said Leonato.

'A moment, Friar.' Claudio's voice rang out; young, strong and confident. 'Let me see this *precious gift*.'

He took Hero's veil and flicked it back over her head; not tenderly, but as one who had bought a picture and wished to see the likeness. Hero smiled bemusedly; for tradition held that the veil should have been taken up at the end of the ceremony, not the beginning. Claudio did not smile, but appraised her coldly. The congregation was silent, waiting, and after some moments Claudio turned away from his bride and mounted the altar steps until he was level with the friar. 'Give me leave a while, good friar.'

Friar Francis, bemused, stepped down and Claudio was left standing over us, for all the world as if he was officiating as his uncle the archbishop had so many times.

'On our recent voyage, on board the gunship *Florencia*, we suffered greatly,' he began, surprising us all. '*Greatly*.'

I looked swiftly to Don Pedro, wondering, as I am sure he was, what the count was about to say of our dread voyage. It was in my mind to break in with a jest; but before I could interrupt Claudio, Leonato did the office for me.

'We all know of your heroism, Count. But perhaps such war stories may be told at the fireside later?'

'I will not try your patience much longer, *Father*,' said Claudio with biting emphasis. 'Think of this in lieu of a sermon, if the good friar will indulge me.'

I recalled his sermons upon the ship; that clear voice, that benign devotion. This was different.

'We had a barrel of oranges to keep the men in health. You have oranges in Spain too, my lord?'

'We do,' said Don Pedro sternly. 'In great number.'

It was then I knew that I had been wrong about the prince; whatever Claudio was about to say, Don Pedro was complicit in it, and anticipated every word.

'On the day we went "north about", we divided the rations of the men. There was a barrel of oranges in the hold. I took one out and held it up in my hand – it looked beautiful – round and gold as the sun.' He mimed the action, and I swear that his voice was so musical and persuasive that we all saw the orange. 'But I pushed my finger through the skin – inside it was black and rotten. The next one was the same, and the next. We had to throw them away, all of them, for though a sound orange might have saved a life, a rotten one can kill an ailing man.'

Claudio now looked at Hero, as though this lesson was only for her; but again, he addressed her father. 'Leonato,' he said, 'we have been your honoured guests last year and this. You have feasted us royally, offered us delicacies from Tripolis and Ragusa and Oran. I ate more at dinner last night than I ate in a brace of months on the *Florencia*. Have you ever, in all those repasts, offered us anything spoiled?'

'Never, my lord!' cried Leonato in confusion. 'I would never serve a guest so in my house.'

'And if you served me a rotten orange, what would you expect me to do?'

With a dreadful premonition, I suddenly knew where this catechism tended.

'I would expect you to refuse it.'

'Then, Leonato, I refuse your daughter.' Beatrice let out a cry, and a gasp rippled around the chapel. 'Her skin is unblemished, I grant you.' Claudio stroked Hero's cheek in a gesture that should have been tender, was not. 'But she is rotten to the very core – pips, pith, flesh, all are tainted.' His stroking fingers moved down and grabbed Hero by the throat. 'And if you press your fingers to the flesh, they sink right through, and inside is contagion, as decayed as a medlar.'

For a moment, we were all frozen in wonderment; then the whole church moved. Beatrice grabbed the count's hands where they squeezed the life from her cousin. Leonato leapt for his daughter, but whether in censure or defence I did not know, for he was prevented by the bear-like embrace of his brother Antonio. Don John's reaction was perhaps the oddest of all; he simply walked out of the church, unhurriedly, discreetly, but with purpose. Only Don Pedro, of the whole company, was still, watching the scene being acted out as if he were at the playhouse.

I sprang forward and clasped Claudio's arms from behind – I was ever stronger than he but today he seemed not of this world; he tossed me about with the strength of a leviathan. I wrenched him away and pressed him against a pillar, while Beatrice cradled her choking cousin at the opposite pillar; so that these two young people, in a dreadful perversion of the sacrament of marriage, were holding up the church. The friar, in the centre of all, bellowed for silence. 'What is this coil?' he cried; and I recalled in that moment that he used to be a soldier.

'Only this,' spat Claudio over my shoulder at Hero. 'What man was it, that you talked with at your window between the hours of twelve and one last night?'

Hero, white about the face but red in the throat where Claudio's fingers had grasped her, began to shake her head and weep.

'Aye,' said Claudio. 'Your guilt seeps from your eyes. What villain shared your bed?'

Leonato stumbled forward. 'My lord, you must be mistaken.'

Now Don Pedro stepped forth. 'No, Leonato. On my honour, we saw and heard your daughter on the balcony of her chamber, talking with a man and embracing him. Upon my honour, I swear it to be true.'

Now I could not be silent. 'What men may do,' I mocked, smiling grimly. No one knew better than I how fallible the prince could be, how little his honour meant. I knew, and Claudio did too, that Don Pedro was not there in the hold on the day of the oranges, for he was craven in his cabin. I did not know, now, why they had formed this strange alliance.

'What do you mean, Signor Benedick?' Don Pedro's tone was a warning.

'Why, that it is no little thing, to swear upon one's *honour*,' I said. 'For a prince to swear so, it is as if a bondsman swears upon his *allegiance*.' We locked eyes like a couple of scrapping toms, but Leonato jumped into the fray.

'I myself would *never* doubt your honour, Prince,' he assured. 'But there must, at the least, be some misprision. My niece is Hero's bridemaiden, and slept with her all night. Lady Beatrice?'

My heart plummeted with dread. Our starlit tryst had condemned Hero. I had spirited Beatrice away from her duty to her cousin. I did not know whether to speak or be silent. My instinct was to speak out, but I did not want to expose Beatrice to these same slanders. But my lady stood, straight as a willow wand. 'As it happens, Uncle, I was from the chamber last night,' she said, clearly. 'But I have for the last week been her bedfellow.'

'Confirmed!' said Leonato.

There was an awful silence, punctuated only by Hero's piteous sobbing.

'We spoke of honour just now,' said the prince softly. 'And it will be to my eternal *dishonour* that I sponsored such a match, and linked my dear friend to a common stale.' Then Don Pedro took Claudio by the arm, and marched him from the church; a dreadful inversion for he should have left with Hero.

I only realised long afterwards that it had never occurred to me to follow them. I stayed, unthinking, with Beatrice. Leonato, with an awful cry, strode across the altar and struck Hero about the face. The poor lady swooned, and it was just as well, for Leonato proceeded to castigate her lifeless form; a terrible verbal muddle about Hero being an only child, about his wife Innogen's death, about his daughter being his hope of the future, a future now gone. The dreadful epithets poured from him: stale, whore, strumpet, hobbyhorse. His brother Antonio pulled him, still shouting, from the church. The drama done, the playgoers left too, gossiping as they went, following their master.

The doors closed behind the congregation and there were just four of us left: Beatrice and Hero upon the ground and the friar upon his knees, where he spent his life.

I leaned over the little group. Hero was so small next to my lady that she near lay in Beatrice's arms like the Pietà. They formed a little circle of devastated womanhood, with the friar and me standing outside; well meaning but excluded from this primal, female distress. Hero's eyes fluttered and opened, and Beatrice embraced her with relief.

Hero looked up at her trustingly, like a child who has woken from a nightmare. 'Beatrice? Am I wed?'

Beatrice shook her head. 'No, dearest.'

And then I saw – we all saw – the dreadful realisation dawning upon Hero; that her nightmare was real. She wept anew. 'How could he say that of me?' And there was no way to know whether she spoke of Claudio or her father. Beatrice shushed her like a child, but had no answer to give. 'How can I go back there?' Hero whispered. 'How can I live with such shame?'

'You need not.' It was the friar who now spoke. 'I think it best that you stay here for a while. You are right that such shame is too great for a living woman to bear; but a dead one may bear anything. We will give it abroad that you fell lifeless upon the count's words. Meantime those who love you can right your wrongs.' He looked pointedly from Beatrice to myself, then back to Hero. 'Come. I will take you to my celleress – she will fit you with a habit.'

Hero followed, meekly, leaning on the friar's arm.

The plaster face of St James looked down on us from the rood screen, his face lit with pride, well pleased with his chivalrous knights and their deeds today.

Act V scene v

The chapel in Leonato's house

Beatrice: Benedick and I were alone at the altar.

The irony was not lost upon me; we had planned to be standing exactly here, to be joined by the friar in matrimony. The prayer book was on the steps where it had fallen from the good monk's hand, his place in the marriage mass lost. Somewhere in those pages was enfolded that particular form of words that would have bound us for ever; special, binding runes that could take a man and a woman and couple them unto death. But different words had been uttered here on this altar; dark, terrible words. Accusations, slanders.

'Words, words, words,' I said. 'Words kill on this island.'

'But, Beatrice.' Benedick came to me and pushed his hand into my hair. 'Hero is not dead in truth. Her demise is but a device of the friar's.'

'Don't you understand? She *is* dead,' I said. 'Her honour was everything, and it is gone. In Sicily even the *suggestion* of dishonour is enough to stain a woman for life. She has been publicly denounced as a whore in church – at the *altar*. Who will take her now? She is utterly undone.' I began to shake. That barbaric test of my maidenhead that I'd endured in my father's castle, was that better or worse than this southern way? In the north, noblewomen had certain freedoms, but must endure such examinations before marriage. In the south a spotless *reputation* was all; and I would not believe that Hero had jeopardised hers with the slightest lightness of conduct. 'The count must have made an error,' I stated flatly.

Benedick ran a finger down the rough stone pillar. 'He, the prince, Don John, all of them must have seen *something*.'

'Two of them have the very bent of honour,' I said. Benedick did not reply. 'I know nothing of the third, for he is too like an image and says nothing.'

'And he left the church as soon as may be. Perhaps he is the root of all.'

'Yet how could the prince and Claudio speak so?'

'You said it yourself. The prince has the *bent* of honour only,' he said enigmatically.

I was too agitated to take his meaning. 'If I had not this trinity of pretty villains to blame,' I said, low voiced, 'I would make myself a fourth. I should have been in her bed.'

'You cannot regret our meeting!' Benedick cried.

'No. Never that. And yet . . .'

He came to me and took both my hands in his. 'As for the princes, I do not know. But I feel it in my marrow that Claudio was mistaken; and there is no sin in mistaking. I will make enquiries.'

I slumped, suddenly, sitting down heavily on the stone steps. 'It hardly matters,' I muttered. 'The sin is not in the mistaking. The sin is in the rejoinder.'

Benedick sat beside me on the church steps, his shoulder pressed to mine. 'Could you explain your meaning?' he asked, gently.

'If there has been some misprision, and if we discover that Claudio was tricked, then what? He is not guiltless, whatever the case.' I sprang to my feet and pointed to the sacred steps we stood upon. 'How could he bring her here, all the way here to the altar, and accuse her in public, to shame and dishonour her in front of not only her kin but all her household too? How could he tell everyone, from her father to the boy who cleans her boots, that she has known the heat of a bed?' I began to pace the nave in my agitation. 'Say he was mistaken, what then? Should my cousin take him in hand, and lead him to the altar once again? Who could forgive so much? Who could overlook such words? What woman could forget being held about the throat until the marks of his fingers are imprinted there? Or being spat upon? Or being called so many different names for whore?' I shook my head, and a little diamond star fell from my curls to the stones. I ignored it. 'I had not known there were so many different words for the same sin. The words were worst of all, worse than the blows. The friar said it all; he exhorted us to let Claudio think she had died upon his words. Well; she did. His slanders ran her through more keenly than a blade. Hero the maid *is* dead. And now Claudio must pay.'

I walked away from Benedick for a moment, the heat of my own anger frightening me. My heart raced – but I did not swoon. I felt as a man must feel as he goes into battle. Had Benedick felt this way when he leapt from ship to ship at the armada, when he had seen combat so terrible that he would never speak of it?

I looked at the familiar statue of Mary holding her son's beating heart in her plaster hand. The heart was a ruby as big as a gull's egg, cut and faceted and red as congealed blood. I remembered one such from the Vara; the Sacred Heart. Hero had been dressed as the Virgin that day. And now her purity had been called into question. I had had enough.

I knew I had a self-serving character, had thought of little else but mine own heart for the last year. I had sat silently in the courtroom and watched a good woman be condemned for witchcraft. I had forgiven Tebaldo's killer for the sake of peace, for which mercy my other cousin Giulietta had thanked me upon her knees. But I could not let Claudio's transgression go by. I wished I could wink at his actions, marry Benedick in secret and take him back to Villafranca. But who would speak for Hero now, if I did not? My cousin had just lost her mother, the last and only strong woman in her life. What would be left to her if I abandoned her now, dishonoured, disenfranchised, dispossessed? I knew I had reached my sticking place; that here, at last, was something more important than the joining of our two hearts. I must gamble upon Benedick's love for Hero's sake; for the sake of all my sex.

I took a deep breath. 'They eat hearts here, you know. In Sicily.' I tried to quiet my own beating organ, to keep my voice steady. 'They have a tradition of blood vengeance. It is swift, without drama. And threats are spoken softly and without emotion; but they are always, *always* carried out. When you say you will eat someone's heart, you are ordering someone's death.' I kept my eyes on the ruby. 'Murder, the end of another human being. And when you speak this dire utterance, you are making a pledge; either that you will carry it out, or a kinsman will carry it out on your behalf. But it will be done.' I looked up at Mary, sorrowing, benign, untroubled by the offal in her hand. 'Guglielma Crollalanza said it, do you remember?'

'Who?'

'The poet's mother, as she burned at the stake. She said it to Claudio's uncle, the Archbishop of Monreale. And now I will say it to Claudio.'

I turned and looked at Benedick. My voice was shaking, but I said the thing in the Sicilian way; quietly, no emotion. I spoke not to God, nor his mother; but to Claudio, wherever he had gone to cage his fury. '*Ti manciu 'u cori, Claudio.* I would eat his heart, if I could,' I said with deliberate relish. 'I would eat his heart, yes, in the very marketplace, so that everyone from the Governor of Messina to the boot-boy could see me do it. I would choke down every gout of flesh, every artery, and drink the attendant blood.'

Benedick put his hand over my mouth, gently, as you might treat a cursing child, to stop the terrible words pouring forth.

'Shush, shush! Dear Beatrice, you are beside yourself. We speak of Hero, not the dark lady.'

I tore his hand away, hard, hurting him. I would not be silenced like a child, nor be muzzled like a dog, or bridled like a scold. 'Yes, yes!' I cried. 'We are speaking of her! Of *both* of them! It is the same case – a man slanders, a woman dies. Well; Claudio's uncle paid his price. A bold assassin dispatched the good archbishop. And now Claudio must pay too; if there is a man who will assume the office.'

I saw his tanned face drain of colour. 'What are you saying? What are you asking of me?'

Now I clasped his hands within mine. 'Kill Claudio.'

He looked at me of a sudden as if I was a stranger. 'I? Not for the world.'

I dropped his hands. 'I said that words could kill. You kill me to deny it.'

'On the *Florencia*, he was my comfort and my friend; and more than that, he became my brother.'

I raised my chin. 'To be *my* friend henceforth, you must challenge my enemy. Otherwise, we are done.' I went to his side, and laid my hand upon his rough cheek. 'Once, you thought *me* inconstant,' I said softly. 'Once you took the word of a man, over that of a woman. There was no difference in birth in the case – one was a prince, the other a princess. The difference was only in our gender. You were wrong then, and even your prince admits his error. Now I ask you this thing because it time to set *right* that wrong. It is time that someone believed a woman. Believe Hero. Believe Guglielma Crollalanza.' I put my hand to my heart. 'Believe *me*.'

We had found ourselves before the altar again. He took my hand from my heart and placed it on his. 'Do you believe, in your very *soul*, that Claudio has wronged Hero?'

I said the words I'd hoped to say, in another life, before the sky had changed. '*I do.*'

He knelt then, in a gesture of allegiance, as he must have done to Don Pedro a dozen times. And I knew then he would challenge Claudio. He did not look at me as he rose and strode down the aisle.

'Wait,' I called. I followed him down the nave, and took the *settebello* card from my bodice. Despite my fury, I knew it was no little thing that I asked. I pressed the card into his hand, for he was truly the worthiest knight. He looked into my eyes and nodded.

Act V scene vi

Claudio's chamber in Leonato's house

Benedick: I went directly to find Claudio, solemn with determination.

I crossed the sunlit court and climbed the stone stair to the count's chamber, unsheathed my sword and entered like a whirlwind.

I saw the count at once, sitting beneath the window, feet splayed, head in hands. He raised his head and the sun gilded his wet cheeks. He was weeping. My martial footsteps stuttered. I had expected to find him bullish, pent and pacing.

I knew then that, for him, Hero had died in truth. I remembered how much he would think of her, talk of her on the *Florencia*. She had been his star to guide him home. I remembered too, with an uncomfortable little niggle like a burr stuck beneath chainmail, that Claudio had told me of an inconstant mother, who had taken a lover behind his father's back and abandoned her son in boyhood.

Sitting beneath the casement Claudio was so diminished; no longer the monster that we had seen at the altar, but so like the boy I'd brought to Messina the previous summer, that my heart shrivelled within me. It occurred to me for the first time that we are angrier with those we love than with any other persons in our lives, that Claudio's dreadful outburst came from the bitter pain of perceived betrayal – by both Hero and his mother – and that his fury proceeded from the death of a dream. I looked at my naked sword in my hand.

I had no stomach for the business, but I must carry it forth.

I looked to Don Pedro. He looked as stern and pious as those portraits in El Escorial; but he was far guiltier than Claudio. He may have been innocent in this business, but he knew what had passed on that mountaintop a year ago, when he called a dancing woman a witch and sent her to the fire.

'Gallants,' I said with biting irony; 'this is a heavy day. You both travelled from Spain to Scotland and back, and did not take one soldier's life. Now you are returned you have between you killed a sweet and innocent lady.' I could have been speaking of Signora Crollalanza or Hero.

I saw Claudio's eyes widen – word had not reached him, then, that Hero was dead. It did not seem to matter; his demeanour did not noticeably worsen upon the news, his spirits had nowhere to sink. His world had already ended – the loss of Hero's physical life was no more dire to him than the loss of her chastity. As I'd thought, he'd already been mourning for his dream. He put his head back in his hands, where it had been when I'd discovered him. 'Yes,' I said. 'Hang your head. For your slanders ran her through as surely as a blade.'

Don Pedro spoke, haltingly. 'I am truly sorry for it. Sorry for the whole business. But, Benedick, we *saw* her with our own eyes.'

'Ah! Yes,' I said, 'upon your advice I believed my own eyes once before; now I know that appearances can lie just as men can.'

'Have a care, Benedick. I am still your prince.'

'No longer,' I said. 'I have taken an oath that supersedes yours. I must thank you for your many courtesies and discontinue your company.' I lifted the medal of St James from about my neck, picked up his right hand from his side, placed it in the palm and closed his royal fingers over it.

He let it fall by the riband and it swung like a pendulum beating time. He looked at me askance, thinking that I was not in earnest. I had jested so many times before, but today I had left off my motley and donned my armour.

Once he collected my expression he laid the medal down on a side table. The scarlet ribbon coiled like a snake. He talked to the little pile.

'But Benedick, there was no mistaking. My brother showed us all.'

'Your brother Don John?' My voice was rich with scorn. 'A man you could not even entrust with your estates?'

'We know too that *one* transgression may be forgiven,' he said carefully. 'I scourged my brother personally for his mismanagement, in the square at Zaragoza. He would not fail me again.'

I snorted at such stupidity. 'You do not think a man that you shamed so publicly would more likely harbour thoughts of revenge than loyalty?'

Don Pedro was silent.

'And where is your brother now?' I asked grimly.

'He is gone – likely now he knows there will be no wedding he has returned to Aragon to take up the stewardship he once neglected.'

No wedding. The words sounded like a knell. 'So, in short, he is fled,' I concluded. 'Does that not speak of a conscience spotted with guilt?'

'No, for we have the Watch searching for the lady Hero's seducer. And, when we find him – mark me – we will have him confess the vile encounters that they have had a thousand times in secret.'

'Since we arrived three days ago? When Beatrice had until last night been her bedfellow?'

Once again, the prince was silenced.

'God knows your countrymen know how to trick out a confession,' I said, 'with your irons and your fires. But such renditions are as nothing to the guiltless honesty of that poor maid. In fact, let us begin the trial now, for we have the true villain here.' I crossed the room to Claudio and wrenched his chin upward in my hand. 'Stand up as you are a man! Defendant – have you nothing to say?' I was stern, but my voice faltered with disappointment in him.

He was silent, and fixed me with his sorrowing eyes. It was as if he had spent all his words at the altar.

'Well; the lady is likewise dumb,' I said evenly. 'And as she died upon your words we shall never hear her testimony. Others must speak for her.'

'You?' asked the prince in surprise.

'Yes. I speak for her, and my sword speaks for me.' I pulled Claudio to me, till we were nose to nose. 'Tomorrow I will meet you at dawn,' I jerked my chin towards the open window, 'down in the courtyard there, to call you to account. Be ready.'

I released his jaw and turned on my heel. Just as I laid my hand upon the latch Claudio spoke at last. 'What's Hero to you?' he demanded. 'Or you to Hero?'

I turned slowly and looked at him. There was a world of pain in his question, a boyhood of female abandonment. I almost felt pity; for he was jealous; jealous of my kinship with a corpse. 'She is a lady,' I said. 'That is enough.'

The next morning, as the sun began to peep over the sea, I was already in the Roman courtyard, waiting for Claudio.

I walked the ancient, tiny tiles, my eyes on the intricate designs, pacing about the tiled head of Medusa. She watched me with her black eyes, and I watched her.

I had been to matins at the chapel, and afterwards descended to the crypt where my lady tended her cousin, and kissed Beatrice fifty, a hundred times in farewell. I was not afraid of Claudio's sword, was not afraid of any man's sword for I knew my own skill; but I was as superstitious as any man on this island, and did not wish to tempt the Fates. So I duly said a last goodbye to Beatrice, and my valedictory manner added fervour to her kisses.

My rapier hit my legs as I paced, reminding me with every step of my fell purpose. I was caught in a cat's cradle; if I did not challenge Claudio, Beatrice would have none of me. If I did and was slain, we would be parted for ever anyway. I huffed, and my breath clouded in the cool dawn. Then I caught a motion at my eye's edge – was it Claudio come? – and saw the singular sight of a ragged man, dressed in hooded clothing, climbing up the vines below the prince's window.

I crossed the court in a heartbeat, grabbed the intruder's ankle and challenged him. 'Hoy! What are you about?'

He kicked out at me. 'A matter of honour,' he spat. 'Let me be.'

'If there was any honour in you you would use the door like an honest man.' I grabbed him by the feet and he tumbled down, bringing most of the vine with him. There was a brief fierce scuffle and I found myself at the pointed end of a mean little dagger, sharp as a marlinspike. But I was armed for a duel, and my spirits were pent and ready for a fight, so I soon had him pinned against the rose plaster walls between my shortblade and rapier. I pressed my elbow to his windpipe and threw back his hood. I uncovered a face that I recognised; with deep-set eyes, wispy hair, a short dark beard and a pearl-drop hanging from one ear.

'Signor Crollalanza!'

'I do not know that name any more,' the poet hissed. 'Now I am Cardenio, like my father before me.'

I looked about me, for the Watch were very keen since Hero's failed wedding. 'What is your business here?'

'The same as yours,' he said. 'Murder.'

I heard a sound in the chamber above, and the light of a candle warmed the window. 'Come,' I said.

I had him by the scruff, his liripipe wound around my hand, and marched him up the stone stairs to my own room, kicking a brace of drowsy hounds out of the way. I thrust him into a chair and bolted the door behind us. I did not light a candle but the sun had reached my window, and now I could see him clear.

I had not known him very much before, but even I could see he was much changed. His beard was fuller now and unkempt, the hair very thin on top and matted about the ears. His face was as tanned as mine and drawn too. His eyes were not soft and dreaming like those of a poet and lover but black and fathomless like chips of obsidian. The eyes of a desperate man; the eyes of a murderer. I could not countenance, now, that I had once thought he would be Beatrice's husband, and could not believe that I had wasted all those jealous hours in bitter envy of him.

I flung a water skin at him and watched him drain it. He sat, easy and confident in my chair, and I stood like an attorney to question him. 'I will ask you again. What do you here?'

'I told you. Murder, like you. A matter of honour, like your own. And I am doing a woman's bidding, just as you are.'

'You are come for Claudio's life?'

'No, not he. I would not steal another man's office – that score is yours to settle. And it was not the Lady Beatrice who sent me, but another, now dead.'

'Your mother,' I said. It was not a question.

'She laid the blood feud on the archbishop, the viceroy and Don Pedro.'

I remembered the guilty grandees at the inquisition. But there had been another tribune: 'And Leonato?'

'Him she spared, through her love of his wife the Lady Innogen. But he was given a warning.'

I had heard tell of it – three Spanish ostlers butchered and laid out in the very courtyard where I'd found Crollalanza. I looked beyond him, through the window, in the direction of Monreale.

Could see again the prelate on the bed, eyes open, mouth oozing poison.

'You dispatched the archbishop, did you not?'

'Never ask a Messinese what he does after the sun goes down,' he replied. But I had my answer. He was the lone assassin, in a monk's hood. The Ragged One. *Cardenio*. Cardenio was not a man but a title, passed from father to son through generations of the blood feud. Folk heroes, brigands, assassins.

'And the viceroy?'

'He has taken to his bed, and will not rise again. He has a growth upon his lung that grows like a canker in a hedge. God has taken care of him; or the Devil. One of them.'

'But then . . .' I spoke almost to myself, 'Don Pedro will be the next viceroy.'

'No, that he will not,' said Cardenio-Crollalanza vehemently.

I understood. 'Then it is the *prince's* life you seek.'

'The late mistress of the house had the right of it. My fellows tell me that on the day you left for the armada, she banished him from the house for his crime.'

I remembered it well; the Lady Innogen told Don Pedro not to return to her house while she was alive.

'Sadly, the lady beat him to the grave, but he shall follow shortly.'

I thought of the prince. I had no longer any love for him, but I had no wish to see him die. He had died for me in a sense already, when he'd lost his nobility. I was struck by the comparison to Hero. Women lived only through their chastity, men through their honour. 'Must it be this way?' I asked. 'So much has already been lost.'

Crollalanza's lip curled with scorn. 'And yet I see him here, in his velvets, eating his haunches of venison, just as he did last year. So what exactly has the prince lost?'

'His fortune. His war.' *His honour.*

'Aye,' he said. 'His war. Well, our family snatched that victory from him, and his king too.'

I narrowed my eyes against the rising sun. 'What can you mean?'

He was silent for a time, looking at me; and at length he spoke. 'In London,' he said, 'where my father now lives, there are storytellers on every corner. You may give a groat upon the street to such a bard and he will tell you a tale. A year ago,' he said, 'you gave my father and me a piece of eight for our passage to Naples. He embarked, I did not; but for your kindness, and your coin, I will tell you a tale – perhaps the last one I shall tell. I will not say if the story is true or false, and if you tell your brothers of Saint James I will deny it with my last breath.'

He stood and looked out of the window, in the direction of the port. I kept my hand on my rapier's hilt, but did not now think he would harm me. 'It is a story of an old man who took a night ship to Naples, leaving his son behind him. He spent the passage to Naples writing a message in the night cabin of the captain, who was his friend.' His voice was changed, to a musical, beguiling lilt. There was some magic in his tone which made the story live; I could see the old man busy with his quill, the lantern swinging in his cabin, the roiling seas outside. 'He wrote on a ribbon of parchment, in indelible ink, letter by letter. The message was as long as the cabin. The old man rolled it and dripped a candle upon it; the wax massed like a seal and grew into a mound, and he shaped it into a ball with his old hands.'

I nodded. I had heard of such things; sometimes on the armada secret orders were sent between our ships in this way. 'The recipient melts the ball of wax to read the message upon the ribbon. That way he can be sure that he is the first one to read the missive.'

Michelangelo nodded in turn. 'The old man changed ship at Naples, for he was to sail that night for England. He went there in seven days. In London he met with certain of his family there,

who concealed him while they arranged a very special audience. He was conveyed secretly to the Palace of Whitehall, and
he put the ball of wax in the hands of a man called Francis
Drake, commander of the English navy.'

I could picture the missive, a little red planet of wax, making
its progress from hand to hand. 'And what did the message say?'
I asked, though I had guessed.

'I shall not say, for if I do not tell you cannot know when asked.
But I will tell you diverse words – the name Philip, the month of
August,' he turned and looked back at me, and the expression in
his eyes shivered my ribs; 'and the word armada.'

'So you were spying for the English queen, last summer,' I
said, bluntly.

'Not at first. But I gleaned certain information, and formed a
theory. I thought that if my father began his sojourn in England
by giving up such a nugget of intelligence, he would be guaran-
teed safe haven.'

And I had given him the money for passage. Fortune's wheel
spun about my head. I had saved the very man who had given
fair warning to the English queen of the armada's approach. If I
had given up Signor Cardenio senior to the Spanish, would
Philip's ships have landed at Kent unassailed, and won the day?
But then I remembered the driving winds, and the rains, and the
disastrous incompetence of the Spanish nobles. I reflected that
the goddess Fortune likely knew what she was doing.

His story done, Michelangelo Crollalanza sat down heavily in
my chair, the dagger he'd worn to dispatch Don Pedro clinking
against the buckles of his baldric. I remembered that he used to
wear a pen where he now wore the knife. 'May you not . . .
write against the prince?' I said weakly. 'For a man's reputation
is as dear as his life.'

He snorted. 'That is my father's office. Under the English
queen's protection he can give rein to his polemics against the
Spaniard. He is creating a legend as black as ink.'

'Then can you not be satisfied?'

He shook his head, his black eyes upon me, never shifting his gaze.

'I saved you once. What makes you think I will not take you straight to the Watch this time?'

The hard eyes softened a modicum. 'And yet, I do not think you will. I think you know what he is.'

I lowered my gaze.

'He made a pretty show at the wedding yesterday, him and the count.'

I could not deny it.

'And it would avail you nothing to betray me. If I am cast into jail, others will do my part – such is the custom of the blood feud. There will be another Cardenio. The isle is full of Archirafi, from my mother's house, and Crollalanzas from my father's. Our family trees are forests and our blood runs in the rivers.' He tucked his dagger below his doublet. 'Besides, the Watch are busy with a bigger fish in their net. I practically walked through the gate unchallenged.'

'What is their business so early in the day?'

He looked at me, calculating. 'They have apprehended the villain who conspired to dishonour the lady Hero.'

'Who?'

'Borachio, the prince's man. And with him Conrad, his companion.' I breathed out slowly – those Aragonese brothers of the bottle; one fat, one thin, both wicked. 'The author of all was Don John, who is fled, but it matters not; Borachio confessed everything. How he caused the maidservant Margherita to clothe herself in Hero's gown, and meet him upon the balcony of her lady's chamber. There he called Margherita by Hero's name, and they performed their mummer's play to a willing audience.'

I could see now how it had been; a puppet show enacted while Beatrice and I were wooing at the Roman baths. This information was precious – I thought I could see, now, how to twist this sorry tragedy about. 'I will broker a deal with you,' I said. 'I will take you through the gate as my kinsman, and convey you safely to the road. In return you will defer your grim task for,' I calculated, 'three days.'

He stood, and walked close to me, fingering the dagger under the doublet. 'Why?' he said. 'Now I might do it pat; dispatch him straight, before the sun is fully up.'

His voice was seductive, persuasive, just as it had been when he was telling his story. But I had no stomach for Don Pedro's murder, no more than I had now for Claudio's. 'If you do this thing, the household will be turned upside down, the Spanish will decamp, and I will never wed . . .' I stopped suddenly.

'The Lady Beatrice,' he supplied.

'Yes.'

'And she returns your affections?'

'Now, yes.'

He considered for a moment. Then his shoulders slumped a little in acquiescence. 'Very well,' he said. 'Don Pedro has his stay of execution. For the coin you gave my father and for the love Beatrice gave my mother.'

Once we were clear of the gate and the Watch, he turned to me on the dirt road and took my hand in farewell. For a moment it was almost as if we were friends. He looked at me directly from under his hood. 'Beatrice always did return your affections,' he said. 'She loved you constantly; last year, this year. Ask her of a sonnet she wrote, once, upon the dunes; in the company of a poor scribbler.' He sounded, once again, like a poet; the bitter edge to his voice had gone.

And he walked away, into the grey dawn, drawing close his hood as he went, down the Via Catania.

Act V scene vii

The chapel in Leonato's house

Beatrice: I visited Hero the morning after the wedding in the little crypt of the chapel.

The celleress melted away when I appeared, and left me with my cousin. Hero was dressed in a grey habit and was holding a darkwood rosary. She was telling the beads between her fingers ten by ten, the Apostle's Creed, the Paternoster, the Ave Maria. I wasn't sure whether she'd even seen me. I waited until she'd passed the little pendant cross twice, and then came forward and took her by the shoulder.

She looked up and her face was as grey as the wimple. Her eyes were shadowed and her skin sallow, and her dark luxuriant sheet of hair hidden completely beneath the coif, not even a strand to be seen. I saw her then as she might be in the future; as a nun. What other path was left to her? What life was left to the unmarriageable, the unwilling to marry? It was the path that had been chosen by Paris's cousin Rosaline Capuletti, the path I'd once contemplated myself. Hero was devout, it was true, but this was not the life she had chosen. It had been chosen for her; for she had been rejected by one man for such a particular sin that she would now be rejected by all. Even Leonato – the one man who should have stood up beside her – had repudiated his daughter, and struck at her life with his own hands. I remembered then my own father, telling me baldly that if I were not found to be chaste he would be 'childless'.

My thoughts tended so much upon fathers that when Hero

raised her head and whispered, in a voice hoarse with prayer, 'I have lost him,' I thought it was Leonato she meant.

I sat beside her on the little truckle. 'There has been some mistake,' I said. 'This counterfeit death is calculated to turn the blade of my uncle's anger. All will be explained and he will take you into his house once more.'

'Not my *father*,' she said, her voice stronger now. 'Claudio. I have lost Claudio.'

I was so amazed that I was struck dumb.

'I want him, Beatrice.' It was an odd utterance from a nun's lips. 'Do you remember all the stories you told me last summer?' She smiled, her mouth twisting wistfully. 'I used to think that my story would end happily, with Claudio and me joined to live happily for all eternity.' I remembered Michelangelo Crollalanza's definition of a story that ended with marriage. A comedy.

'I was a child last year . . . and this?'

I could not answer but I thought, This year, you are a shade. A maid that lived but did not live, walled up in this stone purgatory. There was nowhere cold in Sicily but it was cold in this crypt, as cold as a tomb. And a story that ended with death was a tragedy.

But had the story ended? Hero still loved Claudio, but what profit could proceed from such a preference, for a man who had rejected her and spoken to her with such hatred? But then I heard a whisper as soft as shrift murmur around the cold stones. *Lady Tongue. Harpy. Lady Disdain. Benedick reproved you so, and rejected you, and you love him still.*

As if I'd summoned him Benedick appeared at the door, leaning on the jamb with a look of sympathy softening his gaze. My heart turned over. 'Forgive me, lady,' he said to my cousin. 'Lady Beatrice, a word.'

I went with him up the stair to the chapel, and he drew me down beside him in a pew.

'She still loves him, then?'

I did not trouble to hide my perplexity. 'Yes.'

'Well, she may have him yet. Claudio was mistook,' he said, 'and a cleverer piece of villainy I have never heard. The villain Borachio embraced *Margherita* on Hero's balcony. It was all a design of Don John's. Margherita was wearing one of Hero's gowns, and a coif that she was wont to wear in her hair, and the villain called her Hero loud enough for all to hear.'

'Margherita!' All was explained; the maidservant's disappearance and reappearance, her counterfeit slumber.

'Do not blame the girl; she was gulled into the disguise.'

'I do not blame her. Men are to blame for this tragedy.'

He did not deny it. 'And here is a most singular fact; the plan was hatched to deprive *Don Pedro* of his bride. Hero was meant for him all along.'

'So the prince *did* propose to Hero that night of the masque!'

'Yes. And when Claudio took the prize, Don John carried forth with the plan, thinking that a slight to Don Pedro's favourite was still a slight to his brother.'

I looked up, in wonderment. 'How did you learn this?'

'I questioned the varlet himself at the gatehouse, for the Watch have him clapt in chains. And now that his patron is fled, he has decided it is politic to give up all he knows, like a most obliging villain. But the kernel of the truth I had first from one that you know – Michelangelo Florio Crollalanza.'

'Michelangelo! Then he is back!'

'He never left. But he no longer plays the poet; he is a hard and desperate man, a brigand.'

'Is he here?'

'Gone,' he said. 'But there might have been another death today; he was out for the prince's blood.'

'Don Pedro?'

'Yes. In the name of his mother.'

So Michelangelo had come for the prince's heart – a true Sicilian. 'And you dissuaded him?'

'For now.' He would not explain further, but changed his tack. 'Besides, there are matchings to achieve, before any dispatchings.'

I took his hand, for there was something that must be said before we left the subject of the prince. 'Don Pedro proposed to me too,' I said. 'That morning in the gardens when he told me of your mistaking, and the *Scopa* cards.'

Benedick clenched his hand around mine, hurting me. 'I should have let the poet dispatch him,' he hissed through his teeth. 'I should have lifted the latch and let him in – I should have folded back his princely ruff and guided the very blade into his throat.'

I prised his fingers loose, gently. 'Shush, my love. Does not his confession of the wrongs he did us mitigate the forehand sin?'

He stood, agitated, and began to pace. 'Sin! His sins are many! So numerous I could not recount . . .' He checked himself; turned and sat, breathing hard as if he had been running.

'What is it? Tell me?'

He pressed his lips together and shook his head. 'I may not. I have withdrawn my service from him, but I once gave him my word, and I cannot withdraw that, though other men may do so. Only death may release a vow. Or . . .' He stopped suddenly, and took my hand again.

'Or?'

'If the person you promised releases you.' He reached into his doublet, and drew out the *settebello*. He put it in my palm, and we both looked at the seven colourful coins on the face. I knew what the gesture meant before he spoke.

'Beatrice, I cannot kill Claudio. He made a mistake. I made one once, and spent my worst words upon you. Would you have had me die for my slanders?'

'No,' I whispered.

'Would you have Claudio die?'

Now my anger had diminished, I knew I did not want the count's life. I had no appetite for his heart. I tucked the *settebello* into my bodice, next to mine. 'No. I would not have him die. But,' I said, holding up a hand to pre-empt his embrace, 'he must repent. Does Hero's father know the truth of the matter?'

'The Watch made their report, but they are such haphazards that I had to make another, before he was fully furnished with the facts. I told Leonato all, and that Hero was alive and well. He is even now on his way here, to comfort his dear daughter.'

I caught the irony in his tone, and wondered how to face my uncle. I had avoided him since the wedding mass, for if anything his conduct had been worse than Claudio's. He had believed, upon the instant, the slanders of the two gentlemen, and struck Hero to the ground without once asking for her testimony. He had taken the word of a brace of nobles with whom he had been acquainted for a summer's lease, against a daughter he had known for seventeen years. He had wished Hero dead, and, which was worse, had wished her never born. A morsel of me did wonder how he would bring her back into his grace without loss of face, now the error was proven.

As if in answer to my question Leonato burst through the door, his cloak and sleeves trailing, swept past Benedick and myself, and clattered down the stone stairs to the crypt. By tacit agreement we followed, and reached the doorway in time to see Leonato scoop Hero from her bed, and clasp her to his breast. 'My Hero!' he said, choking. 'My innocent child; I knew all along that you were belied!'

His bearded brother Antonio, who had followed wheezing behind, sniffed happily, a tear rheuming his eye. 'Wondrous!' he spluttered.

'Yes,' I said heavily from the doorway. 'Most affecting.'

'And you will still marry the count?' My uncle's first question to his resurrected daughter did not surprise me one jot. 'He was innocent in this, as was the prince; the fault of it all lies with Don John the Bastard, who is fled to Aragon.'

It was time for me to intervene. I walked forward. 'Not without repentance, Uncle.'

My uncle looked up, bemused. 'But she made no real error – a few Hail Marys upon her knees shall meet the case.'

The friar entered the cell at this instant, and Leonato appealed to him. 'Brother Friar, my daughter would make confession before her wedding. Are you at leisure for a shrift?'

'Not *Hero*,' I said with biting emphasis. 'It is the *count* who must repent.'

'Claudio?' My uncle was all amazement. 'But he and the prince were themselves mightily abused by John the Bastard. He made an honest mistake.'

'Mistake it may have been, but there was no honesty in it. He spoke words to your daughter that should have you reaching for your sword, not your wedding suit.'

Leonato looked, for a moment, shamefaced – recalling, I hope, that his own words at the altar had matched Claudio's for venom. 'Then, Niece, what do you suggest?'

I walked to the bed, and some instinct made me speak low. 'Let us preserve, for now, the fiction that Hero is dead. Let us tell Claudio he is to marry another – but he can neither see her nor speak to her before he takes her in hand.'

'Yes!' said Leonato. 'We shall tell him he is to marry my brother's child, heir to both our fortunes. Brother Antonio, will you serve?'

'No, Uncle.' I sensed that Leonato's guilt gave me a little more latitude with him than usual. 'He is *not* to be offered an heiress, nor a beauty. He was offered before a flawless maid with a fortune and a fair face and he rejected her most cruelly. Let us offer him a woman he does not know at all. No fortune, no chastity, no loveliness, no nobility. He must take a woman, just. Any vice of our sex may lurk beneath the veils, and he must accept us for all that we are. Then, and only then, may he claim the prize he lost.'

'What will this serve?'

'He wants beauty and money – let us see how how he shifts when he is offered neither. Let us measure how sorry he is. And before all this, he must mourn she who is gone.'

'But Cousin, I am here!' Hero was bright cheeked and merry eyed again, quite different from the grey little spectre I had nursed a quarter of the bells ago.

'And so you are. But *Claudio* does not know that you live.' I cupped her face; her newly radiant beauty was framed in the wimple like the bevel of a looking glass – *sans* hair, *sans* ornament, the delicately modelled features of her face were more striking than ever. 'What man would lose such a prize, and marry another the next day, unmoved? No, he must visit your tomb tonight, do obeisance to your bones, and mourn – *truly* mourn – from evening until dawn. And then, on the morrow, he must make his judgement of three veiled ladies; I will make one, Margherita – for her sins – another, and you, Cousin, will be the prize.'

Benedick stepped from the shadows. 'I will do any modest office to help the lady Hero to live again.'

The friar stepped forth. 'And I.'

I looked pointedly at my uncle, where he sat with his arms wreathed around Hero. He shrugged and sighed all at once. 'And I.'

'One thing more,' I said. '*All* of Messina must know she is innocent. They all saw her belied at the wedding, now all must see her redeemed at her funeral. We should invite the general populace to the wake, and Claudio must admit his mistake, for all to hear. I myself will devise diverse words for him to proclaim.'

'Niece,' wheedled my uncle, 'is it necessary to shame the count so?'

I turned on him. 'Shame?' I cried. 'What of Hero's shame? Shall her slander live, and walk around, increasing richly with every whisper and shred of gossip, while her chaste memory dwindles in the grave? No, Uncle. The truth must have its day.'

Leonato, as I'd known he would, agreed to my device. Benedick went to tell Claudio of his reprieve and the conditions of his penance, and I went back into the nave to say a private word to Mary.

For there would be prayers said this night not just for Hero, but for a woman whose ashes *did* lie in the monument, a woman who *had* been slain by slander, and rendered into dust by the fires of faith. I looked up at the plaster Virgin, who'd been patiently holding on to her son's offal all this time. I touched the ruby heart, and it was quite, quite cold.

Act V scene viii

Leonato's family tomb at the Cimiterio Monumentale

Benedick: The procession of torches reached as far as the eye could see, a golden serpent winding high up the hill until the flames nearly merged with the stars.

The night was warm, but Claudio wore a full cope of black, as velvet as the dark. Below the hood his face was as pale as glass.

We trudged dolefully up the mount, with the lutenists singing their melancholy songs, and I marvelled at how this piece of theatre that we had constructed could act upon the spirits. Beatrice, also in black, walked beside Leonato, whose old eyes were rheumy with tears. For this night alone, for all of us, Hero was dead. Something had gone from us – an innocence perhaps.

At length we reached the *Cimiterio Monumentale*, with the glittering bay laid out below us. All colours were muted as if the very pigments themselves mourned for Hero. The trees were agate, the sky indigo, the volcano ochre, their shades leaching into the sea and land; libations of grief.

We stopped beside the little tomb of milky stone. The curlicued iron gates had so recently been opened to admit Hero's mother, and dead flowers for Innogen still clung to the wrought metal. Inside the tomb votive candles burned in a false wake for Hero.

Claudio passed his torch to me and I took it, stern faced. In the days that had passed since I had given him his reprieve we had reverted to our relationship not of shipboard but of last summer. He was now a green boy again, and I his elder, so among the things to mourn tonight was the loss of our brotherhood.

But in exchange I had found something infinitely more dear. Claudio went to my lady now, and Beatrice, her face shrouded by her cowl, handed him a scroll. Claudio knelt before the gates and broke the seal on the scrip, unrolled the parchment, and read the words aloud, his voice constricted with unshed tears.

> *Done to death by slanderous tongues*
> *Was the Hero that here lies:*
> *Death, in guerdon of her wrongs,*
> *Gives her fame which never dies.*
> *So the life that died with shame*
> *Lives in death with glorious fame.*

He speared the paper on one of the iron curlicues on the gate, so that the words could remain there until the weather took them. I looked from these runes of grief to Don Pedro, directly, accusingly; as if drawn, his eyes met mine, but he dropped his gaze first.

'*Hang thou there upon the tomb,*' finished Claudio. '*Praising her when I am dumb.*'

The last syllable choked him completely; his voice cracked and he could speak no more. He nodded to the friar, who raised his reedy voice in a solemn hymn. And then his features seemed to collapse, and the count wept. His breath, the very breath that had killed Hero, was expelled from him in great, racking sobs. I wondered whether he had cried like that when his mother left – I would warrant that he certainly had not cried like that since. It was passing strange, for there was nothing unmanly in his grief; I thought more, not less, of him for this manifestation.

I looked to Beatrice. I wanted to know whether she saw what I saw. Her hood had slipped back a little, her face golden in the light of her torch. Claudio, though he did not know it, was soon to be her cousin, and I hoped she could someday forgive him for his transgressions. Her eyes met mine; of all the changed colours I had seen that night, only her eyes retained their profound blue, true as summer skies. She nodded, very slightly, clearly moved. She recognised real grief, real remorse. Claudio had taken only the first steps along the path to penance, but he was on the way to being forgiven.

I thought then: *Hero should have been here.* Not many of us get the opportunity to attend our own funeral, but she would have seen something in Claudio's remorse that would have touched her closely. And yet, we could not have risked her presence, for if she had been seen, our scheme would have been undone.

The friar's hymn ended with a heavy refrain, the mourners turned and the golden serpent wound away down the hill. I thought that the prince, who had looked shamefaced throughout the ceremony, would insist upon staying for the vigil. But he was one of the first to leave, his eyes darting quickly from side to side. He drew his hood closely about his face and shuffled himself into the pack of mourners. He looked hunted.

Claudio and I were alone that night. On that dark hillside, with the glittering bay below as though the stars had fallen, I had the time and space to think. In the many long dark hours that followed I thought of death, of mine and Beatrice's.

She had told me once of the tombs in her father's city, tombs she used to pass as a child, knowing she would one day rest there. And although I thought this southern monument was no bad place to lie, with the bay below and the smoking mountain above, I knew that, in truth, the only place I wanted to spend eternity was at Beatrice's side, rotting in the northern soils of Verona until our bones combined.

I watched, and dozed, while Claudio prayed. He prayed all night like a true penitent; his head bent, his hands clasped so tight that his knuckles showed white, his lips ever moving. And then at last the sky paled, and with the dawn everything resumed its proper colour, painted in by the busy sun. All the grey, and the black, and the thoughts of death were chased away by the colour. My spirits lifted. It was Claudio's wedding day, and mine too.

I went to fetch the penitent, and it was then I saw that we had not been alone at all. I saw another figure rise stealthily from the brush beyond the tomb – a ragged, hooded brigand. I knew we were in no danger for he raised one hand to me and walked away, ever upwards towards the fiery mountain. Then I knew the author of the scrip that Beatrice had given to Claudio, and knew that the words were not written for Hero. Michelangelo Florio Crollalanza had spent a night's watch not for Hero's sake, but for his mother's.

Act V scene ix

The chapel at Leonato's house

Beatrice: I saw the congregation through a veil of lace.

Hero, Margherita and I waited in the shade of the little chapel, while all of Messina gathered in the garden outside. We all wore white, with veils of snowy Sicilian lace worked with exquisitely rendered flowers and curlicues and butterflies. I surveyed the scene through a rose and a dragonfly.

Through the open door I could see that the pews had been carried out and ranked along the yew walk and decorated with wreaths of rock rose and ginestra. All was to be different from the terrible, interrupted wedding of a week ago – the ceremony would be conducted, as in olden times, on the church steps, and all the town would witness Claudio's penance.

I saw the count approach from the house. For the first time in our acquaintance he had left off his purple. He was dressed in humble cambric, like a peasant. He had not, today, troubled with pomades and scents, his hair was unkempt, his cheek unshaven. He looked like a true penitent, and he wore his shirt of hair remarkably well.

It was Benedick who was the most noble this day, for in contrast, he was wearing a doublet of fine silk which I had not seen before, as grass-green as his eyes. Then I saw the gilded garter bearing arms and I realised – these were the colours of his Duchy of Leon. Duke he might be, but he looked like a king. My foolish heart swelled. The livery of St James was gone, and with it his air of servitude. Now he served no man.

Only Don Pedro still wore the scarlet and the black, and his suit of clothes was now too big for him. He seemed shrunken and diminished, and his eyes darted about shiftily. I thought then that he must not enjoy his complicity in this very public penance – perhaps he thought it not seemly in a viceroy-in-waiting.

The pipers struck up; it was time.

Margherita hung back a little, hugging the shade of the chapel. She had embraced the Church, for it was to be her home. No man in Sicily would take her to wife now, so the friar had offered her a novitiate in his order. She had accepted gratefully enough, for she could continue to live here on the estate, and be by her mother Orsola. After today's performance she would wear a veil every day, assuming the very habit Hero had only this morning cast off. Bride, bachelor, nun, I thought sourly; the Holy Trinity offered to our sex.

As Claudio, the prince and Benedick reached the steps the friar led us forth and I stood on a lower stair to add to the confusion of our heights. We were still, and silent, and a like hush fell over the crowd. We might have been the three graces visiting earth, but I could think only of the goddesses who had offered themselves to Paris.

But this Paris was not a prince, nor a spoiled mortal. This Paris was a man, a man in humble weeds, who knelt at our appearance and bowed his head.

'I understand you are all orphans of this island,' murmured Claudio, 'all of low birth, all of no fortune.'

'It is so,' confirmed the friar sternly.

'Then, good ladies,' said the count, still looking at the ground, 'it is not for *me* to choose one of *you*. I have sinned; I have blood upon my hands. Any one of you would be more than my deserts. Therefore, do *you* elect between you, which one shall have me, but only if you like of me.'

I had expected today to hate him and scorn him, but what I

felt for him was pity. For a man of birth and fortune to take this leap into the dark was something exceptional. Nothing could mitigate his dreadful actions of a week ago, but with his behaviour at the funeral and now at this new wedding, he had made some amends. I was glad – so glad, for Hero's sake – that I could begin to like him again.

Hero now stepped forward, tears dropping from below her veil like diamonds to adorn her gown. She gave him her hand and helped him up.

Claudio raised his eyes. 'Let me see your face.'

'No,' said Leonato, more sternly than I had ever heard him speak to his guest. 'You shall not.'

Claudio gave a little nod. 'If you will accept me, lady,' he said softly, 'I am yours.'

And the ceremony took place with them just like that, Claudio in his penitent's weeds, Hero veiled. Her breath filled the lace and it lifted and bellied like a sail. Claudio was shambling and hesitant, and it was Hero who had to lead him, standing tall and straight, her voice strong and confident. I thought for a time that she was attempting to disguise her speech to preserve the fiction we had constructed; but then I corrected myself. This was a new Hero; the Hero who lived was different to the one that was gone. And I thought then of her mother Innogen, and of Guglielma Crollalanza too, and of how proud they would be.

And then, at last, Hero took off her veil – the lace floated to the stone. The moment moved me greatly – for although I knew, of course, that it was she, even to me it seemed miraculous that she had opened those iron gates, toppled those monumental tombstones and returned through death's door.

'Hero?' Claudio touched her cheek, as if to be sure she was real. 'You're alive?'

'I died,' she said, 'but now I truly live.'

Claudio embraced her so hard I feared that he would chase the breath from her in truth. '*My Hero.*'

She pushed him away gently so she could be heard. 'Your *wife*,' she said. 'But never *your* Hero. Henceforth I am mine own.'

He smiled and bowed, they kissed, the people cheered. Everyone hugged one another, and for a moment I lost sight of Benedick in the melee till I heard his voice. 'Friar, wait.'

Friar Francis turned, still holding the book.

'Which one is Beatrice?'

My heart stuttered.

'Do not you know?' asked the friar, smiling.

Benedick mounted the steps, towards Margherita. 'Here is one,' he said softly, and kindly, 'who made one mistake, but as God loves all sinners, she will make a fine wife for Christ.'

Then he walked to me, close, closer; I breathed heavily, and felt a blush mount to my cheek, for there was just a shred of lace between my mouth and his.

'And here is one,' he said, 'who is possessed of a fury, whose tongue runs away like a buckshee horse and who is wrong more times than she is right. And because she is as flawed as an ill-sounded goblet, she will make a fine wife for a man.'

I fumed, the congregation laughed, and the friar smiled. 'And are *you* that man?'

I waited for his declaration, for the outpouring of his heart, for the sweet words he had unpacked when we were alone on the night that the Roman pools filled with starlight. But something was amiss; he choked and stuttered, and muttered denials.

Impatient, I tore the veil from my head, and my tousled curls fell anyhow about my face. 'Rather ask what woman would accept such a man! For who would take a groom who tattles endlessly like my lady's eldest son, but whose pronouncements contain little wit and no matter?' I turned my back on him, playing to the crowd. 'A poor player who can rehearse his lines but cannot speak them when the time comes for him to step upon the stage. Give these poor people their money back, and have done.'

I smiled grimly at the cheers and laughter from the crowd, and bowed as if I were an actor. When I straightened Benedick was beside me, just as if we were about to be married, if only we could clear this one last obstacle of our own stubborn wills. We stared at each other, jaws jutting forward, mouths set stubbornly, eyes afire. The friar looked amused. 'So you do not love him either?'

Now that it came to the point, I was stuck for an answer. I had never in my life struggled for words, but I simply did not know how to say what I wanted to say.

'Well,' said the friar, in mock resignation, 'there will be no more weddings today, if there is no love in the case.'

Still I was silent, although desperate to speak. The truth was, I could not take the final step. Would I lose myself? Would I lose everything that was meant by the name of Beatrice? I did not know how to capitulate without surrender, to yield without defeat.

But as it transpired, I did not have to find the words. Hero, little Hero, my quiet mouse of a cousin, stepped forth, waving a paper. It looked familiar, and my hand flew to my bodice; yes, the sonnet was gone, there was no scratchy parchment beneath my stays, nor telltale crackle when I took my breath. My sonnet, composed on the dunes with Michelangelo Crollalanza and written to Benedick, was now in Hero's hand.

'I dare say there *is* love in the case,' she crowed, brimful of her new confidence. 'For here's a paper written in my cousin's hand, and stolen from her bodice, containing her affection for Benedick.'

'And here's another,' announced Claudio, his good humour

returned; 'a halting sonnet written on the *Florencia*, in the margins of an almanac of stars. The direction reads "to my dearest Beatrice".'

I leapt forward to snatch my sonnet from Hero's hand, but my hampering skirts made me slow. Benedick had taken it and was reading it over before I could move, and batted my reaching hand away. Given no choice, I crossed to a smiling Claudio, and took the paper from his hand.

It took me a little time to read the writing, for Benedick's fist was worse than any schoolboy's, and the motion of the ship and the salt sea spray had hampered his calligraphy. But my eyes adjusted, and the words sang forth, heartfelt and true, drawing tears from my eyes. There was his love, set down in words – ink, wonderful, powerful ink that could print from a press upon a pamphlet, or join two souls upon a marriage contract, or sign a death warrant; that same ink could write down love, capture it and liberate it at the same time.

We looked at each other. 'Well,' he said softly. 'Here's our own hands . . .'

'. . . Against our own hearts,' I finished.

And then we did not have to find any more words. They were all written down in the blackletter of the prayer book. The friar spoke the form of service, we spoke the responses; someone else's words in our mouths.

And we were wed.

Then there was another whirl of kissings and embracings; we were carried high upon shoulders about the garden and conveyed to the house, for feasting, dancing and the sweet wedding night beyond.

By some strange accident of the procession, and by virtue of the width of the palazzo door, we went two by two into the house like the beasts into the Ark. Claudio and Hero first, then Benedick and myself. The friar and Leonato, the household, the congregation. Even the musicians walked in pairs. Before we turned into the great hall I looked back once and saw Don Pedro left in the garden.

He was entirely alone.

I woke with the sun, in a golden sea of bedsheets.

There in the midst was an island humped beneath the covers. My harbour and my home. My treasure, my America, my Indies. My Benedick.

His skin was golden too and I took a moment to look at him greedily, closely, inch by inch. I could see the fuzz of stubble gilding his cheek, the darker hair on his chest disappearing below the coverlet. His curls tumbled over his forehead, long lashes fanned upon his cheek and his merry mouth was adorably serious in repose.

I hid my own wanton smile in the coverlet. I'd had no idea how it could be when a man and a woman lay together. We'd tossed that ocean well last night, we'd made those waves our-selves, heights fit to topple us and troughs fit to drown us. And now the waters had stilled and it was day, I could not bear a moment more without him. I kissed a corner of his jaw where it met his cheek. He woke.

We kissed for a quarter of the bells before we even spoke.

'Good morrow, Duchesa de Leon,' he said; and I considered then – for the first time – that he was a nobleman, and a rich one too. I trusted that it was not too much to hope that my father would be well content with a son-in-law who combined a duke of Spain, a prodigious fortune and a native of the Veneto in the same person.

'Good morrow, Principe di Villafranca,' I replied, to remind him that the good fortune was not all on my side. And we smiled together.

It was the sound of the bells that made me turn to the

window, and if I had not, God knows how long it would have taken me to realise that we were not alone.

A figure sat upon the balustrade of the balcony, facing into the chamber, watching us. I felt a jag of fear, remembering the murder of the archbishop.

The sun was so bright behind the intruder's back that for a moment I could not see his face. I pulled up the coverlet to shield my nakedness – and tugged on Benedick's arm. He blinked at the light, but recognised the figure before I; for he had seen the trespasser more recently. 'Crollalanza!' he said.

Michelangelo hopped down lightly and padded into the chamber. Uninvited, he sat down on the corner of the mattress, as comfortably as if a newly-weds' marital bed was his own parlour. I did not know how to greet him, for not only was the situation most irregular, but I felt I did not know this man.

Gone was the carefree poet of last year. His skin was as tanned as Benedick's and I could see, for the first time, his Moorish heritage writ in his face. His expression now had a downward tendency – eyes, lips, brows, all turned down at the corners. The loss of his mother had etched new and bitter lines upon his face; two twin troughs of grief sat between his brows. He was dressed in the ragged brown fustian of a brigand, his neck wrapped now not by a ruff but a series of concentric hoods and cowls. The pen and bottle were gone from about his neck, and in their place hung a mean little dagger. The only thing that identified him as Michelangelo Crollalanza was the pearl that still shivered at his left ear. I knew at that moment that his mother must have given the pearl to him, or else he would have eschewed such an ornament by now.

He did not greet us, or we him – the oddness of the tableau seemed to render all normal niceties void.

'And on the third day he rose again,' said Benedick, his voice heavy with irony. 'Are you come to dispatch the prince?'

Michelangelo shook his head slowly. 'I thought upon what

you said; that there are other ways to die. I met a man in the port – Gaspar da Sousa, do you know him?'

I did not recognise the name, but Benedick visibly flinched. 'I do,' he said slowly. 'He was the pilot of the gunship *Florencia*.'

'Yes. I met him by chance at the Mermaid in Messina, and stood him a drink. I recalled the name of his ship from Tuscany's fleet, and asked him if his commander had been an honourable prince by the name of Don Pedro. He answered that his commander had indeed gone by that name, but there was no honour in him. I listened to the tale he had to tell, then came to Don Pedro with it. I told the good prince that if he stays another day, all men shall know what I know.'

Now I was intrigued – what dark secrets had Michelangelo uncovered to hold against the prince? The poet nodded at me. 'Your cousin, lady, could tell you how quickly slander spreads around this island. Gossip goes faster than Prester John, virtue slower than a pilgrim.' He took out his dagger and began to toss it hand to hand, the blade winking and spinning in the air. It was unnerving.

'But Don Pedro,' persisted Benedick. 'He shall not die?'

'One day God shall ordain to be his last,' said Michelangelo, sounding much more like his old self. 'But not today. I chose to banish him instead.'

Banishment instead of death, I thought. It was a merciful sentence I had employed once myself. 'Banishment is death, if you are forced to leave that which you love,' I said, thinking of Giulietta; pining in Verona for the young Montecchi in Mantua.

'Lady Beatrice,' he said, addressing me directly for the first time. 'You always did take the point so admirably. Don Pedro must leave Sicily today and with it all hopes of preferment. I have told him that if he ever sets foot on this island again, I will kill him.'

I believed him. 'So now he will never be viceroy,' I murmured.

'No – he has chosen quite a different path. He is to go for a pilgrim, and walk to Compostela.'

I looked at Benedick. Santiago de Compostela, back in Don Pedro's native Spain, was the spiritual home of his saint, James the Great. *Matamoros* – the Moor-slayer.

'What?' My husband's eyes flew wide.

'It was his idea. I think he wants to go. But he wishes to speak to you,' Michelangelo also looked at Benedick, 'before he takes his leave. And now,' he sheathed his dagger again, 'I must take mine, before the overzealous hounds of the Watch catch my scent.'

'Where will you go?' I asked.

'England, if I make it so far, to join my father. He has a house in London, by the riverbank.'

He rose, and I felt a sudden pang. I was leaving for Villafranca later in the day to return to my father and introduce him to the reason why I could not now be married to whomever he chose. It was unlikely that I would ever see Michelangelo Florio Crollalanza again. It had been a sudden reunion, and as sudden a leave-taking – and though we were no longer friends, we had been once. I wanted to say something in valediction, somewhat about his mother, or the sonnet that we'd written together, but I could think of nothing sensible. So I asked him, 'Will you write again?'

He smiled, quite like the old Michelangelo. 'Now my blood feud is done, I may yet exchange my dagger for a pen.'

'Will you write of your . . . mother?' It was almost a whisper.

His face was grave again. 'Not yet,' he said. 'One day. I will begin not with a tragedy, but a comedy. Your own story, perhaps.'

I thought of our story; the heartache, the loss, the separation. The death, the despair; the nameless secrets Benedick was keeping in the name of honour. 'Are our antics comic, then?'

'You are wed, are you not?' Now his expression tended upwards. His eyes, his mouth, his brows; the tragic mask turned comic again. 'You loved one summer, quarrelled, parted and then wed the next. You travelled hundreds, thousands of miles in between. You girdled the earth; you circumnavigated a great round O and came back where you started. *Tanto traffico per niente.*'

It was a Sicilian tag, but I understood it well enough. *Much ado about nothing.* Put like that, it did seem a nonsense – I smiled at Benedick and he smiled at me; the waste of a year seemed easier to bear with a comic slant upon it. And we were together now; all had ended well.

'The prince stays for you at the gate,' said Michelangelo. 'I will see you anon.' He bowed to us like an actor making an exit, vaulted neatly over the balcony and was gone.

Act V scene x

Leonato's gardens

Benedick: We dressed as swiftly as we might and walked hand in hand through the gardens to the gatehouse.

The sun was only just rising, sleepily, and the flowers were beginning to wake and give off their scent. The dew rimed the lawn with crystals, the grasses were spears of emerald. Beyond the walls the sea was sapphire and foam sat upon the waves like a net of pearl. Everything was bejewelled.

And then we got to the gatehouse, and saw, among the glory of my first morning as Benedick the Married Man, a man of ash.

A pilgrim stood there, leaning on a crooked staff taller than himself. He wore robes the colour of sand, and a broad-brimmed hat with a silver scallop badge pinned upon the front. His rope belt was knotted thrice for the Trinity. He wore simple pattens on his feet, and over the whole he wore a rough cream cloak with the hood drawn up over the hat. I peered into the cowl; it was Don Pedro.

He greeted us with a wave of his staff, but wore no smile. Beatrice, with an instinct I loved her for, hung back as I met him beneath the postern. For the second time that day no greetings were exchanged. We had sailed beyond such shallow waters.

'I hear them, Benedick,' he said to me, low voiced, with no preamble. 'I hear the woman in the flames, I hear the sailors groaning with hunger. My sins call for me in my dreams. All's gone awry, but in Compostela I'll begin to heal.'

'I pray that you do.' And I meant it. I could not absolve him; that was God's business. I could only hope that he would find some peace from those voices. But I did have one more thing to ask him; a notion that had rolled around my head like distant thunder since the fruitless wedding day.

'Did you ever tell Don John, your brother, of the trick you played upon me? When you led me to the beach, to see my lady in the arms of another?'

I had been struck, many times, by the similarity in the way in which Claudio and I were gulled, a year apart, by a pair of brothers.

He furrowed his forehead and I saw then that he wore a smudge of penitent's ash between his brows. 'Yes. I may have told him in an idle hour along the road, as a jest.'

I knew then how it had been – Don Pedro had boasted of his wiles to his brother, and Don John had served Claudio in like kind, bringing him to note an innocent embrace. I looked to the heavens. A *jest*. I'd sailed on a ship of fools from Spain to Scotland and back, and lost a year of my life with Beatrice. As the poet had said, we'd circumnavigated a great round *O*, and come back to where we'd started. But, looking at the prince now, grey as the ash, I could forgive him. He had so little, and I had everything.

'Commend me to your wife,' he said, as if his thoughts marched with mine, nodding gardenwards to where Beatrice stood in the shade, smelling a nosegay of roses. 'You may tell her now,' he said, 'it no longer matters.'

I took his meaning, and did not know what to say.

He smiled sadly. 'My ship waits.' He held out his hand to me. In it was a medal on a ribbon. Next to his subfusc garb the gold and scarlet sang, and winked knowingly in the sun. 'You gave this back to me twice in your life. Might I ask that you keep it this time, as a remembrance of me?'

A treacherous lump rose to my throat. 'It would be my honour.'

He raised his chin a little to look his last upon me. I do not think I had ever seen him look so noble. 'Once a knight of Saint James, always a knight of Saint James.'

He clasped my shoulder briefly, bowed to my wife where she stood in the shadow of the arch, and walked through the gatehouse.

I put the ribbon round my neck and dropped the medal beneath my clothes. The disc was still warm from the prince's hand. I returned to Beatrice and we walked back, sober now.

The friar was sweeping the steps of the chapel where we'd wed the previous day, and stopped to lean upon his broom and wish us joy.

'We have just taken leave of a pilgrim, who takes the silver road,' I told him.

'Aye; Don Pedro,' said the friar, with less surprise than I'd expected. 'I blessed his sandals at matins, for he leaves tomorrow.'

'Today,' my wife corrected, 'we said our farewells even now.'

The friar's sandy brows drew together in a frown. 'There are no ships today. It is God's day; they do not sail.'

He was right; we had wed the day before on a Saturday, and on Sundays, ships did not sail. I felt a sudden chill, as if the sun had hidden behind a cloud.

I took Beatrice's hand, pulling her urgently.

'Where are we going?' she asked.

'Somewhere you know well.'

Act V scene xi

The dunes at Messina

Beatrice: Benedick was right, I knew the place well.

Here I'd seen a Moor couple with his white wife. Here I'd sat with a poet and written a sonnet. Here I'd lain below Benedick as he'd pressed my form into the sand. Here I'd seen a dark lady burn her husband's seditious pamphlets. Here I'd embraced her son, and been spied upon by a prince.

We came to the dunes short of breath, for Benedick seemed anxious, hurried. The sun glittered upon the waves, and found the powdered crystals in the sand. In the bejewelled landscape, there was only one dull patch – a heap of dun garments where the waves met the shore. A body?

Benedick ran forward so swiftly that my hand broke from his. I followed him, heart thumping. But all was well – it was only a pile of clothes. Benedick sorted them with a shaking hand – a sand-coloured robe and cloak, plain pattens. And a broad-brimmed pilgrim's hat, pinned with a silver badge of St James. I took his hand again. 'All is well,' I said, 'all is well.' A foolish litany. For then I saw the footprints. They were the perfect impressions of naked feet, and they led into the sea, then . . . nowhere.

Benedick rushed into the waves, wading as far as he could. I stood, one foot in the sea and one on shore, shielding my eyes and looking beyond him, desperately seeking in that gilded path of sunlight the telltale dot of a bobbing head. But there was nothing but a reverent staff, dipping on the surf like driftwood.

'Come back,' I cried, terrified for that moment that the sea would take Benedick too.

And he did. He waded back to me, his face stricken with grief, and smashed his hand with frustration upon the water. I pulled him from the surf and we sank down, sodden, upon the sand. For once in his company, I had no words. We sat in a stunned silence. The sun beat down and warmed us, the tramontana blew his hair about, drying the curls. Only his eyes were still wet. And then he began to talk.

Of a prince who was not a prince, but a coward. A prince who cut an anchor and sent a shipful of men to their deaths, and then hid, craven, in his cabin. A prince who made his fellows swear to be secret, so his reputation would stand untouched.

'His sins weighed him down in the end,' he concluded. 'They pulled him down into the deeps.'

I remembered more sins, farther back; of the business of Guglielma Crollalanza. I thought of Michelangelo; had he known Don Pedro would take this path – not the silver road to Compostela, but the golden path into the sea? Either way, the blood feud was paid, and Don Pedro had met his end.

Suddenly, I knew what to say. 'The prince did redeem him-self,' I said. 'He told me of your misprision, and of the *Scopa* cards. If he had not, I would always have doubted you.' I took his face in my hands, turned him to me. 'I think he loved you in his way; and now, I shall love you in mine.' I kissed him, tasting the salt on his lips, the salt of the sea, the salt of his tears. He put his sodden arms about me and held me so tight to his chest I could barely breathe; but I did not care. Then I exclaimed, as I felt something sharp pressing upon my chest. I loosened my grip and felt in my bodice. I took the *settebello*, sodden and crumpled, from my gown, and held it out to him.

We looked at the card; purchased in the north and first bestowed in Sicily, it had passed from me to him and back a dozen times. It had been to Spain, to Scotland and now it had returned to Sicily. It had been the symbol of our merry war; but who was the victor? Who would keep the spoils, this saturated, sad piece of coloured card?

Then we looked at each other and began to smile. Hand to hand, complicit, we tore the card neatly in half; three and a half coins each.

And put each half in our bosoms, next to our hearts.

APPENDIX

Beatrice's Sonnet

O! never say that I was false of heart,
Though absence seemed my flame to qualify,
As easy might I from my self depart
As from my soul which in thy breast doth lie:
That is my home of love: if I have ranged,
Like him that travels, I return again;
Just to the time, not with the time exchanged,
So that myself bring water for my stain.
Never believe though in my nature reigned,
All frailties that besiege all kinds of blood,
That it could so preposterously be stained,
To leave for nothing all thy sum of good;
For nothing this wide universe I call,
Save thou, my rose, in it thou art my all.

Benedick's Sonnet

Not from the stars do I my judgement pluck;
And yet methinks I have Astronomy,
But not to tell of good or evil luck,
Of plagues, of dearths, or seasons' quality;
Nor can I fortune to brief minutes tell,
Pointing to each his thunder, rain and wind,
Or say with princes if it shall go well
By oft predict that I in heaven find:
But from thine eyes my knowledge I derive,
And, constant stars, in them I read such art

As truth and beauty shall together thrive,
If from thyself, to store thou wouldst convert;
Or else of thee this I prognosticate:
Thy end is truth's and beauty's doom and date.

AUTHOR'S NOTE

In the course of research for this novel I visited a bustling little market town. The town itself is unremarkable except for a few historical buildings in its very centre. The thing that marks this town out from all others is its most famous son. The citizens talk of him as if they know him, with affection and palpable pride. 'Oh yes,' said an elderly man to me on the street, 'Shakespeare was from here.'

But this was not Stratford-upon-Avon, far from it.

This was Messina, Italy.

The actor Mark Rylance, Shakespearean extraordinaire and first artistic director of the Globe Theatre, says: 'Anyone who claims to have written the plays of Shakespeare needs to show some Italian travel documents.' I myself am in absolutely no doubt that in his 'lost years' Shakespeare, whoever he was, spent at least some of his time in Italy.

But what if we go a step farther? What if Shakespeare *was* Italian? This is the controversial theory put forth by Professor Martino Iuvara.

In his book *Shakespeare era Italiano* (2002), retired Sicilian professor Iuvara claims that Shakespeare was, in fact, not English at all, but Sicilian. His conclusion is drawn from research carried out from 1925 to 1950 by two professors at Palermo University. Iuvara posits that Shakespeare was born not in Stratford in April 1564, as is commonly believed, but in Messina as Michelangelo Florio Crollalanza. His parents were not John Shakespeare and Mary Arden, but were Dr Giovanni Florio, and Guglielma Crollalanza, a Sicilian noblewoman.

Crollalanza, literally *Crolla* (Shake) *lancia* (spear) according to Iuvara, studied abroad and was educated by Franciscan monks who taught him Latin, Greek and history.

Because of their Calvinist beliefs, Michelangelo Florio's family was persecuted by the Inquisition in Messina (then under the Spanish yoke) for alleged Calvinist propaganda. It seems that Giovanni Florio had published some sort of invective against Rome and the Church. The family supposedly departed Italy during the Holy Inquisition and moved to London. It was in London that Michelangelo Florio Crollalanza decided to change his surname to its English equivalent, and for his first name he 'Englished' his mother's name Guglielma, to make William.

Iuvara's evidence includes a play written by Michelangelo Florio Crollalanza in Sicilian dialect. The play's name is *Tanto traffico per niente*, which can be translated as *Much Ado about Nothing*. He also mentions a book of sayings written by a writer, one Michelangelo Crollalanza, in sixteenth-century Calvinist northern Italy. Some of the sayings correspond to lines in *Hamlet*. Michelangelo's father, Giovanni Florio, once owned a home called 'Casa Otello', built by a retired Venetian admiral known as Otello who, in a jealous rage, murdered his wife.

Michelangelo Florio Crollalanza decided to flee Italy because the Inquisitors had already pursued his father, and ended up in England. Contemporary Londoners even reported that Shakespeare 'had an accent', and portraits of him show a dark man with Mediterranean appearance.

In 2008 the mayor of Sicily petitioned Prime Minister Tony Blair and Queen Elizabeth II of England to recognise Michelangelo Florio Crollalanza as the true author of Shakespeare's plays.

You might think all this an interesting idea or you might not believe a word of it. You might think both things. Maybe the story of Michelangelo Crollalanza is true. Or maybe it is just that; a story, to add to the authorship debate, to deepen the mystery surrounding the identity of Shakespeare.

And of that, I feel sure, the real William Shakespeare, whoever he was, would have approved.

Marina Fiorato
London, 2014

Beatrice and
Benedick

A READING GROUP GUIDE

TOPICS FOR DISCUSSION

1. *Beatrice & Benedick* could be described as a prequel to William Shakespeare's play *Much Ado About Nothing*. If you were already familiar with the play, how did knowing the ending affect your enjoyment of the book? Have you read other books which are prequels or sequels to classic works?

2. How important is it that much of the book is set in Sicily? Does the island have a character of its own?

3. What part do Moorish characters play in the book? How does their presence define those who come into contact with them?

4. What does the book say about the concept of Nobility? Which characters are truly noble, and which are not?

5. How does Benedick's sea voyage change him?

6. Beatrice is an unconventional woman. How does she use her independent spirit to get what she wants? How does her conduct compare to that of Guglielma Crollalanza?

7. What is the significance of the religious characters in the book? How would you contrast the characters of Friar Francis and the Archbishop of Monreale?

8. What does the book tell us about father figures? What are the qualities or failings of Leonato Leonatus, Giovanni Florio Crollalanza, and Bartolomeo della Scala?

9. How does Michelangelo Crollalanza change through the course of the story?

10. Drama and public spectacle play a significant role in the book. How do the puppet show, the fencing match, the Naumachia and the Vara procession feed into the plot? Can you think of other instances in the book when the characters are playing a part?

11. Did Beatrice and Benedick's 'merry war of wit' lose them a year of married life? Or did they need to be apart before they could be together?

12. Consider the characters of Don Pedro and Claudio. Which one do you prefer? Do either of them find redemption?

ACKNOWLEDGEMENTS

As I am of Northern Italian provenance, I was a little nervous of Sicily and 'The South', and could not have imagined the wonderful welcome and invaluable assistance I encountered on that matchless island. I made friends for life, and, like Beatrice, I will always return.

Thank you to Katharine Dix at the exquisite Hotel Villa Angela in Taormina, who tirelessly arranged my trips to Syracuse and Messina.

Thanks also to Angelo Greco, from *The Magic of Sicily*, who took me up to the summit of Etna, and also to his cousin's farm – where my children picked oranges – and to his friend's olive press (and his other friend's bar!)

In Palermo, I must thank the Argento family, the members of which have run a jewel of a puppet theatre in the shadow of the duomo for hundreds of years. They very kindly let me poke around backstage, and even hold and operate one of the puppets, a martial fellow who was nearly as tall as me!

Also in Palermo, I am grateful to Francesca Sommatino from the University of Palermo, who spent an afternoon showing me round the Palazzo Chiaramonte, which houses the cells which the victims of the Inquisition decorated with wonderful drawings during their imprisonment.

Closer to home, I am indebted as ever to my wonderful editor Kate Parkin at Hodder, who is always there to gently nudge me back on track when I show signs of wandering off! And I owe my eternal gratitude to my agent Teresa Chris, who guides me as surely as Beatrice's star.

Also at Hodder thanks must go to Swati Gamble for getting

the final manuscript into shape, and Emilie Ferguson for spreading the word about *Beatrice & Benedick*.

Of the books that I read in the course of my research one above all deserves a mention – Richard Paul Roe's *The Shakespeare Guide to Italy: Retracing the Bard's Unknown Travels* (Harper Perennial 2011) is a fascinating analysis of the geography and cultural detail of Shakespeare's Italian plays.

I have watched many wonderful performances of *Much Ado About Nothing* over the years, but the one I referred to most in the process of my writing was the Branagh/Thompson film (Kenneth Branagh 1993), which remains, for me, the definitive filmed version.

I must thank my brother-in-law Richard Brown, who knows more about seafaring than most books.

Thank you to my children; Conrad (*'I am a gentleman, sir, and my name is Conrad.'* – Much Ado IV ii) and Ruby, who never mind being dragged around churches and palaces so long as there is a *gelato* at the end of it.

And finally I will end this book as I began it, with a dedication to Sacha. I share my *settebello* with you.